JACK'S CAROUSEL

Can love overcome deep prejudice?

A novel

SHIRLEY A. RORVIK

Cover and frontispiece by Charles N. Rorvik

WESTBOW
PRESS
A DIVISION OF THOMAS NELSON

WestBow Press books may be ordered through booksellers or by contacting:

WestBow Press
A Division of Thomas Nelson
1663 Liberty Drive
Bloomington, IN 47403
www.westbowpress.com
1-(866) 928-1240

Because of the dynamic nature of the Internet, any web addresses or links contained in this book may have changed since publication and may no longer be valid. The views expressed in this work are solely those of the author and do not necessarily reflect the views of the publisher, and the publisher hereby disclaims any responsibility for them.

Scripture quotations are taken from The Holy Bible, New King James Version Copyright © 1982 by Thomas Nelson, Inc.; or from The Message Copyright © 1993, 1994, 1995, 1996, 2000, 2001, 2002 by Eugene H. Peterson.

All characters in this novel are fictional. I have taken liberties with certain details about Missoula, Montana, and the Carousel for Missoula. I hope I have captured the enchantment of this authentic carousel.

ISBN: 978-1-4497-7389-2 (e)
ISBN: 978-1-4497-7387-8 (sc)
ISBN: 978-1-4497-7388-5 (hc)

Library of Congress Control Number: 2012920881

Printed in the United States of America

WestBow Press rev. date:11/19/2012

Also by Shirley A. Rorvik, illustrated
by Charles N. Rorvik
Picture Book
Pickles' Predicament

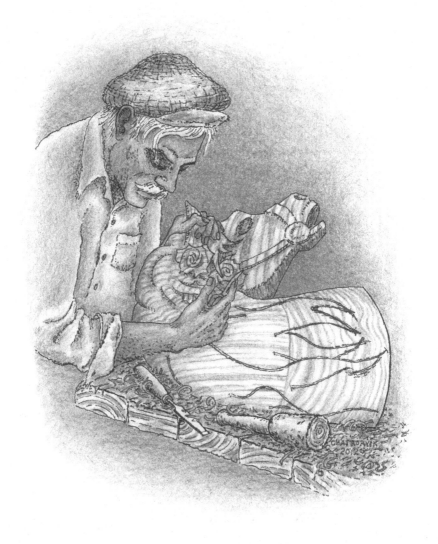

Jack carving carousel pony's head

for
Tim and Bryan
and
Dawn and Jane

God judges persons differently than humans do.
Men and women look at the face;
God looks into the heart.
1 Samuel 16:7 The Message

ACKNOWLEDGMENTS

Heartfelt thanks to Chuck Kaparich, who welcomed my invasion of his busy garage workshop. Mr. Kaparich is the creator of the delightful Carousel for Missoula. Thanks also to Bob Cherot, who graciously invited my husband and me to spend an afternoon touring his workshop and admiring his beautiful, handcrafted carousel overlooking Flathead Lake.

Loving thanks to my husband, Chuck, for encouraging my scribblings, despite the often empty cookie jar.

PROLOGUE

A nebulous band of morning light appeared behind Mount Sentinel just as the slim, brunette woman wearing gray sweats parked her Cadillac under a green canopy of maples on a quiet residential street. She got out and walked away from her car as though beginning a daily exercise routine. She hurried past tidy yards with lemon-yellow snapdragons, climbing Blaze roses, and fragrant petunia beds. The sound of her brisk footsteps accompanied the soft hiss and spray of underground sprinklers.

At the corner, she crossed the street and skirted around a few cars in the hospital parking lot. She quickened her pace, entered the deserted lobby, and took the stairs to the third floor. She knew the nurses would be in the report room at this hour, and the night aides would be yawning as they neared the end of their shifts.

Silent, unseen, she moved toward a room halfway down the hall, went in, and eased the door shut. Her nostrils flared at the antiseptic smell overpowering the patient's subtle body odors.

Claire Emerson lay with her eyes closed, intravenous lines plugged into both hands, a translucent feeding tube inserted into one nostril, and a urine collection bag suspended below the bedcovers. A massive stroke had transformed Claire from an attractive, sophisticated woman into a comatose victim.

The younger woman brushed her manicured fingers across Claire's forehead and kissed her cheek. Then she slid her hand into her sweatpants pocket, pulled out a small, unmarked bottle, and unscrewed the lid. She hesitated, wondering if God would forgive what she was about to do. Then she shrugged. God didn't care about her anyway.

CHAPTER 1

Four Years Later ...

After a pleasant January thaw, winter returned in February. Skiffs of snow swirled along the curbs of Jack Emerson's once-affluent neighborhood. Barren Dutch elms paralleled the sidewalks on both sides of the narrow street. Nikolas Kostenka eased his faded 1968 Oldsmobile around an icy corner. Jack, in the passenger seat, tugged at the tips of his mustache and waited until his friend completed the turn. Then he resumed the conversation about their evening's work at the community Carousel.

"Thought I'd finish carving the forelock and eyes tonight, but no go. Too many interruptions." Jack glanced at Nikolas. "Did you know all those kids would be there?"

Nikolas nodded. "The lady in the gift shop—you know, the one who sometimes helps sand the ponies—she said the children were celebrating a birthday. To visit the Carousel was a special surprise. Especially because they observed us at work." Nikolas stroked his full, grizzled beard. "I did not mind their visit."

"Hmph. Well, I did. Couldn't get any work done. Questions, questions. And that one kid kept taking my chisels." He shook his head. "Probably dulled every blade."

"Ah, yes, that boy. You should have seen him in the paint room." Nikolas' voice softened. "Even our lovely lady with eyes the color of the ocean raised her voice to him."

Jack frowned. "What? Who're you purring about?"

"You know."

"You think I check the color of every woman's eyes?"

"But this one, you know."

"You mean Kennocha?"

1

Nikolas arched one black, bushy eyebrow and smiled. "Ahhh, yes. Kennocha Bryant. I am right, am I not? Her eyes are the color of the ocean."

Jack snorted. "I know what you're up to, you nosy, old Russian. But you'll get no reaction from me." He paused. "Besides, how about you and those two women after church last Sunday? The way you were making eyes at them ... Why, they were young enough to be your great-great-granddaughters."

Chuckling, Nikolas halted at a stop sign, carefully looked in both directions, and drove on. "You exaggerate. They are young, yes, but not too young. Know this, my friend, younger ladies prefer gentlemen our age. We are more settled, more mature, more distinguished—"

Jack whooped. "Distinguished! Me, maybe, but not you." He grinned at his friend and waited for his comeback.

"You change the subject. We were talking about Miss Bryant."

"You were. I wasn't."

Nikolas pulled into the driveway alongside Jack's white clapboard home on the corner. A spacious yard with several tall maples surrounded the blue-shuttered, two-story house. "Perhaps you do not need to tell me much. I see what I see. And I am glad. Four years Claire has been gone. It is time for you—"

"You see what you want to see. Martha's been gone longer than Claire, and you're still alone. Fine one you are to talk." Ignoring Nikolas's chuckle, he said, "You want to come in for a cup of coffee?"

"What, and have caffeine disturb my slumber?"

"Cocoa then."

Nikolas peered at the dashboard clock. "No, it is after ten. Time for me to go home."

Jack groped for his gloves and pulled them on. He snugged a red woolen scarf around his neck. "There's a John Wayne movie on tonight—*Rooster Cogburn*. I'll make popcorn ..."

Nikolas raised one eyebrow. "With butter?"

"And a little salt. C'mon, you old Russian. It's not so late."

Sighing, Nikolas eyed the clock again. "No, no. I cannot. We worked too late tonight."

Jack's shoulders slumped. He pulled his scarf up around his ears, pushed the car door open, and stepped into the frigid, windy night. Bright moonlight, seizing openings between fast-moving clouds, cast distorted shadows of barren elms onto the street.

Jack leaned into the car and said, "I'll drive tomorrow. The usual time?"

"Not tomorrow, my friend. Sunday—the Lord's Day. I would pick you up for church—"

"No, thanks. I went with you last week."

"Potluck social afterward."

"No, Nikolas, maybe another time." Jack shivered. "Freezing out here. I'll see you Monday." He closed the car door and waved as Nikolas slowly drove away.

Jack hurried through the gate, went up the back steps, and searched his pockets for his keys. A gray and white tabby appeared at his feet. "Well, it's about time you showed up. Where were you this afternoon, Missy?" He located his key, unlocked the door, and pushed it open, stepping aside for the cat to streak by into the warm kitchen. Jack went in, locked the door, and hung his keys, jacket, and scarf on the hooks by the door.

Thinking of Nikolas, Jack mused, *Probably should go to church more often with him. But I don't need any self-righteous, husband-hunting widows trying to latch onto me. Like that one who came after me the minute she heard Claire was in the hospital. And she was supposed to be one of Claire's friends. Hmph. Some friend.*

Although he barely admitted it to himself, at times Jack actually enjoyed the freedom of living alone. Claire had gotten downright cranky after he took an early retirement. Like she hadn't wanted him around so much. His ideas of taking her fishing and camping had never materialized. She preferred soft beds, bone china, and high heels.

Then suddenly, the stroke. And just when she was beginning to show signs of recovery, death. "This sometimes happens," the doctor had said. Jack felt betrayed, lost. After a year or so, Nikolas urged him to let go. Move on. Jack tried, sometimes.

Now, inside his warm, cozy home, Jack prepared for bed. Unbuttoning his woolen shirt with frayed cuffs and draping it across the back of a chair, a little smile teased his lips. He remembered how Claire fussed about his work shirts and then gave a satisfied nod when he wore something she favored—like the year she splurged and bought him a blue, Armani shirt. "Matches your Paul Newman eyes," she said.

Jack gave a soft snort and headed for the shower. *Movie star. Last thing I want to look like.* He scrutinized himself in the bathroom mirror. *No bald spots, plenty of hair. Smoke gray. No, silver.* He smiled at his foolishness and slapped his belly. *No flab.* He twitched his upper lip, pleased with the new, neatly trimmed mustache. He fancied it made him look younger than the bushy growth he'd had for years. Claire liked his mustache. That's what counted.

After his shower, Jack returned to the bedroom, opened the bottom drawer in the maple highboy, and pulled out a pink tricot nightgown. As his fingers caught in the delicate fabric, he frowned and shook them loose. Woodworking had roughened his hands, but he hated that greasy stuff Claire used to insist that he rub into his calloused skin. He lifted the lace-lavished garment to his cheek, remembering Claire's lingering rose scent. *Sometimes I can feel her right in this room.* He sighed, replaced the nightgown, and pulled his own faded flannel pajamas from the second drawer.

An hour later, lying in bed with W. Phillip Keller's *Still Waters* propped open on his chest and the purring cat curled up at his side, drowsiness flowed into Jack's limbs like liquid warmth. His eyelids closed.

The sound of someone pounding on the back door startled him awake. He threw off the covers, burying the cat, glanced at the clock, and swung his feet over the side of the bed. *After midnight. Probably one of those college kids next door. Locked himself out of the house again. Good thing for them Mrs. Adams gave me a spare key when she moved downtown. Good thing for her, too.*

The cat sneezed, scrambled out from under the bedspread, and began grooming her fur.

"Sorry, Missy." Jack patted her head and pulled on a gray, plaid robe with threadbare elbows. He tightened the belt and groped for his slippers.

The knocking became more insistent.

"Whoever it is, they're not about to give up. C'mon. Let's see what's going on." The cat leaped off the bed and minced out of the room, tail high. Jack followed, his slippers making a soft scuffing sound on the carpet. He flipped on the porch light and pulled the curtain aside to peer out.

"What the—" He unbolted the door and yanked it open. A blast of cold air hit him.

"Hi, Granpop."

Scott Giroux, Jack's sixteen-year-old grandson, stood shivering on the porch, duffel bag in hand. "Scott!" Grinning, Jack pulled the boy into the room and wrapped him in a bear hug. Then he stepped back, placed his hands on Scott's shoulders, eyes level with his, and said, "Am I getting forgetful, or what? I didn't know you were coming.

Where're your folks?" Jack glanced beyond the teenager's shoulder toward the door.

"Just me, Granpop." Scott shoved his hands into the pockets of his Boise high school letter jacket and looked away. "Got anything to eat? I'm starved."

"Of course, of course. Come in. Take your coat off. Sit down. I'll see what I can find." Aware of his grandson's nervousness, questions raced through Jack's mind. He opened the refrigerator and rummaged. "Here's a pork chop leftover from supper ... and macaroni and cheese." Jack backed away, balancing covered dishes and a carton of milk. He nudged the refrigerator door shut with his foot. "You here for school? Debate team?"

Last year, when Scott won his state's title in debate, he made the trip here with his teacher to compete against winners from other states. Jack had gone to the event, proud to see his grandson competing, not minding that he didn't win again. *Must be why Scott's here now—another school event. Or is it? Why is he getting here so late? Who dropped him off here? Why doesn't the boy answer me? Why is he avoiding my eyes? And what about that hair? Used to be the same nice, rich brown color as his mother's. Looks like he bleached it on top, like he's wearing a giant mushroom cap on his head. Kids!*

Clattering dishes caught the tabby's attention, whiskers alert. Her immaculate fur was offset by one ragged ear, scarred from some battle only she knew about.

"Hey, kitty. C'mere." Scott stood, scooped up the cat, and allowed her green-eyed scrutiny. He laughed as, satisfied, she rubbed her head under his chin. He stroked her and was rewarded with a deep purr.

Jack punched "Start" on the microwave oven and turned to see Scott wipe away a tear with the back of his hand. With exaggerated nonchalance, his grandson tossed a shock of blond hair off his forehead. Jack pulled at the tips of his mustache, wondering.

To ease the sudden awkwardness, he said, "That cat. Thinks she has to eat every time I open the refrigerator. You'll have to share the macaroni and cheese with her, but she turns her nose up at my pork chops. Thinks I use too much pepper."

Scott smiled and sat down with the purring cat on his lap. "What's her name again?"

"Miss Lavender. Inspired by an Ogden Nash poem. Mostly, I just call her Missy." Jack set a plate of warm food in front of his grandson and resisted an inclination to boot the cat to the floor. He loved animals but not that close to the kitchen table.

Watching Scott, Jack said, "Slow down, boy. The way you're shoveling in that pork chop, you're going to choke. How long since you ate?" Scott looked like a squirrel with cheeks full of nuts.

The teenager chewed and swallowed. "Uh ... I had a Snickers and Coke yesterday." Scott leaned toward the floor with a piece of cheese-coated macaroni between his fingers. The cat promptly hopped down, delicately accepted the tidbit, and began nibbling.

Jack considered the boy's rumpled, soiled appearance. He leveled a look at his grandson. "Did you run away from home?"

Scott hesitated, wiped his plate with a piece of bread, and stuffed the bread into his mouth. He got up and deposited his dirty dishes in the sink, shuffled back to the chair, and sat down again. He peeked at his grandfather from beneath long bangs. "Yeah. Rode the bus here from Boise. Walked here from the bus depot."

Arms folded across his chest, Jack waited.

Scott rubbed his forehead, a pained look on his face. "Everybody thinks we're like, perfect, y'know? Just because Dad's making it big time at the bank, and Mom's on every stupid committee ever invented. And because she has one of those stupid bumper stickers, 'My son's an honor roll student.'" He wrinkled his nose. "Like that makes a difference. But our life isn't what you think. What they try to make everybody believe. It stinks!"

Jack tensed. *I thought those kids had worked out their problems before they left Springfield.* After a moment, Jack said, "I'm listening."

Scott stared at the linoleum. "Mom and Dad fight all the time." He fidgeted, cracked his knuckles.

"Go on." Jack watched Scott's face, hoping for some sign of youthful exaggeration.

The boy continued, "It's worse when Dad's drinking. Mom is worse than girls at school. Moody. And she's ... well, she goes ballistic, you know? And she's always on some weird diet. If Dad's sober, he handles it. Otherwise ..."

Jack frowned. "Otherwise?"

Scott sniffed several times and blinked rapidly as though fighting back tears. "Dad gets mad. Then the yelling starts. Then ... it gets worse. Dad blows up ..." He wiped at his eyes. "Sometimes, I think she does it on purpose."

No, can't be. Not Marah. Jack collected his thoughts, focused on the immediate problem, and shoved his feelings down deep. "What brought you to this? Running away?"

A new expression registered on Scott's face: anger. He scowled, got up from his chair, and distanced himself from his grandfather. Leaning against the kitchen counter, he folded his arms. "Got sick of it, that's all." He shoved his hands into his back pockets. "Can I stay?"

Jack ran a thumb over his mustache. "For now, yes. Your folks know where you are?"

Scott shook his head.

Jack nodded toward the wall phone. "Give them a call."

"Now? It's ..." he looked around for a clock. " ... late ... midnight or something."

"Two o'clock. Your folks probably aren't getting much sleep, worried about where you are." *So why haven't they called me, let me know he was missing?*

Scott made a wry face, but after a moment's hesitation, he picked up the phone, punched in his home number. Several seconds later, he spoke. "Mom, it's me ... at Granpop's ... the bus ... no!" Abruptly, Scott thrust the phone at Jack and tromped through the dining room into the darkened living room.

"Marah, what's going on?"

"Oh, Dad, what a relief to know he's with you. I thought he was at Larry's house."

"How long has he been gone?"

"Um—since Wednesday night."

"Wednesday? And you didn't know where he was? This is Saturday night!" When she didn't respond, he continued, "Why did he run away?"

"Oh, you know how it is with kids. We had an argument, that's all. He got rebellious. Every kid thinks about running away."

"But this kid really did it. Why?"

"Look, Dad, it's a family problem. Just send him home tomorrow. I'll wire you the money for an airplane ticket. Really, Dad, it's nothing to be concerned about."

Jack raised his voice. "He's my grandson. He came here. I am concerned." After a beat he said, "Let me talk to Vic."

"He's out of town. Why do you want to talk to him?"

An uneasy feeling gnawed at Jack's gut.

"Dad? Are you there?"

"I'm thinking ... Tell you what. Let's give it a day or two. Can he afford to miss school Monday, maybe Tuesday?"

"Yes, but I don't know what good that will do."

"Give the situation time to cool down. Whatever it is. Besides, the kid looks beat." Jack paused at an odd sound from the receiver. "What?" He waited. "Thought you said something."

"No, I—uh, go ahead, what were you saying?"

Jack grunted. "Yeah. Well, Scott looks like he hasn't slept much in the last few days. He'll be okay here. Get rested up."

After a short pause, Marah said, "All right, Dad. Can I talk to Scott a minute?"

"One other thing, daughter. I want to talk to Vic as soon as he gets home."

Long pause. "I'll tell him."

Jack covered the mouthpiece and called toward the living room, "Scott, your mother wants to speak to you."

Scott yelled, "I don't care. I don't want to talk to her."

Jack sensed he shouldn't push it. "Just let him be for now, Marah."

After he hung up, Jack let the cat out and spent several minutes tidying the kitchen and pondering. Then he went into the living room.

A streetlamp cast weak shadows through the picture window onto the beige and brown carpet. Jack's house—his and Claire's first and only home—originally belonged to an upper-class family sixty years ago. Without a generous wedding gift from Claire's aunt Maggie, they'd never have been able to afford it on their wages at DeWolfe Department Store. Money was tight at first, but they'd never regretted going into debt for the solid old house. After the children were born— first Paul, followed by Marah five years later—it was perfect.

Now that he was alone, Jack sometimes thought of selling out, buying a little cabin up toward Hidden Lake, somewhere he could cast a lure minutes away from his front door ... maybe, someday.

He found Scott curled up on the padded bay window seat, hugging a cream-colored throw pillow against his chest.

Jack sat down beside him. "You must be tired." He patted his grandson's shoulder. Scott winced and pulled away. "What's wrong? Shoulder hurt?"

"Nah, just tired." Scott stood. "Haven't slept much. Okay if I go to bed?"

"Of course. Upstairs, remember? Both rooms are made up—take your pick. My bedroom's on this floor, down the hall next to the bathroom." Jack got up, moved toward the arched doorway to the dining room. "I'll see if her feline highness is ready to come in for the night. Be up in a minute to see if there's anything you need."

Scott followed him through the house to the stairs off the kitchen. Jack continued to the back door and flipped on the light switch. The outdoor light usually brought the cat running on these cold winter nights. Sure enough, moments later, she meowed at the door. He picked her up and petted her while her feet warmed against his body. When he put her down, she headed for her dish on the floor and began crunching.

"Don't you ever get full, cat?" Chuckling at her insulted look, Jack went upstairs.

When their children were young, Jack and Claire had turned the landing area into a reading nook, benches built into two corners, surrounded by bookcases. Claire had made sturdy cushions from old jeans and papered the wall in a red, white, and blue stars-and-stripes print. He'd mounted reading lamps on the walls. The bookshelves still held Paul's and Marah's collections, a documentary of their growing-up years—Little Golden Books, Dr. Seuss, Nancy Drew, Hardy Boys, Jack London, Louisa May Alcott—and piles of magazines—airplanes, true adventure, fashion, romance. On the end of one shelf was a white Bible, Marah's, still as new looking as when she'd received it from Nikolas and Martha for her eighth-grade graduation. Separate doors, one off each side of the reading area, opened into the two bedrooms.

Paul's room overlooked the street at the front of the house, and Marah's faced the backyard. Gabled windows provided a place for window seats.

Someday, he might turn Marah's room into a study. Nice place to sit in the old rocker with a book and look out over the flower garden and pond he'd made for Claire.

Someday. Not yet. He still enjoyed visiting the kids' rooms once in a while. Marah's frilly curtains and doll collection, Paul's airplanes and hot rod models. In Paul's room, he'd look around at the posters and cluttered shelves and remember how it used to be, before their second child was conceived.

From time to time, haunting memories disturbed Jack's sleep, but he shoved them away. He rationalized that the occasional ache in his gut was from something he ate.

As expected, Jack found Scott in Paul's former quarters, with its airplane models and mountain-climbing photographs.

"Did Uncle Paul ever climb any of these mountains?" Scott stood before framed prints of Mount Everest, the Matterhorn, and Mount McKinley. When he was Scott's age, Paul dreamed of becoming a mountaineer.

Shirley A. Rorvik

"No, but he did bike around in Europe one summer. Before he joined the air force." Jack lifted a corner of the denim patchwork quilt to see if he'd remembered to put clean sheets on the bed after Paul's brief visit last month. Yes, but he'd forgotten the pillowcases. He went back downstairs, Scott's voice trailing behind.

"I'd like to do that. Bike tour. Camp out. With a dog."

"You got a dog?" Jack called from the linen closet under the stairs.

"Nah, Dad won't let me. But someday I'm gonna have one." As Jack reentered the room, Scott asked, "Can I take a shower?"

"Of course. Feeling a little smelly after the bus ride, eh?" Jack chuckled.

Scott made a wry face. "For sure." He pulled off his shirt, sat on the edge of the bed, and bent to pull off his shoes.

Jack stared at his grandson's bare back, where inflamed flesh swelled under a thick, rough scab on his shoulder blade. The wound was about two inches long, at least a quarter-inch wide. Jack moved in for a closer look. "What happened here, son? That's a nasty cut."

Scott jerked upright, his face flushed. "Nothin'."

"*Something* happened."

The boy squirmed. "Uh—accident at school. No big deal." He stood and tossed his shirt over his shoulder, covering the wound. With a nervous glance at his grandfather, he started toward the door.

Jack held up his hand. "Wait, let me get a better look at that." Scott slowed, and Jack pulled the shirt away. "Somebody hit you? What'd they use, an axe?"

Silence.

"You get in a fight?"

Scott leaned against the doorjamb and closed his eyes. "I don't want to talk about it right now, okay?"

Jack saw tears in his grandson's eyes before the boy turned away and bounded downstairs. He called after him, "Be careful you don't tear that scab off in the shower. I'll bandage it when you're done."

Frowning, Jack tugged at his mustache. He scanned the room as though it held clues. Nothing much belonging to Scott—shoes and socks, a duffel bag, jacket.

Jack picked up the bag and poked around. Paperback copy of *Moby Dick.* Dog-eared magazines—*Car and Driver, Popular Science, Playgirl.* He jerked back involuntarily. *What the—?* A bare-chested young man on the cover, bronze skin glistening, faded blue jeans riding low on the hips, half unzipped. *What kind of magazine is this? Would've thought*

10

Scott would have Playboy, *that's what Paul used to sneak in at this age.* Jack fanned through the pages, thinking it might be a fashion magazine for teenage boys. He halted at a photo of male nudes. Jack shook his head and tossed the magazine back with the others. He'd worry about that later.

He continued pawing through the bag. Sweatshirt, jeans, couple pairs of undershorts, and socks. He pulled out a wadded-up khaki shirt, shook it out, and held it up by the shoulders. *Enough pockets to make a passable fishing vest.* He turned it around. *What's this? Blood?* In back, on the upper-left shoulder, a jagged tear and a lot of dried blood.

He stared at the shirt, trying to figure out what might have happened. With no answers, he rolled it up and tucked it under his arm. He'd soak it cold water, try to get the blood out. But not until he got some answers from his grandson.

He glanced around. Scott's jacket hung over a chair; his billfold lay on the dresser. Jack hesitated. *No, I won't look any further. The boy has to tell me what happened.*

The cat sauntered in as he walked out of the room. Jack bent to scratch her ears. "Abandoning me tonight, are you? Just as well. Our boy needs company, I think." The cat hopped onto the bed, kneaded a spot to her liking, and began grooming her fur.

When Scott came out of the bathroom, Jack was sitting at the kitchen table, reading the newspaper. He looked up as the boy approached. "You like pizza? Here's a coupon. Maybe we'll use it tomorrow." He used a paring knife to cut out the Pizza Hut coupon.

Scott toweled his wet hair. "Man, did that feel good."

"Got any dirty clothes? I'm going to throw a load in tomorrow."

Scott grinned. "Smelled that bad, did I?"

Jack grinned back.

"Yeah, Granpop, I'd appreciate that. Didn't bring much stuff."

"Planning on a short visit, are you?"

"Don't need many clothes. I can get by."

"Let's take a look at that wound." Jack slipped the pizza coupon under the sugar bowl and folded the newspaper.

Scott sat down and twisted his head around for a glimpse of his back. "Guess it needs a Band-Aid, huh?"

Jack grunted and scowled while he gently pressed around the wound. "Probably should have had stitches, but it's starting to mend now. You'll have a scar to brag about. I'll put some antibiotic and a bandage on it. Sit tight a minute." He went into the bathroom and came out with a tube of ointment, a roll of tape, and a box of gauze bandaging.

Scott's eyes widened. "Not that bad, is it?"

Jack gave him a devilish look. "Want me to use duct tape instead?"

Scott laughed. "No, thanks."

As Jack cared for the wound, he asked, "You ready to tell me why you ran away?"

No answer.

"Something to do with this cut, huh? Bet the other guy looks a lot worse."

Scott hung his head.

Jack didn't press for an answer.

First aid completed, Scott yawned and headed for the stairs. "Thanks, Granpop. I'm going to bed. G'night."

"Good night, son. Sleep well."

Later, restless and unable to sleep soundly, Jack sat up on the edge of his bed and scratched at chest hairs bristling above his pajama top. He rubbed his face with both calloused hands and smoothed his mustache with his thumbs. He massaged the ache in his lower back. *Ah, that feels better, but now I'm wide-awake.*

He peered at the illuminated clock on the nightstand. Four thirty. He slipped his icy feet into his slippers. He'd have to put an extra blanket on the foot of his bed if Miss Lavender continued to sleep with Scott.

He pulled on his robe and slowly opened the bedroom door. Hoping not to disturb Scott, he eased into the hallway and peeked into the bathroom. Empty. Beyond that, the other main-floor bedroom Claire had converted to her sewing room. Jack had left it that way, as though she might return one day and pick up where she'd left off. He rarely opened that door.

He crept into the kitchen, tiptoed to the foot of the stairs. No sounds from the second floor, but a pair of eyes glowed from a white, furry face. Miss Lavender sat on the fourth step, observing him. No secrets with that cat around.

He poured a glassful of milk and tucked a box of cheese crackers under his arm.

The cat rubbed against his bare ankles. "Mee-yow-owl-l-l."

12

Jack hissed, "Sh-h-h!"

"Meow."

"That's better. Yes, you can have some. Now, c'mon." With his free hand, Jack plucked the garage keys off the hook by the back door and went out, the cat racing ahead down the shoveled path, snow piled high on either side. Jack shivered. *Br-r-r! Forgot my coat.*

The night sky glowed above downtown lights, but away from the city, it hung like sequined black velvet. Jack forgot his chill as he paused for a frosty, refreshing breath, his glance sweeping across the deep horizon. Sunday school lessons drilled into him as a youngster again came to his mind, familiar words he had often repeated over the years on clear nights, whether in his own backyard or near his tent pitched alongside a rippling mountain brook, about how almighty God laid the foundation of the earth and made the heavens. And once again Jack wondered, *How could it be that the Almighty, who did all that, should care about the likes of me? But Scott, he's just a boy. What happened to my grandson, God? What am I supposed to do?* Jack stood gazing at the stars for several minutes, hoping for some insight, some flash of wisdom. Nothing happened.

Shivering now, Jack hurried to the side entrance of the garage, where the cat waited impatiently, raising alternate paws off the cold concrete step.

"I'm coming, I'm coming." Unlocking the door, he pushed it open, stepped inside, and flipped the light switch. Miss Lavender scampered in and headed for the rag rug in front of the woodstove. She gave Jack an expectant look.

He set the crackers and milk on a nearby shelf. "Any coals left in there?" The cast-iron door swung open with a squeak. Jack stirred the sleeping embers, the poker clunking against the edge of the firebox. "This'll take right off, Missy. Get us warmed up in no time." He gathered a handful of kindling from the wood box, placed it on the coals, added a couple of small, split logs, shut the stove door with a *clang,* and adjusted the chrome-handled damper. He sniffed, satisfied that the faint wood smoke smell wasn't signaling a poor updraft in the stovepipe.

He pulled up the rickety rocking chair and sat down on the cushioned seat with his feet on the rug, knees near the stove. He poured a little milk from the glass into a chipped dish and set it on the floor.

Miss Lavender sniffed it and turned her green eyes back to him.

"How do you want your crackers tonight, Missy? Al dente or al soggy?"

Like a prairie dog, the cat sat up on her haunches, her tail straight out behind her on the floor. She reached one white front paw toward Jack. "Meow."

"Al dente. Very good, madam. Here you are." He offered a cheese cracker to the cat. She daintily took it in her teeth, hunched down on the rug, and began eating.

As Jack and the cat enjoyed their snack and listened to the crackling fire, he looked around the shop, relaxing in the warmth radiating from the stove. *Best thing I ever did, closing off this end of the garage, insulating and sheet-rocking it. Glad I finally sold Claire's car. All I need is the pickup. This room is just the right size for my saw and workbench and plenty of shelves for tools and supplies. Cement floor's cold, though. Someday I'll get a carpet remnant to cover it.*

A feeling of pleasure brought a slight smile when he looked at his current project—a miniature carousel horse, replica of the full-sized one he was carving for the downtown Carousel.

The big one's named after you, Claire. My Clarissa Mae. He sighed. *I miss you so much, Claire. Okay, truth is, I miss you especially now. Maybe you could figure out what's going on with our grandson.*

Placing his empty glass on a shelf, Jack stood up to check the fire. Miss Lavender hopped onto his warm chair cushion and curled up. "Humph. Some manners you have." He stroked the cat's back. "Okay, I'll just get to work."

Since Claire's death, hardly a week went by that Jack didn't get up in the middle of the night and come to the shop to work on his carvings. After a snack, of course. If he forgot, the cat reminded him.

Jack pulled a stool up to his workbench, switched on the lamp, and picked up the five-inch-high horse. With the smallest blade of his pocketknife—the same one his grandfather had given him nearly sixty years ago—he began trimming the horse's flank to give it life and motion.

Working with his hands enabled Jack to concentrate on his problem. *Who's Scott protecting? Vic? Drinking messes up a man's judgment. But that cut on the kid's back ... Vic couldn't do that to his own son; he's not that kind of man. Then who? Where'd Scott go when he left home? Must have hung around in Boise a couple days.* Jack recalled an article he'd read about runaway teenagers living on the streets. He visualized Scott sleeping under the bridge, like he'd seen itinerants do downtown. *Probably got in a fight with someone of that caliber. So why won't he—or Marah—tell me? Or is it Vic they're protecting?*

With no answers, Jack forced his attention onto his work. He dusted wood shavings off the miniature horse and held it at arm's length. *Coming along pretty good.* His thoughts turned to the Riverfront Park Carousel. *Hope Clarissa Mae turns out as well.*

Working at the Carousel made living worthwhile. Life had become peaceful, promising, even. An image of Kennocha Bryant filled his mind, and he smiled. Kennocha—long, wavy, red hair, sea-green eyes, just like Nikolas said. Jack chuckled. *Not that I'd ever admit it to him. How old is she? Looks to be about Marah's age; too young to be interested in the likes of me. But there's that bit of gray hair at her temples. Maybe she's closer to my age than I think. Does it matter?*

A pang of guilt struck. *Claire, I still love you. Always will. But I'm lonely. I need a woman around, someone to hold, someone to talk to, like now, about Scott.* Aloud he said, "Is that so bad, God? Am I being unfaithful to Claire?"

Suddenly, he felt old. He muttered, "How's a man supposed to know what to do? About anything? I don't want to get involved in Marah's family problems. If that's what's going on. But Scott's wound is too serious to ignore."

Miss Lavender hopped down from the chair, strolled across the floor, and leaped onto Jack's lap. She thrust her head under his chin until Jack set aside the wooden horse and stroked her. She settled against his chest and purred while he talked.

"Missy, the boy should be with his family. In school. Teenagers always overreact. I could let Marah get that airplane ticket for the boy. Then drive over in the spring myself, see how things are going." He scratched the cat's ears absentmindedly while he considered the idea. "Yes, Missy, that's what I'll do."

Having reached a decision, Jack tucked his arm under the cat's haunches and stood up. "Time to bank the stove and get to bed. I'll tell our boy in the morning that he's got to go back home.

CHAPTER 2

Monday morning while Scott still slept, Jack drove across town to pick up Nikolas at his eastside home. On their way downtown, Jack filled in his friend on what had happened since Saturday evening.

Nikolas shook his head and clicked his tongue. "My, my. Such a sad thing. It is God's will that Scott came to you."

"Don't know about that, but I'll be glad when he's back home. Where he belongs." Jack tapped his thumb on the steering wheel, waiting for a traffic light to change.

"When will that be?"

"Soon as I can get hold of Marah, tell her to wire the money for a plane ticket."

"You are going to let the boy go?"

Jack threw him an irritated look. "What's wrong with that?"

A deep frown creased Nikolas's face. "This is not right. Nothing will be resolved. You must talk to the boy's parents."

"I can do that later. When the roads are better. Drive over and see how things are going."

When Nikolas didn't respond after several moments, Jack glanced over to see the big man smoothing his beard over his chest, still scowling. Not a good sign.

As Jack turned off Front Street and drove down the short hill to Riverfront Park, Nikolas said, "Your grandson ... his parents ... something is very wrong. Keep him safe. With you. God has sent him—"

"Nikolas." Jack raised his voice. "My mind is made up." He pulled into the parking lot in front of the brick and glass Carousel building and turned off the motor. Both men got out, neither looking at the other.

Two rooms at the rear of the building served as work centers: one for carving wooden ponies, friendly gargoyles, and dragons; and the other for painting the creations. A storage room adjoined the paint room. The workrooms' large, interior windows faced the center attraction: forty colorful ponies mounted on a gleaming hardwood platform.

The artisans who'd created the ponies had given them individual personalities and trappings. Merrilee—a golden palomino with daisies intertwining her mane and tail. Noble Knight—an armored, satin-black steed, strong and courageous. Princess—a white Arabian with smartly arched neck and red, tasseled reins. Chief—an Indian pinto, strong legs ready to gallop across the plains. Buster Brown—a toddler-sized pony on the inside row, his chocolate-colored eyes friendly and warm.

The horses seemed alive, watching, eagerly awaiting the calliope's magical music to bring them to life amid shouts and laughter of young and old riders—toddlers through great-grandparents. No two ponies were alike, yet there was a sense of unity, a reflection of the spirit of cooperation among the many volunteers who created the Carousel.

The fragrance of fresh-cut basswood greeted Jack when he opened the woodshop door. He glanced over his shoulder and saw Nikolas disappear into the paint room.

A balding man in navy sweats sat at a scarred wooden table, chisel in hand, a basswood horse head in front of him. "Hi, Jack. You're just in time. Give me a hand with this, will you?"

"Glad to. What's the problem?"

"This mouth. Thought I knew how to start his teeth, but now I'm not so sure."

Jack studied the piece and picked up a chisel and a wooden mallet. "Here's what I'd do. Start here." Jack placed the blade against the horse's mouth and tapped the end of the chisel with the mallet. In a few seconds, an upper lip and rough-hewn teeth emerged beneath Jack's skilled hands. Jack handed the man the tools. "See?"

"Yeah, I see where you're going."

Jack gave the man a friendly slap on the shoulder. "You can do it."

At his own workstation, Jack picked up a nearly completed horse head from a shelf and pulled out his pocketknife. Soon, he lost track of time, absorbed in his work, relaxed, and content.

After a while, Nikolas came in, lifted a set of pony legs from a hook on the pegboard wall, sat down opposite Jack, and began sanding.

Jack cleared his throat. "Sorry I bit your head off." He shoved aside some wood shavings and waited for a word from his friend. When Nikolas didn't respond to his apology, Jack looked up to find mischievous black eyes fixed on him.

Puzzled, Jack said, "You look mighty pleased with yourself. What've you been up to?"

"She's here."

"Who?"

White teeth gleamed through the black and gray beard and mustache. "The lovely lady with hair the color of a Siberian sunset."

Jack snorted. "What would you know about Siberian sunsets? You haven't been in Russia since you were in diapers." He bent to his carving.

"Ah, but my father lived nearly his whole life in Russia. I am quite certain he saw such sunsets. I remember what he said."

Jack winked. "Or you made it up."

Nikolas placed his hand over his heart, a mock look of pain on his face. "You doubt me?"

Jack chuckled. "Have you ever given me any reason not to?"

"You digress. I was speaking of a certain young lady."

"You're too old for her."

"Aha. You misunderstand. I was thinking of you."

Jack shook his head. "No schemes. Told you that before." Shavings flew under a quick puff of air from Jack's pursed lips.

"My friend, I just want to help. You grieve too long."

"I'll decide that." He scowled. "Besides, I haven't forgotten the last time you fixed me up on a date."

Nikolas's face clouded. "Yes, I misjudged that particular lady's intentions." His eyes gleamed. "But this one is different. Kennocha Bryant is special."

Jack grunted and bent his head to hide a smile.

That evening, Jack tried again to reach Marah and Vic. No answer. *Tomorrow's soon enough, I guess. Wouldn't hurt for the boy to stay another day or two.*

Tuesday morning, Scott moped, so Jack assigned chores. Scott helped split and stack firewood and then he filled the wood box by the stove in the garage.

Miss Lavender had become the teenager's frequent companion. The cat's unusual compliance to Scott's attention—not at all like the feisty feline Jack had grown used to—made him suspect the animal sensed the boy's despondency. She understood suffering.

The bedraggled, half-grown cat had appeared at his back door about a year after Claire died. Had she been there, Claire wouldn't have allowed the filthy, sickly looking animal in the house. But Jack felt sorry for the cat; her appearance matched his own emotional and mental state. He took her in, fed her, and provided a cozy box for her to sleep in underneath the stairs. For three days, she ate and slept, with only occasional ventures outside to tend to her needs. She began grooming herself on the fourth day and hadn't quit since. The white on her breast and face gleamed, and the gray and black stripes on her back shone. Her mitten paws looked like ermine fur in winter.

With her restored energy and health, her personality began to blossom—generally independent with delightful, and rare, moments of warmth. Jack's house became her castle, the yard her domain. Jack had never been more pleased with his adoption of this kitty than now, to see the bonding between his grandson and the cat.

Wednesday afternoon, Jack's fingers itched to get back to work on his carving. Encouraged by Scott's willingness to work alongside him, he said, "Want to go to the Carousel? See the horse I'm carving?"

The teenager shrugged, nodded.

Jack went to the garage, lifted a soft, old towel from a nail on the wall, and dusted off the hood and windshield of his red Chevy pickup. Not that the vehicle was particularly dirty. Maybe a little airborne dust from the workroom when the adjoining door was open. Hardly enough for anyone but Jack to notice.

He raised the garage door, climbed behind the wheel, and started the motor. It caught on the first crank and idled smoothly. Scott shuffled into the garage, his Boise State cap pulled low over his eyes, his mouth turned down. He glanced up as he neared the pickup, and his face brightened.

After Jack backed out, Scott lowered the garage door and hopped into the passenger seat. "You still have this ol' truck! What is it? A '54?"

"Close—'55." Jack pulled out into the street.

"Not the original paint, though." Scott ran his hand over the seat. "Upholstery neither. You do it?"

"Not everything. Friend of mine who has a body shop did the paint job six or eight years ago. Did the upholstery myself. With your grandma's help." What Jack didn't say was that Claire had resented the money he spent on his old pickup. Her help was grudgingly given, her relief evident once the project was completed.

"Yeah, Mom's good at that stuff, too." Scott gave his grandfather a sidelong look. "She let me help do the living room. Have you seen it? Since we changed everything?"

Jack tugged at his mustache. "Let me think—seems like it was maroon or something when I last saw it. Dark. That's what I remember."

"You should see it now. Mostly blue and white. Winter white, Mom calls it. She let me do the blue pillows. I picked out the stuff, cut it out, and everything. Mom sewed them, though, 'cause she wanted some kind of binding or something on the edges."

"I remember it looked downright glum before. Glad to hear you and your mother brightened it up."

Scott's chin dropped to his chest. "Yeah."

Jack drove a couple of blocks in silence, puzzled at his grandson's sudden mood change. He changed the subject. "Wish your grandma could've seen the Carousel."

"You mean you didn't always do this? Only after Grandma died?"

Jack nodded. "Gave me something to do. Filled in the hours."

Scott seemed to consider this. "How many horses have you made?"

"Just finishing up my fourth. Izsak Miksa starts everyone out in the sanding or painting rooms. Then we work up to carving."

"Shock Meeshack who?"

"EE-zhahk, first name, MEEK-shah, last name." Jack glanced over at his grandson. "I haven't told you this story? Izsak is the reason this town has an authentic, full-sized, operating carousel."

Scott settled against the door of the pickup, pushed his cap to the back of his head, and fixed an interested gaze on his grandfather. "Yeah?"

"This all started several years ago, when Izsak wanted to carve a horse in his grandad's memory. Seems the old gent was a maker of fine furniture in Hungary. But in the early 1900s, when he came to the USA, the country was flooded with men like him. A glut of expert furniture builders. So he turned to making the horses for merry-go-rounds."

"Big comedown, huh? From fancy furniture to merry-go-round horses?"

Jack smiled. "Hardly. Ever see a genuine, old-time carousel? Dentzel, Looff, Philadelphia Toboggan Company—"

"Huh?"

"Carousel manufacturers back East. Big thing in those days. Philadelphia-style horses carved to look realistic. Somebody once said the only thing those merry-go-rounds lacked was the smell of a stable and the sound of a whinny. That's how good they were."

"You guys do it like that?"

"We're trying. Not as good as the masters, but pretty good. Wait 'til you see. You can judge for yourself."

Jack eased to a stop on the icy street at a traffic light. As the signal turned green and they went through, he continued. "Before the Great Depression, there were lots of amusement parks in this country, especially on the East Coast." He glanced at his grandson. "You've heard of Coney Island?"

"Yeah, in New York. Like a big carnival or something."

"I don't know if anyone knows for sure how many carousels there were on Coney Island during those years, but Izsak's grandfather knew of one fellow who had about a dozen of his own in operation."

"I never knew they were such a big deal. I just thought it's like, carnivals, fairs, you know?"

"Lots of these new citizens, the skilled woodworkers, took to carving these horses, working for the bigger companies. After a while it was like a contest—who could carve the most intricate, patriotic horses."

"Patriotic?"

"Just like today, people getting complacent. Thinking they had it made. Wanting to be entertained. Not much thought about the nation and their freedom. But the immigrants were thankful to be here. They loved this country. So they worked patriotic themes into their carvings. Horses decorated with flags and buntings and banners. Shields with heads of presidents carved into them. Military horses."

Jack pulled into the Carousel parking lot. "'Course, there were the fancy, frilly horses, too. Flowers and ribbons and jewels. And other animals—lions, rabbits, giraffes. You name it. But mostly horses." He turned off the motor and looked around. "Don't see Izsak's pickup here today. You'll get to meet him another day."

Scott eyed the building with a center-peaked roof. "The merry-go-round's in there? A whole building just for that?"

"That's right. The calliope, too. Izsak started out making just one pony in his garage. Then his idea grew into a whole carousel for the town. People got interested. Some wanted to help carve and paint the horses. Others gave money."

"Rich people. Like the ones Mom's always hitting up for whatever cause she's working on." Scott turned his head away, and gloom returned to his countenance.

Jack ignored the mood change and continued. "Wealthy folks, yes, but others, too. Service clubs—Rotary, Kiwanis. Schoolkids. Families. Then the city got involved after a while, donated this piece of land. An architect designed the building for free; a contractor gave supplies and his time." Jack gestured to include the building and the small park surrounding it. "Wasn't long before we had this. All volunteer effort."

"You mean you don't get paid to do this?"

"Nope. No one does. Not in money, anyway."

Scott looked impressed. "Cool."

They climbed out of the pickup and stood for a moment while Scott looked around. The Carousel building sat near the bank of the Clark Fork River, now partially frozen. Less than a quarter-mile away, the Higgins Avenue Bridge spanned the river, one of several bridges connecting both sides of the city.

Scott gestured toward the structure. "Bunch of homeless guys live under a couple of the bridges in Boise. They do that here, too?"

Jack thought of the wound on his grandson's back. "So I've heard. Once in a while you see them loitering around. Especially upriver, near the university. Rough-looking bunch." He paused. "If someone, say a teenager, got too close, they might give him a bad time, huh?"

Scott shrugged and pointed to the north end of the bridge where an old, eight-story, brick building with a marquee stood. "Movie theater?"

"Yes. Restored from the 1920s. Restaurant, too. Apartments in upper levels. Pretty fancy, from what I hear. Nikolas tells me one of our new painters lives there. Kennocha's her name."

Scott looked bored and shivered.

Jack said, "C'mon, let's go in."

"Is it open? I mean, for people to ride?"

"Mm-hmm. Year-round."

They entered through the brass-trimmed front door and passed from the small lobby into the main Carousel chamber.

Scott's mouth dropped open; his eyes lit up. He stood riveted, his face glowing with wonder. "Far out! Like, wow! This is *nothing* like the carnival junk. This is awesome, Granpop!"

CHAPTER 3

Forty horses and two chariots stood on a carousel platform, illuminated by over a thousand lights under the overhead canopy. The prancing steeds shone with bright paint and colorful trappings: an elegant, white pony with golden mane and the American flag draped at her side; a spunky, bucking pinto; a shiny, black, armored charger with a school mascot carved in a shield adorning its rear flank; a Norwegian Fjord horse, complete with rosemaling on the saddle blanket. Each pony was unique, filled with life and motion. Eyes watchful, anticipating, as though ready to spring into life the moment a rider climbed on and the music began.

Light bounced off gleaming brass plating around the base of the circular platform and the shiny poles where the ponies were mounted. Beneath their hooves, the highly polished hardwood floor mirrored a kaleidoscope of color. Ornate carvings—gargoyles, dragons, and cherubs—decorated the canopy above the suspended platform.

Grinning, Scott spread his arms wide. "Granpop, this is terrific! Man, I thought it'd be like any old merry-go-round, you know? Like the ones at the state fair. They're nothing like this. I didn't even know anybody ever did stuff like this. It's so-o-o cool!"

Jack' chest burst with pride.

Scott examined a galloping dapple gray.

"He's Messenger, a Pony Express horse."

"They have names?" Scott stroked the wooden pony's neck.

Jack nodded. "Every one of them. Not only that, but each one has a special story behind it. You'll learn more as you meet the carvers and painters. Let's go back to the workroom."

From the glassed-in workroom, Nikolas waggled a beefy hand. Jack returned the greeting with a half salute.

"Remember Nikolas Kostenka?"

"Yeah ... with the funny accent and perfect grammar. My English teacher would be, like, wowed."

Scott walked into the woodshop and sniffed. "Smells good. Hi Nikolas." Nikolas ignored Scott's outstretched hand and wrapped him in a hug. Scott grinned. Then, blinking rapidly, he bit his lower lip and wandered around the small room, studying unfinished heads, necks, bodies, and legs. After a moment, he said, "Looks like an auto parts store—for horses."

Nikolas and two other men stood beside a pair of sawhorses. The men were applying clamps to a freshly glued, complex array of flat-planed boards with precision-cut right angles. None of the wood grains ran parallel to adjoining pieces.

"Looks like a wood puzzle," Scott said. "Granpop, how come you don't just use one big hunk of wood?"

"Couple of reasons, son. One, these basswood boards don't come in pony-sized hunks. They're all different sizes, just like the trees they come from."

"So you glue them together to get a big enough piece."

"Right." Jack pointed to a seam. "And see this? The grain doesn't go the same direction at the joints."

Scott studied the arrangement of boards. "I get it. So it won't warp out of shape."

Pleased, Jack nodded. "Also adds strength."

Scott watched the gluing and clamping operation. The whole unit resembled a hollowed-out rectangular box. As Nikolas tightened the last clamp, the teenager gave him a skeptical look. "That's gonna be a horse?"

Nikolas wiped his hands on his carpenter's apron. "That it is, my boy."

"How come it's hollow?"

"For strength. And to seal away sentimental treasures for posterity."

"Yeah, sure."

Jack said, "All us carvers do it."

The other two men working on the horse body voiced agreement.

Scott asked, "What're you gonna put in it, Nikolas?"

Nikolas arched a black eyebrow and pursed his lips. "That is a secret." He folded his hands prayer fashion and rolled his eyes toward the ceiling. "Only the good Lord knows. And my closest compatriots— who will also deposit secret items."

Scott's eyes narrowed as though to test the older man's seriousness. Apparently convinced, he said, "Cool. I like that idea."

26

After Jack, Nikolas, and the other men discussed the day's work, Jack picked up a wooden horse's neck and eyed his grandson. "Think you'd like to try your hand at sanding?"

"Sure." He took the wooden neck Jack offered. "Hey, it's kinda light. I thought it'd be real heavy. What kind of wood did you say this is?"

"Basswood. Or linden. Same thing. Good for carving." Jack handed Scott several squares of sandpaper. "Start with this one, the coarser grain, work down to the finer grains. Have you sanded before?"

"Yeah, in shop class. Made a desk caddy for Mom. Kind of liked doing it. Wood feels good, smells good, you know?" He began sanding in long, even strokes, and the scratching sound developed into a rhythm.

"I can tell you're a natural." Jack picked up the head, a separate piece, and opened his pocketknife. After touching up the knife edge on a leather strop, he went to work on the horse's ears, visualizing an alert, forward position.

Other carvers wouldn't think of using a pocketknife, but Jack had his own style. Until detail work demanded chisels with curved blades for flower petals and intricate parts, he relied on his faithful old pocketknife. His friends called it "Jack's magic blade."

He glanced over at Scott and felt his worries evaporate, satisfied with the boy's absorption in his work. He seemed to have a feel for the wood—alternately sanding, dusting, and smoothing with his hand to feel the rough spots.

After a while, Scott said, "Mom's got those quail you carved on the mantel at home. They're cool. I'd like to do that kind of stuff. Birds and animals. And cars. Sports cars." He held the neck at arm's length to examine his work. "You ever do horses before you went to work here?"

"Just miniature ones. Nothing big."

Scott looked up. "Did you have to start out sanding, too? Like everyone else?"

"No, I started with carving. Not the heads, at first, but the neck and legs." Jack switched to the smallest blade on his knife. "Usually, one person does the head and body for a horse. Personalizes it. Other carvers might work on the legs and neck. Sometimes, one person does the whole thing."

Scott walked over to stand by Jack. "What's yours going to be? Have you picked out a name yet?"

He trimmed a tiny, rough edge and said, "Yes, this is Clarissa Mae. After your grandmother."

"Hey, neat. Grandma would like that."

"This little pony will have a cascade of roses behind the saddle and smaller roses on her bridle."

"Was that Grandma's favorite? Roses? I remember she was always crawling around in her flowerbeds. Wearing that big straw hat."

"Um-hm." Jack smiled, remembering. "She loved her rose garden." He scrutinized his work.

Scott said, "What color? The horse, I mean."

"White?"

Scott tilted his head. "For Grandma, yeah, white. And all colors of roses. That'd be cool."

Jack nodded and paused to give Scott a wink and a knowing smile. "According to our knowledgeable friend Nikolas, the new painter is especially good at painting flowers. Shades them so they look real. I might ask her to do Clarissa Mae's."

"You know her? The painter?"

Jack's smile broadened. "Met her once. Caught a glimpse or two of her around here." To himself, Jack added, *Wish I knew how to get to know her better without making a darned fool of myself.*

Scott picked up a curl of wood and wrapped it around his finger. His expression was pensive as he studied his grandfather's face.

Over the course of the afternoon, the door to the workroom opened and closed as other volunteers came and went from time to time. Jack barely noticed until he happened to look up from stropping his knife and saw a stranger. Memories of his job as supervisor of the men's department at DeWolfe's Department store were awakened as the well-dressed man entered the room.

Late forties, Jack guessed, looking like he might have just come from a photo shoot for a full-page menswear ad. Understated wealth and rugged good looks—dark hair, high cheekbones, strong chin. An earth-tone herringbone wool blazer, size forty-two long to Jack's practiced eye, over a forest-green turtleneck. In Jack's days at DeWolfe's, the man's Levi's would have been considered too casual for the jacket, but nowadays, he reflected, anything goes.

The stranger caught Jack's eye, strode across the room, and offered a handshake. "Bevan O'Brien."

Jack returned the handshake and introduced himself. The visitor was probably interested in buying a carousel pony. From his appearance and attitude of self-assurance, a few thousand might be what the man expected to pay for a custom-made pony. Izsak set his price high, but he earned it.

The other man's eyes quickened with interest. "Jack, the famous wood-carver. I've heard a lot about you."

Caught off guard, Jack didn't respond.

Bevan glanced around the room. "Maybe you can help me. I'm looking for Kennocha Bryant. I was to meet her here, but I haven't found her."

As though someone had jerked a cord anchored to the top of his head, Jack's spine straightened and his shoulders squared. "Kennocha?"

"Yeah. She said to meet her in the Carousel workroom at five."

Jack resisted the impulse to tell O'Brien she hadn't come in today. Instead, he said, "Did you look in the paint room?"

Bevan arched an eyebrow. "Tell you the truth, I didn't know there was one. Kennocha carries on about this place so much, I tend to tune it out."

Jack gestured with his thumb. "Next door. She paints, you know."

"So she does. Thanks, Jack."

Staring at the man's retreating back, Jack felt Nikolas's eyes watching him. He set the strop aside and returned to his work, avoiding an interchange with Nikolas. For now.

After a while, Nikolas pushed himself to his feet with a groan and patted his ample belly. "A man could get skinny doing this. No time to eat."

Jack snorted. "I've never known you to miss any meals."

"I was going to invite you to partake of my oven stew, but now I shall just ask Scott."

Squinting at his old friend, Jack leaned toward his grandson. "What d'you think? You gonna risk it?"

Scott grinned. "Sure, if he'll eat it first." He stood, yawned, and stretched. "I'd eat anything right now."

Nikolas pulled at his ear. "I am hurt. To think my dearest friends question my culinary skills." He arched one eyebrow. "You will see. It is an excellent stew."

Jack gathered his tools. "In that case, we accept." After he finished tidying up his workspace, he picked up the horse neck Scott had sanded. "Nice job, son."

The teenager's face lit up. "Thanks. It was fun."

"Okay, let's finish cleaning up around here. Looks like we're the last to leave. There's a broom in the corner. You want to sweep, Scott, while I pick up this other stuff?"

Later, as Jack and Nikolas left the building, Jack looked over his shoulder for Scott. The teen trailed behind, his gaze lingering on the Carousel. Nikolas drew Jack's attention.

"I know you. You are thinking she is too young for you."

"Who?"

"You know who. Kennocha. Of course, she is just right for me."

Jack eyed the big man beside him. "Just right? As I recall, you old Russian, you're three years older than me."

"Ah, yes, but I am younger in my heart. Besides, did you not tell me that you are not interested?" Nikolas clasped his hand over his chest. "Ah, my heart pounds with anticipation of how I shall romance her."

"Your heart pounds over every good-looking woman. I wish you'd get married and settle down again. Martha would rather know you're behaving instead of running around, chasing women."

Nikolas chuckled. "Only in my imagination, my friend. As you know." He paused. "At least my thoughts are occupied with capturing one of the fairer sex. What is your excuse? Claire has been gone longer than my dear Martha, may she rest in peace." He bowed his head for a moment before he continued the attack. "You never give any lovely creature a chance to catch you."

Jack moved ahead of Nikolas with a purposeful stride. "I'm not ready yet. Furthermore, my private life is none of your business, you old meddler. Besides, you've got it backward. Martha's been gone longer than Claire. Now, c'mon. Let's go eat that rotten stew of yours."

Scott caught up to Nikolas, and Jack overheard him say, "Granpop has a girlfriend? He never told us."

"No, my boy, not yet. Perhaps never. He holds on still to your grandmother."

At the pickup, Jack called over his shoulder, "Let's go, you two. I'm getting hungry."

At Nikolas's house, after a hearty meal of oven stew and biscuits from scratch, Nikolas produced a homemade apple pie from the pantry. Scott piled his slice with ice cream and went into the living room to watch a rock concert on television. The two men stayed in the kitchen.

Nikolas refilled their coffee cups and sat down. "I am glad to see you have not sent the boy home."

Jack scowled and pressed his finger into a pastry crumb on his plate. "Can't get hold of them about the airplane ticket. So I decided to drive him back myself." He forked a bite of spicy apples and flaky crust into his mouth.

Nikolas ate quickly, a dark scowl on his face. With the last bite poised midair, he said, "I have a proposal. You go talk to Marah and Vic alone. Leave the boy here. With me." He paused. "You assess the situation, then decide about the boy. Perhaps he would be better off with you for a while. Perhaps until the end of this school year."

Jack grunted and sipped his coffee. "That'd be—what—three, four months? No, can't do that. A few days, yes. But not that. Wouldn't be good for the family, let alone me. I'm getting too old to have a teenager around that long." He raised his eyes to meet Nikolas's disapproving look. "Okay, go ahead. I know you'll chew on me."

Nikolas contemplated. "No, my friend, I cannot reprimand you. I would feel the same. You and I—it has not been easy for us, being alone. Now, at last, we have adjusted. We can jest with one another about lovely ladies, but the truth is, we have come to enjoy living alone, eh?"

Jack nodded, swallowing the lump in his throat.

Stroking his beard, Nikolas continued, "But on the other hand, a teenager would challenge you. Perhaps even revitalize you."

Exasperated, Jack shot upright. "Revitalize? You old fart! You should talk!"

A rumbling laugh rolled from deep inside Nikolas's chest. "See, it is working already." He dabbed at the tears running down his cheeks with a blue-bordered handkerchief. Between chortles, he said, "If it works for you, I may try it myself. I have grandsons who are Scott's age. Their mother would be very pleased to have me take them off her hands."

At home that night, Jack threw a load of clothes into the washer. Scott's smelly socks brought back memories of Paul's youth. *What is it about teenage boys' feet? Paul used to come home from football practice and shed his clothes in a pile near his bedroom door.* Jack's mustache prickled in recollection of the odor when he ventured into his son's room. *Wonder if my feet stunk like that? Me and my four brothers. My poor, dear mother, God bless her soul. Bending over a galvanized tub, scrubbing clothes on a washboard.*

Thursday morning, Jack found Scott curled up with the cat in his favorite place in the living room, the bay window. After four good nights' sleep, a gallon of milk, pizza, hamburgers, and good home cooking, the teenager's color had returned to normal, and the black circles under his eyes had faded. But in idle moments, like now, he seemed sad. Homesick?

Jack sat down in an olive-green, thread-bare recliner—his stubborn rebellion against Claire's everything-new decorating scheme. "Son, I think it's time we called your folks again."

Scott shrugged and looked away.

"We need to get you home, back in school."

With a sudden movement that caused the cat to leap away, Scott swung his feet to the floor. Gold flecks in his brown eyes shot fire as he glared and snapped, "I'm not going home! If you don't want me here, fine. I'll go someplace else." He stomped toward the door.

The sharp crack of Jack's voice stopped him. "Young man, come back here."

Slowly, Scott turned.

Eyes boring into his grandson's, Jack said, "Come here and sit down."

The teenager shuffled to the bay window bench and sat, his expression defiant.

Jack said, "In the first place, it's not a matter of whether I want you here. My first concern is what's best for you." He paused. "In the second place, I want to know why you ran away. You won't talk about it, your dad didn't call; your mother is evasive as you are. This has got to stop. Somebody better start talking."

Scott flinched. "I can take care of myself."

Jack leaned forward and gripped the arms of his chair. "I intend to get to the bottom of this." He waited while Scott tried to stare him down. Jack saw the defiance in his eyes weaken.

"Dad doesn't ..." Scott shook his head. "You don't ..." The boy's hostility melted. "Granpop, I *can't* talk about it." He rubbed the back of his neck. "I just want to forget it." He fought for control but lost. His shoulders shook with choked-back sobs.

Jack's stomach curled into knots. He got up, sat down beside Scott, wrapped his arm around him, and pulled him close. After a few moments, Jack said, "Son, I can see it's hard on you, but running isn't the way to deal with problems. When something so serious happens that a kid runs away from home, you need adult help to figure it out. Someone you trust. If not me, some other grownup. A school counselor ..."

A low moan escaped Scott's lips. He rubbed his eyes. "Please don't send me home. I ... just can't."

"Listen." He gave his grandson a gentle shake. "I'll be there with you. To talk to your parents."

"Promise?"

"You've got my word. Okay?" Scott nodded. "Okay. Let's take this one step at a time. Now, let me take another look at that wound."

"It's healed up."

"I want to see it."

Scott grumbled, "Oh, all right." He pulled off his shirt.

Jack examined the skin around the bandage, didn't see any flaring redness, and the bandage showed no drainage from the wound. "Healing up good. We'll take the bandage off tomorrow." He patted Scott's good shoulder and stood up. "Now, I'm going to call your mom, tell her we're coming over."

"When?"

"We'll go Friday—tomorrow."

Scott's reddened eyes widened in alarm. "Can't we wait? 'Til the weekend, maybe? Or next week?"

"No, son. Let's get this done." He went to the phone in the kitchen, muttering to himself, "Those two are going to give me some answers or else." As soon as his daughter came on the line, he said, "Marah, I'm bringing Scott home tomorrow."

"Oh ... good."

Her voice didn't sound convincing. In fact, she almost sounded disappointed. He continued, "Is Vic back from his trip? We need to talk—all of us."

"Well, yes, but—"

"No buts. Neither you nor Vic have called to explain why your son ran away. I want some answers."

"I understand your concern, Dad, but it's easily explained. You know how teenagers are. Don't you remember when I ran away from home?"

Jack remembered. "You were five. You were pouting because your mother wouldn't take you to the playground. Your journey was three blocks. You were a child, Marah, not a teenager." Jack paused and let his next words fall like a judge's gavel. "And you didn't have an unexplained wound from some violent act."

Marah gasped.

Jack continued. "We'll be there tomorrow evening. You tell Vic that I expect both of you to be home. Understand?"

Her voice was low. "Yes, Dad. I'll tell him. We'll be here. And don't worry about that cut on Scott's back. He—"

Jack's sharp voice cut her off. "That's enough." He ended the call. Replacing the phone, something nagged at him, something Marah said. *Cut on Scott's back ... did I say it was on his back? No. So, how does Marah know?*

CHAPTER 4

In Boise, Marah felt restless after her father's abrupt hang-up moments before. She stirred skim milk into her coffee, gripped the cup in both hands, and leaned against the kitchen counter, her brow furrowed with worry. *Dad's like a bulldog, won't give up. What did Scott tell him? Why can't they just leave things alone?* She slammed the cup onto the countertop, grabbed her purse, and hurried out the door. She didn't know where she was going. She simply knew she had to move, do something, anything. If Vic hadn't left for work by the time she got back, she'd just tell him she had to run to the grocery store for something.

A soft howling sound in the yard drew her attention. A child crying? She listened. No ... a puppy. She began walking slowly around the yard, bending to peer under bushes. At the sound of a faint rustling noise, Marah turned. There, under the garden bench, a tiny, quivering puppy. She knelt, speaking softly to coax the animal into the open. She ignored the cold, damp grass. A wet, dirty, brown and white puppy limped toward her outstretched hands, favoring a front paw.

"Oh, you poor little thing. Come here, baby, come on." Yipping and whining, the puppy approached, its eyes imploring. Oblivious to the filth and dampness, she scooped the pup into her arms and cuddled it against her chest. "You're so cold. And probably hungry." She placed her cheek against its head and felt it tremble. "Don't be afraid. I'll take care of you."

Marah shot a furtive look toward the house to be sure her husband wasn't watching. She whispered to the puppy, "I'll have to hide you someplace. Just until he's gone." Rising to her feet, she felt a sense of panic. "He won't let me keep you. Where can I hide you? My sewing room? No, he might hear. I'll have to put you in the cellar for now."

Holding the puppy close, she sneaked into the house, into the large kitchen pantry, and through the door that led to the cellar. She tiptoed down the old wooden stairs, pausing and holding her breath at each creak. In the storage room, she searched for something to make a bed. She grabbed an old woolen jacket hanging on a nail and stuffed it into a cardboard box. Then she set the puppy in the cozy nest. Marah stroked the pup's grimy fur. "We'll have to give you a bath. Now, be still while I find you something to eat."

She returned to the kitchen and filled a small bowl with bread and milk. With an anxious glance at the clock, she put the bowl in the microwave for a few seconds and then stirred the mixture to break up the bread. *This will have to do for now,* she told herself. *I'll go get some dog food later, after Vic leaves.* She took the bowl down to the puppy. As she placed it inside the box at one end, the puppy scrambled over and began lapping hungrily.

"You little cutie. I hope you'll fill your tummy and take a nap. We don't want Vic to hear you." She stroked him again and went upstairs, closing the stairwell and pantry doors firmly behind her.

In the kitchen, she pulled open a lower drawer and searched for the bibbed apron with a wide ruffle to cover the muddy streaks on her cashmere sweater. Scott had given the apron to her for Mother's Day several years ago. She never wore such things, but she couldn't bear to part with her son's gift. She shook out the blue apron with bright yellow sunflowers and held it at arm's length. *Yes, this will do.* She slipped it over her head, tied it behind her waist, and adjusted the ruffles to cover her sweater.

Marah had just finished washing her hands at the kitchen sink when she heard her husband's approaching footsteps. She busied herself, wiping the already immaculate countertop.

Vic fastened silver cufflinks into his shirtsleeves, pulled on his suit jacket, and asked, "What are you going to do with the pup you sneaked into the house? Where is it?"

Marah froze. Then she took a deep breath and said, "In the cellar. He's so cute, darling, and so wet and cold. I just want to—"

"I know, you want to keep it. Just make sure you take care of it. I don't have time to be walking a dog."

Marah found her voice. "I will, Vic. I'll take care of him. Scott will help me. He'll be so excited to have a puppy."

Vic reached into the cupboard for a thermal travel mug. "You'd better get it out of the cellar. Pretty chilly down there for a wet pup." He pried off the lid of the mug, poured in a generous splash of Jack Daniels, and topped it with hot coffee. His eyes met his wife's questioning look. He smiled. "Starter fluid. Big day today."

She murmured, "Every day's a big day. Your breath—"

"Smells like coffee." He tasted his brew and nodded in satisfaction. He glanced at her apron and cocked one eyebrow but didn't comment. Instead, he asked, "Who was that on the phone a little while ago?"

"Dad. He's bringing Scott home tomorrow."

"Good. Kid's missed too much school. Don't know why you to let him go visiting this early in the semester. He could've waited until spring break."

Marah avoided her husband's eyes. "He can miss a week without falling behind. He's smart." She paused. "Dad wants to talk to us. About Scott."

"What about him?"

She shrugged and continued cleaning the countertop. She held her breath, hoping Vic wouldn't press for answers.

He kissed her cheek in passing, briefcase in hand. "I've got to get going. Don't make any dinner for me."

Watching her husband's prized, silver, Mercedes-Benz disappear down the street, Marah breathed easier. She'd long ago given up wondering about his prolonged dinner meetings.

No man she'd ever met made her pulse quicken the way Vic did. Not that he was terribly handsome—his lips were too full for his narrow chin, his eyes too close-set. But he was lean and attractive. Today his suit matched his slate-gray eyes and complemented his dark hair accented with silver at the temples. His slight limp, from a college football injury, only added interest, making him more appealing. If only his interest in her hadn't waned, maybe she wouldn't have ... But she didn't want to think about that now.

Marah pulled out a stool at the kitchen island and sat down. She leaned her forehead onto one hand and massaged it as if to erase the faint wrinkles. *How am I going to tell Vic? Will he blow up in front of Dad? Or wait until we're alone?*

"Oh! The puppy!" She hurried down to the cellar and picked up the box with the sleeping puppy. He awoke as she set the box in a corner of the family room. He stood on his hind paws, tail wagging, his front paws scratching at the side of the box. She picked him up and cuddled him under her chin. "You little sweetheart. What shall I name you? I know, we'll wait until Scott comes. He'll want to give you a name." She laughed as the puppy licked her chin. Then she gently set him back in the box. "I have to go buy you some puppy food. And a bed. And some toys. You'll be fine in your box bed until I get back." Marah hurried to take off her apron, tidy her hair, and grab her purse. She left the house, happy to have something to think about other than the problems facing her.

CHAPTER 5

Friday morning, anticipating an early start for Boise, Jack went upstairs to wake Scott. He rapped on the bedroom door and pushed it open. Bed made, room tidy, but no Scott. No duffel bag. Nothing of Scott's. Jack took a deep breath and suppressed a feeling of panic. *I was too hard on him. He's run away again.*

Jack searched the house, calling, "Scott?" *Maybe he left a note.* Jack looked in every possible place and a few unlikely ones. Nothing. *When did he go? Had to have been during the night while I was asleep. No, the cat would have jumped onto my bed after he left. Must have been this morning, while I was in the shower. Did he have enough money for a bus ticket?* Jack grabbed the phone book and found the number for the bus depot. A description of the teenager yielded a negative response from the ticket agent. Jack paced, thinking hard. *Where would the boy go? Maybe he's hiding.* Annoyed and worried, he headed for the garage.

"Scott, you in here?" His workshop was undisturbed, but something told him to look in the garage.

The pickup was gone.

Furious, Jack stormed back into the house and looked on the key caddy near the door. House keys were still there, but the pickup keys were gone.

Pacing angrily, Jack thought, *What to do now? Call the sheriff? Where would he go? Does he even know how to drive? Yes, probably does. Where is he?* Heart pounding, Jack pulled a chair out from the kitchen table and plopped down. His head hurt. He closed his eyes, rubbed his face and forehead with both hands, and tried to think. *Call the police. Maybe he's hiding in town. But he doesn't know anyone here except Nikolas.* Hope flickered. *Would he go to Nikolas?*

The back door opened, and Scott stepped in. Relief and anger flooded Jack when he saw his grandson standing there, duffel bag in hand, looking sheepish. Jack glared at him, jaw clenched.

Scott thrust the pickup keys toward him. "I'm sorry ... I, uh ..." He dropped the keys on the table and shoved his hair away from his face. "I can't run away, Granpop. Not from you. I'll go with you to Boise. But I can't promise I'll stay."

Except for icy spots in shaded areas, Highway 12 was bare until they had traveled about thirty miles and began climbing over the mountain pass. Here, deep snowbanks lined the roads. At the top of the pass, the roof of a visitor center peeked out from under marshmallow-crème piles. Descending into the canyon, their tires crunched on sand and gravel scattered across the icy, winding highway.

Finally, they stopped for lunch in a small town. Afterward, Scott slept the rest of the way into Boise while Jack drove and pondered.

Why haven't Marah and Vic shown more concern over their son running away? Why does Scott evade my questions? Will Vic be there tonight, or will he pull his usual stunt—"business meeting"—and leave? Can't let him do that.

For a few minutes, Jack was distracted by the beauty of the winter scene—snow-covered cabins hunched in the forest beside a rapidly flowing stream. Quiet, peaceful. Jack's thoughts momentarily moved to a higher level. *Nikolas says God cares. So why isn't He helping me figure this out? Maybe He is. God, make Vic be there this evening. Make him and Marah talk to me.*

Darkness had fallen by the time they reached the Giroux house in one of Boise's premier neighborhoods. The restored Victorian, with its elegant lead-glass front door, occupied a corner lot, its wide, pillared porch facing a gracious boulevard. The front porch light was on, but Jack drove around to the back. Lights shone in the kitchen and family room.

Deliberately, Jack angled his pickup directly behind the open double garage door, blocking Vic's silver Mercedes and Marah's white Cadillac. *No one's leaving until I get some answers.* He turned off the motor, glared at the luxury automobiles, and muttered, "Conspicuous consumption."

"Plastic," Scott mumbled.

The teenager's eyes were half-open. Jack suspected he'd been awake for some time, even though he had remained slouched in the corner. "Plastic?"

Scott sat up and nodded his head toward the Mercedes. "Dad's car. Flagship model, he says, but it's mostly plastic."

Jack didn't care if it was cardboard. "C'mon, son, let's go in."

Scott got out, but he didn't move toward the house until Jack did. Then he followed at a distance, his face like stone.

Jack paused on the sidewalk when the backyard was suddenly illuminated. Motion sensors, he supposed. Fancy house, fancy gadgets. He looked around, waiting for Scott to catch up. "Not much snow here, eh?" He eyed the limp rosebush leaves and brown remains of last summer's flowers. A wrought iron garden bench beneath a cluster of trees in the corner looked neglected, forlorn. A small pond with a rock fountain sat quiet, its surface opaque with a thin layer of ice. He looked at Scott. "Ready?" The boy nodded.

The sound of a blaring television hit them as the back door flew open and Marah rushed out. "Scott! Oh, my precious, let me see you. We've missed you so."

Jack moved aside. Scott stood rigid, glaring at his mother, fists clenched at his sides. Marah threw her arms around him, but he remained frozen in place.

"Darling, what's the matter? Aren't you glad to see me?" She reached up to brush a strand of hair from his eyes, but he jerked his head and took a step back.

Vic walked out onto the porch. "Knock it off, Marah. Leave him alone." He came down the steps. "Hello, Jack. How was the trip? Slide over the pass in that pickup of yours?"

Jack met his eyes and returned his handshake. "Roads weren't too bad. I've got a couple gunny sacks of sand in the back for weight."

"Oh, yeah. I've seen guys around here do that too." Vic gestured toward the house. "Come on in." He turned toward the house with another sharp glance at his wife and held the door open.

Jack waited until Marah and Scott went in. He followed, curious to see if Vic would greet his son. As he stepped into the family room, he heard Vic address Scott.

"Maybe you'd like to go up to your room? Let your mother settle down? We'll have a talk about school after a while."

Jack tugged at his mustache and kept his thoughts to himself. He watched Scott hurry through the kitchen and disappear into the dining room on his way toward the staircase. He still hadn't said a word. Not even a hello to his parents. *The boy isn't only hostile,* he thought, *he's also scared. Of what?*

Marah lingered at the kitchen counter, her eyes following Scott. Both she and Vic were dressed to the hilt. Marah's brocade suit, the color of ripe peaches, made her skin look like porcelain. Her dark brown hair shone under the fluorescent kitchen light. She reminded him of Claire many years ago.

Seeming to sense her father's scrutiny, Marah turned to meet his gaze. *Those eyes,* Jack thought. *Claire's were hazel. Marah's are brown. With gold flecks. Unusual. Scott's the same, but his with something different inside, something more ... innocent. Youth,* he supposed.

Vic turned off the television and picked up a glass from the coffee table. Ice clinked as he raised it. "Jack, can I fix you a drink?"

"No, thanks."

"Marah told you we have a dinner engagement tonight?"

Jack frowned. "No."

Vic threw an irritated look at his wife. "Well, she should have. My client from Japan. He's been here several days, but he flies out tomorrow. His wife is with him. We're taking them out to dinner tonight." Vic paused to sip his drink. When he continued, his voice took on a sarcastic edge. "My darling wife has known about this all week."

Marah gave a nervous laugh. "Oh, Dad, you know how it is. Sometimes these things never materialize. That's why I didn't say anything."

Vic snorted and sat down in a large leather chair, indicating the sofa to Jack with a wave of his hand. The man's well-cut, three-piece, gray suit and wine-red tie reeked of success. Money. Silver links gleamed at his shirt cuffs. He crossed his legs, revealing shining black oxfords, and gave his father-in-law a measured look.

Jack had the feeling he was enjoying this. He considered putting the younger man in his place, telling him about his wealthy customers at DeWolfe's. Men whose successes easily overshadowed Vic Giroux's. Men who treated Jack like a trusted friend, taking his advice, asking his opinion on more than just suit fabrics and styles. Even though he was momentarily tempted, Jack wouldn't lower himself to play Vic's games.

From the kitchen, Marah chattered. "I hope you didn't have dinner. I made a seafood casserole for you and Scott. And salad and French bread. It's all ready." She began setting out dishes.

Matching Vic's gaze, Jack let his daughter's words drift by and addressed the man opposite him. "Why did Scott run away from home?"

Vic's glass halted in midair, his mouth open. "What?" He lowered the glass and stared at Jack.

Jack narrowed his eyes. "You heard me."

Abruptly, Vic got up and strode into the kitchen. "Marah, what is this? You told me the kid was visiting your dad. What's this about him running away?"

Marah shrunk against the refrigerator. "Vic, I … didn't want to worry you, so I thought I'd wait—"

"He's been gone all this time, and you never told me he *ran away*?"

Marah edged her way toward the sink, putting the island table between her and her husband. "He … wasn't there all the time. Just since—" Her eyes appealed to her father.

Jack stood in the family room, incredulous at the scene unfolding before him.

Marah continued, "Since Saturday. Right, Dad?"

Vic's voice rose. "The kid's been gone a week. Where was he? Before he got to your father's house?"

"At Larry's. I mean, I thought he was at Larry's, but—"

Vic gripped the back of a stool and leaned forward. "You *thought?* You don't know?"

"No … I—I just talked to Larry's mother yesterday. She told me he hadn't been at their house."

Vic spoke slowly, deliberately. Each word fell like the strike of a hammer. "So. You don't know where your son was for three nights."

Cringing against the edge of the sink, the color drained from Marah's face.

Jack started forward.

With a loud crash, Vic shoved the stool against the table, whipped around, and marched through the dining room doorway. He stopped just out of sight around the corner and yelled, "Scott! Get down here! Now!"

Jack glanced into the dining room. His son-in-law stood before the liquor cabinet, mixing himself another drink. Jack folded his arms and waited.

Vic returned, glared at Marah, and took a long drink.

Scott shuffled into the kitchen, hands buried deep in his pockets. His eyes darted from Vic to Marah.

Vic took a step toward him. "What's this about you running away? Where were you?"

Scott stared at him, his jaw set in a stubborn line.

"Answer me!" Vic gripped his glass, knuckles white.

Jack knew this tactic wouldn't work. "Vic, let's slow down here."

When Vic turned toward Jack, Scott darted behind him, heading for the back door. Jack's quiet, authoritative voice detained him. "Scott, come back here, son."

Scott looked at his grandfather but didn't move. Jack walked over and put his arm around him. He spoke quietly, firmly. "Go on back to your room and wait for me. It'll be all right."

Scott shot a quick glance at his father and obeyed.

Vic drained his glass, shrugged back a sleeve, and looked at his Rolex. "I don't need this kind of theatrics now." He glared at his wife. "You know how important this client is. My mind has to be clear for the meeting tonight. You could have prevented this problem." He lifted his glass and saw it was empty.

Marah moved around the table toward him, her expression imploring. He brushed by her, glass in hand. Marah reached for his arm. "Darling, let's put all this out of our minds for now so we can think about the dinner meeting. We need to leave in a few minutes." She reached for his glass. "Why don't you wait, dear?"

He pulled his arm away and continued on course. Jack heard the sound of a cabinet opening in the dining room and then the clink of glass against glass. He shook his head in disgust and looked at his daughter. "Were you here when Scott left home?"

Marah fiddled with her diamond ring and hedged her answer. "Dad, you know how it is with kids ... emotional, always exaggerating." She sighed. "I was worried sick about Scott, but if he had to run away, I'm glad he went to you. You can't imagine how relieved I was when you called."

As Vic reentered the room, Marah slipped behind him into the dining room. Jack wondered if she was going upstairs to see her son.

Vic called to her departing back, "We've got about five minutes."

Jack's mustache prickled. "You have anything to say?"

Vic snorted. "About what? Ask your daughter. I guarantee you I don't know."

"How did Scott get the wound on his back?"

"What wound? Is that what the kid told you?"

"Mess of pus and scabs when he showed up at my house."

Vic set his glass on the counter so hard that amber liquid slopped out.

Marah reappeared. "Look at the time! Vic, we'll be late! I'll get my coat and purse. Is the car out, darling?" She hurried away.

Jack's eyes narrowed. He tugged at the tips of his mustache, watching the sudden flurry of activity as Marah rushed toward the foyer, and Vic headed for the back door. Jack's next words stopped Vic. "What did you hit your son with?"

Vic halted, hand on the door. He gave Jack an inscrutable look and went out the door.

Moments later, Marah returned to the kitchen. The fear Jack had seen in her face earlier had been replaced with a look of conspiracy. In a low voice she said, "Dad, Vic's drinking has gotten worse. He says he can control it, but—"

The back door flew open. "Jack, you'll have to move your pickup." His eyes glinted, darting from Marah to Jack and back to his wife. "What's going on here?" He stepped inside. "What lies are you telling, Marah?"

Her temper flared. "You can be sure it's not lies if it's about you!"

His bitter voice raked the air. "Trying to make me the scapegoat, are you?" He moved forward.

Marah's eyes blazed. "Oh, Mr. Innocence! As though you never laid a hand on your son!"

Jack had heard more than enough. He stepped between them and gripped each one's shoulder. They fell silent and stared at him. He spoke in low, measured tones. "No wonder your son ran away."

Marah started to speak, but Jack' expression silenced her. He said, "You two go ahead with your dinner. I'll talk with you tomorrow. Separately. Vic, at your office?" His look drilled into his son-in-law's face.

"Yeah, Jack. I'll make time … I'd like to talk to you myself." He thought a moment. "Ten thirty? Can you stick around that long?"

"I'll stick around until this is resolved." He locked his eyes onto Marah's. "Daughter? First thing in the morning?"

"I—I have a meeting … it's pretty important."

Jack snapped, "More important than your son?"

"Uh, no. I'll cancel it."

Jack dropped his hands, looked beyond Marah and Vic, and caught a movement in the kitchen. Scott came into view. His face looked stricken. His eyes met Jack's.

"Granpop, would you give me a ride to my friend's house?"

Marah whirled. "Scott—"

Vic interrupted. "Where do you think you're going?"

Defiant, Scott said, "I'm not staying here."

Rage filled Vic's voice. "You can't come in here and tell us what you're going to do. You'll stay right here. No more of this running away!"

Jack moved between the couple and their son. "Just a minute, here." His scalp prickled as though an unseen presence stood beside him. Suddenly, he knew what he had to do. "Scott and I will get a room tonight. We'll talk tomorrow, after everyone's cooled off."

"A room? A motel?" Marah said. "You can't. You have to stay here."

Vic shoved his hand through his hair. He jerked his sleeve back and looked at his watch. "Shut up, Marah. He's right. Tomorrow will be better. I'm so uptight now I can't even think straight. And I've got business to take care of tonight—"

"But, darling—"

"Marah, I told you this client is important. Get your priorities straight. Put all this out of your mind. I want you in tip-top shape tonight. You've got to entertain his wife. You can fall apart tomorrow."

Jack's gut twisted at his son-in-law's words. *Priorities. Scott clearly ranks second, or lower, in his father's life. Marah probably isn't much better. What's happened to these people? Just a year ago, I thought they'd settled their differences. Never knew of any problem with Scott. What's going on here?* He took his grandson's arm. "Let's go, Scott."

CHAPTER 6

Relieved to be away from his daughter and son-in-law, Jack felt half-dazed. Scott slumped against the pickup door. *Got to pull ourselves together.* "Let's go get a milkshake. Know of a good place?"

Scott shot his grandfather a look and then sat up straight as he seemed to sense Jack's intent. "Yeah, Yogi's. Turn left at that next corner."

Over milkshakes—chocolate for Scott, butterscotch for Jack—they quizzed one another on the various makes and models of cars in the parking lot while a petite, attentive waitress made eyes at Scott. A friendly argument ensued and ended in laughter as Jack conceded. *If I were his age, I would have at least smiled at the waitress. Poor kid's probably too worried to notice the girl.*

As Scott sucked his glass empty with a noisy slurp, Jack stood and stretched. "Let's go find a place to sleep tonight, son."

Remembering another time years ago, when he and Claire had spent a weekend here, Jack headed for the familiar location, but he soon realized that the quaint motel had been a victim of progress.

He splurged on one of the newer motels near the river.

"Hey, Granpop, we could, like, order in pizza and watch a movie."

"Pizza! We just had—" Jack paused. "Yeah. Good idea. You pick the movie; I'll order the pizza. But no pineapple. Canadian bacon and mushrooms. Deal?"

Scott laughed. "Deal."

Even though he said he'd seen it a couple of times, Scott picked *Jurassic Park.*

"Sure you don't want something different?"

"Nah, you'll like this, Granpop."

Scott was right. With the thunder of T-Rex's footsteps hunting its human prey, Jack lost himself in the adventure and devoured two slices of pizza before he realized what he was doing.

Later, while Scott snored softly in the next bed, Jack recalled the weekend, years ago, spent with Claire in Boise.

When Jack and Claire had announced their twentieth anniversary getaway to their children, thirteen-year-old Marah sighed. "A second honeymoon—how romantic."

Eighteen-year-old Paul, parked backward on a kitchen chair, protested. "Boise? Why don't you guys go to Hawaii or something?"

"We can't afford that," Claire said. "Besides, Boise is special to us." She smiled at Jack.

His heart melted. Even after twenty years, she could still do that to him. "Sure is. Spent our first honeymoon there. We were practically penniless. Lucky to even get out of town. But Mr. DeWolfe Sr. gave me the weekend off and tucked a fifty dollar bill in my pocket." He chuckled. "We ended up in a little motel by the river. Pretty nice in those days. Hope it still is."

Marah squealed. "You mean you're going back to the very same motel? It's still there?"

"Probably a dump by now," Paul muttered with disgusted look at his sister.

"Is it, Dad?"

"No, daughter. I called. It's been remodeled. Inside, anyway. Outside, it's probably the same six-unit, plain brick motel."

"Wow, a real classy joint." Paul made a wry face.

Claire ruffled her son's hair. "Never mind. We like it. It's quaint. Spectacular rose beds in front of each unit and the office. Romantic."

Jack stepped up behind her and wrapped his arms around her. With a wink at his kids, he nuzzled her neck. "Indeed," he whispered.

Marah blushed and looked away.

Paul groaned. "Oh, please."

That weekend, Jack and Claire found the outside of the small motel unchanged. The loquacious desk clerk assured them the honeymoon unit had been remodeled and would be quite suitable for an anniversary weekend.

The moment Claire stepped into the small room, she was enchanted. "Oh, Jack, look! It's so sweet!"

Jack looked around. Sweet? Well, he guessed so. Shiny fabric everywhere in a cluttered print of what his mother used to call cabbage roses. Green and pink. White wicker furniture. A closet-sized bathroom with pink towels. Definitely decorated by a woman.

Claire cooed and exclaimed over everything, while Jack struggled to find room for their suitcases. That done, he turned to his wife and let himself be caught up in her mood as she responded to his kisses.

After a while, lying in bed, Jack listened contentedly to the sound of Claire's voice. From the comfort of her pillow, she verbally rearranged the room.

"Those two chairs would look better side-by-side, don't you think, Jack? More cozy, intimate."

"You make it intimate, sweetheart," he murmured. He slid his hand around her waist.

She laughed and pushed him away. "Not now, darling. Let's go shopping." She jumped out of bed and dashed for the shower.

Disappointed, Jack got up and squeezed into the shower with her. At home, she rarely allowed this anymore. Several minutes later, laughing, they climbed out of the shower, toweled dry, and dressed.

That perfect weekend, Claire made Jack forget old wounds and doubts. He resolved to do everything in his power to preserve their closeness. Let go of his bitterness. He vowed to himself to bury the past.

Jack had been working at DeWolfe Department Store for several years when the elder DeWolfe announced that his son, Richard DeWolfe Jr., would be joining the business as vice president. From the beginning, the younger DeWolfe's arrogance raised Jack's hackles.

Coming from a wealthy family, the man had never held a job until now. He'd traveled overseas after college graduation and only returned because of his father's upcoming plans for retirement. Jack, on the other hand, had worked all his life. After completing high school, he landed a stockroom job in the prestigious DeWolfe Department Store, where the elder DeWolfe recognized his potential and soon placed him in the men's department as a sales clerk. That's when Jack met and fell in love with Claire, who was clerking in ladies' ready-to-wear.

By the time Richard DeWolfe Jr. joined the company, Jack was the manager of the men's department, although the elder DeWolfe still handled the buying, not because Jack couldn't, but because the older man relished this part of the business. He had occasionally boasted to Jack that Missoula's most powerful men had DeWolfe Department

Store to thank for the image they presented. Jack allowed the old man's self-gratification, never mentioning the special orders he'd placed himself, because some clients didn't like the selection on the racks.

One Christmas season, the suave Richard Jr. and his timid wife, Frances, hosted a party for the store's department heads in their elegant residence on Farview Heights. Claire had splurged on a low-cut, red dress. Toddler Paul happily spent the night with their close friends Nikolas and Martha Kostenka and their children. DeWolfe's tri-level house overflowed with people, food, and liquor. Frances, a conscientious hostess, fluttered about, while her husband entertained attractive women.

After two hours, Jack and a few others, wearied by the party, gathered their coats. But Jack couldn't find Claire. A snide hint from an inebriated fellow leaning on the bar sent Jack to DeWolfe's den on the lower floor. He found Claire and Richard lounging side-by-side on a fur rug in front of a blazing fireplace, drinks in hand. Jack was stunned. If the woman had been anyone other than his own wife, he might have laughed at the contrived setup. Jack strode across the room, grabbed Claire's hand, and pulled her up. Her drink spilled onto Richard's chest. Richard started to rise, but Jack planted his foot on the man's chest, shoving him back, and then turned on his heel and left with Claire in tow. She fell asleep in a drunken stupor on the way home. The next day, she said she remembered nothing. Jack didn't believe her.

A month later, employees anticipated the announcement regarding the prized first-floor manager position. Several people assured Jack he would get the job, but some thought old man DeWolfe would allow Richard to make the final selection. Jack held little hope the son would send any good fortune his way after the Christmas party incident.

The elder DeWolfe would tour the store before the meeting, after the doors were locked for the day. In preparation, employees scurried about rearranging crystal, adjusting mannequins, and aligning neckties.

Jack was especially proud of his department and personnel. When a customer walked into the men's department, he knew all his needs would be met—from socks, work clothes, and casual wear to white pleated shirts for black-tie galas. Jack set an example of treating all customers with equal respect and attention. Among his most faithful customers were not only lawyers and bankers but also a handful of railroad and lumber mill workers, who knew Jack carried durable work clothes that saved them money in the long run. They all trusted

Jack, whether their collars were white or blue, their nails immaculate or grease-embedded.

After the store closed for the day, Jack ignored the elevator, as usual, and went up the back stairs to turn in his daily report to the office. The narrow, wooden stairway had escaped remodeling a few years ago. The steps creaked as Jack ascended in the dim light. His toe bumped something on the landing halfway up, where the stairs made a sharp turn. He reached down into the shadows and picked up a bulging envelope.

Stepping under a light fixture on the wall, he looked for identification on the manila envelope. It was blank, the flap open. He looked inside: a roll of currency and several folded sheets of paper. He pulled them out. Daily department reports. Well, that solved this mystery—these things belonged in bookkeeping.

As he refolded the papers, his own handwriting caught his eye. He glanced at the report—last night's figures. He recalled the totals. Not quite record sales, but good. His ads on men's jackets had brought in brisk business. He glanced at the bottom figure and did a double take. This was several hundred dollars less than the amount he recalled. He stared at the numbers. It looked like his handwriting, but Jack knew it couldn't be.

Quickly, he glanced through the other reports. Home appliances. Betty told him last night she'd had good sales, but this report showed less than a hundred dollars. He checked a few more. Roland's and Alice's. Jack couldn't remember exactly, but he was sure these reports were too low. He pulled out the bundle of cash and thumbed it. Mostly twenties; some larger. He estimated a couple thousand dollars. He slid the bundle back into the envelope and pulled out a bank savings passbook: Richard DeWolfe Jr. Odd that it should be here. Suspicion heightened as Jack scanned the entries. Random deposits every month; the final balance, five figures. Realization hit as Jack sucked in a deep breath and let it out. He replaced everything in the envelope and leaned against the wall, thinking. *The filthy weasel, faking sales records, stealing from his own father, cheating all of us.* Jack continued up the stairs. At the top, he glanced at the bookkeeping office door and then continued along the corridor to the elder DeWolfe's corner office.

A half hour later, the meeting convened. Jack wondered if anyone noticed the strain on the elder DeWolfe's face. Vice President Richard DeWolfe Jr. stood to make the announcement about the new floor manager. Heads turned toward Jack. He noted the encouraging smiles, but he also saw the younger DeWolfe's disdainful glance. Jack knew he didn't have a chance.

Richard Jr. began, "As you all know, the floor administrator is one of the most important positions in the store."

As he droned on, people fidgeted. Richard Sr. appeared distracted. Finally, the younger DeWolfe said, "I am pleased to announce Morley Johnson is the new floor manager."

Around the table, people stirred, murmured. After a moment, Jack began applauding to break the silence. Others followed suit. Before Richard DeWolfe Jr. sat down, his eyes met Jack's in a look of smug satisfaction.

The following week, the company's accounting firm began a storewide audit. Soon after that, Richard DeWolfe Jr. departed, supposedly to travel for several months on company business. But Jack knew better. He stored the secret away in his heart, along with the other black mark against the man. He would never forgive him for either offense.

Failing health forced Richard DeWolfe Sr. to announce his retirement a year later. With no other heir, son Richard stepped into his father's position as president of DeWolfe Department Store.

Shortly before the elder DeWolfe's last official day, he summoned Jack to his office. "I appreciate your discretion, Jack. No one within these walls knows of my son's shameful deed except you and I ... and the auditors, of course. Thank you." He paused. "I have arranged for a substantial raise for you as the men's department solitary buyer. As you undoubtedly realize, I chose to handle punishment and redemption privately. My son will not infringe on your territory, and your annual bonus will reflect an increase in the percentage of your department's sales from now on." He offered his hand. "Your position here is secure, Jack."

When Jack and Claire returned from their twentieth anniversary weekend in Boise, Claire's youthful mood and sweetness lingered for a while. But eventually, their lives returned to an ordinary routine. Paul graduated from high school and began an air force career. Marah aspired to become an interior decorator. Her numerous activities and part-time job kept her constantly in and out of the house until two months into her senior year in high school. Without warning, the apple of Jack's eye became withdrawn and moody. He could make no sense of it.

"What's bothering our daughter?" Jack asked. "What happened to all her friends? She's in her room most of the time when she's not in school or working."

Claire shrugged. "Moodiness. Maybe her friends dumped her. Her weight is getting out of control."

"Her weight? Nothing's wrong with her weight. She looks good."

"She's getting flabby."

"That's ridiculous." Jack narrowed his eyes. "Are you telling me that's why she stays home so much and doesn't have friends over? She's worried about her weight?"

Claire tilted her nose up, sniffed. "She'd better worry about it if she ever hopes to catch a rich husband."

"Is that what you've been telling her?"

"I've just warned her, that's all. She's dieting now. You'll see a change in her."

The change Jack saw in his daughter over the next few months wasn't what he'd hoped for. She lived on salads, grapefruit, and hard-boiled eggs. Both Marah and her mother ignored Jack's objections that the girl was getting too thin. Not only that, he suspected she was taking diet pills.

Jack was proud of his daughter when she landed a part-time job at DeWolfe Department Store, home furnishings, without Jack's intervention. Claire hadn't worked for several years, so he felt certain she had nothing to do with it. When the department manager allowed Marah to arrange showcases, Jack thought his daughter's future looked promising. He fancied she might even end up as the store's interior decorating consultant after college.

During her second year in college, Marah met and fell in love with Victor Giroux, a graduate student. Her eyes sparkled as she talked of a fancy wedding after Vic completed his degree and got a job. Jack liked Vic and believed Marah would be in good hands.

Vic graduated and became a loan officer in a Springfield, Oregon, bank. First step on his career ladder. Against Jack's advice, Marah abandoned her own career dreams, quit college, and married Vic. She glowed with happiness. All he really wanted for his children and their families was safety, security, and happiness. And it seemed both his son and daughter had all that.

Until Claire died.

Now, in Jack and Scott's Boise motel room, Jack awoke late the morning after *Jurassic Park* and pizza with a kink in his back. He looked over at the next bed. Scott still slept, curled into a ball, hugging his pillow. *Like he used to when he was a little tyke, scared of the dark. Now he's scared of his parents.* Anger surged through Jack's veins. *No kid should have to go through this kind of misery.*

Scott rolled onto his back, yawned, and stretched. "Are we checking out now?"

"No, we'll have breakfast and then go see your mother. Just in case, I reserved this room for tonight, too." At that, Scott scowled and dragged himself out of bed, grumbling all the way.

An hour later, Jack and Scott pulled up in the driveway of the gracious Victorian house on the corner. Inside, Scott immediately went up to his room, avoiding his mother. Jack sat on a stool at the kitchen island, determined to get some answers from his daughter.

CHAPTER 7

Jack watched Marah pour fresh-brewed coffee while she chattered.

"How do you like my kitchen, Dad? This was the first thing we remodeled after we bought the house. Bay window, new cupboards, and tile."

The expanse of white tile reminded Jack of a hospital. The wine-red grouting and matching narrow trim inside the window helped relieve the sterile white, as did the glass-door cupboards. He liked the array of houseplants and blue bottles on the bay window's sill. He glanced at his daughter. "What's in those bottles? Looks like leaves."

She picked up a fish-shaped bottle standing on its tail. "Olive oil and herbs. Oregano in some, rosemary in others, and garlic or thyme."

"Decoration?" Jack recalled some strange things—like bunches of dried weeds—his daughter had used to decorate her house in Springfield. Jack remembered that after one of their visits, on their way home in the car, Claire had commented, "Marah has a real flair for the original. She would do well as a professional decorator." Jack had muttered, "It's original, all right."

Now, Marah said, "They're decorative, but functional, too. I use the flavored oil for salads. With a little balsamic vinegar or fresh lemon juice."

"Sounds pretty good." Jack's gaze wandered around the room and noted the spots of color here and there—dried flowers, a fruit basket, colorful bowls; probably souvenirs from their trip to Italy. Or Costa Rica. Too gaudy for Jack's tastes, but he knew she'd worked hard to create this effect. "Your kitchen looks very nice, daughter."

She smiled. "Come see the rest of the house." She walked toward the arched doorway leading to the dining room.

Jack stopped her. "Later. Right now we have to talk." He pulled out a stool and sat.

Slowly, she came back, pulled out a stool on Jack's right, her back to the doorway. The hem of her skirt cascaded to the floor in graceful folds of black, gray, and white.

Jack cupped his coffee mug and waited for his daughter to speak.

"This is so ridiculous, Dad. It was such a little thing." She pushed her black sweater sleeves up to her elbows. "I wanted Scott to clean out the foyer closet. He got smart and sassed me." She poured fat-free French vanilla creamer into her coffee. "We argued. Next thing I knew, he was saying he hated me, hated his father, didn't want to live here anymore. And he left." She took a deep breath, lifted her cup, and sipped, her eyes wide-eyed innocence as she looked at Jack over the rim of her cup.

The words, so carefully spoken, sounded rehearsed. Had Vic concocted this story? "Where'd Scott go? You said this happened Wednesday. He showed up at my place Saturday night. Where was he?"

"He didn't tell you?"

Jack shook his head.

Marah's gaze dropped. She murmured, "I don't know."

"How'd he get the cut on his back?"

Marah swung her feet around and stood. She picked up the coffeepot. "Ready for more?"

Extending his cup, Jack watched her closely. She seemed composed. Perhaps she believed the story—her story, or Vic's?

"I don't know anything about a cut. Probably happened at school." She arranged bananas, oranges, and apples in a ceramic bowl and set it in the center of the island, avoiding Jack's eyes. "Couldn't be too serious."

"Serious enough that he should have had stitches."

For a split second, Marah looked at him, fear in her eyes.

"You sure you don't know how it happened? You knew it was on his back, so you must know—"

"No! I—" At a slight sound behind her, Marah looked over her shoulder.

Scott stood in the dining room doorway, his face hardened in anger. He glared at his mother for several long seconds. His mouth worked as though about to say something, but suddenly, he bolted through the kitchen toward the back door.

Voice sharp, Jack asked, "Where are you going?"

The boy hesitated a moment, his hand on the door handle. "Dunno."

Jack stood, reached into his pocket, and pulled out the motel room key. He tossed it to Scott. "Here. I'll see you later, after I talk to your dad."

Scott caught the key midair, mumbled, "Thanks," and left.

Turning to face his daughter again, Jack saw she was trembling. "Don't worry. He won't run out on me." He sat down and waited until she regained her composure. "Did you look for Scott Wednesday night?"

Marah fiddled with a marquise-cut emerald ring on her middle finger. "I didn't think he was running away. I mean, it was just an ordinary argument. You know how it is, Dad." Her eyes met Jack's. "Remember that time when I tried to sneak in the house after curfew? You caught me, and I tried to lie my way out of it."

"I remember. And now I think you're trying to lie your way out of this. You know more than you're telling me." He paused a beat. "Are you trying to protect Vic? Scott said Vic hits you. Did he hit Scott?"

Marah's face paled. Tears began running down her cheeks. She folded her arms on the table and buried her face, sobbing.

Jack stood. "Marah, I want to help." He put his hand on her shoulder. His heart melted. He wrapped his arm across her shaking shoulders and gave her a gentle squeeze. "Daughter, please. Whatever it is, tell me."

He pulled back as she suddenly jerked away and stood up, mascara mingled with tears streaking down her face.

"You wouldn't understand. No one does." She wiped at her face with the back of her hand. "Go away, Dad. Leave me alone." Abruptly, she pushed past him and hurried into the family room.

Stunned, Jack stood in the kitchen and listened to the sound of her footsteps ascend the stairs to her sewing loft. Slowly, he moved toward the back door and went outside. He climbed into his pickup, started the motor, his heart heavy. *Something is very wrong in this family. God help me.*

The receptionist at Gem State Bank directed Jack to the wide, carpeted stairs leading to an overhanging balcony. As he reached the top, Jack's glance took in an immense dark-blue rug bordered in gold-colored oak leaves. Potted trees and ornate chairs complemented the carpet. Two desks—cherry, to Jack's practiced eye—faced the stairs in a pleasing arrangement. Only the first desk was occupied at the moment.

The attractive young woman smiled. "May I help you, sir?"

"Jack Emerson. Vic Giroux is expecting me."

"Oh, yes, Mr. Emerson. Right this way, please." She walked toward the middle of three widely spaced doors. *The top dogs,* Jack supposed. She knocked lightly above a brass nameplate and opened the door. "Mr. Giroux, Mr. Emerson is here." After Jack entered, she closed the door softly behind him.

Vic met Jack in the center of the room, his hand outstretched.

As he shook hands, a smell reached Jack's nostrils. Whiskey.

"Have a seat, Jack, over here." Vic gestured to a pair of leather club chairs in front of a gas fireplace, facing one another across a beveled-glass coffee table.

Jack glanced at publications on the table as he sat down. The *Wall Street Journal, Fortune 500, Business Week,* and others.

Vic sat in the other chair. "You and Scott slept well?"

"Well enough."

"I'll pick up the tab for the motel."

Jack hesitated and then nodded. He looked into his son-in-law's eyes and said, "I'm taking Scott home with me."

Vic's head jerked back in surprise. "Now, wait a minute. You can't come in here and tell me—"

"I just did."

Hard lines formed around Vic's mouth. He spent several seconds arranging the magazines on the table in a precise stack and said, "You know, Jack, this really isn't any concern of yours. We can handle—"

"Wait a minute. Let's get this straight." Jack placed his hands on his knees and leaned forward. "It became my business when my grandson arrived at my house Saturday night. He left your house three days earlier. He wouldn't say where he'd been, but judging from his appearance, he had a rough time. He hadn't eaten a decent meal in days. The kid came here to Boise with me under protest. He swears he'll run away again if anyone tries to make him stay here. I love that boy, and I care what happens to him."

Vic rose abruptly and paced, rubbing the back of his neck.

Jack continued. "The reasons he's given for running away are vague. Marah's just as bad. The kid says he can't talk about the cut on his back. Marah can't look me in the eye when I ask her. You walked out the door when I asked you." He kept his eyes on Vic. "You're all hiding something. What happened to Scott's back? Why'd he run away?"

"Okay, okay. You've made your case." Vic halted and looked at Jack from the center of the room. "This isn't easy." He began pacing again.

"I'm not sure myself what the whole story is. I think Marah knows. But she won't tell me. I get the same stuff you do from her." He sucked in a deep breath and let it out. "Okay. Here's what I've pieced together."

Vic dropped into the leather chair across from Jack, elbows propped on his knees. "Marah and Scott had an argument. Whatever happened between them, it had to have been serious. Really serious. Scott worships his mother. Used to." He rose, went to his desk, started to sit, changed his mind, and stood in front of the window. His back to the room, voice low, he said, "If you want to believe the rumors, Scott walked in on something."

The leather chair creaked as Jack pushed himself to his feet. He crossed the room to stand in front of Vic's desk. "Idle gossip has nothing to do with this."

Vic turned, his face somber. For the first time, Jack sensed genuine concern. Seconds ticked away. Vic seemed to be studying Jack, as though debating how much to say. Finally, he spoke. "Marah's changed, Jack." His voice sounded sad. He looked away, staring out the window.

"Let's get back to Scott."

Vic's head jerked around. "This *is* about Scott. And me. Our family. She's not there for us anymore. Not like she used to be. Before her mother died."

Exasperated, Jack said, "What's *Claire* got to do with this? What are you talking about, man?"

Grasping the top of his swivel chair, Vic yanked it back and sat. He drummed his fingers on the armrests. "Okay, it's not just that. Claire's death, I mean. Just before that, when we lived in Springfield ... I admit I made some mistakes. I'm sure you know. Marah took Scott and stayed with you and Claire a couple of weeks. But we worked it out and got back together. I tried to make up for it. Thought we were doing okay. Seemed close again. Then everything changed. After Claire's stroke. And funeral." He looked up, his eyes imploring. "My wife wasn't the same woman when we got back home. She'd turned bitter. Hardened. She just didn't care anymore—about anything."

Jack eased into a chair in front of the desk. He felt like a heavy, cold fog was closing in on him. The two weeks before Claire died were a blur of pain in his memory. It had taken him over two years to regain some sense of normalcy in his life, but now his son-in-law stirred the banked embers of misery back into life. He didn't want to think about Claire's last days ... or her death.

Marah—changed? How? He recalled that she hadn't shown grief over her mother's death. She seemed numb, unfeeling. But sometimes people reacted that way. The emotional release would come later, probably after she was back in her own home. After the funeral, she didn't come for a visit every couple of months like she used to. He figured she was grieving, like he was. Now Vic was saying she didn't care about anything. Once again, anger arose. He didn't need this. He wanted to get the problems with Scott resolved and get home. Jack folded his arms, leaned back in his chair, and looked across the desk. "Is there a point to what you're saying, Vic?"

The man's eyes turned hard, his voice sharpened. "The bottom line is Marah's having an affair." Vic's chair spun as he rose abruptly.

His mind in a daze, Jack watched the chair's slowing revolutions. *Round and round. One story after another. First Marah, now Vic.*

Vic paced from one end of the room to the other. Coins jingled when he shoved his hands into his pockets. He kept rattling them as he paced. "Near as I can figure out, Marah's new boyfriend is—"

Jack leaped to his feet. His chair tipped backward to the floor with a dull thud. "Enough rumors and gossip!" He struck the desk with his fist. "This has nothing to do with Scott's running away!"

Vic stopped pacing, his mouth agape. "Jack, don't you see? It has *everything* to do with why Scott ran away. He *saw* them."

The two men locked eyes.

At last, Jack looked away. He uprighted the chair and leaned on its back. Blood pounded in his ears and throbbed in his throat. In a blur, he realized Vic could be right. If the boy found out, that would explain Scott's hostility toward his mother. But would it make him run away? Somehow, it didn't ring true.

Dizzy, still holding the back of the chair, Jack stepped around it and sat down. He leaned back and closed his eyes. Moments later, he opened them to find his son-in-law watching him.

"You okay, Jack?"

"What do you think?" Jack sat up, straightening his shoulders. "Couple of things missing from this picture. You say your wife is having an affair. You say your son ran away from home because the boy discovered the affair. Scott has a wound on his back. What are you doing about all this?"

Muscles tightened in Vic's jaw. His eyes narrowed. He picked up his coffee mug and drank deeply.

Relentless, Jack pressed harder. "You're drinking too much. You think I can't smell the whiskey? Is this your escape from dealing with your family problems?" Jack's unwavering eyes met Vic's glare.

"What I drink and when I drink is my business. What do you think I am? An alcoholic? I don't need to drink. I can quit any time."

"That's what they all say." Jack stood and strode to the door. "I'm telling you, cut down on the booze. Send your friend Jack Daniels packing, and work on your home front. Or you'll lose it all."

At the motel, Jack found Scott stretched out on his stomach, watching TV. Jack picked up the remote and clicked it off. Scott rolled over, his head propped on his hand, a quizzical expression in his eyes.

"Well, son, I just came from a meeting with your dad. Seems your folks have some problems to work out between them."

The teenager sat up and cast a sidelong look at his grandfather. "Yeah, I guess so." He picked up the remote, flipped it end over end in his fingers. "They fight a lot."

"How does this fit in with your running away?"

Scott ran his fingers over the buttons on the remote, turned it over, and fiddled with the battery compartment. His voice came out low. "I dunno."

Jack waited, but Scott remained silent. He recognized the closed expression on his grandson's face. No answers now. Maybe later, when the boy felt safer. Jack took a deep breath. "Think you can put up with an old man and a cranky cat for a while?

Scott's head shot up. "I can stay with you?"

Jack nodded. "I'd be very pleased to have you." He smiled.

Scott let out a whoop, bounced off the bed, and tackled Jack in a big hug.

Jack tousled his hair and hugged him back. *This will work. It has to. God, please help me make it work.* For the moment, Jack shoved away the thought of his lost solitude. After all, a couple of months wouldn't be so bad. He'd get used to it, enjoy it. He loved his grandson. As for Vic and Marah, Jack was fed up with them. Maybe a few months without their son would give them the jolt they needed.

CHAPTER 8

That evening, Marah heard the news.

Vic said, "Jack and I talked today." He took a glass from the cupboard, looked at it a moment, and put it back. He turned, and bracing his hands on the tile countertop, faced Marah. "Call the school tomorrow and get Scott's records transferred. He's going home with Jack."

Marah felt a tightening in her throat and chest. "No."

Vic continued. "He'll stay until school's out. This is best for everyone. You'll go with me to Japan now that Scott's taken care of. We'll be gone about eight weeks. Don't know when yet, probably next month. Have to get the details ironed out. Sakura likes you. She invited you to come. Jack and Scott will be by this evening to get the kid's things. No scenes, understand?"

Marah nodded.

The tension in Marah's chest eased. Vic would be gone for two months; Scott would be with her father. She didn't intend to go to Japan, but she knew better than to say so now. She'd figure out later how to get out of it.

CHAPTER 9

That evening, when Vic greeted Jack and Scott at the door, Jack noticed the absence of a whiskey glass in his hand. The man wrapped an arm around his son. Jack saw Scott stiffen, but he allowed his father's embrace.

"Well, son, what do you think? Did I bring in enough luggage?" Vic gestured toward the pile on the floor. "Figured you'd want to take a few books, so I brought in this bag, too." Dropping his arm from Scott's shoulder, Vic picked up a sturdy blue bag with reinforced straps. "And you can put your shoes in this." He scooped up a zippered gym bag.

Scott nodded. He stuffed the bags under one arm and grabbed the large suitcase off the floor. He started toward his room with the load.

"Oh, Scott," Marah reached for him, her expression pleading.

Vic stopped her short. "Don't start, Marah."

Her hand fell to her side, and Scott hurried away. Marah turned beseeching eyes to her father.

Before he could change his mind about taking Scott away, Jack said, "I'll give him a hand."

He found his grandson haphazardly stuffing clothes and books into the bags. "Here, let's fold these shirts. They'll fit better. And we won't have to iron them. Your grandma taught me that." He began folding jeans and shirts.

Unmindful, Scott grabbed a couple of sweatshirts from his drawer and pushed them into a bag. "Can we go tonight? Back to Missoula?"

Jack fished out the sweatshirts and tossed them back to Scott. "Fold 'em. We'll leave in the morning, soon as the sun's up long enough to melt a little ice off the highway. I don't like driving at night in the winter. Too risky."

"I just want to get out of this dump."

"Slow down a minute. Let's talk about this." Jack sat on the bed and pushed the suitcase aside for Scott.

His grandson rolled his head back and groaned. "Granpop—"

Jack smacked the bed with the flat of his hand. "Park."

Shoulders drooping, Scott plopped down on the bed and studied his feet.

"You know what I'm going to say, don't you, son?"

"Yeah, I guess so."

"Okay, so you tell me."

The teenager flopped back on the bed, arms stretched above his head. He stared at the ceiling and tapped his foot. "You're gonna say I should be nicer to my parents, because I won't see them for a long time."

"That pretty well sums it up. I'd add that you shouldn't do something now that you might regret later. Part on good terms. You'll feel better about yourself." Jack reflected that he should take his own advice.

"Okay, Granpop. I'll try." Scott scrambled to his feet and jerked open a dresser drawer. He scooped up a load of socks and undershorts and dropped them in the suitcase. "But I don't want to stick around here very long."

Nor do I, Jack thought.

Downstairs, looking composed, Marah barely glanced at Jack and Scott when they brought down the luggage. Her voice light and cheerful, she said, "Have you had dessert? I made a lemon pie." Without waiting for their answer, she went to the china cabinet for plates. "Let's have it in the living room. Go sit down. I'll bring it in."

Scott's eyebrows shot up. "Living room?" he muttered. "When did we get so important?"

Vic played the perfect host. "C'mon, son. Jack." He led the way into the formal living room.

Jack's feet sank into the soft, blue carpet. The quail family he had carved from juniper years ago decorated the Italian marble mantel above the white fireplace, flanked by French horn candle sconces. Vic sat in a tapestry-covered chair, and Jack eased onto the ivory brocade sofa. Scott prowled, finally settling on the hearth.

Marah entered, carrying a silver tray laden with platinum-rimmed porcelain cups and plates of creamy lemon pie piled high with golden meringue. She set the tray on the coffee table beside a graceful Lladro figurine of a young woman with a harp, her dress caught in a breeze. "I'll be right back with the coffee. Scott, dear, what would you like to drink? Milk? A Coke?"

"Yeah, Coke."

Jack cocked an eyebrow toward his grandson.

"Please," the boy added.

Moments later, Marah returned with another silver tray, a silver coffeepot, and a crystal goblet filled with cola and ice. Jack surveyed the elegance, his jaw tense. His daughter missed her mark if she thought all this would impress her son—or her father. Nor would it erase the tension of important things left unsaid. Jack berated himself for failing to get to the bottom of the problem, but regardless, he wanted Scott and his parents to part on peaceful terms.

Everyone began eating, avoiding one another's eyes.

Suddenly, Marah said, "Scott, dear, I forgot to tell you—we have a puppy."

Head down, Scott mumbled, "I didn't see any puppy."

"What should we name him?"

Scott raised his head slightly. "Can I see—"

Looking nervous, Marah glanced at Vic. "Tina's taking care of him now, because ... your father and I are going to Japan for a few weeks." She looked at Vic again, took a deep breath, and said, "When we get back, I'll bring him home." She seemed to breathe a sigh of relief when Vic didn't comment.

Vic's fork chimed softly against his plate as he set it down. "How's that community project going, Jack? Merry-go-round, isn't it?"

Jack nodded. "Coming along very well. In full operation for some time now." *Several years, in fact, if you'd been paying attention.* "We're making new horses to replace the ones that have worn-out or need repair. Scott went with me the other day and helped out."

Marah beamed a smile at her fidgeting son. "Oh, darling, that's wonderful. What did you make?"

"A pile of sawdust." Scott turned to his father and changed the subject. "Dad, can I take the old computer? I could use it in school."

"Take the new one, son. More RAM. Your mother never uses it anyway."

"Okay, thanks." Scott wolfed down the last of his pie, gulped his cola, and stood. "May I be excused? To get the computer and stuff?" He glanced at his mother but directed his attention to his father, waiting for permission.

Vic answered, "Of course. Take some blank disks, too. There's a new box in the drawer." Scott left the room.

A few minutes later, Jack noticed his grandson heading for the pickup with his luggage. When he came back, he stuck his head in the door.

"It's all ready to go, Granpop. I put my bike in, too, for later, when the snow's gone."

"Got anything to cover things in case it snows?"

"Yeah, an old plastic tarp. It's got some little holes in it, but I can make it work. Then all I have left is the printer. I'll put it up front with the computer. Monitor's on the floor by my feet, and the keyboard."

Jack nodded. "Okay." He accepted a coffee refill from Marah and sized up his daughter and son-in-law. *They're putting on quite a show of generosity and hospitality. But no real connection with their son. What will become of Scott? Am I doing the right thing by taking the boy away? Would it be better if this family remained together?* He recalled Nikolas's urging to keep Scott with him. *Well, God, Nikolas is in better standing with You than I am, so I'll follow his good sense—and my own instincts.*

He knew what Claire would have said—they needed counseling. She'd gone to a number of sessions herself. For what, exactly, she wouldn't say. He supposed Claire's unhappiness concerned her usual dissatisfaction with their daughter. Their beautiful Marah.

Why had Claire insisted on that name anyway? At the time, Jack thought "Marah" sounded special, for a beautiful baby. Years later, Claire told him where she'd gotten the idea—from the Bible. That surprised him, because he didn't know she ever read the Bible. He did sometimes, privately, especially Proverbs. He remembered the harsh sound of his wife's voice and the downturn of her mouth when she told him, when Marah was sixteen or so, what their daughter's name meant in Hebrew. "'Bitter.' It means bitter. And it fits," she'd said.

Jack had reasoned Marah was going through normal adjustments for a young girl growing into womanhood, so he dismissed his wife's outburst as typical mother-daughter conflict. But he never understood why, when Marah was born, she would want to give an innocent baby a name that meant bitter.

Now, looking at his daughter, thinking of the present circumstances, Jack wondered, *Does a person's name affect who or what they become?* Jack recalled Nikolas's beaming face when his granddaughter was born last year. He'd said—what was it?—oh, yes, Nikolas said, "Ashley, my first granddaughter. Her name means 'peaceful.' She will be a blessing to us all." Then he quoted something from the Bible—one of those big prophets—Isaiah. Something about quietness and strength. *Nikolas has a verse for everything,* Jack mused. *I wonder if he could find a good verse for Marah's name? Something other than bitter.*

Scott returned, the printer in his arms and a couple of books on top, tucked under his chin. "I'm ready, Granpop."

Jack stood and grabbed the books. "I'll carry these. Thank you for the dessert, Marah, Vic. We'll be on our way now."

Marah frowned. "You're not driving home tonight?"

"No, we'll leave in the morning, but we won't be seeing you then."

His daughter quickly got up and wrapped her arms around him. She spoke softly, "Thank you, Dad. I know Scott will be safe with you."

Jack's eyes filled with tears, and he held her tightly for a moment. She clung to him. His voice gruff with emotion, he said, "Get your life in order, daughter." Jack broke away and offered a handshake to his son-in-law.

Vic gripped Jack's hand. "Thank you, Jack."

Their eyes met, and for a moment, Jack almost trusted him.

Jack turned to see Marah attempt to hug Scott. The boy stood rigid, no move to set down the printer. He allowed a brief, awkward hug from his mother and then pulled away. Everyone followed him into the kitchen. At the back door, Scott looked at his father. Vic stepped forward and wrapped the boy and printer in an embrace. Then he opened the door, and Scott went out. Jack followed. He turned at the gate to give a final wave to Marah and Vic as they stood on the porch, watching them go.

Inside the pickup cab, Scott sat with his head down, looking through a box of floppy disks. Jack started the engine and drove away.

CHAPTER 10

Two weeks later, Jack lay in his bedroom, listening to creaking floorboards and thumps above as Scott moved about. *Lifting weights. At bedtime, of all things. Not doing homework, certainly. Can't complain about that, though. The boy is self-disciplined about his studies, brings a stack of books home every night.*

Jack rolled onto his side, bunched up his pillow, and reviewed the changes since they returned from Boise. The worried frown had disappeared from his grandson's face. He seemed happy, helped out with the school newspaper, joined the debate team. Lately, he talked about finding a job after school. Showed incentive. The only thing that worried Jack was that the boy didn't seem to have many friends. Didn't attend sports events or anything else except debate. He'd mentioned one kid, Danny, and said they might get together to work on some social studies projects.

Jack flopped over onto his back and massaged his scalp with thumbs and fingertips.

The worst thing was no privacy.

Now his feet itched. Kicking the covers off, he propped one foot on his flexed knee and rubbed his toes.

He enjoyed Scott's company—most of the time. And his grandson was safe here. The boy had gotten over the moodiness that had draped him like thick fog the first few days after they returned from Boise. And if he found a part-time job to occupy some of his free time, all the better. Paul and Marah had jobs when they were teenagers. Jack had worked nearly all his life, and he saw no reason why the present generation shouldn't do likewise.

The floorboards above stopped creaking. *Scott must be in bed.* Yawning, Jack pulled up the covers and soon drifted off to sleep.

A sudden moderation in winter temperatures coaxed Jack out of his woodworking shop into the bright morning sunshine flooding his backyard. He squinted and looked across the still-snowy expanse toward the street. He needed to stretch his legs. A walk would do him good.

Fifteen minutes later, he cut across the parking lot of Greenough Park and strode toward the footbridge. His glance took in a new, red Toyota four-runner parked near the bridge. "Hmph," he snorted. *Probably another one of those transplanted Californians. Think they need four-wheel-drive just to live here.* He hoped he wouldn't encounter them on the trail, wearing clothes straight out of L. L. Bean catalog and having the mistaken notion that they fit in with the local crowd.

Jack paused on the wooden bridge, leaned on the rail, and looked into the clear, flowing creek. Sunlight danced on the water and bounced off ice crystals in the snowy banks. He moved on and quickly reached the trail leading into the forest of cottonwoods, willows, and pines bordering Rattlesnake Creek. Beyond the trees, covering the surrounding hills, comfortable homes and paved streets populated the gulch. But here in the park, the city seemed miles away. Jack walked up the meandering, snow-packed trail, enjoying the solitude. Chickadees fluttered along, chirping a merry song. In the cold stream, water ouzels dipped and strutted, hunting for food.

After several minutes, he came to a fork in the trail. The main path led up a slight incline and continued to another bridge at the far end of the park. Jack turned onto the less-used path leading down to the water. Ice flakes fell from the tall, straw-colored grass flanking the shaded trail as his pant legs brushed against the frosted stalks. He ducked under overhanging bushes and felt a chilly shower sprinkle down his neck. At a small clearing on the creek bank, he stopped to survey the scene.

Directly across the creek, several huge, snow-covered boulders sheltered a quiet little cove sealed in ice. Upstream, now-barren bushes stood with their branches buried in snow, bordering the sleepy stream that gurgled over red, green, and gray stones.

Jack stepped forward for a better look and was surprised to glimpse a pair of boots immersed ankle-deep in the creek, denim jeans tucked into the laced tops. Bushes and trees concealed the rest of the standing figure. Jack concluded some youngster had given into the temptation of wading. How old was the child? Old enough to be out here alone, wading over slippery rocks in frigid water? He walked along the bank and around the bush until a girl with red hair pulled back in a ponytail under a baseball cap came into full view, her back toward him. She wore a puffy, blue, quilted jacket over her jeans. She seemed to be studying the bush. Jack shook his head. *Kids.*

"Say, young lady, aren't your feet freezing?"

The girl nearly lost her footing as she turned to look at Jack. He caught his breath. *Kennocha!*

The woman smiled. "Oh, hello. Didn't hear you come up." She carefully picked her way toward the shore where Jack stood. "Yes, now that you remind me, my feet are getting numb. I'm not sure if I still have toes." She scrambled out of the shallow water, brushed snow off a large rock near Jack, and sat down. "Oh, my mittens are wet. No wonder my hands feel like ice." She pulled off the mitts, fumbled with her shoelaces, and finally succeeded in pulling off one boot. She rubbed her toes.

Impulsively, Jack said, "Here, let me." Kneeling, he propped her stockinged foot on his thigh and gave her foot a brisk massage.

"M-m-m. Feels good."

"Let me have the other one, too." Jack pulled off her boot, propped her foot on his knee and massaged it. "No wonder you're getting cold. Your socks are damp. Wool socks work better. Keep your feet warm even if they get wet."

She gave him a rueful smile. "So much for waterproof boots." She sighed and closed her eyes while Jack rubbed her toes. "Oh, that feels heavenly."

Jack was mesmerized. What a beautiful woman. Her jacket, unzipped to the waist, showed a red plaid flannel shirt and navy turtleneck. Strands of coppery curls, threaded with gray at the temples, exploded from beneath her denim cap. Her skin looked creamy and smooth. A V-shaped scar, about a half-inch in size, to the left of her chin caught Jack's eye. He found it interesting—appealing even. Freckles scattered across her nose looked like a dash of nutmeg on whipped cream. The wrinkles in the corners of her eyes deepened when she smiled.

"What were you doing in the water?"

She grinned. Pointing toward the creek and bushes, she said, "See that spider web?"

Jack looked. "No."

"Lean this way. Light must be wrong from where you are. I can see it."

Jack leaned closer. Her outdoorsy fragrance pleased him. His heart beat faster. "Yes, I see it now. In that second branch above the water. Small web. Sparkly."

"Isn't it beautiful?" She smiled. "If only I could weave ice crystals into my lace." Her gaze traveled over his face, swept him from head to toe, and then lingered again on his face. She didn't seem in the least self-conscious.

Surprising himself, Jack flirted. "You're a woodland nymph, weaving magic."

She laughed. "No, my grandmother's lace is magic. Mine is quite ordinary."

"You really make lace?" Jack thought it was an art lost long ago to machines.

Pulling on her boots, she nodded. "My grandmother taught me. It's been carried on for generations in our family."

Like a teenager fumbling for the right words, anything to continue the conversation, Jack asked, "You spend a lot of time with your grandmother?"

"Yes. Whenever I can. She raised me. Said I was hopeless, too much a tomboy. She said I'd never learn lace making." She chuckled. "Gran knows me. She said the right word—'never.' I vowed then—at age thirteen—to be the best lace maker in the family."

"And are you?"

Again her lilting laugh. "Not a chance. Gran still holds that title." She cocked her head and gave him a mischievous look. "But I'm very good." She scrambled to her feet.

Jack rose, ignoring the pain in his knees. Wouldn't do to look old.

She stuck out her hand. "I'm Kennocha Bryant."

Jack returned the handshake. "Jack Emerson." She wasn't tall, barely up to his chin. "You come here often?"

"Yes." She studied him a moment. "You look familiar. Do I know you from someplace?"

Remembering how he'd routinely sought glimpses of her at the Carousel, Jack felt too embarrassed to tell her where she'd probably seen him. He avoided her question. "I like to come here when it's not crowded."

She nodded. "I know what you mean. People and dogs. Don't get me wrong—I love dogs. People, too, for the most part. But not too many of either when I'm out here in this heavenly spot."

"That must be your Toyota in the parking lot."

"Yes. I just got it. Isn't it awesome?"

Awesome? Jack restrained his opinion. "You're not from California. Your accent is east of the Mississippi."

She grinned. "From the tone of your voice, I can tell you're a born and bred western man."

Jack grinned back. "Almost. Born in Minnesota, been here since I was eighteen."

"I'm from upstate New York. Just moved here a few months ago." As she stepped onto the trail, an expression of dismay went over her face. "Oh, dear. I sat on that rock so long, I melted the ice." She grinned. "Now I have wet feet and a wet seat." Momentarily rubbing her derriere, she walked down the trail.

Jack followed, surreptitiously admiring the view.

She glanced over her shoulder. "Does your wife ever come here with you?"

"She passed away suddenly a few years ago. Stroke."

"I'm sorry."

Before she could ask any more questions, Jack blurted, "Your name is lovely. Irish?"

"Aye, and that it is," she lilted. "Named after me grandmother, I am." She laughed. "Don't mind me. I love my Gran's accent, but I'm a poor imitation."

Jack thought anything she said sounded wonderful. He wanted to keep her talking. "Sounds good to me."

The narrow trail they'd been following joined the main path at the bridge. She glanced at her watch. "Oh, I have to hurry. So easy for me to lose track of time when I come here." She turned. "It's been nice visiting with you, Jack." Her green eyes sparkled. "And thank you for the foot rub. I'm not in the habit of letting strangers do that."

Again, Jack surprised himself. "Oh, I quite regularly rescue beautiful young women from wading in the ice-cold creek in February."

She arched an eyebrow and tilted her head. "I know where I've seen you—the Carousel."

"Practically live there. I'm one of the volunteers."

"Me too. I just signed up." Her face brightened. "Oh, you're Jack of the famous blade! The expert carver."

"And you're the expert painter."

"Well, let's just say I've had some experience at painting." She looked at her watch again. "I wish we could talk longer, but I really have to hurry now. Perhaps I'll see you at the Carousel later."

He smiled. "I hope so. I'm usually in the woodshop. Have a good day, Kennocha."

With a wave, she trotted across the bridge, following the road to the parking lot. Jack watched until she disappeared around the bend.

Leaning on the bridge rail, Jack stared into the moving waters and let his thoughts flow. *Claire ... I'll always love you, but you're gone. I need someone ... someone warm, someone who laughs ... likes what I do ... someone like Kennocha Bryant.*

Jack stood up, gave the rail a slap, pulled his shoulders back, and lifted his chin. He felt a lot younger than he had an hour ago.

Late that afternoon, Jack went to the Carousel, found the carvers' corner of the parking lot empty, and let himself in the back door with a key. Others would show up soon. Meanwhile, he relished the solitude. The smell of wood and the familiar clutter in the carving room felt almost as good as his own workshop at home.

He lifted his wooden pony's head from a shelf and examined it all around. Forelock needed a little more work, but today he wanted to finish the rose cascade. He returned the head to its shelf, picked up three flower carvings one at a time—two completed small ones and one larger, unfinished cascade. He examined each, nodded his satisfaction with the smaller pieces, and returned them to the shelf. He settled onto a stool at the workbench, pocketknife in one hand, cascade in the other. His blade coaxed delicate rose petals from the basswood, while his mind rehashed the fragments of information he had picked up in Boise a few weeks ago

Vic says Marah's having an affair, and Scott found out. Marah says she and Scott had a normal parent-teen argument. Scott won't say anything except that his parents argue a lot. When they lived in Springfield, Marah and Vic nearly split up over Vic's affair. Marah left him for a while and stayed with us. If I'm to believe Vic, now Marah is committing adultery.

Jack paused, remembering. A chill swept over him when he recalled Claire's words to their daughter: "Give him back his own medicine." Jack was shocked. He was positive Marah did not heed that ill-spoken advice then, and he fervently hoped she wasn't now.

Much as Jack despised Vic's philandering, he'd always believed his son-in-law played it straight with him face-to-face. No lies. Not even when Jack had confronted him about his cheating. *So it wouldn't be like him to lie now, would it?*

Jack recalled how miserable the man had looked that day in his Boise office, when Vic had voiced his suspicions about his wife. Vic wouldn't fabricate something like that. His pride wouldn't allow it—would it? In Vic's mind, his cheating—if he got away with it—was common to men. But to have his wife cheat? Not acceptable. Jack lowered the knife and the rose cascade, and closed his eyes. Marah's image filled his mind. He loved her in that special way a man loves his only daughter. He was proud to be her father, but tiny cracks of doubt worried their way into Jack's confidence in her. Her failure to deal with Scott's pain couldn't be ignored. After a moment, he picked up the blade and began the finishing touches of a leaf tucked under a rose. *Whatever is happening between Marah and Vic, Scott is caught in the middle. Torn loyalties. No wonder he's built a barricade around himself to hide his confusion, pain, and fear. Nikolas was right, had to get the boy out of there.* Jack rounded out the inner whorl of the rose with a tiny concave chisel.

Vic's drinking more than I've ever seen him do before. Liquor fouls up a man's judgment. If he was drunk and struck Scott with something ... but what would make that deep cut? If he'd been sober, he probably wouldn't have done it at all.

But why is the boy so cold toward his mother? Did Marah witness an attack and fail to intervene? Such betrayal could turn the boy bitter. Marah said she didn't know anything about Scott's wound. But on the phone, when I called her before we went over, she seemed to know. In fact, she knew it was a cut on his back. I didn't tell her that. So how did she know unless she saw it happen?

The base of the leaf under the rose presented difficulty. He needed to trim out just a bit more. He tried the pocketknife. Distracted with his troubled thoughts, the tip of Jack's blade slipped, and he sliced his finger. He grunted at his carelessness and grabbed the cleanest looking rag lying on table to wipe off the blood running down his hand. The cut continued oozing, so he applied pressure, propped his elbow on the table, and leaned his head on his hand.

The door to the workroom swung open, and Nikolas came in.

"Aha, caught you napping, did I?" Nikolas grinned at Jack.

"Napping? Me? I haven't picked up your trick of sleeping on the job, you old fox." Jack went to the well-stocked first-aid cabinet and wrapped a Band-Aid around his finger.

Nikolas hung up his coat and went to the shelf of Jack's work. "This one is finished?" He held a small bunch of wooden roses. In his burly hands, bristling with black curly hairs, the carving looked fragile and pale.

Jack nodded. "That other one, too. And I'll have this cascade ready shortly." He resumed shaping the stubborn leaf.

"I saw Kennocha come in the back door. We could see if she wants to start on this bouquet."

"We?"

"Um-hum." Nikolas looked at Jack out of the corner of his eye and stood, carved flowers in hand. "Come. She will paint your roses."

Jack arched an eyebrow and shot his friend a quizzical look as he grabbed the other small rose piece off the shelf and followed. Entering the paint room, Jack's pulse quickened at the sight of the petite, slender woman in blue jeans and a sunny yellow T-shirt, her back to them as she sorted through tubes of tint on shelves above a workbench. A few curls had escaped the narrow blue ribbon that held most of her long, red hair at the nape of her neck.

"Miss Kennocha, we have brought a new task for you," Nikolas said.

She turned and smiled. "Oh, good. I finished the pinto's saddle. Ready to start a new job."

Her voice rang mellow and musical to Jack's ears.

As she walked across the room, Jack admired her rounded hips and small waist. He pulled his attention away from her body. Her eyes met his, her gaze frank and friendly ... and perhaps more?

"Hi, Jack. Good to see you again."

He grinned. "Your feet dry?"

She grinned back.

Nikolas looked from one to the other, raising questioning eyebrows.

Jack, ignoring Nikolas's inquisitive expression, took the carving from him. "These are ready to paint." He extended them to Kennocha.

Handling them with care, the woman examined the detailed petals and leaves. After a moment, she looked at Jack and said, "You are an artist."

Jack's mustache prickled with pride.

Kennocha placed the carvings on a table, stepped back, squinted at the roses, her hands stuck in her hip pockets. Jack tried not to stare.

She tilted her head, still studying the roses. "Are there other decorations? Tell me about the horse, its color, its name. Is there a special story behind it?"

When others had asked Jack similar questions, he gave minimal answers, not wanting to bother explaining. He surprised himself now as he said, "The horse's name is Clarissa Mae, in memory of my wife, Claire. This pony has lots of roses, because Claire loved them." *Why am I telling her all this?* Jack gestured toward the carvings on the table. "These are for the bridle. I'm working on a cascade to go behind the saddle now. Then I'll do a garland of roses for the breast collar."

Kennocha smiled. "Sounds lovely. What was your wife's favorite rose?"

Jack pulled at the tip of his mustache. "Hm-m. Tell you the truth, I don't know."

Nikolas moved in closer. "Did you not want many colors?"

Jack glanced at his friend. "That was Scott's idea." Casually, he stepped between Nikolas and Kennocha. "She liked yellow best. You know, the ones with the orange edges?" Jack looked into Kennocha's eyes and smiled. So close he could reach out and touch her, he felt captivated by her aura. Jack sensed mutual attraction. His heart beat faster.

She nodded in response to his question. "Yes, I think I know which ones you mean. We already have a couple of ponies with multicolored flowers. Suppose we do these in warm yellows and corals?" She paused. "Tell you what. I'll make a colored sketch and show you before I begin painting." She cocked her head. "What do you think?"

Jack melted. At this moment, he would have agreed to green stripes and purple polka dots. "Good idea."

Kennocha stepped forward, her shoulder lightly brushing Jack's arm, and picked up the carvings. "May I keep these to make the sketch? It would be a couple of days."

"Of course."

Jack and Nikolas returned to the woodworking room. As soon as the door closed behind them, Nikolas pounced. "What is this you talk about? Dry feet? That is not the proper way to talk to a lady." Awakening dawned on Nikolas's face. "Oh, ho. This was from a previous conversation?"

Jack smirked. "Maybe, maybe not."

Undeterred, Nikolas said, "See, my friend, what did I tell you? I knew you would be smitten with Kennocha."

"I'm not smitten." Jack picked up a rag and attacked sawdust on the table.

"Ha. You are—what do they say—twitterpated."

"Twitterpated? That's about as archaic as you are. You'd better sign up for some more English lessons, you old Russian."

Nikolas folded his hands over his belly and chuckled. "You are the one who will need lessons—in how to court a lady. You are rusty. You should have listened to me long ago when I told you to begin practicing. I knew the day would come."

Jack snorted and stomped to the coatrack. He wasn't ready to admit his feelings aloud. He jerked his cap over his ears, whipped a scarf around his neck, pulled on his coat, and scowled at Nikolas. "Got to get home, cook supper."

"Jack ..."

Jack paused at the serious tone of Nikolas's voice.

"This lady likes you, I can tell. You do Claire no dishonor by being interested in another woman. A good, Christian woman. Like Kennocha."

Jack regarded his friend for a long moment. Slowly, he said, "I know, Nikolas. Kennocha is ... special. But I don't know if I'm ready yet. Especially now, with Scott—"

"Scott? He is a big boy."

Jack studied the floor. "Well, maybe you're right. But you saw that fellow the other day—that O'Brien character."

The sparkle faded from Nikolas's eyes. "Oh, him. Bevan O'Brien. Yes, I saw."

Jack adjusted his cap and left.

Outside, wind whipped along the river in the waning light, scattering flurries of powdery snow among the bleak branches of overhanging trees—winter's final blast before crocuses bloomed purple and gold, peeking through crusty snow.

Jack hurried to his pickup, and after the motor warmed up a bit, he eased up the hill to the Front Street intersection. Waiting for a break in the five o'clock traffic rush, he glanced at two figures coming out of a building across the street. The illuminated sign above the door said Sea Horse Club. Whatever that was. A bar, maybe?

Jack blinked and strained for a better look. Scott? What's he doing there? Who's that with him? One of his classmates? Oblivious of the cars rushing by on the facing street, Jack inspected the stranger. Seemed to be about Scott's age, clean-cut, dark hair, thin build, several inches shorter than Scott. The boy turned, glanced across the street, and Jack got a look at his face. Eyeglasses, pale complexion.

Just then, someone else came out of the building and joined them on the sidewalk. Whoever that character was, Jack didn't like his looks nor the way he acted. Nearly Scott's height, shoulder-length blond hair, long black overcoat, high-heeled boots. The guy turned, so his face came into view. Dark lipstick, dangling earrings. His overcoat hung open, exposing a white shirt and tight black pants. Jack glared at the way the stranger gestured, his body movements. If not for the flat chest, he'd have sworn this person was a woman.

What is my grandson doing hanging around with this jerk?

CHAPTER 11

Scott and the two strangers stood in front of the bar with the weird guy doing most of the talking, hands fluttering. Jack glanced around, looking for a parking space. Nothing. A car pulled up behind him and honked. Jack eased forward, but traffic forced him to turn right. Minutes later, he turned onto the street where he'd seen Scott and the strangers. But now the trio was gone. He'd have to question Scott later.

After supper, Jack rolled up his sleeves, plunged his hands into soapy dishwater, and said, "I saw you downtown this afternoon." He rinsed a green bowl and set it in the draining rack.

"I wasn't—"

Jack looked over his shoulder. Scott stood holding a carton of milk and a butter dish. "You were going to say something?"

Wary, Scott asked, "Where'd you see me?"

"Down by Front Street. Coming out of some place called the Sea Horse." Jack deposited two clean plates in the dish rack and picked up a kettle. "Those guys you were with—friends of yours?"

Scott slammed the refrigerator door, rattling glass jars and bottles inside against one another. "Yeah." He picked up his backpack. "Got a lot of homework tonight." Without looking at his grandfather, he hurried out of the kitchen and ran upstairs.

Jack dried his hands, ran his thumbs over his mustache, and followed his grandson.

In Scott's bedroom, Jack sat on a straight-back chair. "Let's talk."

Scott sat on the bed, snapping notebook rings. Then he started scratching the cat's ears.

"What was that place you kids came out of?"

"We just went in there for a Coke."

"They serve alcohol in there?"

"Yeah, so what? Doesn't mean we drink." Scott shot a defiant look at Jack.

"You're under age. Stay out of there."

Scott stood and rolled his eyes toward the ceiling. "Granpop, we weren't drinking. It's not just a bar. It's a place where you go to meet people."

Jack frowned. When Paul was growing up, he didn't go to bars to meet people. "I said stay out of there. You're not to go into bars for any reason. Understand?"

"Yeah." Scott perched his elbows on the dresser, turned on the radio, and fiddled with the dial. A blast of rock music hit the room. Jack cringed. Miss Lavender's ears twitched. Scott, back turned to his grandfather, tapped his fingers to the beat on the edge of the dresser.

Jack's jaw tensed, and his ire rose along with his voice. "Turn that thing off!" Scott complied. "Who were those people you were with?"

"Just a couple of guys—Danny and Marco. Danny's in my social studies class. Marco's just a guy we know. He's a DJ."

"DJ?"

"Yeah. Disc jockey. Plays at dances and stuff."

"He was the one with the makeup?"

Scott's shoulders hunched. "Yeah."

Jack considered this. *DJ—that explained the weird appearance. But what about the gestures? The body movements? Did that go with the job, too? Only one way to find out.* He got up and stood in front of his grandson, arms folded. Miss Lavender jumped off the bed and dashed downstairs.

Scott gave Jack a worried look.

"That Marco—is he one of those queers?"

Scott studied the floor. He shrugged. "Dunno."

"But he could be?"

"Maybe," Scott mumbled.

"I don't want you associating with such people."

"Huh?"

"Homosexuals. I don't want you to have anything to do with perverts."

Scott turned on his heel and marched across the room, holding his head in his hands in an elaborate show of exasperation. "Geez, Granpop. It's the twentieth century." He dropped his hands in an appeal. "This is old stuff. It's not like nobody knows about it. Some people are just born that way."

Jack snorted. "Can't buy that. God doesn't make mistakes."

Scott groaned. "You gonna give me a sermon?"

"Don't get smart with me. It's plain, common sense. Men aren't made to have sex with other men. And there's AIDS. Did you stop to think that might be God's judgment?"

Scott turned and shuffled to the bay window facing the street. He shoved some books aside and flopped down. "Not everybody gets AIDS just because they're gay."

Jack didn't know what to make of Scott's remark. Was he defending homosexuals? Why? Sure, Jack had seen stuff in the newspapers, but he didn't waste his time reading about perverts' problems. Didn't concern him nor his family. Never would. But he supposed Scott heard stuff in school, maybe even knew some of them.

Scott sat up and cleared his throat. "Sometimes I think—" He shook his head. "I mean, I—" He looked at Jack, his face imploring. "Does it matter? I mean ... you gonna kick me out or something if I ... want to be friends with gay guys?"

Caught off guard, Jack rubbed his jaw and thought. *Have to admit, I'm not up to date on this stuff. Maybe Nikolas knows. He's got teenage grandkids.*

He took a deep breath to calm his simmering anger. "Maybe I'm worrying over nothing. After all, you've got good sense. I suppose ... if you've got a friend who buys into that lifestyle, well then, that's his business. I know I don't have to worry about you. But I'd like to meet your friends. Bring 'em around."

Scott mumbled something.

"What's that? Speak so I can understand you."

"I said, I don't have any friends. Not a lot, like you make it sound."

"I realize you're a newcomer in school here, but won't be long before you—"

"Granpop, I don't have a lot of friends. Not here, not in Boise, either." He lowered his head. "Nobody likes me," he muttered.

Jack was more bewildered than ever. He thought a moment. "What about that other boy, Danny?"

Scott looked at him out of the corner of his eye. "What about him?"

"He's a friend, isn't he?"

Scott nodded.

"Then, bring him over." Jack moved toward the door.

Scott picked up his backpack and pulled out a stack of schoolbooks. "Okay."

Scott was upstairs that evening when Nikolas stopped by with a sketch for a new pony. He wanted Jack's advice, but Jack couldn't concentrate.

"My friend, you are troubled." Nikolas began rolling up the paper. "This we will do another day."

"What? Oh, sorry, Nikolas." Jack tugged at his mustache, got up from the table, and with a glance toward the stairs, said, "Come on in here, would you?" He walked into the living room, with Nikolas following.

Nikolas settled into an easy chair while Jack sat on the edge of the sofa.

"What are they teaching these kids in school nowadays about so-called gays?" Jack asked.

Nikolas raised one eyebrow. "My daughter says some schools teach—what do they say—diversity? Yes, diversity. 'Alternative lifestyles,' she said." Nikolas stroked his beard. "But you know ... we see these things on the television ..."

Jack scowled. "But I don't pay much attention. Never had any reason to. What about in church? Sunday school? What do they say about all this?"

"I can only speak for my church. We believe the act of homosexuality is a sin. But it is God's business to forgive sin."

"Now hold on here. You said 'the act.' Are you making some kind of distinction?"

"Some say people are born homosexual. With this, I think I agree."

Jack snorted. "That's garbage."

Nikolas held up his hand. "Consider this. Why would anyone voluntarily decide such a thing? To be homosexual? Think, my friend. Look at what they suffer—prejudice, rejection, and for some, terrible illness." Nikolas paused. "And perhaps the wrath of God, for the Bible says the act of homosexuality is a sin."

"You said that already. So what you're leading up to is that if they're born that way, they're supposed to—"

"Abstain. Celibacy. Yes."

"Hmph. You think anyone really does that? This country's turning into another Sodom and Gomorrah. And if you ask me, that's what AIDS is all about. God's judgment. Do you agree?"

Leaning back, Nikolas's eyes searched Jack's. "No one has ever asked me that before." He closed his eyes and scratched at his chin. "I recall a sermon our pastor gave not long ago about the sin of condemning people who are different from us. He mentioned homosexuals, too. I wrote some notes. My memory is not so good anymore." Nikolas placed his hands on the arms of the chair and prepared to lift himself to his feet. "Let me get my Bible, and I will look up the Scripture references Pastor used."

"Can't you just say what you think? Do you have to use the Bible every time I ask you a question?"

Nikolas tucked his chin to his chest, raised his bushy black eyebrows, and fixed his gaze on Jack. "My friend," he sighed, "what do I know? I must consult the authority on important matters."

"Oh, all right." Jack stood. "I'll get your Bible. Where is it?"

Nikolas sank back into his chair and rubbed his knees. "In the front seat of my car. Thank you."

Jack hurried away and returned shortly. He handed the dog-eared Bible to his friend.

Nikolas spent a few moments fanning through the pages. At last he said, "Ah. Here it is. He unfolded a light blue church bulletin, the margins covered with his handwriting. After he studied it a moment, he opened his Bible, found his place, and said, "First Corinthians, chapter 6, verse 11, says, 'And such were some of you. but you were washed, but you were sanctified, but you were justified in the name of the Lord Jesus and by the Spirit of our God.'"

Jack frowned. "What does that mean?"

"Do you not see? It says, 'Such *were* some of you.' People can renounce the sin of homosexuality just as we must renounce our sins. Our Lord Jesus asks that we confess and repent." Nikolas drew in a deep breath and let it out. "Our Father wants good for us. He gives us the Way."

Jack tugged at the tips of his mustache. "Hmm. So you think people can stop being homosexual."

Nikolas wagged a finger. "The act. Stop the behavior."

"Yes, yes, the act. I'm not so sure people can change that much."

"Ah, but look at the apostle Paul. Remember how he was before the Lord called him to change?"

Jack nodded. "He was a devout Jew, terrorizing Christian Jews. Then Jesus got hold of him. Paul became a Christian Jew himself." He paused. "Enough of all this." He started to get up, but Nikolas held up his hand. Jack put his hands on his knees and stared at his friend. "Now what?"

"Now," said Nikolas, "will you tell me why you ask these questions? Is it Scott? Is he gay?"

Jack jumped to his feet. "Of course not!" He shoved his fingers through his hair and paced across the room and back. "But I saw Scott with a guy this afternoon who looked like a queer if I ever saw one." He sat down and leveled a look at his friend. "What worries me is Scott's reaction when I questioned him tonight." Jack related his conversation with Scott. He paused, smacked his fist into the palm of his hand, and declared, "If Scott's hanging around with people like that, I'm going to put a stop to it. Or send him packing."

"Jack, my friend, let us think about this."

"What's there to think about?"

"The boy is lonely and confused. His parents have failed him. He seeks love. He is not sure about himself and perhaps thinks he is not worthy of love. Perhaps he blames himself for what has transpired with his parents." Nikolas propped his elbows on the arms of the chair, laced his fingers together, and peered at Jack. "You, the grandfather, are the boy's only solid anchor now. But you know how teenagers are. If you tell him he cannot do a thing, you can be assured he will do that very thing."

Jack glared at his old friend. "Not while he's under my roof, he won't."

CHAPTER 12

Jack gave a final swipe to his freshly polished loafers and stuffed the rag back into his shoe kit. He checked himself in the mirror one more time, combed his mustache, and scooped his pickup keys from the dresser. He would meet Kennocha at the Carousel to go over her colored sketches of the pony Clarissa Mae.

Humming "Seventy-Six Trombones," Jack rounded the corner into the kitchen and stopped in his tracks. Marah pushed open the back door, pulling a large suitcase behind her.

"Hi, Dad. Surprise!" Smiling, she crossed the room to give him a hug and a kiss on his cheek. "I've come for a visit."

"So I see. Why didn't you call first?"

She glanced at him from the corner of her eye, pulled off her coat, and flung it over a chair. "Didn't think I had to."

Jack pulled at the tip of his mustache in irritation. "Where's Vic? I thought you two were going to Japan."

"Still in Japan. I stayed home, and I got lonesome. Decided to spend a few days with my son. And you."

Jack stepped around his daughter and headed for the door. "Make yourself comfortable. I have an appointment."

"Appointment? Are you sick?"

Jack arched an eyebrow. "Sick? Course not."

Marah frowned. "Not a doctor's appointment? What then?"

"It's about the Carousel. I'll try to be back before Scott gets home. He has a meeting after school. Debate club." He reached for the door handle.

"What time?"

Impatient, Jack turned once more. "I don't know, daughter. Sometimes these things take a while. I said I'd try to be home before Scott—"

"That's what I mean. What time does Scott get home?"

"Oh. About five thirty. I have to go." He stepped out the door. Hurrying toward the garage, his thoughts tumbled. *Just when things were settling down, now all this. First, Scott's strange friends and even stranger reaction to my questions. Now Marah. Too soon. She should've called. I'd have told her to wait. Scott's not ready for this.*

Jack backed out of the garage and stopped. *I should send her back home.* He shifted into gear. *No, I can't do that. She's my daughter.* He pulled into the street and turned downtown.

Kennocha was in the paint room when Jack arrived. She was studying the sketches of Clarissa Mae she'd spread across the table. She looked up and smiled at Jack.

"Have I kept you waiting? My daughter just arrived unexpectedly from Boise." Jack stood beside her and breathed in her fresh scent. *What is that? Smells like those purple things that Claire planted by the roses. Lavender?*

"I just got here myself. Is this a good time for you? We don't have to—"

"This is good for me." He picked up a sketch of the rose garland and smiled. "Just like I pictured in my mind. Yellow with orange centers and edges. Perfect."

She laughed lightly. "I'm glad you're pleased. What about the saddle? I was undecided, so I tried a couple different ones."

Jack felt like a schoolboy, trying hard not to sneak looks at a beautiful girl. He concentrated on the sketch in his hand as she leaned across the table to reach for some other drawings.

Kennocha pushed a strand of hair behind her ear and stood beside Jack, her shoulder touching his arm. She showed him the two color schemes for the saddle. "What do you think? Deep coral or blue and gold?" She tilted her head to one side as she considered the drawings.

Jack couldn't take his eyes off her. "You decide."

"I think the blue." She picked up a sketch of the halter. "And this? I sketched in a design and thought I'd repeat it on the saddle. What do you think?"

Jack reached for the paper and let his hand touch hers. She didn't pull away. "Couldn't be better. You've done a wonderful job."

Again, her light, musical laugh. "Well, let's reserve judgment until the painting is actually done."

Jack helped her gather up the drawings. Finished, he cleared his throat. "Uh ... would you like to—" He thought fast—*like to what?* Would she think he's nuts if he invited her for a cup of coffee? His stomach tightened. Blast Nikolas anyway! This was his idea! "Would you like to go get a cup of coffee?" Embarrassed, he fumbled with the stack of papers.

Her warm voice and the touch of her hand on his arm made him breathe easier. "I'd love to," she said. "Do you like espresso? Or cappuccino? There's a great little shop close by. We could walk."

Jack grinned. He couldn't help himself. He hadn't the foggiest notion what espresso or that other stuff was, but he knew he'd like it. "Okay, let's go."

Ten minutes later, Jack glanced around inside the cheerful bistro and inhaled the aroma of fresh-ground coffee. Perhaps a dozen people sat talking and laughing in cozy clusters around small tables painted in primary colors. Kennocha ordered a grande, dark-roast coffee, and Jack asked for the same.

At their table, knees brushing as they settled into their chairs, Kennocha stirred cream into her Italian ceramic mug and asked, "You said your daughter's from Boise?"

Jack nodded, tasted his coffee, and restrained a shudder. He poured in a good measure of cream.

Kennocha lifted her cup and looked at Jack over the rim. "I almost accepted a job there before I took this one. Decided I preferred mountains within a closer drive. And lakes. It's been my dream to go camping and hiking and fishing on weekends. Maybe backpacking during summer vacation. Of course," she chuckled, "that dream was more likely to have happened when I was in my twenties, even thirties. Not sure I could really backpack a sleeping bag and provisions now. But I like this town."

"Missoula is a good town." Suddenly, he felt daring. "And it gets better all the time." He smiled into her green eyes.

She blushed. "Thank you."

Jack cleared his throat in the silence that followed. "I've heard you're a teacher. High school?"

Kennocha nodded.

"Let me guess ... art?"

She smiled. "It's my real passion. But I have to eat. So I teach English. Specifically, creative writing for gifted students. And I help with career counseling." She sipped her coffee. "Someday, I may go back to New York and work on a dual degree—art and counseling.

Art would help me stay sane while I'm studying counseling. And Gran would love having me closer again."

Jack didn't want to think about her leaving. "English isn't so bad, is it?"

"No, but what I enjoy most here in school is counseling. Oftentimes helping students choose careers naturally involves some emotional counseling, too. Kids' ideas about what they want to do after they graduate are usually a lot different from their parents' expectations." She shook her head and frowned. "Gets pretty tough for some students." Occupied with her thoughts, she creased her napkin into accordion folds.

Jack watched her and wondered what she'd say about Scott's new friends. "What would you say to parents whose son is running around with the wrong kind of kids?"

Kennocha looked up. "Wrong kind? What makes them wrong?"

Jack squirmed. He hadn't bargained on getting into a discussion about homosexuality on his first date. "Say they're gay."

Kennocha studied him for a moment. "You're not talking about a hypothetical situation, are you?"

Jack could have kicked himself for even mentioning this. He didn't want to talk about his family problems. Kennocha probably would never want to see him again. But, he'd gone this far. "My grandson lives with me. He's sixteen. The other day I happened to see him with a couple of guys in front of the Sea Horse."

Kennocha nodded. "That's known to be cross-cultural."

"It is?" Jack thought cross-cultural meant different nationalities. University influence, he supposed. A bunch of liberals trying to make Missoula into another San Francisco.

"Is your grandson gay?"

Jack bristled. "Of course not."

Kennocha leaned back, palms forward. "Wait a minute, Jack. I didn't mean to offend you." After a beat, she folded her arms on the table. "Look, I'm sorry. I have to admit I'm somewhat calloused about this whole issue. I forget that other people don't deal with it almost every day." She paused. "It's not that I'm judging their lifestyle—it's a personal thing—but when I see the havoc created in some of these kids' lives because of their families' reaction to a gay lifestyle ... parents kicking their sons and daughters out of the home, disowning them ..." She shook her head. "That's not right."

Jack pondered. No doubt about it, if he ever had to face a situation like that, he'd kick the kid out if he didn't straighten up.

Kennocha's eyes looked sad. "Most kids don't tell their parents. They're afraid of rejection. The parents often find out from someone else, or they see their kids with people who exhibit suggestive behavior, wear symbols, or have bumper stickers on their cars. I think they want their family to know, but they're terrified, so they display hints, hoping their mothers or fathers will ask to open the conversation."

Her words sunk into Jack's mind like lead weights on a fishing hole. *Not Scott. Not my grandson.* He sat up straight, took in a deep breath, and smiled. "We've gotten mighty serious here. Let's talk about something else."

She hesitated a moment. "All right."

Soon after, they left the bistro and took the long way back toward the Carousel. The wind whipped Kennocha's hair, but she didn't seem to mind. They walked halfway across Higgins Avenue bridge and stopped to look at the river. After a few minutes, Kennocha shivered, tucked her coat tighter around her throat, and turned to look back the direction they'd come. She gazed up at the old, redbrick Wilma Building at the north end of the bridge. "That's where I live."

"Top floor?"

"No, that suite is reserved for the manager. I'm on the third floor. Bevan—he's the manager—invited me up for a social gathering recently. Even better view than I have."

Inwardly, Jack despaired. *Bevan O'Brien. The guy's practically living on her doorstep.*

They walked back across the bridge and stopped at the entrance to the Wilma.

Kennocha offered her hand. "Thank you for the coffee and conversation." Kennocha gave Jack a coquettish smile. "Would you be offended if I asked you out sometime?"

Jack, holding her hand, did a double take. *Times change,* he told himself. "Not at all." He grinned. "I'd like that."

She smiled. "I'll get to work on Clarissa Mae's garlands this week. You'll have to come by and see the progress."

"I will. I promise." Jack gave her hand a gentle squeeze before he let it go. After she disappeared into the building, Jack walked to the stairs leading from the bridge down to Riverfront Park and the Carousel. He glanced toward the Carousel building as he descended and paused in surprise. *Is that—? Couldn't be. Yes, it is. Marah. In the Carousel parking lot, watching me.* He checked his watch. Scott should've been home an hour ago. Jack hurried down the stairs and strode toward his daughter. When he stood in front of her, he stopped. Her gold-flecked brown eyes flickered, and the tight lines around her mouth reminded him of Claire when she was irritated with him. His daughter's voice sounded accusing.

"Who was that woman?"

Startled, Jack said, "She's one of the volunteers who works on the ponies." He resolved not to let his daughter's mood spoil his afternoon. He headed for the Carousel building. "Come on inside. I'll show you around." He held the back door open for her.

She gave him a searching glance as she went in. "You didn't say you were meeting a woman. Why didn't you just meet her here? If this is where you work on these things. Why did you go to her apartment?"

"Stop it, Marah, you sound like a jealous wife. And I didn't go to her apartment. We were at a coffee shop after we finished up here." Jack shook his head, changed the subject. For the next several minutes, he showed Marah the carving and painting projects. She seemed distracted. He gave up trying to capture her interest. "Did Scott get home yet?"

"He called. That's why I came down here." Her mouth twisted in a bitter smile. "He wasn't exactly overjoyed to hear me answer the phone. Said he was going to the library and not to expect him home until late." She toyed with a scattering of sawdust on the floor, pushing it into a little pile with the toe of her shoe. "Dad, I want to ask you something about Scott. Does he have a girlfriend or a girl he's interested in?" Her foot stopped moving, but she continued to keep her eyes lowered.

"Girlfriend? No. He says he doesn't have any friends here. Hardly any." Jack wondered if he should tell her about the two he saw with Scott. Marah worried him. Could she handle the news that he saw her son hanging around with a gay guy? "He's got a couple of friends."

Marah picked at her nail polish. "Boys?"

"Yes. Why are you asking?"

After a moment, she dropped her hands to her sides and looked at Jack. "Scott doesn't have a girlfriend at home. He hangs out with Larry—an okay kid, but I think he's gay. So I wonder if Scott is—"

"Gay? You wonder if your son is gay?"

"Yes. I think he's avoiding me, because he doesn't want to talk about it." Her voice dropped. "I hoped he'd come right home when he knew I was here."

"It's too soon, Marah. I'd have told you that if you had called first. The boy is barely beginning to get settled in school. It hasn't even been a month." He decided not to tell her about Danny and Marco and the Sea Horse. He needed to find out more himself first. "Whatever happened that caused him to run away, it's going to take some time to heal. He still isn't talking about it. Yet."

"No reason why he should. It's over. We talked about it—Scott and I—it's taken care of. Just a misunderstanding, that's all."

Jack's eyebrows went up. "When did you talk? Not when Scott and I came to Boise."

Flustered, Marah waved her hand as though to brush away the question. "Oh, well, you know what I mean. It doesn't matter. I said it's over." She smiled and took her father's arm. "C'mon, Daddy, I'll take you out for supper. I'm starved. Scott said he'd grab a burger, so we don't have to worry about him."

Jack studied her for a moment. *What is she hiding?* He realized he'd never get it out of her now, not when she called him "Daddy." An old, familiar ploy from her youth, designed to soften him up. He felt uneasy, still suspicious that she was covering up for Vic. Perhaps hoping it was about Vic, not about Scott being gay. *My grandson, a pervert? I can't accept that.*

When they got home after supper, Scott still wasn't home. Jack carried Marah's suitcase upstairs to her old room. When he came down, he found his daughter in Claire's sewing room.

Everything remained as it had been before Claire died: lengths of neatly folded fabrics stacked on shelves, patterns filed in boxes, spools of thread on wall-mounted pegs above the long worktable, the sewing machine still threaded with yellow from the interrupted kitchen curtain project. After Claire died, Jack had folded the unfinished curtains and placed them in the closet. He couldn't bear to walk in and see them lying on the table, hems pinned, ready for Claire to stitch.

Marah sat in the swivel chair in front of the sewing machine, her face pensive. Jack leaned against the edge of the old kitchen table Claire had used for her work surface.

Her voice flat, her face expressionless, Marah said, "I remember when I wanted to sew a dress for my doll. Thought I knew how to operate the sewing machine. Didn't ask Mother. Made a terrible mess. Thread knotted up, tangled around the bobbin case, fabric stuck in the feeder. Mother was furious." Marah pivoted to face Jack. "Know what she did, Daddy? Threatened to lock me in the closet. I ran outside and hid in the lilac bushes until Paul got home from school."

"Your mother wouldn't have locked you up."

A small, knowing smile touched Marah's lips. She whispered, "Oh, yes, she would. And that wasn't the worst of it." She rose. "Come here."

He followed her into the dining room, where she stood in front of the china hutch. She cradled a delicate, gold-rimmed, china teacup, white with pink roses, in her hands. Her strange mood persisted.

"Remember how Mother used to hold the Ladies Auxiliary meetings here? And she'd use these teacups? Her grandmother's, she said. One day I wanted to help get things ready for the afternoon tea party. I was trying to get back into Mother's good graces. I was always in trouble with her, always trying to please her. She said I was a 'bad girl, fat bad girl.'"

Jack started to protest, but she continued.

"She let me put the damask napkins and silver out. Then I decided to surprise her and get out the teacups, too. I had to stand on a chair to reach the top shelf. The last cup was in the very back. Only my fingertips touched it. I jiggled it forward. Too far. It fell out, hit the sideboard, and broke into a million pieces."

Jack watched his daughter. Her face had drained of color, and she stared at the floor as though seeing bits of shattered china scattered about her feet. He reached toward her, wanting to break her mood. Her strained voice halted him.

"Mother heard it. I'd never seen her so angry. I was terrified. Her eyes ... so cold ... She never said one word. She went upstairs, got my porcelain doll, my favorite—remember Susan? I loved that doll more than anything else in the world." Trembling now, Marah continued. "When Mother came back downstairs, she had Susan. I was down on my knees, trying to pick up pieces of the teacup. Mother stopped in front of me. Bits of china crunched under her shoes, her lovely blue pumps with the gold buckle on the toe. She said, 'You knew you were never to touch my grandmother's china. Now you'll pay for it.'" Marah's voice cracked. "She raised Susan up above her head. The lace hem on Mother's slip showed. I wrapped my arms around her legs and begged, 'Please, Mommy, please,' but she just smiled ... an ugly smile ..." Marah paused. "She threw Susan onto the floor and broke her." Marah covered her face with both hands and broke into wrenching sobs.

"Marah, Marah," Jack breathed. He pulled his daughter into his arms and hugged her, groaning, "I'm sorry, honey." He held her head against his chest and stroked her hair.

Why hadn't he known? He searched his memory for clues. He recalled one time asking his daughter where Susan was; the doll wasn't in her usual place on Marah's pillow when he tucked the little girl in for the night and recited prayers with her. Instead of answering, the child had solemnly told him she wanted to say a prayer for Susan, because she had gone away. At the time, Jack simply thought it was a new game Marah had invented. It was normal for her to playact so well that she believed her own inventions. Jack considered the games to be harmless, so he didn't worry. The doll would show up.

Claire didn't tell him about the china nor the doll.

Now, with one arm still holding his weeping daughter, Jack took the teacup from her trembling hands and placed it on the shelf, out of sight. He'd pack away the whole works at his first opportunity, so Marah wouldn't have to be reminded again. Ever. He shut the cabinet door and led her away.

He let Marah get control of herself while he made a fresh, strong pot of coffee. She went into the bathroom and returned a few minutes later, makeup removed, face washed, eyes red. Jack filled their mugs with steaming brew.

"Marah, I'm shocked. Your mother—"

Marah's voice sounded wooden. "It's over. Let's just forget it."

"Claire's cruel punishment was inexcusable," Jack said. "No child should ever be treated like that. Teacups and sewing machines are replaceable. A child's trust is not."

She began crying again.

He reached for her hands and held them in his own. "I'm sorry, Marah. I wish I could take it all away. I don't want to excuse her behavior—it was wrong—but she was a troubled soul in some ways. Never completely happy. I tried, God knows I tried, but a person can only do so much. There comes a point where we each have to decide within ourselves what kind of person we will be. Claire seemed to choose to be unhappy no matter what I did ... what anyone did." He sighed. "May God rest her soul, it's over now." He squeezed Marah's hands. "I can't explain her behavior, but I know she loved you."

Marah jerked her hands away. "No, Dad. She hated me. Nothing you say will change that. She hid it from you and other people, but I knew. I knew. For the longest time, I tried and tried to make her love me. Then one day I realized how useless it was. I'd never be good enough." Abruptly, she got up. "I don't want to talk about it anymore." She looked at her watch. "I'm too exhausted to wait for Scott. I'm going to bed. Good night, Dad." She kissed him on the cheek and went upstairs.

The television nightly news had just wrapped up when a flash of headlights caught Jack's attention. A vehicle stopped in front of the house, a door slammed, and the car pulled away. Moments later, Scott shuffled into the living room lugging his backpack.

"Hi, Granpop. She still here?"

"She? You mean your mother?"

"Yeah, I didn't see her car. Did she leave?"

"No, she went to bed. Her car's in back."

Anger tainted Scott's voice. "How long is she hanging around here? I thought she was supposed to be in Japan with Dad. How come you didn't tell me—"

"Scott, that's enough. I was just as surprised as you." Annoyed, Jack rose and turned off the television.

Scott dropped onto the sofa. "Well, holy cow, Granpop . How come she thinks she can just show up?"

"She used to live here, remember?"

Scott flopped back on the sofa and groaned. "Oh, brother."

"You won't be able to avoid her indefinitely, you know. Where have you been? You're a half hour past curfew."

"Library. Then we got a hamburger." The teenager sat up. "Sorry, Granpop. I just got all freaked out when I called from school and she answered the phone."

"Who brought you home?"

"Marco."

Jack's mustache bristled. "Were you at that place again?"

"No, we just went to Dairy Queen. Man, I had like a million books to pack home. Marco came by the library and offered to give me a ride." He slid his foot in and out of his untied shoes. "I know what you said about Marco, but if you knew him ... and besides, I didn't even go near the Sea Horse."

"You know if you needed a ride you could have called me. As for Marco, you bring him around. Danny, too, remember, and let me judge for myself. Until then, no hanging out with Marco. Understood?"

Head down, Scott looked at Jack from beneath his bangs. "Yeah." He stood. "I'm going to bed. G'night." Suddenly he stopped. "Where's Mom? She sleeping upstairs?"

Jack nodded. "Her old room."

"Oh, man. Can I sleep down here? On the couch?"

"That's ridiculous. Go to bed."

Grumbling, Scott gave his backpack a kick as he left the room.

Hours later, Jack trekked through the cold, cloud-covered night to his garage workshop. No milk, no snack. For once, Miss Lavender didn't complain. She hopped onto his lap as he sat staring into the rekindled fire, thinking.

Marah, so convinced her mother hated her. Jack didn't believe that, but if Claire had harbored any bad feelings, there could be only one reason. He and Claire had a secret, and they had agreed never to tell anyone. Even without that vow, Jack knew he would never tell Marah he was not her biological father. Nor would he ever tell her that he had stopped Claire from aborting her. *Marah said her mother was cruel. Did Claire harbor bitterness in her heart and take it out on the daughter who symbolized her own sin? Why, dear God, why didn't I suspect something? I should have protected Marah!*

CHAPTER 13

Marah didn't come downstairs the next morning until Scott had left for school. She looked composed, beautiful. And too thin. She had pulled her hair up into some kind of twist on the back of her head, and she wore a black pantsuit with a pale gray turtleneck. Jack thought she'd look better in a brighter color, like red, but he kept his opinion to himself.

"Dad, are you going to work on that merry-go-round today?"

"No, thought I'd spend the day with you." He pulled out a griddle. "Pancakes?"

"No, I don't eat breakfast. I have some shopping to do." Marah snapped the clasp on her silver bracelet. "Is DeWolfe Department Store still here? I haven't been downtown in ages."

"I'm surprised you didn't see the store yesterday when you went to the Carousel. It's still there on the corner."

"Hm-m-m. How about Mr. DeWolfe? What was his name? Richard? Wasn't he your boss?"

"That's right. Richard Jr." He cracked an egg into a bowl. "He's retired now, but he's still involved with management people. Haven't seen him in years." *No loss there.* He dumped pancake mix into the bowl, added milk, a grated potato, and his secret ingredient, and beat it all into a bubbly froth. Maybe Marah would have an appetite after she smelled them cooking. "Set the table, daughter."

Marah got a cup of coffee and watched her father pour circles of batter onto the hot griddle. "Did Mom ever tell you about the time he made a pass at me? When I was in high school?"

The spatula Jack was holding clattered onto the griddle. "He what?"

"Yes, he's the one Mother and I argued about. I told you we'd had an argument, remember?"

Jack didn't remember, but he was more concerned now about what DeWolfe had done. "Tell me what happened with DeWolfe." He turned the pancakes.

"He tried to get me up to his office. Well, he did, in fact. I liked working in home interiors, but he wanted to move me to the lingerie department. So he invited me up to his office to discuss it. We sat on that huge leather couch—wonder if it's still there?—and he put his arm around me. I was scared speechless. He told me he liked 'plump and pretty' girls. Then he slid his hand up my leg, under my skirt. I ran out of there so fast I nearly fell over his secretary." Marah laughed, a flat, unfeeling sound. "I think she was listening at the door, the old bag."

"Why didn't you tell me?"

"I told Mother. She didn't believe me at first. Then she accused me of enticing him." Marah uttered a short sound of disgust. "A dirty old man like that. Mother made a big case out of it. Told me it was indecent, like it was my fault. After that, how could I tell you?"

"Was that the end of it? He left you alone?"

"No, he acted like it was a game or something. I never went up to his office again, but he'd catch me off guard in the back room or employees' lounge when no one was around. He never did anything, but I was scared he would. I tried never to be alone, but it didn't always work out. He watched me constantly." She shuddered. "Made me feel like he was undressing me in his mind. Told me I was more beautiful than Mother."

Jack flinched as memories stirred to life.

"After a few weeks, I'd had it. I told Mother I was going to quit and find another job." Marah refilled her coffee cup.

Jack noticed her hands shaking.

She continued. "That time she believed me. She said I wouldn't have to quit my job. She said it would be taken care of. Not long after that, he quit bothering me. So I thought she must've told you, and you got on his case." Marah smiled. "I used to imagine you beating him up. For me. But he was the boss, so I knew you couldn't do that. What did you do, Daddy?"

"Boss or not, I would have. But your mother never told me." Suddenly he smelled burning pancakes. "Dammit!"

Marah's eyes widened. "So, you didn't ...?"

Jack shook his head while he cleaned off the griddle. "No."

She frowned. "But it all stopped so suddenly."

"Your mother must have set him straight herself." *Why didn't she tell me and let me take care of it?* Jack shoved the griddle off the burner and picked up his coffee cup. He gripped it so hard his knuckles hurt.

"Dad? What's wrong?" She put her hand over his.

"I've a mind to go see that filthy scoundrel right now and—"

"Dad! Let it go. It's been years. I'd be terribly embarrassed if you said anything now."

He blinked, relaxed his hands, and worked his jaw to ease the tension.

"Mother never told you? I mean, not anything? Ever?" Marah pulled out a chair from the kitchen table and sat down.

"Is there more? I thought you said he behaved himself."

"He did. I meant … about me. Mother insisted I was at fault. She never let me forget that I caused her shame. It came up again—between Mother and me—right before her stroke." Marah's eyes narrowed as she looked at Jack.

Warily he asked, "What did she tell you? What shame?"

Marah's eyes searched his face. After a moment, she looked away. "Never mind. It's not important." She jumped to her feet. "Let's go to the Carousel. Maybe your friend will be there. What was her name?"

"My friend? Oh, the woman you saw me with yesterday. Kennocha. She won't be there. She's a teacher. Volunteers weekends and sometimes evenings at the Carousel."

Marah looked disappointed. "Too bad. I'd like to meet her."

"Don't know what for," Jack gruffed.

Marah rinsed her cup and picked up her purse.

"Wait a minute," Jack said, "you haven't eaten."

"Daddy, I don't eat breakfast. I'm going shopping."

"Marah!" But she was gone. *What kind of father am I? All that girl does is evade my questions. She throws these stories out and then drops them. If she's trying to drive me nuts, she's succeeding.*

He threw out the burned pancakes, wiped off the griddle, and cooked what was left of the batter.

Miss Lavender came into the kitchen, paused to stretch and yawn, and then caught the scent of one of her favorite meals. She sat down at Jack's feet.

"Meow?"

"You want a pancake, Missy? Just a minute, and it'll be done." He looked at the cat's inquisitive eyes. "What do you think I should do about Marah?"

The cat's ears twitched, and she raised her nose and sniffed.

"I know, all you're interested in is pancakes. Okay, at least I know how to make *you* happy."

Late that afternoon, Marah arrived home from her day of shopping. Scott was doing homework at the kitchen table, and Jack was sitting at the other end, reading the newspaper. He lowered the newspaper and greeted Marah. He noticed that she had surprisingly few packages from her day of shopping. Claire would have brought home a trunkful.

Marah said, "Scott, darling, let's go to the mall after dinner and get you some new school clothes. Do you have a girlfriend yet? Girls like a boy who looks sharp, you know."

"I don't need any clothes."

"But—"

"I don't want anything."

During dinner, Marah tried again. "We could open up a checking account for you."

Scott glared at her. "What for? I don't have enough money here for a checking account."

"I'll deposit some funds for you."

"No, thanks. I don't want anything from you." He stood and gathered up his dirty dishes.

"I'll bring the puppy over next time."

"We don't want a dog. We have a cat," Scott retorted.

Marah sucked in her breath, grabbed Scott's arm, and jerked him around to face her. "I thought you'd be glad to see me. You act like you want me to leave. Do you?"

Scott shrugged and muttered, "Don't know why you came anyway." He pulled away.

After more sparring between mother and son, Jack interrupted. "Enough! Whatever is wrong, it will never be resolved this way. You're like a couple of carousel horses, chasing each other 'round and 'round, nipping at each other, going nowhere."

"I'm goin' to my room," Scott mumbled.

As soon as he slammed his bedroom door shut, Marah said, "Dad, I'm worried about Scott. I don't know how to say this. He doesn't fit in with other kids. In Boise, I mean. He once told me he felt 'different.'" She looked at her father. "You said he only has two friends here. Boys. Dad, do you think … does he seem normal to you? Is he *different*?"

Jack pondered. "I think I know what you're alluding to." His fists clenched. He forced himself to voice the worry that gnawed at his gut. "You're wondering if he's homosexual." Marah nodded. "I think he's too young to know who he really is. Kids like to experiment. Sometimes too much." He leaned against the kitchen counter and folded his arms across his chest, tucking his hands under his arms. "I can't believe he's actually done anything ... like that. He's not stupid. He might have talked about it, you know, a bull session among other boys. But I can't believe he'd do it."

"Dad, you've got to help me. Help him understand that it's just a phase, that he's normal."

"I'm doing what I can, short of threatening him. I won't have him living with me if he's fooling around with that queer stuff."

"I'll work with you, Dad. We'll get this frightful notion out of his head."

"Now, daughter, I want to continue the conversation you started this morning. About you and your mother."

Marah rubbed her temples as she walked out of the kitchen. "Not now, Daddy. Scott has given me a migraine. I just want to take some aspirin and go to bed." She filled a glass with water and went upstairs. Jack sighed and let her go. *I need a couple of aspirin myself.*

The next morning, Scott tiptoed downstairs while Marah slept. Jack watched as the boy wolfed down a bowl of cereal, grabbed his jacket and backpack, and prepared to leave.

"You're going to tell your mother good-bye, aren't you?"

Scott paused at the door and looked over his shoulder at Jack. "She leaving today?"

Jack nodded. "She brought her suitcase down last night—after you locked yourself in your room."

A pink tinge crept up Scott's face. He looked away and fidgeted with the door handle.

"Son, your mother knows you're really unhappy with her about something. You've made your point. Regardless of what she's done—or what you think she's done—" At that, Scott turned and scowled at his grandfather. Jack ignored the look. "She is still your mother and deserves your respect. Telling her good-bye now is the decent thing to do." Jack pulled his jacket from the hook and stepped around his grandson. "I'm going to the workshop. Think about it, okay? And brush your teeth."

Scott let his backpack drop to the floor with a loud *clunk*. "Okay, Granpop."

Jack walked to his shop. A few minutes later, Scott stuck his head in.

"I'm off, Granpop. Bye." In answer to Jack's questioning look, he added, "I did. She was up, packing her makeup junk." He gave Jack a toothy grin. "And I brushed my teeth. Now can I go?"

Jack couldn't hold back a grin. "You scamp. See you tonight."

Marah wasted no time with her departure. She declined breakfast, filled her travel mug with hot coffee, and picked up her purse and cosmetic case. "I've had a lovely visit, Dad."

His eyebrows went up. "Lovely?"

"I'd stay longer, but I have to get home for the spring home show our garden club is planning. Maybe you and Scott could come over."

"No, I don't think so. Don't push Scott. Give him time."

"Push him? I don't know what you mean. I'm not—"

Jack gave her a stern look. "Marah, stop it."

She looked hurt. "Well, time for me to go."

Jack followed her outside to the car, opened the door, and gave her a hug and a kiss on the forehead. "Drive safely. Give Vic my regards."

She slid into the driver's seat. "Dad, that woman at the bridge ... are you ... interested in her?"

"What if I am?"

For a few moments, Marah fiddled with her car keys, face averted. Then she looked up, her eyes intense. "Mom's not been dead that long. It's not right."

Gently, Jack said, "It's nearly four years."

She lashed back, "How can you even think of another woman."

Jack leaned forward. "Marah—"

She jabbed the keys into the ignition and started the motor. Angry, she reached for the door handle. "All right, Dad, I'll mind my own business. But you know how I feel."

She drove away, and Jack heaved a great sigh. He knew this wasn't the end of it.

CHAPTER 14

In the cheerful, busy environment of the Carousel, Jack felt the knots in his back loosen up. He breathed deeply. Wooden ponies carried no hidden agendas.

Nikolas stood before a horse body blank—rough-sawn boards glued together—on the worktable. "Jack, my friend, you will help me, yes? Learn to make a pony?"

Until now, Nikolas had done just about everything except make a horse body from scratch. Jack and Izsak knew he was ready to move on, even though Nikolas seemed to have some doubts about his ability.

Jack hung up his coat. "You already know most of it."

Nikolas held up a hand. "But I want to go over everything again. The big picture, as you say."

"Everything?"

"Yes. From the beginning. Some things I have forgotten."

"Okay, let's go into the lumber room."

They entered a small storage room alongside the paint room. It was filled with side-by-side stacks of rough-cut planks. A narrow aisle separated each double stack and ran around the perimeter of the room. The long sides of the stacks faced the door. The back corner of the room held boxes of sandpaper, saw blades, and hardware items. Nikolas barely fit in the aisles, but he easily reached up and lifted a plank from the top of the seven-foot-high stacks. "This is from basswood trees."

"Around here we call them linden trees. Common term for the lumber is basswood." Each plank was two inches thick, six to ten inches wide; lengths varied from three to six feet.

Nikolas considered the stacks. "You have to let this season for a while?"

"Nope. It's already kiln-dried. Izsak orders it in this way. We keep it in here until we're ready to use it. C'mon, we'll go back to the shop now." When they walked through the painting room, Jack saw two women applying urethane sealer to a painted pony. He automatically looked around for Kennocha, even though he knew she was at school this time of day.

In the woodworking room, Jack steered Nikolas toward two machines off to one side. Long, flexible plastic tubes, like oversized clothes dryer vents, led from the saws to large sawdust-catcher bags in the corner.

"First thing we do is run the boards through a jointer so we have one flat side—the broad side. See?"

Nikolas nodded.

"Then we give them a half turn and run them through again. Now we have a flat edge and a right angle."

Jack handed him a set of protective earmuffs and picked up a pair for himself.

"Okay, put your muffs on and watch." Wearing his own protective gear, Jack turned on the motor and pushed the rough plank against the saw blade. As the wood contacted the spinning steel, a high-pitched squeal emanated from the machine. After a few repetitions, the blade removing fractions of an inch each time, the board became smooth on two adjoining sides, the edge squared.

Jack turned off the jointer. "Okay, now for the planer. This machine makes it easy to get a board with parallel surfaces." He lowered steel rollers, sandwiching the board between rollers and blade, turned on the machine, and pushed the board through lengthwise. He held it up for Nikolas's inspection. "See here, we just took off the high ridge along one side. Now we'll lower the rollers another fraction and cut off another layer." After a couple more passes, Jack declared the board finished, its broad surfaces parallel, the edges squared off.

Pulling off his earmuffs, Nikolas nodded. "This I remember." He struck his philosopher's pose—one hand on his beard, the other on his hip. "This board, it is like life. We are the boards. We must go through adversity to shape us into stronger, more usable people for the Lord."

Jack folded his arms and waited. "Are you done preaching?"

Nikolas grinned. "Yes. What is next?"

"Gluing. Depending on what you're doing—body, legs, whatever— your boards should be similar in length." He walked to the opposite wall. "Here's the body you helped glue the other day." Metal clamps had been placed along the form every few inches.

"Yes, and I wondered, do we ever lay the grain all the same direction?"

"We get away with that on the head, maybe the neck, but the body and legs take the most stress. People sitting in the saddle, kids climbing up on the legs. So they have to be stronger." Jack pointed. "Gluing these together like this, with no two adjoining boards having the grain go in the same direction, gives the whole thing more strength. Also eliminates—or at least significantly reduces—warping."

The door opened, and Izsak came in, his round, ruddy-cheeked face split with a smile. A delicious aroma filled the air, coming from a bulging bakery sack. He announced, "Glazed buttermilk potato donuts today. Still fresh."

Izsak's short stature and broad build belied his strength. Jack had seen him wrap his arms around a short stack of lumber and lift it as though it were a pile of Styrofoam.

While the three men sat on stools enjoying donuts and coffee, they watched visitors trickle into the main carousel room from the gift shop. Several lined up at the telephone-booth-sized ticket window, where a painted dragon guarded the opening in the glass. Below it, a sign, "Rides, fifty cents."

After purchasing their tickets, three young children scrambled for their chosen ponies. One little boy climbed onto the pinto's legs, squirmed his way into the saddle, and settled down with a triumphant grin.

A gray-haired couple, moving carefully, chose a stander for the woman, a prancer for the man. A mother lifted an excited toddler onto a palomino's back, fastened the safety strap, and wrapped her arms around the child.

A young couple claimed a chariot, snuggling together, laughing.

The band organ boomed out "The Carousel Waltz" as the platform began turning, picking up speed. Jack, Nikolas, and Izsak smiled, watching through the workroom window as laughing riders zoomed by, hair flying, holding tightly to the brass poles as the ponies glided up and down and around.

"I never tire of that sight," Izsak said.

Jack and Nikolas nodded in hearty agreement.

Jack wiped crumbs from his mustache and told Nikolas, "We'll get you started on the band saw today. First, you trace the pattern onto the wood block. Outline it with a black marker and then cut it out on the band saw. Gives you a rough shape. After that, it's all hand carving and sanding."

Nikolas shoved in his last bite, washing it down with coffee. "I saw a set of leg forms over there. They are ready to have the pattern traced on and cut out, yes?"

Jack got up and brought over the blocks of glued boards. "Yep, these are ready. Legs need to be strong. You saw those kids climbing on them. See here? Each leg has four boards with a lap joint where the knee should be. See how they overlap? And how the grain goes in different directions? Makes 'em good and strong."

Izsak looked in the donut bag. "You guys want another one?"

Both Jack and Nikolas shook their heads.

"Okay, then. I'm going to see if our riders want some. Be back later."

Nikolas busied himself tracing and outlining the leg patterns. "This is like what my Martha used to do when she sewed. She had a little wheel and some kind of carbon paper to trace onto her cloth."

At the band saw, Nikolas cut out the legs he had traced onto the wood. The long, narrow, vertical blade allowed free movement of the wood as Nikolas carefully guided it with his hands.

After a while, Jack said, "Good. Now you're ready to carve. And you know how to do that."

"If I worked every day, how many days would it take to make a pony from beginning to end?"

"Carving might take three or four weeks. Another couple of days—say, ten hours—to paint it. Then the clear coats. Urethane. Like varnish, but better. Very durable. They apply at least ten coats, maybe fifteen to the places that get the most use."

They looked up at the sound of paper being crumpled. Izsak strolled in, wadded up the bakery sack, tossed it over his shoulder into a trash can, and joined the conversation. "Clear coat gives the horses a deep shine. Beautiful. The more coats, the better they look. You've noticed that the paint is put on with rags or sponges or stippling brushes. They kind of dab it on. Then, after multiple layers of clear coat, the pony's hide almost looks like you could curry it."

Nikolas drew in a deep breath and said, "I am honored to work on this Carousel. It is a labor of love."

Jack and Izsak grinned. "And this is only the horses," they said in unison.

Izsak said, "One of these days, I'll have you spend some time with the fellows who take care of the carousel platform and mechanical operation. And the calliope."

The three men looked into the large central room, beyond the circular pony platform, to the band organ mounted against the wall by the front door. Encased in a castle motif, the calliope featured comical knights on armored steeds in endless pursuit of a grinning, half-submerged dragon in a moat.

Nikolas shook his head and said good-naturedly, "Jack, my friend, I did not know my retirement would end when you persuaded me to volunteer."

Jack grinned. "Have to keep you out of trouble, you old Russian."

After Izsak left, Jack told Nikolas about Marah's visit, but he omitted what she'd told him about Claire. He needed more time to think about Marah's allegations against her mother. How could he not have known? What kind of father was he? Was this somehow tied to Marah's family problems now?

After Jack told him about the tensions between Marah and Scott, Nikolas grunted sympathetically and patted his friend on the back. "I remember you once said they were very close, those two. My own daughters and their teenagers, they had problems, too. But in the end, it all worked out. Let us hope and pray it will be the same for your family." He paused. "As for you and Marah conspiring against Scott, questioning if he is normal, I must say to you, my friend, I think you are treading in—how do you say it?—whirling waters? But let us not talk of that now. I have something to tell you that will brighten your spirits. Izsak held a little meeting yesterday morning. You were not here yet. Did he tell you about it?"

Jack shook his head.

"The fifth anniversary of the Carousel is coming up in a few months—in August. We will have a grand celebration. Izsak said rides and popcorn will be free all day. The three new ponies will be complete." He cast an inquisitive look at Jack. "Yours will be done, yes?"

"I'll be finished with the carving soon. Maybe Scott would like to have a hand in the sanding. And Kennocha already has the color scheme worked out. She said she'll be spending more time down here after school's out."

Nikolas arched a bushy black eyebrow. "Oh? You have made progress, eh?"

Thump. Jack let his big wooden mallet drop to the table. He shot a look of exasperation at Nikolas. "What are you talking about?"

"The last time I saw you," Nikolas said, "you were so twitterpated you could hardly come near Kennocha without stumbling over your feet. Now you talk of her as though—"

Jack snorted. "Don't let your romantic fancies get carried away. We met to go over the sketches. That's all. Had a cup of coffee and talked. Nothing like your overworked mind is conjuring up."

Nikolas stroked his beard and purred, "Ah, but it is coming along, this romance."

Jack ignored that. He picked up his tools and concentrated on shaping the pony's cheek. The mallet tapped out a rhythm, striking the end of the chisel: tap-tap-tap-tap, pause, tap-tap-tap-tap. Under Jack's light touch, thin wafers of wood fell away, and the pony's personality slowly surfaced. By late afternoon, satisfied, he began sanding.

After Nikolas left for the day, Jack lingered, hoping for Kennocha's arrival, but she didn't come. At last he gave up, put away his tools, and went home.

Scott had started supper—frozen pizza. "Hey, Granpop, I was beginning to wonder about you. Were you at the Carousel?"

"Yep. Got the pony's head carved. Sanding now. Lost track of time. I should do this more often, so you'd have supper ready every night, eh?"

While Scott added some finishing touches to the pizza—extra pepperoni and cheese—he said, "I'd like to do that. Take a hunk of wood and make something really cool out of it. Think I could learn?"

"Of course. You have an imagination, don't you? You know what they say about Michelangelo. That's how you make a horse. Or anything else."

Scott slid the loaded pizza pan into the oven. When the microwave buzzed, he took out two steaming tacos. He grinned at Jack. "Appetizers. Want one?"

Jack shook his head and went into the bathroom to wash. He joined Scott at the table. "Think you'd like to help sand Clarissa Mae?"

"Yeah." Scott licked his fingers after polishing off the tacos. "Danny's coming over tonight. We're doing a science project together."

"Good. Looking forward to meeting him." Jack sniffed. "Pizza smells good." He narrowed his eyes and looked at his grandson. "No pineapple, I trust?"

Scott grinned. "Couldn't find any in the cupboard or I might've."

Danny knocked at the front door just as Jack finished his last bite. Scott downed his milk and jumped up.

Jack stood as the boys came into the kitchen. Danny looked thin—too thin to Jack's way of thinking—and pale. His dark, wavy hair fell over his forehead, barely touching his wire-rimmed glasses. Jack offered his hand. "Hi, Danny, I'm Jack." Danny's brown eyes met his as they shook hands. Jack tried not to stare at gold flecks in his eyes. A lot like Scott's.

While Jack and Danny exchanged a few words, Scott gathered up the plates and silverware. "I gotta do dishes. Granpop and I take turns. I'll be done in a few minutes."

"You cooked, Scott. I'll do the dishes tonight. You and Danny go ahead with your project."

Later that evening, after Danny went home, Scott bounded down the stairs and found Jack in the living room, reading the newspaper. "Well, Granpop? Didn't I tell you? He's okay, isn't he?"

"Seems like a nice fellow. Bright. Carries on a good conversation. Where's he live?"

"By the university. Lives with his grandparents." Scott grinned. "Like me, huh?" His expression grew serious. "Except his parents are dead. And his mom was an only child. So's Danny. He's the only family his grandparents have."

"Is Danny okay—health wise, I mean? Doesn't have much color in his face. And he's too skinny."

Scott hesitated. "Guess so. Never misses any school." He scooped up the cat and scratched her ears. "Maybe Marco will stop by this weekend. Then you'll see he's not so bad, either."

The newspaper crackled as Jack turned a page. "Uh-hmm."

Scott started to leave and then stopped. "Last week I wrote a paper for English. A short story. Kennie thinks it's pretty good. Wants to send it to some contest. After I work on it some more."

The newspaper dropped into Jack's lap. "Who's Kennie?"

"My English teacher."

"You address teachers by their first name? What's his last name?"

"Her. A woman. She says we can call her Kennie."

"Odd name for a woman."

"That's her nickname. Real name is something foreign—Irish, I think she said. Hard to remember, so we call her Kennie. She doesn't care. She's cool." Scott cracked his knuckles. "She doesn't let all her classes do that. Just ours, 'cause we're like, smarter, you know. Creative writing's only for 'A' English students. Only about ten of us in there."

"Creative writing? Is her name Kennocha?"

"Yeah, that's it! Kennocha. Hey, you know her, Granpop?"

"I believe I do. She's a painter at the Carousel."

"Yeah, that's probably her. She talks a lot about merry-go-round stuff."

Jack smoothed his mustache with his thumb. "She's a fine person."

"Yeah. Cool." Scott switched gears. "You hungry? I'm gonna get some ice cream."

Jack shook his head, marveling at the boy's appetite. "I'm still full of pizza. You go ahead, son."

All week long, Jack prolonged his daily work at the Carousel, hoping to see Kennocha, but she didn't come in. He wrestled with the idea of calling her. His carving would be done by Friday. Then his next project, along with sanding Clarissa Mae, would be to help with restoration of the older ponies.

As volunteers completed new horses, Izsak removed from the platform the ones that showed wear or had damaged parts. With heavy use, especially in summer months, the ponies were regularly in circulation between the platform and the workshop. Their tails, most made of real horses' hair, suffered noticeably. Children couldn't resist feeling and pulling the long, coarse hairs. Genuine horsetails were getting expensive, and Izsak worried about having to replace them with tails carved from wood as the original ones wore out.

Friday night, Jack was the last to leave the Carousel. He switched off the lights in the workroom just as the front door of the building opened. His heart skipped a beat. A moment later, disappointment. The figure outlined in the doorway clearly was not Kennocha.

"Jack, that you?"

Jack flipped on the workroom light again. Light shone on the face of the Carousel's founder. "Izsak. What brings you down here so late?"

"I was about to ask you the same thing."

"I thought Kennocha might show up. She's going to do Clarissa Mae. But haven't seen her all week."

Izsak tipped his cap onto the back of his head. "She's gone. Her grandmother took sick. Kennocha went to take care of her. New York."

Jack tensed. "She's coming back, isn't she?"

Izsak shrugged. "Dunno. Hope so. Guess it depends on the grandmother's health." He walked into the workroom. "Say, this looks good." He ran his hand the length of Jack's completed pony head and neck. "Fine work, Jack, very fine."

"But—Kennocha—she was going to paint this pony."

Mild surprise registered on Izsak's face. He looked up from his appraisal of the wooden pony. "Someone else will do it. Pick whoever you want, Jack. You're my best carver. Pick the best painter."

Jack thought, *Kennocha's the best.*

Jack found a note on the kitchen table when he arrived home after the disturbing news about Kennocha. "Granpop, Danny and I went to the mall for a burger. Scott."

The living room clock chimed the hour. *Seven o'clock. I should've come home earlier instead of behaving worse than a teenager waiting around for a girl.* A car pulled into the driveway. Jack peered out the window at an old Camaro, red paint faded to dull brick. Doors swung open, and three people got out. Scott, Danny, and Marco. The three straggled into the house, Marco bringing up the rear. Jack leaned against the kitchen cabinet and waited.

"Granpop, this is Marco. Marco, my grandfather, Jack Emerson."

Marco flipped his long, blond hair over his shoulder and stepped forward, hand extended. His falsetto voice slithered out, "Nice to meet you, Mr. Emerson."

Jack returned his limp handshake with a firm grip then resisted the urge to wipe his hand on his pant leg.

Marco's silver earrings dangled above the collar of his satin shirt. He waved his hand like a limp noodle, rings flashing. "Nice place. I *love* your copper canisters."

Jack pulled his astonished gaze away in time to catch a glimpse of Scott and Danny, rolling their eyes at one another.

Marco continued gushing. "I just want you to know, Scotty's one of my very best friends." His earrings swung wildly with his bobbing head.

Scott muttered, "Oh, brother."

"Oh! You've got Italian glassware," Marco crooned. He picked up the old, green glass canning jar where Claire had always stored macaroni. "Don't you just love Italian?"

Scott made a face. "Marco."

Marco turned. "Mm-m-m? What, sweetie?" He glanced back at Jack and said, "I'm used to being called Marnie." He giggled.

Jack didn't know whether to laugh or be outraged. *Is this for real? Helium voice, phony inflection, pretentious. Not to mention his jewelry and clothes.* He gave Scott a look.

"C'mon, Marco. Performance is over." Scott started upstairs, Danny on his heels. "Let's go up to my room." To Jack, he said, "We're gonna listen to some new songs Marco has."

Marco rippled his fingers at Jack. "Talk to you later, Jack-O."

Jack dropped into a chair and put his head in his hands. *Jack-O? This can't be happening. Not in my house. Not my grandson.*

Loud booming from Scott's stereo upstairs jolted him upright. Miss Lavender ran into the kitchen, eyes wide, and meowed at the back door.

"You too, eh, kitty? Let's get out of here." Jack followed her out and went to his workshop. He paused at the door. *I can hear the booming out here. The whole neighborhood can hear it!* He retraced his steps. "I won't have this in my house."

Gritting his teeth, Jack went back into the house, slamming the back door behind him. He marched upstairs into Scott's room, punched the "off" button on the stereo, and glared at the three figures sprawled on the floor listening to the so-called music. "I want to talk to you, Scott."

In the ensuing silence, Jack's glance went from Marco's innocent look to Danny's worried expression to Scott's angry eyes.

Danny scrambled to his feet. "C'mon, Marco. Let's go."

Marco followed in slow motion. He started to extend his hand toward Jack but withdrew it under Jack's glare. They clattered downstairs. Moments later, the car engine coughed to life.

"Come downstairs." Jack turned on his heel and walked out.

Scott clomped downstairs after him.

"Sit," Jack ordered, indicating a chair on the opposite side of the kitchen table.

Sullen, Scott sat.

Jack waited until the teen's eyes met his own. "I agreed to meet Marco. Now I have. You're not to associate with that—that person.

And you're not to play your stereo that loud again." Jack paused. "Understood?"

Red-faced, Scott said, "You can't make me drop my friends just like that."

"As long as you're in my house, I'll have a say about it."

Scott's chair tipped backward and clattered to the floor as he jumped up. "I don't have to stay here! I can find someplace else to live. I don't need you! I don't need anybody!" He grabbed his jacket off the hook, jerked open the back door, and ran out.

Jack dashed for the door. "Scott!" He caught sight of the boy in the corner streetlight, sprinting down the street. Angry, he muttered, "Fine. Go live on the street."

CHAPTER 15

By nine o'clock, Jack gave up trying to read *National Geographic* or watching the public broadcasting special on volcanoes. Instead, he paced the floor. He peered out into the night. *Should I go look for him? Call the police?* He picked up the phone then set it down again. *I'll wait until eleven. Scott's weekend curfew. He'll probably be home by then. If not, I'll call the police. Where would he go? That bar. I could go see if—*

The phone shrilled. He snatched it up. "Yes?"

"Hi, Jack, it's Kennocha."

He caught his breath. *Kennocha.* The sound of her voice soothed his nerves like licorice tea on a sore throat. "You're back. It's good to hear your voice. Izsak said your grandmother was ill. How is she?"

"I think she'll be all right now. Jack, would you like to meet me downtown for a cup of coffee or something? Or here, at my apartment? I just feel like some company this evening. Hope you don't mind my calling—"

"No, no." Jack's irritation with his grandson increased. He cleared his throat. "But I have something of a problem here. Scott left a while ago, pretty upset with me. In fact, when he went out the door, he said he was going to find someplace else to live. Sounds a little far-fetched." *Except that he's done it before.*

"Scott? Is he the grandson living with you?"

"Yes, that's him."

"How old is he?"

"Sixteen."

"Old enough to do it if he really means it. What can I do to help?"

"Wish I knew. Don't know what to do myself except wait. My gut instinct tells me he'll be back. Doesn't make the waiting any easier. But listen, you don't need to hear my problems. How are you? And your grandmother?"

She sighed. "I'm glad to be home. My grandmother ... can be a bit trying if you know what I mean. She's ninety-three, thinks she knows what's best for her. She insists all doctors are too young to know what they're doing. But you don't want to hear all that."

"Yes, I do. Tell me about her."

"She had a stroke two years ago. Scared me. In fact, I almost didn't accept the teaching job here because of that. But she has a strong will to live. They weaned her from the respirator, removed the IV after she started taking fluids and food on her own, and her recovery accelerated after that. Except for a slight limp, she was her old self again after about a year. Up until then, she'd been living alone—happily, I might add—in her big, old, colonial house in Syracuse. Of course, I was less than an hour away. Anyway, when this job came up, Gran knew how desperately I wanted it, but I couldn't go with a clear conscience. She had a fit. We had a huge argument, which resulted in a compromise. She agreed to hire a live-in housekeeper, and I agreed to follow my dreams and move out here. Anna, the housekeeper, is a godsend."

"Good for your grandmother, insisting you go. I'm on her side. But what happened that took you back to New York? Another stroke?"

"No, she broke her hip. She's a rascal. Needed something off the top shelf of her closet and climbed on a chair while Anna was outside for a few minutes. Gran lost her balance and fell. I went back to be with her during the hip replacement surgery. Can you imagine that? At ninety-three? But she's doing fine now. On her feet, using a walker, determined to be rid of it before a month goes by. She's amazing."

"You must take after her."

Kennocha laughed. "I wouldn't mind that. Except I hope I'm not quite so stubborn." She paused a beat. "Jack, I'm tying up your phone line. What if Scott's trying to call you? We'll talk another time, okay?"

"Yes, you're right. But knowing you're home lifts my spirits."

"Call me tomorrow, would you? I'd like to hear about Scott."

"I will. And I'd like a rain check on that cup of coffee."

"You've got it. Thanks for listening, Jack. G'night."

"Good night, Kennocha." He replaced the receiver, reluctant to break the connection.

A while later, something nagged at his mind. Something Kennocha had said about her grandmother's stroke. As though it was just yesterday, memories returned of Claire's hospital room.

CHAPTER 16

Summertime, four years earlier ...

Jack stood at the foot of his wife's hospital bed, where plastic bags suspended from a metal stand sustained her life. Transparent tubing penetrated her body, without her knowledge, without her permission.

The tube that bothered Jack the most was the one leading from the bottom of a quart-sized bag and disappearing into Claire's nostrils, like a snake sneaking through a crack between rocks. Whitish liquid flowed from the bag, through the plastic line, into Claire's stomach. Nourishment, the nurses said. As disturbing as it was to see his wife like this, it was worse for their daughter.

Marah stood by the flower-laden windowsill in Claire's hospital room, staring at the IV stand. Jack's heart wrenched as he looked at his daughter's pale, drawn face.

"This is only temporary, Marah. As soon as she gets stronger and can eat on her own, they'll take the feeding tube out."

Marah's gaze focused on him, her brown eyes unfathomable, the gold flecks dulled. "Will she get better?"

"The doctor is hopeful."

"But not sure."

"Nothing is for certain. Only time will tell."

"I wonder ... if she'll be able to talk again."

Jack's heart felt like lead. No answer came to mind. The doctor had warned him that even if she regained consciousness, she could have residual brain damage. But Jack couldn't bring himself to talk about it, not yet. He pulled up a chair to the bed, sat down, gently slid his hand under Claire's fingers, and watched his daughter.

Marah fussed with a bouquet of pink carnations. She pulled a wilted blossom from the vase, snapped off the head, and squeezed it until her knuckles turned white. Abruptly, she threw it in the wastebasket. "Do you blame me, Daddy? For this?" Her arm swept over her mother's still form.

"Of course not. Why would you even say that?"

"Because ... we had a terrible argument." Marah twisted the carnation stem, her hands trembling.

Bewildered, Jack asked, "You're worried about a disagreement you and your mother had?"

"Dad," she said, her voice insistent, "it happened just before she collapsed." Bits of green leaves fell to the floor from Marah's nervous fingers. She wiped tears off her cheeks with the back of her hand. "M-maybe our argument ... caused the stroke."

"No, Marah, no." Jack stood, crossed the room, wrapped his arms around his daughter, and held her. "What happened to your mother isn't your fault."

She buried her face in his shoulder and clutched him, crying. He rocked her gently back and forth, holding her tight.

After a few moments, Marah pulled away and reached for a tissue. She wiped her eyes and nose, walked to the window, and stood with her back to the room. She sucked in a deep breath, straightened her shoulders, and lifted her head as though pulling herself together.

Jack turned his attention to Claire. He leaned over, kissed her cheek, and sat down. He longed to see her open her eyes and look at him.

He sighed and stroked her arm.

Suddenly, with her back still to the room, Marah said, "Did you want me? Another baby, after Paul was already in school?"

Jack's heart skipped a beat. "Of course we wanted you, Marah. What—"

"No, I mean *you*. Did *you* want me?" She turned to face him.

"Yes, I wanted you."

She stared at him. "Were you and mother happy?"

Exasperated, Jack sat back and folded his arms. "I don't know what you're digging for, Marah. This makes no sense. Your mother and I are happy, we wanted you. *I* wanted you."

Marah's eyes showed disbelief.

A nurse entered the room and spared him further interrogation. The knots in his stomach eased.

Now, Jack sat alone in his living room, waiting for Scott, remembering that day. He recalled what Marah had told him recently about Claire punishing her for innocent childhood mistakes—the jammed sewing machine, the broken teacup.

A heavy weight descended over him, and he wondered what Claire had told Marah during their argument. *Marah couldn't know. Claire wouldn't have told her, would she? Could she have been that cruel?*

Jack rose, paced the floor, checked the time, and looked out the window.

Claire, Marah, now Scott. I just want my family to be happy, to live in peace. Why all this trouble? Why did Scott run away from home? Why is he so cold toward his mother? Why is she so moody? Restless one minute, happy the next.

Is she taking diet pills again? She's obsessed about eating too much. She looks like a skeleton, even her face, like that newswoman, whatever her name is. What's the matter with young women nowadays? Skin and bones isn't beautiful. Kennocha is beautiful—trim but not too skinny. A man likes to feel a woman's softness, not her bones.

Thinking of Kennocha raised another irritation with his daughter. *Marah's getting downright annoying about Kennocha. Paranoid, even.*

Headlights flashed across the window as a car rounded the corner. Jack pulled the curtain aside and watched the taillights disappear down the street. Disappointed, he dropped the curtain, retraced his worried path, looked at the clock, and forced himself to sit down. Eleven ten. He turned on some late night talk show and stared at the screen without anything registering in his mind. His thoughts returned to Marah's peculiar behavior the night before Claire died.

One morning as Jack sat beside her hospital bed, Claire rallied momentarily, opened her eyes, and seemed to recognize him. His hopes elevated.

When Marah came in later, he said, "I started reading a new book to her. I think she likes it. *The Kitchen Madonna.*"

"Somehow I can't see Mother liking anything Rumer Godden writes. Why bother reading to her? She can't hear you."

"You don't know that. They say the hearing is the last to go. I'm sure her eyelids flickered when—"

"Dad," Marah interrupted, her voice sharp, "Mom's mind is gone. She can't respond. Why don't you give up? She's a vegetable!"

After a moment of heavy silence, Jack said, "She's not a vegetable. She's my wife. Your mother." He paused a beat. "I can't give up." His voice broke.

Marah went to him and put her hand on his shoulder. "Oh, Daddy, I'm sorry."

He remained alone at Claire's bedside the rest of that day and on into the early evening, reading aloud to her, dozing off and on. Then Marah returned with a bouquet of flowers picked from Claire's garden. She persuaded him to go home while she stayed. Bone weary, Jack agreed. Just a couple of hours, he thought, then he'd come back.

At home, without bothering to undress, he fell across the bed and slept. Hours later, he awoke to the back door opening and the sound of soft footsteps. Jack rolled over and sat up. Marah stood in his bedroom doorway. "What time is it? How is she?"

"Very early morning. Go back to sleep, Dad."

Jack rubbed his eyes and struggled to focus on his daughter's face. His head felt stuffy, like he'd been sleeping in a room with no ventilation. He massaged the back of his neck, rolled his shoulders, and yawned. "I didn't mean to sleep so long. Did she wake up again?" He peered at Marah's face.

"No. Not even when that doctor came in and checked all her tubes." Marah came in and sat on the side of the bed. "I don't like him."

Jack yawned again and stretched. "Who?"

"That doctor."

"Dr. Norman?" He rubbed his eyes. "Why don't you like him?"

"He's too—I don't know—too cold or something. I wouldn't put it past him to pull out Mom's respirator."

Now Jack was wide-awake. "Marah! He's a doctor! He saves lives; he doesn't murder people."

"Is it murder when a person is like Mom is? What guarantee do we have that she will ever be normal again? Why make her suffer so long?"

Jack shifted on the edge of the bed to face his daughter. "I told you, she opened her eyes this morning—yesterday morning—and I'm sure she recognized me."

"Did she try to speak? Or move her hand?"

"No, but—"

"You want her to respond so much that you read things into spontaneous body movements. That doesn't mean her mind's engaged. That she's aware."

Jack couldn't meet his daughter's eyes.

Marah leaned toward him and put her hand on his arm. "Besides, isn't it more merciful to let her go? You want to keep her alive, on that artificial life support system, for yourself. For a false hope that she'll be like she was before. She won't, Dad. She'll never be the same." She got up. She started to leave the room but turned back. "That feeding tube ... that gross-looking white stuff ... she can't live on that forever." From the doorway she said, "I'm going to bed. You should go back to sleep. It's too early to get up."

As she walked into the hallway, Jack heard her say, "I used to love her, too, you know."

"You love her, you mean," Jack called after her. "You love her! Not used to! She's still alive!"

Jack took a quick shower, dressed in clean clothes, and left for the hospital. The nurses were accustomed to his coming and going at all hours over the past weeks, so he was sure they'd let him see her now.

In the hospital, walking down the corridor, a sense of alarm quickened Jack's step when he saw a commotion near Claire's room. He broke into a run but stopped short when the doctor stepped out of the room, saw him, and held up his hand.

Jack tried to force his way around the man, but Dr. Norman held his position. "What's wrong?" Jack demanded.

"Let's talk." The doctor took Jack's arm and tried to lead him away toward a seating area at the end of the hall.

He pulled away. "I want to see Claire."

The doctor caught his arm and held on. "Jack, Claire is gone."

Jack's knees buckled. He reached for the wall to steady himself. "No! No! She was getting better. She opened her eyes yesterday. She looked at me. I'm sure of it."

"Okay, Jack, okay." Dr. Norman took Jack's arm and steadily pulled him away. "Come on, let's go sit down. Give the nurses a few minutes and then you can go in."

Numb with shock, Jack went along and dropped into a chair, his head in his hands. "My daughter—she just left here. Claire was fine then. How could this happen? How?"

In his living room, momentarily forgetting about Scott, Jack stared with unseeing eyes at the talk show on the television screen, hearing nothing, his mind reliving that last terrible morning.

Marah had taken the news stoically. Her calm demeanor had seemed out of character, but his own pain was so great, he had barely given it any thought at the time. Now, he considered her strange lack of emotion, wrestling with unwelcome thoughts. *My daughter seems like a stranger to me ... a bitter woman, hanging onto the past like a sack of garbage, dumping it into her life now, pawing through it, letting the stink out, jeopardizing her family. Vic says she's having an affair, and Scott found out. Is this what he's hiding? I don't understand how it could have come to this. I don't know what to do about it. Scott. Where is that boy?* He got up, turned off the television, and paced again.

The anniversary clock chimed twelve times. Jack went to his pickup.

He drove slowly past the Sea Horse, peering at every person in the vicinity. He found a parking space five blocks away and walked back. He paused when he came to a faded red Camaro pulled up at the curb in front of the bar. *Marco's car.* Jack steeled himself and went inside.

Earsplitting music and a cacophony of voices made him take a step backward. He thought of the noisy saws at the Carousel and concluded they were mild compared to this.

Jack pushed his way to the bar, where he had a view of the room filled with an odd collection of people. He stared. Men wearing makeup, women's clothing, and multiple earrings; others dressed like they'd just gotten off a construction job, in mud-covered jeans and paint-splattered coveralls; men in white shirts and loosened ties; a scattered few with nose rings, bare-chested to show off nipple rings; an occasional cowboy.

Jack felt like he'd landed on an alien planet. *Are they losing their minds? Or am I?*

"Can I help you, sir?"

Jack turned.

The bartender leaned toward him. "Can I get you something?"

"Nothing. I'm looking for someone."

"Who? Maybe I know him."

Jack fought back an uneasy feeling that Scott might be a familiar face here. "No, I think I'm in the wrong place." He started to move away.

"Jack-O! Hey, dude, what's happenin'?"

Jack recognized that sing-song voice. He turned.

Marco swayed his way through the crowd to Jack. He was wearing a purple satin vest and a pink shirt. His eyes were outlined in black, and his lips looked glossy pink.

Controlling his revulsion, Jack said, "Have you seen Scott?"

"You mean like tonight, here?"

Jack nodded.

Marco put one hand on his hip and the index finger of his other hand on his chin. He rolled his eyes toward the ceiling. "Let me think." He paused a heartbeat. "I don't remember." He whirled around and called to a thirty-ish-looking guy in Levi's and a black T-shirt sitting at a nearby table. "Hey, Mikey, you seen Scotty?" Mikey shook his head. Marco raised his voice and glanced around. "Anybody?"

Jack tensed. *They know Scott.*

Heads turned; people eyed Jack. No one had seen Scotty.

Eagerly, Marco asked, "Want us to go look for him?"

"No, thanks." Jack worked his way to the door and left. Outside, he sucked in the cool, fresh air and shuddered. He hurried toward his pickup. *These are the kind of people Scott wants to hang around with? They're all a bunch of weirdos. Except a few, like that guy Marco called Mikey. He looked normal. What's he doing in there? Are they all fags?* Head down, Jack continued down the dark, deserted street. His back felt uncomfortable, kind of itchy, like he was being followed.

One November before Paul joined the air force, the two of them had set up camp near Willow Creek Reservoir and hunted elk in Sunburst Canyon. After an unsuccessful day, they'd headed back to camp through fresh snow just before dusk. Both of them were tired and hungry and nearly dragging their feet. Jack was in the rear, and he remembered feeling uneasy. He stopped a couple of times, peering over his shoulder, trying to discern movement through the brush or low-hanging evergreens. He couldn't see anything, but he felt certain they were being followed. By whom? Or what?

In the morning, when they headed back up the trail, Jack took the lead and studied their tracks in the undisturbed snow. He found the answer. Mountain lion. If either of the men had been alone on the trail, the big cat might have attacked if it was hungry enough.

Now, Jack recalled that feeling of being followed. But this was Missoula. No mountain lions on these streets. So why did he feel so uneasy? In his heart, he thought knew the answer. So he faced it: *my grandson is probably homosexual.* He felt like he'd passed through a forbidden, frightening door and let it slam shut behind him. No turning back.

Inside his pickup, he pondered what to do next. He had to find Scott. He rejected the notion the boy might be hiding out under a bridge. He surely wouldn't risk another injury like the one on his back. If that's where it had happened in the first place. Jack still had no answers to that question. *Where would he go? Danny's house? I should have asked Danny's last name. Marco or someone might know.* Gritting his teeth, Jack got out of the pickup and walked the five blocks back toward the bar.

Marco's Camaro was gone.

Nothing to do now but call the police.

Minutes after Jack arrived home, he picked up the phone but replaced it when he saw a police car pull up in front of his house. *Is Scott injured? In trouble?* Heart pounding, he hurried into the living room, turned on the porch light, and opened the door.

Two figures stepped out of the car. Relief washed over Jack when he saw that one was his grandson, upright, walking. Not injured. He recognized the policeman, a high school buddy of Paul's. Ernie had been an easygoing, polite teenager who hung out here so often he was like family.

The officer spoke as they stepped onto the porch. "Hello, Mr. Emerson. This young fellow belong to you?"

"He sure does, Ernie." Jack stepped aside. "Come on in."

Ernie waited until Scott entered the house, then he followed and closed the door. Scott stood to one side, head down, hands buried in his pockets.

Jack looked at him. "You okay?"

Scott raised his head enough to see beneath his bangs. "Yeah," he mumbled. "Can I go to my room?"

Jack glanced at Ernie. The policeman nodded slightly.

"Yes," Jack said. "I'll be up to talk with you later." Scott left. "What's going on, Ernie? Do we have a problem?"

"No. I was checking out a possible burglary report at the Carousel. Turned out to be your grandson. But he wasn't trying to break in. Just hanging out. Said he was going to sleep there tonight, in the doorway. He seemed pretty distraught and trying not to show it."

"We had a disagreement earlier this evening. I don't approve of one of his friends. Scott rebelled and took off out of the house like a young colt through an unlatched gate." Jack pulled at the tip of his mustache. "I'd been out looking for him. Just got back. I was about to pick up the phone to call you fellows. Never thought of checking the Carousel."

"The boy says he's living with you."

"That's right. For the time being anyway. Trouble at home. He needed some stability. What's more stable than an old man like me, eh? But I haven't raised any teenagers in many years."

Ernie smiled. "As I recall, you did a fine job. Paul—an air force officer. You were practically a father to me, too. I'm not in the Pentagon, but I'm doing all right."

"Got a minute?" Jack motioned toward an easy chair. "Sit down. I'd like to hear about you." Ernie removed his cap and perched on the edge of the sofa. Jack sat in the chair. "I read that you married the Molenda girl some years ago. Good kids."

"Sure did. Abby and I have twin boys, sixth grade. Abby teaches third grade at Paxson. We bought a couple of acres south of town. Kids have a horse." He grinned. "Remember when Paul and I wanted to become pro rodeo riders?"

Jack laughed. "How could I forget? You two didn't know the first thing about horses."

"I still don't. But Abby does, and she taught the boys." He fingered the bill of his cap. "I haven't seen Paul in ten years or more. Does he get home very often?"

"Once in a while, on the fly. He calls pretty regular, about once a month. Wants me to move to Virginia, but my home is here."

"I remember reading about Mrs. Emerson. Sorry to hear that." He paused. "How's your daughter—I forget—Marah, is that right?"

Jack hesitated. *If I say she's fine, he'll know better. I just told him Scott's home life is unstable. Why's he asking? Just being polite? Or filing it away in the back of his mind in case Scott gets in trouble? That's what I'd do if I were a cop.* He sighed. "I wish I knew, Ernie. Obviously, things aren't good, or my grandson wouldn't be living with me." He made a wry face. "Hmph. And then the boy runs away tonight. So much for stability under my roof."

"I wouldn't worry too much about that," Ernie said. "Scott looked pretty miserable when I found him. And when I said I'd take him home, he darned near beat me to the patrol car." He rose. "I've got to get going now, but I want you to know, Mr. Emerson, if either of my boys ever ran away, I'd be very relieved if they came to someone like you for help."

Jack got to his feet and stood still for a moment, not knowing what to say. He felt he'd failed Scott. Ernie stuck out his hand, and they exchanged a firm handshake. Jack was embarrassed to feel his chin quiver. *He knows I was just as miserable as Scott. I couldn't bear losing that boy.* "Thanks for bringing him home, Ernie."

"No problem. Let me know if I can help in any way. See you around."

After he left, Jack stayed in the living room for a few minutes, collecting his thoughts. *Was I too hard on Scott? But that Marco ...* He shuddered. Then he recalled that Marco offered himself and others to go look for Scott. *If Marco had gone to look for him, he probably would have brought him home. I think he was genuinely concerned, despite his behavior. Come to think of it, several of those guys at the Sea Horse looked concerned. They like Scott.* He paced around the living room, scratching his head. *That doesn't mean Scott's a pervert.* He dropped onto the edge of the sofa, put his elbows on his knees, and held his head. *Who am I kidding? What if he gets AIDS? He'll die.* He groaned. *God, help me. I can't let him be homosexual. Can Marah really help? I doubt it. She's evasive, too unstable to help me get him out of this stuff. Does she love her son enough to try?*

Several moments passed before Jack pulled himself together and got up. *I don't know what to say to Scott right now, but I want to see him. Just to make sure he's okay.*

Upstairs, Scott was in bed, the lights out. Jack switched on the small bedside lamp. The boy lay still, facing away, covers pulled halfway over his head. Miss Lavender poked her head up from her cozy spot at Scott's side. She blinked against the light. Jack scratched her ears and patted Scott's back. The boy felt tense, probably feigning sleep. "I'm glad you're home, son. I love you. Good night."

He turned off the lamp and walked toward the door. He paused when he heard a muffled voice.

"I love you too, Granpop."

Jack rose as usual, around six thirty. After he showered, he stepped into the hallway, heading for his bedroom with a towel wrapped around his middle, pajamas flung over his arm. He sniffed. *Coffee?* Barefoot, he padded around the corner. In the empty kitchen, a gurgling coffeepot greeted him. A carton of eggs and package of bacon sat on the counter, ready to go into the pans on the stove. The toaster was plugged in, a loaf of bread nearby, and the table was set.

Smiling, Jack returned to his bedroom, got dressed, and then went into the living room. Scott was sprawled on the sofa, watching a documentary about the US Air Force. When Jack entered the room, the boy clicked off the television and got up.

"Hey, Granpop. I made your coffee. Two scoops?"

"Just right. You in charge of breakfast this morning?"

"Yeah." Scott had a sheepish smile. "I've been a real jerk. I'm sorry." He headed for the kitchen. "Hope you like your eggs scrambled, 'cause that's all I know how to do."

"Scrambled sounds good to me. With a little shot of Tabasco?"

"Sure, why not?" Scott opened the package of bacon and covered the bottom of the biggest cast iron frying pan with bacon slices. He had six left, so he lined the sides of the pan with them.

Jack restrained himself. *It's only bacon. Probably first time he's ever cooked it. Leftovers are good in sandwiches.* He remembered the teenager's appetite. *If there are any leftovers.*

Next, Scott got out a large mixing bowl and began cracking eggs into it.

"I'll go get the newspaper," Jack said. He needed something to do while Scott cooked for an army. His grandson was turning the bacon when Jack returned to the kitchen. Another frying pan was filled with bubbling, scrambled eggs. Jack noted a generous sprinkling of black pepper. "Bacon smells good. I'm getting hungry." He poured a cup of coffee, sat down at the kitchen table, and opened the newspaper. "Let me know if you want any help."

A moment later Scott spoke. "Last night—when I left here—I went by the Sea Horse," he said, his attention on the bacon. "Marco was there, but he didn't see me. I thought he and Danny were—" He shot a quick glance at his grandfather. "Like best friends, you know? But Marco was with this other guy, like Danny didn't matter. Made me mad." Scott jabbed at the bacon as he glanced over his shoulder.

Jack grew very still. *He admits he went into that bar again. Disobeyed me. But he's trying to tell me something here. I need to listen.* He sensed Scott was waiting for a reaction. "I went there last night," he said, "looking for you."

Scott turned around, his eyes wide. "You did?"

Jack nodded. "Go ahead, finish what you were telling me about Danny and Marco."

"I didn't stay there. At the Sea Horse. I walked around downtown for a while. Then I went to the Carousel. Wished I could get in and ride those ponies. Listen to the music. Forget about everything, you know? I wished you were there, too, Granpop."

The bacon sizzled and popped.

"If I had been, I'd have unlocked the door, and we'd have turned on the music and all the lights and grabbed a couple of ponies. I know what you mean, forgetting about everything. Sometimes I feel that

131

way, too. I want to climb on that big bay and forget about everything else."

"I'd choose the black stallion, Noble Knight."

"You know, son, the trouble is we'd just go around and around. Never really get anyplace. In real life, we have to get off, get out there, and deal with whatever is coming our way."

Scott set the pan of scrambled eggs on the table and took a plate from the cupboard for the bacon. "Yeah, well, you were right about Marco. He's a two-faced jerk. But Danny's not."

Jack got up, put bread in the toaster, pulled off a couple of paper towels from the roll, and handed them to his grandson. While Scott folded the towels to fit the plate and placed the slightly blackened, very crisp bacon on top, Jack said, "Maybe there's a good side to Marco. Danny struck me as a good kid. I have no problem with him. Except he needs fattening up." He gave Scott's arm a playful punch. "He needs you to cook for him."

That evening, Danny came over, and the boys made a huge bowl of buttered popcorn. They settled in the living room to watch movies.

Jack picked up the phone near the kitchen and stretched the cord to its limit to get out of earshot in the living room. He dialed Kennocha's number. Warmth stirred his belly when he heard her voice.

"Jack, I'm so glad you called. Your grandson, is he home?"

"Yes, everything's fine. Scott cooked breakfast this morning, and his room looks like a recruit's barracks." Jack chuckled. "As Nikolas says, good things can come from bad."

Kennocha laughed. After a beat she said, "I warned you I'm not bashful about asking a man for a date. Would you like to get together this evening?"

"And I'm not bashful about accepting from a beautiful woman. I'll come over. Do you have anyplace in mind you'd like to go?"

"No, we'll figure that out after you get here, okay?" Kennocha gave him her apartment number and hung up a few minutes later.

Jack quickly shaved, showered, and put on clean clothes. He spent several minutes grooming his mustache while Miss Lavender sat on the bathmat and watched.

"What do you think, Missy? Will I do?"

The cat's whiskers twitched, while her green-eyed gaze remained fixed on him.

"Thank you. I'm glad you approve."

He headed for the kitchen, the cat racing ahead. "Okay, I'll find you a tidbit." He opened the refrigerator door, broke off a piece of bacon, and offered it to the cat. "Payment for your personal consultation, Miss Lavender."

With the cat happily nibbling her treat, Jack plucked his pickup keys from the hook by the door. *What am I going to tell Scott? Can't tell him I have a date; he'd probably think I'm going senile.* After a moment's thought, he jotted down Kennocha's phone number on the grocery list notepad and left it lying on the table. Then he went into the living room.

"Hey, you guys, I'm going over to a friend's house for a while. I left the phone number on the kitchen table if you need me. I won't be too late."

Engrossed in a car chase scene, Scott barely nodded. "Okay, Granpop. See you later."

Relieved not to be bombarded with questions, Jack hurried away.

CHAPTER 17

At the Wilma Building downtown, Jack ignored the elevator and took the marble stairs to the third floor. Kennocha opened the door before he rang the bell. The surprise must have shown on his face.

She laughed. "I was watching for you. I was pretty sure you'd park down by the Carousel. I can see the parking lot from here."

"I didn't even try to find a space on the streets around here. There's always a place for me at the Carousel."

He'd expected a small apartment and was surprised to find a spacious living room with large windows overlooking the Clark Fork River. He gave a low whistle. "Very nice. Used to be a bunch of cramped offices in this old building."

Kennocha smiled. "I never saw them before, of course. I heard there was a waiting list for these apartments even before the remodeling was completed."

"How long did you have to wait?"

"Fortunately, since Bevan is a friend, I knew about them before they were advertised."

That guy again. What am I doing here?

As if reading his mind, Kennocha said, "Bevan's from New York. My hometown, in fact. We knew one another in high school. Our parents were good friends. Gran plays bridge with his mother." She moved toward the living room. "I don't really feel like going out, so I thought we could spend the evening here. Still feeling the tension of New York, I guess. Do you mind?"

"Not at all. This is more to my liking, too."

"Make yourself comfortable while I finish the hors d'oeuvres."

Jack watched her walk away, wondering why she bothered with him when she undoubtedly could have Bevan O'Brien. She wore a pair of dark jade slacks with a silky blouse in a lighter shade. Her red, curly hair fell loose around her shoulders. As she disappeared into the kitchen, he looked around the living room. His intrigue with the woman deepened.

A large area rug instilled warmth in the room with its Navajo patterns in warm reds and blues on earth-tone backgrounds with narrow, black accents. A Ponderosa pine coffee table, with natural-looking flaws among dark knotholes, sat in front of a buckskin leather sofa. Jack's eyes roamed over the walls. A bookcase flanked one window. On the other side hung a large, framed painting of buffalo at rest, snowy hills in the background. He squinted to read the brass plaque: "Hidden Valley" by Nancy Glazier. He stepped back and admired the painting for several minutes. Then he moved to the adjoining wall where a collection of smaller paintings hung, including three of wild horses, their colors bright and unnatural. A blue and white pinto caught his eye. He leaned closer to read the title: "Carousel Horses," by Nancy Glazier.

"Ahhh." Suddenly, the colors didn't seem preposterous at all. He stood back, tugging the tips of his mustache, studying the paintings.

"Like them?" Kennocha swept into the room with a bottle of wine and glasses. She set them down and left again.

"I do like them," he said. "This is what the ponies would do if they could jump off the carousel. Run wild and free across the prairies."

"Exactly," she answered from the kitchen. "I'll be done here in a minute."

"No hurry. I'm enjoying myself." He continued his survey of the room.

Facing center again, his eye fell on the most remarkable piece of furniture he'd ever seen. He walked around the chair to examine every angle. Upholstered primarily in smooth, tan leather, it had large accents of brown and white animal hide, short hair intact, covering the lower back, the front of the arms, and the entire lower third of the chair. Six-inch leather fringe was sewn into the seams where smooth leather met hairy hide. He scratched his head when he noticed the objects on the floor beside the chair.

A pair of well-worn, broken-in cowboy boots sat on one side, with a bouquet of realistic silk sunflowers and weeds bursting out of their tops. On the other side, a small wagon wheel topped an old wooden nail keg. Positioned horizontally, the wheel's wooden spokes supported a smoky glass top where a unique juniper lamp sat. The lamp's a leather-laced, linen lampshade was partially draped with dark red buckskin.

Still staring at the chair and its accessories, and scratching his head, Jack jumped when he heard Kennocha's voice behind him.

"Go ahead, laugh. Everyone does."

He whirled around, saw the glint of humor in her eyes, and grinned. "I've never seen anything quite like this."

"That's the idea. I like unusual things. Outrageous, even. Good conversation pieces, don't you think?"

Jack watched her set down the tray of recognizable food: cheese, salami, and crackers. "Does your decor have a name?"

She laughed. "It's a mixture that defies labels. New American West, according to the furniture dealer." Turning back toward the kitchen, she said over her shoulder, "Would you pour the wine while I get the food out of the oven?"

Jack saw a bottle of merlot on the coffee table, alongside two stoneware goblets glazed in a veil of red and purple. He picked up the corkscrew. *Hope I remember how to do this. Beer, I can handle. Should have Nikolas here; he's good at this sort of thing.* Jack chuckled as he removed the cork. *No, no. Wouldn't want Nikolas around now.*

Kennocha came back with a platter of stuffed mushroom caps and something that looked like cheesy biscuit balls.

"I'm starved," she said. "Had a sandwich earlier, but it's disappeared." She kicked off her shoes and curled up in a chair upholstered in dark red suede.

Jack handed her a goblet. "A toast," Jack said, "to your grandmother's health and your safe return." Their eyes met as they touched the rims of their goblets.

"Thank you." Kennocha took a swallow, set her glass down, and popped a mushroom into her mouth. "Tell me about your grandson."

Jack sat on the sofa and built a bite-sized sandwich of crackers, salami, and Gouda. "For one thing, I found out he's in your creative writing class."

"He is?" She thought. "Scott ... Scott Giroux? Recently transferred from Boise? Of course!"

"That's him."

She tilted her head and studied Jack as though trying to make the connection. "He must resemble the other side of the family. I would never have guessed him to be related to you."

"Scott's his own man. Just looks like himself. His mother, Marah, is my daughter."

Kennocha reached for a cracker. "Do you have other children? Grandchildren?"

"An older son, Paul. He and his wife, Lynne, have two beautiful daughters, Cheri and Deidre."

"What does he do?"

"Air force, career man. Lieutenant colonel, assigned to the Pentagon."

"Cheri and Deidre are older than Scott?"

"No, younger. Let's see—Cheri is twelve, and Deidre is nine."

Kennocha replenished their wine. "You probably don't see them often, living so far away?"

"Unfortunately, that's right. Haven't seen my granddaughters since my wife died. Nor Lynne. Paul travels occasionally and visits me whenever he can."

"It's hard, being so far away from family. I miss my Gran terribly at times. But, I love living here."

"Would she move west to be near you?"

Kennocha shook her head. "She'll never leave Syracuse and her house. I'm sure she believes the city couldn't function without her. She makes a regular practice of writing letters to the city's traffic control department. Tells them where to set crosswalk flashers. Objects to synchronized traffic lights. Says they turn streets into racetracks. She's quite articulate and extremely opinionated. Her body may be aging, but her mind is not."

He smiled and reached for a cheesy biscuit ball. "I'd like to meet your grandmother."

She balanced her goblet between her fingertips. "Yes ... I think you will one day." She sipped and leaned back in her chair. "Now tell me more about Scott. Does he have siblings?"

"No."

"What does his father do, and his mother?"

"Vic's a bank officer. Marah does a lot of volunteer work. And social activities—community concert, garden club. I don't know what all." A shadow drifted over Jack's light mood with thoughts of Marah and Vic.

Kennocha said, "Scott's a good student. Very talented writer."

"So I hear. That's how I found out he's in your class. He wrote a story?"

"Yes. A short story. Very poignant. I think he would have a good chance of placing in the contest. However, he doesn't seem terribly interested in entering." A frown creased Kennocha's forehead. She set her wineglass on the coffee table and leaned her elbows on her knees. "Scott's parents—are they—" She stopped. "Do you mind my asking?"

Jack set his glass down and shook his head.

She continued, "I sense there are problems. At Scott's home in Boise. Would you shed some light for me?"

He debated how much to tell her. He began, measuring his words. "A few months ago, we—no, I—decided it would be better for Scott to live with me until the end of the school year. Marah and Vic have some problems to work out between them."

"How did Scott take that? Being uprooted?"

Jack cleared his throat. "The boy had run away from home. Came to me. After a few days, I took him back to Boise. But after seeing the situation in his home, I realized he'd be better off with me for a while. His parents agreed. Scott was ... relieved."

"What prompted him to run away?"

"That's a mystery yet to be solved. Scott refuses to talk about it." He paused. "Vic has a drinking problem. But there might be more to it than that. Marah and Scott had an argument, apparently. Not clear in my mind yet what happened. Scott ran away after that." Jack looked into Kennocha's concerned eyes. "Either his parents really don't know why their son ran away, or they just won't talk about it. I'm hoping the boy will tell me on his own when he's ready. I can't let him go home until I know."

She took a deep breath. "Forgive me for prying, but ..." She paused a beat. "Scott and I have talked. I had no idea he was your grandson. But it wouldn't have mattered. My job is to help students sort out issues." She leaned forward, her face earnest. "You can help me, Jack, to help Scott. And I think I can help you answer some questions."

"How?"

"Scott talks about his father some. But when I ask about his mother, he freezes up."

"There's tension between Scott and his father."

"But what about his mother?"

For a long moment, Jack didn't answer. "That's what puzzles me. They've always been close. until now. Even Vic doesn't know what happened." *He doesn't really know. He has suspicions, that's all.* Conflicting emotions arose: his love for Scott and his desire to defend his daughter. And his inner need to be honest with Kennocha. "Marah said Scott was being rebellious."

Kennocha's voice turned soft. "Jack, I think I know where we can find an answer to why Scott ran away."

Faint sounds of traffic from the busy street below filtered into the room. Off to his right, Jack heard the ticking of a clock. A heavy weight descended onto his shoulders. His eyes met Kennocha's. "How?"

She got up. "I'll be right back." A few minutes later, she returned with some typewritten pages. "Normally, I wouldn't share a student's writing without his permission. But under these circumstances ... This is Scott's story. The one I hope he'll enter in the contest. It's a first draft. He hasn't turned in the final yet." She handed it to Jack. "Their assignment was to write in the first person; it could be a true story or fiction about a person who changes as a result of some big event in his life. Scott says this is fiction, but I've wondered. Go ahead and read it. I'll make some coffee."

CHAPTER 18

The movie ended, and Scott and Danny headed for the kitchen. After they grabbed a couple of sodas, some cheese sticks, and a bag of chips, they went upstairs to Scott's room. Danny settled on the bed with his back against the headboard and nibbled on mozzarella cheese. Scott turned on the stereo then sprawled across the end of the bed on his belly, soda and chips on the floor within easy reach.

Danny said, "You know what I'd like to see? *Bent.* It played on Broadway." He held out his hand. "Toss me the chips."

Scott tossed the bag, rolled onto his side, and propped his head on his hand. "What's that about?"

"Persecution of gays in Germany."

"Under Hitler? I've read about that." Scott made a wry face. "But I don't think I want to see a play about it. Sounded horrible. Gimme some chips."

Danny tossed the potato chip bag back to him. "I'd still like to see it. Y'know what else? I'd like to write a play about guys like us. Here and now."

"Who's your English teacher? Maybe she'd let you do it for extra credit."

Danny wrinkled his nose. "Elmer Fuddy-Duddy."

Scott laughed. "Okay, forget that idea." After a moment, he said, "Hey, Danny, are those guys leaving you alone now? You know—Karl and his gang?"

"Yeah, pretty much. They call me 'queer' and 'pervert' if the principal isn't in the hall. But I'm watching out for them. Trying to avoid the creeps."

"Good. I don't trust those jerks." Scott laced his fingers together and cracked his knuckles. "Karl elbowed me in the ribs a couple of days ago. Y'know, after assembly? But I got him back a minute later. Slugged him in the stomach before we went upstairs. Mr. Hutchinson came by a second later and saw Karl winding up to hit me." Scott grinned. "Ordered him to get to class and to stop by his office before he went home."

"Lucky!"

Scott sobered. "Yeah, I know. I might be able to handle Karl, but if all five of them corner me, I guess I've had it."

Both boys fell silent for a few minutes. Then Scott asked, "Do your grandparents know?"

"I think they suspect it. How about your family?"

Scott rolled onto his back, tucked his hands under his head, and stared at the ceiling. "No, I'm scared to tell them. I thought I could tell Granpop someday, but now I'm afraid he'd kick me out after he had such a big fit about Marco."

"When?"

"You know, that day Marco brought us home."

"Oh, yeah. And Marco put on his fag act."

A sharp knock on the front door caught Scott's attention. He jumped up and peered out the window at the street below. Streetlights revealed a faded red Camaro. He groaned. "It's Marco. What should I do?"

The knocking continued. Marco called, "Scot-ty ba-by. Lemme in."

Danny's face twisted into a grimace. "He's been drinking."

Scott rubbed the back of his neck and paced between the window and the bed. "Oh, man ... Can't leave him out there yelling. Mrs. Gustine across the street will call the cops."

Marco yelled again, pounding on the door.

"I'll try to get rid of him." Scott hurried downstairs.

He opened the front door a crack to a swaying, grinning Marco. "You can't come in. Go home, Marco."

Leering, Marco leaned against the doorjamb. "Oh-h-h, big bad wolf gonna get the cute little boy?" He reached in, and Scott stepped back. Marco stumbled in.

"You can't stay!"

Marco gave him a pleading look. "Scotty, dear, I need to use your bathroom." He laced his fingers in mock prayer and bent his knees. "Ple-e-e-z-e."

Skeptical, Scott looked him up and down. "Well, hurry up."

He followed Marco through the living room. Just as they reached the hallway, Danny called down from the upstairs landing.

"Is he gone?"

Scott groaned again.

Earrings bobbing, Marco whipped around and went to the foot of the stairs. "Danny?" Then he turned accusing eyes onto Scott. "You didn't tell he me was here. Does your grandfather know?" He didn't wait for an answer but went up the stairs, two at a time.

Scott followed slowly. *How am I gonna get rid of him? If Granpop finds him here, he'll blow his cork.* He walked into his room to find Danny standing by the door with a disgusted look on his face. Marco was perched on the window seat, smiling. Scott glared at him. "You said you were desperate to use the bathroom."

"Oh, I don't have to go now. What are you boys doing while Grandpa's away, hmmm?"

Danny said, "You're rude. You know that, Marco? And you're a cheat. We don't want anything to do with you!"

Marco sniffed and turned his nose up.

"Like I told you," Scott said, "you can't stay."

"Why not?"

Danny folded his arms across his chest. "Because you acted like such a jerk when Scott introduced you to his grandfather. Or have you forgotten that we had to leave in a big hurry that day?"

"Oh, that day." Marco shrugged. "I was just having a little fun. Besides, I saw your grandfather at the Sea Horse the other night, and we got along fine." He stood. "You got some more pop downstairs?" Without waiting for an answer, Marco clattered downstairs.

As soon as he disappeared, Scott whispered to Danny, "How are we gonna get rid of him? I'm gonna be in big trouble if Granpop sees him."

Danny nodded. "I know. I'll ask him to take me home."

"He's drunk! And your car's out back—"

"I'll tell him it's—"

Suddenly they heard Marco on the stairs. He entered the room and halted, looking from Danny to Scott. "Conspiring against me?" In one swift motion, he flopped onto the bed, adjusted the pillow against the headboard, and popped open the soda can and took a swig. He smacked his lips and fixed an eye on Danny. "Good little Christian boys don't talk behind people's backs. And they don't play together, either."

"Oh, come off it," Scott said.

"He always gets that way when he's been drinking," Danny said. "And he's not as drunk as he's pretending to be." He scowled at Marco.

Marco shrugged. "Got me in the door, didn't it?" He gave Danny a long look. "Playing house with Scotty?"

Scott clenched his fists at his sides.

Danny's face flushed. "No! It's none of your business anyway." He shook his head and turned away.

Marco snickered.

Danny whipped around to face him. "You just don't get it, do you? Even if we were—doing it—we sure wouldn't be doing it here. Not in his grandfather's house."

"Oh, you'd go to your house?"

"No! That's not right, either."

Marco got up and stood in front of Danny. "Getting awfully self-righteous, aren't you? All that church stuff getting under your skin?"

Scott looked at Danny. *Church stuff? I didn't know he was religious.*

Danny stared at his tormentor. "Maybe you should try it."

"Oh?" Marco's eyebrows rose, and he sneered. "How did you manage to find a church that allows—heaven forbid—gays?"

"It's Nikolas's church. They don't treat me any different than anybody else." Danny looked away. "Besides, you don't know anything."

Scott was braced for another retort, but suddenly the fight seemed to drain out of Marco. Silent, he walked to the window, his back to the room.

Scott and Danny exchanged puzzled glances.

When Marco spoke again, his voice was low, and he sounded sober. "I know a lot more than you think." He turned to face them. "You want to hear how it really is? A couple of years ago, I'd just come out of another stinking relationship and decided to go home. Back to my parents' place. I remembered how happy they always were together, how they seemed to be in love even after all those years. I wanted a relationship like that." He sat down on the edge of the window seat, leaned on his knees, and laced his long fingers together. "They were glad to see me. Prodigal son returns and all that. I went to church with them. Same church they'd been going to forever. They knew everybody. You know the scene, hugs, handshakes, good ol' boy stuff all around. Until the fine people of the church saw me. I even dressed in ordinary clothes for the occasion. Then it got real quiet, and everybody just went and sat down. And whispered. And sneaked looks at me." Marco's eyes filled with tears.

A shiver ran down Scott's spine.

"The story gets better," Marco said. "That same afternoon, the preacher and two elders came to my folks' house. I found out that Mom had asked her women's Bible study group to pray for me. So everyone thought they knew all about me. These guys wanted to lay hands on me and pray for me." His voice became bitter. "Bottom line is I wasn't welcome in their church until I publicly repented of my sins." He glared at Danny. "So don't tell me I don't know anything about—" he spat the word out, "*Christians.*"

Silence hung in the room.

Scott squirmed. His parents didn't go to church anymore, and he barely remembered Sunday school. He didn't know what to think about Marco's revelation.

Danny sucked in a deep breath and let it out. "Our church—the one I've been going to with Nikolas—isn't like that. They treat everybody the same. And in youth group, sometimes we even talk about stuff. You know, discrimination, persecution, people with AIDS. Nikolas says God loves everyone. Sexual orientation doesn't matter."

Marco didn't respond. He stood, drained his soda, tossed the can toward the wastebasket and missed. He ignored it and walked toward the door. He paused. "But do they know you're gay, Danny? And do they believe you're *born* gay?" He gave them both a long look.

Neither answered him. Scott felt at a loss, and Danny seemed confused.

Marco left without another word. The boys heard the front door open and close. Moments later, Scott watched out the window as he drove away.

Scott ran his hand through his hair and broke the silence. "Whew. I didn't know Marco could be so serious."

"Me neither. I've been around him when he's drunk, really drunk, and he can quote the Bible as good as Nikolas. But I don't know if it's really the Bible or if he's making it up. He gets so sarcastic, I just don't want to listen."

"I feel bad for him," Scott said. "That part about those guys from his parents' church."

"That's what I didn't like about my grandparents' church. I felt like dirt every time the priest talked about sinners. Maybe I was being paranoid, but I always felt like he was looking right at me when he talked about homosexuals." He sat down on the edge of the bed. "Sometimes I think my grandmother suspects it." He doubled his fist and struck the mattress. *Whump!* "I hate feeling like I'm living a double life! I want to tell!" He gave Scott a wide-eyed look. "I mean, what're my grandparents gonna do? Kick me out? I don't think so. I'm all they've got."

Scott breathed deeply. He didn't want to think about consequences now. Instead, he grinned at Danny to break the mood. "Yeah, you're spoiled. You're the only guy I know with a TV, stereo, six Polk speakers, a desk, a PC, and a laptop. All in your bedroom. Which is bigger than my whole house, practically. Man, you could tell your grandparents you want to marry Marco, and they'd say it was okay."

Danny laughed. "I don't think they'd go for me marrying another guy, especially Marco." He sobered. "And really, I love my grandparents. I don't want to hurt them. They're basically all I've got, too."

"What d'ya mean, basically? There isn't anybody else, is there?"

"There's Uncle Stanley."

"Yeah, but you told me he's not your real uncle. So he doesn't count."

Danny shrugged. After a moment he said, "What do you think your parents would say if you told them?"

"My dad already hates me. I used to think about telling Mom. Before I left home." His voice hardened. "I'm glad I didn't."

Danny looked up in surprise. "Why? What's the deal with your mother? How come you never talk about her?"

Scott examined his thumbnail. Ignoring Danny's question, he said, "She'd tell Dad, and he'd blame her, take it out on her. He always does when he thinks I've screwed up. Then he'd probably find some way to blame me for what Mom did."

"Huh? What'd your mom do?"

Scott picked up Marco's empty can from the floor and pitched it into the wastebasket with his own. "Nothin,'" he mumbled. "I mean, he just always blames me for stuff."

Danny didn't seem to be listening. "Y'know, some guys never tell. Like my friend in San Diego. He never told his family."

"That old guy? 'Uncle' Stanley?"

Danny flushed. "He isn't that old. Not really old-old, you know. He's forty-three."

"He looked ancient in that picture you showed me."

Danny's voice dropped. "He's been sick."

"What's wrong with him?" Scott stared at Danny, but his friend looked away. "Has he got AIDS?"

"He says it's his stomach or something. He's getting better. He wants me to come down and stay with him this summer."

"Are you going?"

"I'd like to ... if I can talk my grandfather into it. He doesn't like Stanley. Even though he was my parents' best friend."

"Well, if your grandfather doesn't like him, you'd better not go. We were gonna go camping this summer, remember? You want me to find someone else to hang out with?"

"No, but I kinda want to go to San Diego, too." He looked at his wristwatch and jumped up. "It's almost eleven. I have to go home."

Scott wondered about his abruptness. *Why is he so defensive about Stanley? What's the deal with that guy anyway?*

After Danny left, Scott channel surfed but didn't find anything interesting. He wandered into the kitchen and rummaged through the refrigerator. Nothing. He searched the freezer, hoping for a frozen pizza or carton of ice cream, but he didn't find either. He looked at the clock. Almost midnight. *Where's Granpop?*

He heard a meow at the back door and let the cat in. He watched her groom herself. "You beat Granpop home, kitty. Wonder where he is? Must be at Nikolas's house. D'you think he'd bring us some of Nikolas's brownies?" He dialed the number Jack had written down. When a woman answered, he hung up, startled. He checked the list of numbers Jack had posted near the phone. This one wasn't on it. He found Nikolas's number and dialed.

"Hey, Nikolas. Did I wake you up? ... Oh, good movie, huh? ... No, nothing's wrong. I just thought, well, is Granpop there? He said he was gonna visit a friend. ... Yeah, I thought it was you. But I dialed this number he wrote down and some woman answered." He laughed. "Guess so. But you know what's funny? She sounded just like my English teacher, Miss Bryant ... Yeah, Kennocha ... No kidding? Granpop? ... But she's my teacher ... Yeah, okay ... Nah, I won't tell him" He laughed again. "Okay, Nikolas, our secret. G'night."

Granpop and Miss Bryant—I wonder if they're talking about me? What if she tells him about my story? Sometimes I want to tell him. But what good would it do?

CHAPTER 19

Jack heard Kennocha grinding coffee beans. He glanced at the typewritten sheet she had handed him and noticed a few smudged spots in the middle of the page, where the words "he" or "him" had been inked in by hand. He settled back on the leather sofa and began to read.

I was scared, and at first, I didn't think I could go it alone, but I made up my mind to never give up.

The biggest thing is to realize that even though someone you really respect and love tells you you're dirt, that doesn't mean it's really true. You have to believe in yourself, even when someone you really believe in turns out to be a liar.

It's like, you're driving down this road, and this person is sitting beside you, helping you find your way in this strange country. We come to this crossroads. She says, "Never go down that road. It's wrong, and it'll get you in big trouble."

So you believe her. Then later, you find out she went that way afterward, even though she knew it was wrong.

It eats at your gut 'til you can't stand it anymore, and pretty soon you have to ask her, "Why?"

I can tell you right now, it's better to pretend you don't know what road she took. Once the words are out, anything can happen. It'll never be the same again.

It's like, you have to start all over again, figure out who you can trust. And you have to figure out who you are. While you're doing that, you might discover some new things about yourself.

It's not easy, starting over. Sometimes you just want to give up.

But I made it. I didn't do it alone. One person who helped was a teacher who listened to me. I mean, listened like maybe I had something important to say. Another person is someone I've known all my life, but at the same time I didn't know him. The best thing is, this person never lies to me. I can trust him. That means the most. My grandfather.

Jack shivered and wiped his eyes. He got up and walked to the window. Certain words from Scott's essay stuck in his mind. "Scared ... liar ... never be the same ... figure out who you are." Images drifted in and out of Jack's mind. He felt like he was trying to find his way through a murky fog, where truth was obscured by vapors of lies, half-truths, and silence. *What is it that Scott doesn't want to talk about? How did he get that wound on his back? Why did Marah ask if we wanted her? What did Claire tell her? What is my daughter hiding? Is she the liar Scott wrote about?*

He stared down at the river. Streetlights along the bridge cast patches of light in the water below, revealing a dark, gray-green current with scattered ice. Headlights zipping back and forth across the bridge created a blinking rhythm through the vertical bars along the rail. A nagging thought from somewhere deep in his mind rose to the surface in cadence with the blinking lights. *It's true, it's true, it's true.*

He felt dizzy for a moment, as though he'd been riding the carousel 'round and 'round, faster and faster, calliope music blaring in the background. Rational thoughts impossible. Stop the music! Stop the carousel!

He drew in a deep breath and shook off the peculiar feeling. He became aware of Kennocha at his side when she put her hand on his arm.

"Jack," she said softly. "Let's have a cup of coffee. We can talk about this."

Several moments passed. Finally, Jack said, "The teacher. That's you."

"Yes."

"I'm ..." His voice cracked. He cleared his throat and tried again. "I'm glad he trusted you." He turned to her. "It's his mother, isn't it?"

She looked long and deep into his eyes. "I don't know, but yes, I suspect it is, because he doesn't want to talk about her. Because you said they argue when they're around one another." She squeezed his arm. "I'll help you try to learn the truth ... if you want me to." Suddenly, she hugged him, her cheek against his shoulder.

Jack held her. She felt good. Not just physically good, but more. He felt a sense of hope. Together, he and Kennocha would help Scott. He pulled her closer. Her hair felt soft. She smelled good. His heart beat faster.

Kennocha gave him a soft, brief kiss and gently pulled away. She took his hand and pulled him toward the kitchen. "C'mon. You pour the coffee while I cut the blueberry cheesecake."

CHAPTER 20

Mid-April ...

In Boise, Marah glared at Vic across the center island in their kitchen. "Why all the questions? Don't tell me you had nothing to do in Japan but wonder what I was doing."

"You've had a lot of freedom since you kicked Scott out."

"I didn't kick him out. You and Dad decided to move him to Missoula. I didn't."

"Right." Vic's voice dripped with sarcasm. "Nevertheless, you haven't exactly acted like a distraught mother since he left. Your social schedule defies my imagination. And you spend too much time with Tina."

"She's my friend."

"She's a druggie. Those diet pills you got from her—are you still taking them?"

"She's not a druggie. And there's nothing wrong with those pills."

"How many a day are you popping now?"

"What difference does it make? You want me to stay thin, don't you?"

Vic looked disgusted. "Use your head, Marah. You could get addicted to that stuff, if you aren't already." He switched topics. "What do you do all day?"

"You know what I'm doing. The community good works you're so fond of. Concert committee, hospital auxiliary—"

"Wait a minute. Hospital? When did you start that? This have anything to do with your new boyfriend?"

Her voice icy, Marah said, "I don't have a 'new boyfriend,' as you put it. You should be glad I'm in the auxiliary. The more I do, the better you look. Right, darling?"

Vic's mouth clamped shut in a tight line. After a few seconds, he strode into the dining room. Marah heard the liquor cabinet open and the sound of glass clinking against glass. Trembling, she hugged her arms against her waist.

Highball in hand, Vic returned. He stopped short, feet braced apart, and leveled a look at her. He took a long drink from his glass. "I want Scott home."

"What? We said we'd let him finish the school year and—"

"You made such a scene over having him leave, I thought you'd be anxious to get him home." Vic drank deeply. "Or would that put a crimp in your so-called community service?"

"Of course not. It's just that—"

"I've changed my mind. He belongs here at home." He set the now half-empty crystal tumbler on the center island. "Call your dad and tell him."

Her eyebrows went up. "Now? You're so anxious, you do it. I'm going upstairs." Marah walked through the family room and up the stairs to her sewing loft, where she could hear every word if Vic used the phone in the kitchen. He never came up here. She was safe.

CHAPTER 21

Jack answered the phone and heard his son-in-law's voice. After brief small talk, Vic got to the point.

"I want Scott to come home. As soon as possible."

Jack's pulse quickened. "You and Marah have solved your problems?"

"The kid's got to learn to get along at home."

He didn't answer my question. "There's no hurry. Scott's not a problem here. He's adjusted well in school, and I've enjoyed his company."

"No. I'm not going to baby him. He's had too much of that already from his mother. He has to come home. I'll let you know the arrangements in a few days. First I've got to get my work wrapped up on this Japan project."

Jack's uneasiness increased. "Scott's not here right now. If you call back in an hour or so, you'll catch him."

"You go ahead and tell him."

"No. You'll have to do that yourself, Vic." The call ended.

Jack and Scott were just finishing supper when the phone rang. Scott leaped up and answered with a cheerful "Hello." Then his face fell. "Oh, hi, Dad ... What? Did you talk to Granpop? ... But I'm not ..." His voice grew louder. "I don't care what Mom wants. I don't care about her." His tone dropped. "Yeah, I hear you." He slammed the phone into its cradle and shuffled to his chair. He plopped down, elbows on knees, chin on fists. A scowl creased his face.

"Guess your dad told you."

"Yeah."

"Came as a surprise to me, too."

"You want me to go?"

Jack thought a minute, carefully choosing his words. "This isn't a matter of whether I want you to stay or go. What I want is for my family to be happy. Live peaceably with each other. It's right and fitting for parents and children to be together. I'm not going to push you out, but I don't have the final say. Your parents do." He paused. "Do you want to go home for a while? See how things work out?"

Scott's head drooped. "It'll never work. Things aren't the same anymore."

"What things? What do you mean?"

"Mom—" Scott shook his head. "Oh, nothing."

"Son, I read your story."

Scott's head jerked up. He stared at his grandfather for an instant.

"Thanks for trusting me. I mean that." Jack paused. "Now I'm going to ask you to trust me a little further. Tell me what happened that caused you to run away."

The boy leaned down, untied his shoes, pulled up his socks, and retied his shoes. Finally, he mumbled, "You wouldn't believe me."

"I love you, Scott, and I trust you. Try me."

CHAPTER 22

After Marah and Vic returned from their dinner engagement, she hurried up the curved staircase off the foyer to the master bedroom at the end of the carpeted hallway. Vic had been moody all evening. She feared a confrontation.

She quickly undressed, kicking off her pumps and tossing her clothing over a chair, contrary to her usual neat habits. Vic entered the room just as she stepped into her nightgown. He moved in slow motion and avoided looking at her—a signal she knew all too well. His anger had been smoldering for hours, ever since his call to Scott. She worried about what their son might have said that drove Vic into this mood.

Vic reminded her of a panther. He stalked his prey, lithe body movements smooth, quiet, focused. Despite her fear that she was his target tonight, Marah felt stirrings of arousal.

She crawled into their king-sized bed as Vic went into the adjoining bathroom and closed the door. She pulled the ivory satin comforter up to her chin and savored the brief minutes alone. Her gaze wandered around the master bedroom of her dreams. Pale green plush carpet, beveled-glass dressing table with brass trim, and near the window, an ivory velvet chair that complemented dark green, brocade drapes. She heard the click of the bathroom door and closed her eyes, feigning sleep. She sensed Vic's stealthy approach on the plush carpet.

"What happened between you and Scott the night he ran away? The kid used to be on your side all the time. Now he acts like he hates your guts. Why?"

Marah stirred. "I don't know. He's just behaving like a normal teenager. Breaking the apron strings."

"What about that wound on the kid's back?"

She mumbled, "I never saw it. Probably just some lie to get his grandfather's sympathy ... you know how kids are ..." She rolled onto her stomach. Moments passed. She willed herself to breathe evenly.

Voice low and deliberate, he said, "A couple months ago, in the dead of winter, Jack drove over three hundred miles to talk to us. He's nobody's fool. He must have had good reason."

Suddenly, Marah felt the comforter yanked away. Her husband leaned into her face. Heart pounding, she half turned onto her side and gagged at the smell of whiskey on his breath.

"Why'd Scott run away? You're hiding something, aren't you?"

Forcing herself to remain composed, Marah got out of bed and stepped around her husband to pick up her satin peignoir. Voice calm, she said, "No." She ran her fingers through her hair and turned to face him, letting her wrap fall open. "Darling, let's talk about this in the morning." When he didn't answer, she stepped closer and slipped her hands inside his unbuttoned shirt. "Let's just go to bed now. It's late."

Vic's hand whipped up and struck Marah's face. She stumbled and fell into the chair. He spat out, "You're lying!" He raised his hand again.

She screamed, "Vic, no!"

He grabbed her shoulder and forced her to look at him. "Tell me the truth."

"Vic, that hurts ... let go ... please, let go ..." *Try to reason with him.* "We had an argument. About school. I grounded him. He got mad. I thought he went to Larry's house. I didn't realize how upset he was until later. When he didn't come home for dinner."

"Why'd you tell me he was visiting your dad?"

"I didn't. You assumed—"

"And you let me."

"You were so busy, I hardly saw you." Marah squirmed under Vic's grip until he released her. She stood and moved toward the window, positioning herself behind the chair. She assessed Vic's expression and continued. "You had a business meeting that night, remember? After you got home so late, I decided to wait and tell you in the morning. But then you left again." Marah willed her lips to form a tentative smile, gambling he'd been too drunk to recall anything. "You remember, don't you, darling?"

Vic blinked several times and swayed on his feet. "Nice story. Very tidy," he rasped. "I'm going to fix a drink. When I come back, you tell me all about this so-called problem at school." He sneered. "When has Scott ever had school problems?" He stepped out of the room, paused, and turned back, steadying himself with a grip on the door frame. He

158

pointed a swaying finger at Marah. "The kid is too perfect. He's hiding something. Just like his mother."

Vic's footsteps sounded heavy and faltering as he went downstairs. Marah fumed. *Hope he falls and breaks his neck. What does he care about what goes on in this house as long as we look good to his friends? He doesn't care about me. His whole life revolves around that bank. If he'd been a better father, Scott wouldn't have run away.*

Marah moved across the bedroom to examine her face in the dressing table mirror. Her fingertips touched the tender area on her jaw. *Will it bruise? Wish it would. I'd go home, and Daddy would take care of Vic.* She heard a noise downstairs. *Vic falling, probably, he's so drunk.* She listened. *I hope he doesn't knock over my new Ficus plant.* Marah heard the steps creak under Vic's weight. She moved closer to the window.

The sound of ice tinkling against glass signaled Vic's return. He entered the room, a golf club dangling from one hand. Marah's throat constricted. She cringed.

He laughed. "You think I'm gonna hit you? I should. Why didn't you tell me you put a tree down there? I tripped over it." He shook the club head in her face. "This thing was stuck behind it."

She stared at the brownish-red stain on the heel.

"Who put it behind that stupid tree?"

"I—I don't know. I told Scott to clean out that closet. I wanted him to get his golf bag and stuff out of there." She stopped as a grimace formed on Vic's face.

"Was this before or after your fight with him about school?"

"After—no, before. Oh, that's right!" Marah forced out a short laugh. "That's what the fight was about. The golf clubs. He got smart with me. Didn't want to put them away. So I—"

Vic's eyes bored into hers. "So you what, darling?"

Marah swallowed. "I ... don't remember. We argued ... he left ..."

Vic slammed the steel head onto the floor. Amber-colored liquid slopped from the glass in his other hand onto the plush carpet. His face twisted in fury. "You're still lying. I can see it all over your face, you tramp." He advanced.

A flame of hatred ignited in her chest. Anger overpowered her fear. "Don't call me that."

A sardonic smile twisted his face. "Truth hurt, slut?" He paused to swallow what was left of his drink.

"Don't call me names." Marah's voice rose. "What right do you have to question me about Scott? You're a lousy father. You're never here.

And how about all the times you've threatened your son? Drunk out of your mind."

Vic roared, "You're the one who argued with him before he ran."

"I just wanted him to shut up!"

Vic's eyes narrowed. "Shlut ... shut up abou' what?"

Marah's heart beat faster at her near slip. His slurred words told her that he was close to passing out. *Keep him at bay. Calm down. Buy time.* "About the closet. The mess he'd made in there." She turned away, moved slowly to the chair, and sat down. *Take a deep breath. Give him space. Don't look at him.* "You know how mouthy he can get sometimes. He was just getting too smart-alecky, that's all." She picked at her frosted nail polish. From the corner of her eye, she saw her husband stumble to the bed and flop down.

"We'll finish thish discush—dishcuh—thish talk t'morrow." His eyes closed.

Marah waited until snores gurgled up his throat. Quietly, she retrieved the golf club and tiptoed downstairs to the kitchen. After she scrubbed the stain off the club head, she returned to the foyer, opened the closet door, and pulled out Scott's golf bag. With an anxious glance up the curving staircase, she slid the club into the bag, shoved it to the back of the closet, and closed the door. She listened for Vic's snores then quietly walked back to the kitchen, got a glass of water, and went upstairs to her sewing loft. She turned on a small lamp, retrieved her pills from the back of her thread drawer, and spilled two into her palm. After she swallowed them, she curled up on the loveseat with a mohair afghan.

Fingering the afghan, Marah recalled when her mother made it and presented it to her at a bridal shower eighteen years ago. Could her mother have guessed even then that Marah would have many nights separated from her marriage bed—endless nights huddled on a sofa or in a chair, listening for threatening footsteps, dreading whiskey-soured breath? *Would she have cared? No, she only cared about Paul. I meant nothing to her. I'll never forget the day I found out how much she despised me, the day I wanted to go with Paul and his friends to Flathead Lake.*

She didn't tell her mother she had a crush on one of Paul's friends when she begged to go. "Why can't I go, Mother?"

"You're too young. They're all in high school."

Marah brooded. "If I was in high school, I could go, couldn't I? Why didn't you and Daddy have me sooner, so I could do things with Paul, anyway?"

Claire gave her a hard look. "We didn't plan to have you at all. You were an accident."

A few days later, Marah asked Jack, "Daddy, was I an accident? Mother said you guys never wanted me."

Jack looked startled. Then he wrapped his arms around her and waltzed her around until she giggled. "You're no accident. You're my angel. God sent you to me."

She believed him. But she believed her mother, too.

On the loveseat in her loft, Marah snuggled down, safe from Vic at least until morning. She lay in the semi-dark, thinking about her secret. If Vic knew what really happened the day Scott left, she would pay a terrible price. If Scott had not been hanging around with that Larry, it never would have happened. Marah's life had been exciting and promising until that night Scott ran away.

When Marah, Vic, and Scott moved from Springfield to Boise two years ago, she had begged God for a new beginning. Guilt-ridden, Vic gave his word. She hoped he'd stop sleeping around, but she had to be satisfied with less physical abuse. She could have tolerated hidden bruises if her husband would stop philandering. She hated the pitying looks she got from other women, women who knew about Vic's cheating.

In Boise, she and Vic attended social functions and enjoyed the admiration, the envious looks. Together, she and Vic made a striking impression—both with dark hair, Vic with gray eyes, Marah with brown; his olive complexion both complemented and accented Marah's fair skin. They dressed in understated elegance. They lavished charm to garner praise.

A little over a year ago, Marah knew they had been accepted into the elite social crowd when they received an invitation to the New Year's Eve party at the fabulous Singleton mansion, overlooking the city. Ever sensitive to more than a flicker of interest in men's admiring glances, Marah's eyes lingered when the hostess introduced her to the handsome Dr. Warren Addison. Intent on her best behavior, her mind registered his equally lingering look and filed it away. No flirtations tonight.

But a few weeks later, lonely and bored, ideas churned in Marah's mind. She called to make an appointment to see Dr. Addison, tearfully describing a lump she'd found on her breast; she needed to see him as soon as possible. The receptionist squeezed her in late in the day, apologizing that the doctor was already running behind schedule.

Scott and his friend Larry planned to grab burgers for supper and then attend a foreign film for extra credit in literature class. They'd undoubtedly end up at Larry's house afterward. Lately, Scott had been pushing his curfew when he knew his dad was at a board meeting. Vic's board meetings had been running past midnight, although by now, Marah was sure his meetings were excuses. Discretion ruled Vic's behavior ... to a point. She smiled. His fractured promise suited her plans perfectly.

She didn't mind that she had to wait a long time to see the doctor; she was his last patient of the day. She heard him tell his receptionist he would handle Mrs. Giroux and send her for a mammogram. He told the woman to go home, he'd lock up. Although she didn't know about any remaining patients or the rest of the staff, Marah felt certain no one would be around after the nurse directed her to his office. No one except Dr. Addison.

Hours later, she drove her Cadillac into their empty garage. Vic hadn't arrived yet, but with a light on in the family room, she knew Scott was home. For a moment, she felt alarmed. Then she relaxed. *I can handle Scott.* She lingered in her comfortable car, inhaled the familiar leather scent, and thought of Warren's office and his leather sofa. She closed her eyes and savored the thrill of her evening. She could hardly wait for their next meeting, only this time she wouldn't have to arrange to be his last patient of the day. He wouldn't have to tell his staff he'd lock up. No, next time, he said, they'd meet at a safer place. He'd call her.

Smiling, she got out of the car and walked toward the house, feeling whole again and only slightly tarnished.

That was just over three months ago. Now, in her loft safely away from Vic, she tried not to think about what happened later that evening. She pushed the memory down deep inside and resolved to erase it from her mind.

She recalled the scene with her husband a little while ago and thought again about divorce. She and Warren had continued their secret meetings, but so far, he hadn't shown much interest when she mentioned leaving Vic. He seemed satisfied with their sexual rendezvous, but she wanted more. She wanted security, a man who wanted her, no one else.

Marah pulled the afghan around her and hugged a pillow. Aloud, she whispered, "I just want someone to love me for real, for keeps."

She sat up abruptly. *The puppy.* She threw off the afghan, jumped up, and hurried down to the basement.

"Tippy," she called softly, "where are you? Come baby, come to Mama."

The pup scampered out of a corner, where he'd been chewing on an old boot. He wriggled in delight and licked her chin when she picked him up.

"You little cutie. Did you miss me?" She sniffed and wrinkled her nose. "We have to change your newspapers. Tomorrow." Holding the pup close, Marah returned to her sewing loft, whispering, "You love me, don't you?"

CHAPTER 23

Toward the end of April, springtime fragrances filled the air in Jack's neighborhood. Nature's brushstrokes brightened city parks and trash can–lined alleys. Tender blades of green sprouted around the base of fence posts and stop signs and filled sidewalk cracks. Purple crocuses and yellow daffodils knew no class distinctions, as they blossomed throughout the town, from the landscaped gardens of old, distinguished, university-area homes to weather-beaten, untended houses on the north side of the railroad tracks.

One morning after Scott left for school, Jack walked to the Carousel, enjoying the fine day and contemplating the pleasures in his life,

At the top of his list, Kennocha. She became more dear to him every day—and he to her, he hoped. He wanted to spend more time with her, but devotion to her students occupied much of her free time.

Next, Scott. He enjoyed his grandson's company, and he was studious, lively, and well-behaved—most of the time.

Then, the Carousel. He'd finished carving Clarissa Mae, and Kennocha had applied the primer coats. Somehow, Jack felt he couldn't really close the door on his life with Claire until the pony was completed.

Finally, like a strong thread running through the fabric of his life, his good friend Nikolas. They'd known one another over thirty years and had seemed to instinctively understand one another from the beginning. Jack admired his friend's deep faith and now, more than ever, wished he was more like Nikolas in his confidence in God.

Jack crossed Front Street, started down the hill, and glanced toward the parking lot in front of the Carousel. He was the first of the volunteers to arrive. Inside the building, Jack climbed onto the circular hardwood platform and studied the dapple gray, one of the originals. The pony's once thick, genuine horsehair tail had become a short, bristly tuft. One ear had broken off.

Engrossed in his examination, Jack jumped when a hand clamped onto his shoulder. He whirled around to find Nikolas's bushy, black eyebrows meeting in a scowl above his nose.

"Sir," Nikolas said, "do I know you?" He squinted. "Oh, my friend, Jack, it is you. I had forgotten what you looked like."

"What kind of remark is that?"

"In the old days, once a week I could count on you to come over to my house. We would play cards and talk politics. Now, never. Even here, you do not want to talk to me." He winked. "You only want to talk to a certain lovely lady."

Jack grinned. "Jealous, are you?"

"No-o-o. But I am inquisitive. Your relationship is developing?"

"I didn't say that."

Nikolas persisted. "But if you were, ah—developing a relationship, shall we say—you would tell your best friend, would you not?"

Jack cocked his head. "Why would I tell you? The biggest gossip in Missoula. You're worse than an old woman."

Nikolas wagged a finger at him. "Ha. Just as I thought. Cupid's arrows have struck your heart."

"See, there you go. Jumping to conclusions."

Nikolas winked and nodded at someone behind Jack. Before he could turn around, he heard a familiar voice.

Kennocha used her schoolteacher voice. "Just what are you two up to?"

Jack turned, smiling, and tucked his arm around her waist. She leaned into his side. "This Russian rascal is accusing me of trying to romance you," Jack said. "Would you set him straight?"

"What do you think, Nikolas? You've known him a long time. Should I fall for his amorous attentions?"

For once, Nikolas was speechless. His stare darted from Kennocha to Jack. He placed a hand over his heart. "I am very happy to see this." He took Kennocha's hand in his big paw. "You have won his heart. That I can see." Eyes twinkling, he turned to Jack. "You are lucky you saw her first. If I had, you would not have had a chance. She would be swept off her feet by my charm." With a flourish, he bowed before Kennocha and planted a kiss on the back of her hand.

"All right, that'll be enough of that, you old fox," Jack protested. He pulled Kennocha's hand away and stage-whispered to her, "You can't trust this sly immigrant."

She laughed. "This is fun, being fought over by two handsome gentlemen." She gave Jack a quick hug. "I had to run a school errand, but I couldn't resist stopping by. Now I have to get back to work. See you boys later."

Both men watched her graceful sway between the ponies as she made her way off the carousel and left the building.

One Saturday night a few weeks later, Jack showered, shaved, and splashed on cologne. He put on the navy slacks and white dress shirt he hadn't worn since Claire's funeral. He fussed with his hair and mustache until he tired of it and threw the comb down. From the back of his closet, he pulled out a tan sport coat with suede elbow patches. Claire used to complain that it wasn't his best color, but he liked the jacket. It felt comfortable. And it had been expensive, even with his employee discount—one of the advantages of being manager of the men's department at DeWolfe Department Store. He adjusted his burgundy tie and stepped in front of the mirror. *Haircut was worth the five bucks.* He stepped back for a full-length view. *Not bad for an old man.*

He strutted into the kitchen.

Scott looked up from his car magazine and gave a low whistle. "Hot date?"

"You might say that."

"Sure hope she likes Old Spice cologne." Grinning, Scott crossed one foot over his knee and rocked back on the legs of his chair.

"Too much?"

"Well, just not my style. You're cool, Granpop. I never saw you wear that jacket before."

Suddenly doubtful, Jack asked, "Is it too old-fashioned?"

"Not for a guy your age."

"Just how old do you think I am, you young pup?"

A devilish gleam in his eye, Scott said, "Old enough to be my grandfather."

Jack playfully cuffed Scott on the back of his head and marched out the door. "Don't wait up," he called.

Scott yelled back, "Tell Kennie hi for me."

As he ate the last bite of his succulent steak at their candlelit table, Jack eyed the bottle of Cabernet Sauvignon and wondered if he should indulge in a third glass. He raised his eyebrows in a questioning glance at Kennocha. She nodded, and he refilled their glasses.

When Kennocha lifted the glass to her lips, the wide sleeve of her sheer jacket slid down to her elbow. Jack had never seen a more beautiful evening ensemble. The silky fabric of her slacks and sleeveless top seemed almost liquid, the way it flowed with her every movement. The color was perfect—a sea green that made Kennocha's eyes look the color of a deep alpine lake.

He felt good. Unlike his first date with her, this time he avoided possibly controversial subjects, like Scott's gay friends. Their conversation was light, even flirtatious at times. He felt more confident about her feelings for him. The evening had blown his budget, but he had no regrets.

Kennocha's next words dampened his euphoria.

"Have you talked with Scott about his essay?"

Mentally putting romance on hold, Jack said, "Yes, briefly. His father called a couple of weeks ago, demanding that Scott come home."

"Oh, no."

"Scott said he doesn't want to go. I told him I'd read his story and asked him to talk to me about it." Jack sighed. "He refused. Said I wouldn't believe him. I think he'll tell me later."

"When does he have to leave?"

"Vic said he'd let me know as soon as he wrapped up some deal he's working on at the bank. Knowing Vic, his demand might have been an impulsive decision influenced by alcohol. He might be having second thoughts by now. How long does it take to wrap up a deal? Maybe he'll save face by letting his son decide. Scott still tells me he won't go home."

Kennocha squeezed his hand. "You're a good grandfather, Jack."

A short time later, in Kennocha's apartment, they chatted while he watched her make coffee. She had removed the sheer jacket. She looked sensuous, irresistible. Jack took two coffee mugs out of the cupboard.

Kennocha finished her task, leaned back against the sink, and wiped her hands on a towel. Her eyes met his, and neither spoke. In two strides, he stood before her, leaned down, and gently kissed her. Encouraged by her warm response, he pulled her close and kissed her again. She wrapped her arms around him and returned his kisses. His pulse quickened.

For an instant, Jack felt guilty as he thought of Claire. He pushed her out of his mind. *This woman in my arms is the woman I love.*

They lingered through their next kisses, and Jack thought about nuzzling her neck. He didn't have a chance to pursue that thought.

Kennocha gave him a little smile and a gentle push. "I'll pour the coffee. Let's just talk."

Hoping she meant about them, their relationship, he asked, "About what?"

"Something safe." She chuckled. "I know, I'll make sundaes."

"At midnight?"

She dug in the freezer for the ice cream. "Sundaes are good anytime. Get some bowls down, would you, please?"

Jack rubbed his stomach, wondering if he could eat another bite. "Okay. A small one for me, please." He set the bowls on the counter and got out some spoons. "You and Scott are a pair. He can eat practically a whole pizza and still have room for ice cream."

An hour later, belly miserably full, sexual tensions eased but not forgotten, Jack said, "Now, I'd better go home." Kennocha walked him to the door. He took her face in his hands and lightly kissed her forehead, the tip of her nose, and then her lips. "Before my principles weaken."

About a week later, on Sunday evening, Jack, Kennocha, Scott, and Danny sat around Nikolas's kitchen table, eating his home-cooked fried chicken, mashed potatoes, and white gravy. Kennocha brought coleslaw and baked beans. Jack brought the dishwashers—Scott and Danny.

Nikolas licked his fingers one by one and examined them. Satisfied, he reached for another chicken thigh.

When the platter was passed to Jack, he declined. "One's enough for me. How about you, Danny? You've hardly eaten a bite."

"No, thanks, I'm not hungry."

Jack wondered if the boy felt well, but he resisted the urge to pry. He just wished Danny looked stronger.

Between bites, Nikolas asked, "Izsak has started you on a new project?"

Jack wiped his mustache on a napkin. "Wish it was a new project. Easier than what he wants me to do." He cleared his throat. "Seems that since I'm his oldest carver," he leaned toward Kennocha, "in seniority only, you understand, he wants me to do something in this anniversary fanfare."

Scott looked up from his plate. "What fanfare?"

Jack acquiesced to Nikolas, who waited until the ancient refrigerator concluded its start-up performance with a low whine, several chugs and rattles, then a steady, loud hum.

Nikolas plucked a chicken tidbit from his beard then said, "It is the fifth anniversary of the Carousel. It will be a fine celebration. You see," he addressed the teenagers, "we have—or very soon will have—completed three new ponies. That means three old ponies can come off the carousel and go into the shop for restoration. When we introduce a new pony, it is always an occasion. This year, we have three finished all at once." He held up a greasy finger. "Also, there will be—what do you call it—live music? A band—in the outdoor theater."

The boys' eyes lit up. "Yeah? Who?"

"That I do not know. But there will be many people and much food and much music."

Scott and Danny chorused, "Cool!"

"And," Nikolas continued, "we will introduce our new ponies. Is that where you come in, Jack?"

"Whatcha gonna do, Granpop?"

Jack mixed green peas into his mashed potatoes. "Izsak wants me to talk little bit. How I got involved in the Carousel. Don't know why anybody'd be interested in that."

Kennocha squeezed his arm. "I'm interested. Try it on us."

Encouraged, he thought a moment then began. "I'd kind of hit a slump in my life a few years ago. Up until then, after I retired, I'd been busy with carving small animals and birds. Even thought about starting a new career. The fellow who owns Hellgate Gallery invited me to do a showing. People liked my stuff, especially the birds." Jack paused. "But after a while, I just didn't care anymore." Jack paused again, unsure of how much to say.

Nikolas picked up the story. "But someone remembered the quail ..."

"Yes," Jack continued, "old Harry down at the lumberyard. He'd seen the quail family—"

Scott interjected, "The ones Mom has on our mantel at home?"

Jack nodded.

"They're really cool. Everybody likes those, Granpop."

Jack's eyes met Kennocha's. Yes, she had noticed, too. Scott's spontaneous mention of his mother and home was like a tiny crack in the door to his vault of silence about his home life.

"Harry knew Izsak," Jack continued, "and when Izsak told him about his dream for a city carousel, Harry told him about me. Izsak came by to see me one day. Invited me to take a look at what he'd started in his garage. In those days, that's all there was—Izsak's dream and one half-finished pony in his garage. In fact, there wasn't even a park by the river. That all came later." Jack pushed his plate away. "I took one look at the pony Izsak had going, and my fingers itched to get out my pocketknife. I agreed to help make his dream come true."

Danny asked, "Had you ever carved horses before?"

"Just a couple small ones, when I was a kid. Birds were my forte."

"You needed a new challenge," Kennocha said.

"A few months after I got involved, two other guys joined us. Pretty soon we had three or four ponies coming to life in Izsak's garage."

Kennocha smiled. "And you had something to look forward to every day."

Jack nodded. "Little kids in Izsak's neighborhood used to come over and watch me carve. Full of questions, excited about having a merry-go-round. Some of them told their teacher, and she got them going on a fund-raising project. Pennies for Ponies, they called it. The newspaper did a story on it. Then the townspeople started sending in donations. Everything snowballed after that. The city got involved and set aside that piece of land for a park. An architect and a local builder donated their services. Lumberyards and hardware stores donated supplies. Izsak's dream of Riverfront Park Carousel became a reality."

Scott asked, "How about you, Nikolas, did you start when Granpop did?"

"No, I am almost a newcomer to the Carousel."

"First," Jack said, "I had to convince him he could carve something besides roast beef and turkey."

"I am only just learning to carve a pony on my own. In the old days, when I was young, I helped my father build furniture. I would have no problem if horses looked like desks or tables." He reached for a chicken wing.

Jack chuckled. "Or food."

CHAPTER 24

One morning when rain streaked the windows and clouds hung low with no promise of sunshine, Jack tackled a job he'd been putting off. He boxed up all of Claire's clothes in their closet and in her dresser. After Claire's funeral, Marah had offered to pack up her mother's things and donate them to charity, but Jack couldn't bear to part with them. Until now.

When he came to the drawer with her nightclothes, he hesitated. Kneeling on the floor by the drawer, he scooped up her nightgowns and inhaled. *I used to think I could smell Claire's perfume, but these things just smell dusty now.*

Thinking about his recent dinner date with Kennocha and his sensual stirrings at her apartment afterward, Jack recalled his guilty feelings, as though he were betraying Claire. *I've finally met a woman I love, but Claire stands in the way. Nikolas is right; it's time to let go.*

He pulled out the drawers and dumped their entire contents—nightgowns and underclothes—into a box with other clothing destined for the thrift shop. A weight lifted off his shoulders. He started to close the lid, but something black and lacy caught his eye. *What's this? Bikini underpants? Lace brassieres?* He pulled out matching undergarments in red and black. *Claire hadn't worn underwear like this since our honeymoon. When did she buy them? For our twentieth anniversary? But she didn't wear them. Why? I thought she was happy during our anniversary getaway.* He sighed. *I'll never know.* He dropped the garments into the box, closed it, and started on the next drawer.

Finished with Claire's things, Jack eyed his own side of the closet. *Yes, it's time to get rid of some of my old clothes. The ones Claire used to complain about, saying they made me look old. Even Scott said so a while back.*

By the time he finished in the bedroom, he had packed six boxes for charity and had vacuumed every inch of the closet, floor, and dresser drawers. Then he dusted off the furniture and removed the dust catchers—Claire's jewelry boxes, perfume bottles, and framed photos, including one of herself. The one of Claire went into his dresser drawer. The remainder, he put in a separate box for Marah to go through.

Miss Lavender wandered in and sniffed at the boxes.

"What d'you think, Missy? Did I overdo it?" Purring, the cat rubbed his ankles. "No, I did right. It was time." The cat arched her back, begging for a scratching. Jack obliged. "Know what I'll do? Get myself some new clothes. A couple of shirts, a pair of pants, maybe even some new shoes." He chuckled, recalling Kennocha's apartment. "Or cowboy boots."

With several hours before Scott arrived home, Jack resolved to finish the job. The cat curled up on his bed before he went down the hall and entered Claire's sewing room. Jack had never seen the cat in that room, which always seemed odd to him. Miss Lavender made herself at home in all the other rooms—except Marah's—since Claire died. *Strange. Well, that's a cat for you.*

He walked into the sewing room. *This will be easier. Or will it? Claire slept in the bedroom, but this is where she spent most of her time at home. Her room. Pretty much off limits to me and the kids.* He switched on the small portable radio beside her sewing machine. Bach's "Toccata in D Minor" slithered into the room. Jack muttered, "That's all I need. Haunted house music." He tuned into a country music station and heard Randy Travis singing about digging up bones. "Might say I'm burying bones, not digging them up."

He hadn't been in this room since Marah had sat here and tearfully recounted her childhood experiences. He still had difficulty believing Claire could have been so cruel. He put the recollection out of his mind.

Humming along with Randy Travis, Jack quickly emptied the shelves, filling boxes with folds of fabrics, patterns, and sewing paraphernalia. He'd put these in the attic and ask Marah if she wanted to through them before he gave them away. He'd already asked Paul, Lynne, and the girls. He set aside the two pincushions the girls remembered. He'd mail those and anything else they might want. Lynne was creative, too, but her gift was in painting.

As his work progressed, Jack considered what to do with the room now. *Could let Scott make it into a hangout for him and his friends ... Keep the boys here on the main floor. They could play their stereos, and maybe we'll haul the old television out of storage in the garage. No, I should take that old TV to the dump. I'll talk to Scott. Could buy him a new one, but if he helps pay for it, he'll appreciate it more. Take some ownership in this room.* The more he thought about it, the better he liked the idea. He'd let Scott have a say in how to furnish it, even let him paint it if he wanted to. He glanced at the pale pink walls. Yes, he'd want to paint it.

Long after the radio played several more tunes, "Diggin' Up Bones" still ran through Jack's mind when he sat down at Claire's sewing cabinet and pulled open the top drawer. He found it filled with bobbins and spools of thread. He dumped them into a box. The next drawer held a tracing wheel and paper, gauges, and other sewing tools. He added them to the box.

The third, and last, drawer revealed sewing how-to books. At the bottom, he found a spiral notebook filled with Claire's handwriting, the letters so perfectly formed it was almost as if she'd drawn them. His heart skipped a beat, seeing her familiar handwriting. As he stared at the script, a flash of longing and loneliness swept through him. He pushed it away and began leafing through the book.

He'd had no idea she kept such a careful record of her sewing projects, every entry dated. It began with an Easter outfit she'd made for Paul when he was just a year old. Jack remembered the suit. Sapphire blue, matching shorts, vest, and bow tie. Claire had made herself a dress from the same fabric. He'd taken a snapshot of them that Easter Sunday. He'd felt like the happiest man on earth.

Jack paged through the notebook entries, reading here and there, thinking Marah might like to have it for a keepsake. Curtains, pillow covers, more clothes for Paul. Dresses, skirts, and blouses for herself. Claire had included detailed descriptions of the articles and the fabrics, the substitutions, and alterations she made for each project. She'd glued small fabric swatches by each set of notes.

Recalling photos of Marah as a child he still kept in his billfold, Jack expected to find entries about the dresses Claire had made for their daughter. One of his favorite snapshots was of chubby Marah at age two in a yellow sundress, her dark hair curling around her face.

But Claire's record stopped about a year before Marah was born. After that, nothing but blank pages. *Wait, here's more toward the back. Odd that she would have skipped all those pages.* Jack located the first entry of this section, dated some forty years ago, and began reading.

January 6—I would never have planned this to happen, but now that it has, I believe it must be Fate. I feel so alive and beautiful. He lavishes me with gifts like I've never

175

seen before. Perfume and jewelry and bras and panties. I giggle as I write that. No man has ever given me such intimate things before. Especially not Mr. Practical Jack. They're very sexy. Of course, I have to hide them.

I know it's wrong, but it's so exciting. I'll do this just for a little while to break the monotony of my life, then I'll stop. I get so tired, trying to keep up the house, take care of a four-year-old, cook, wash, and iron. It's so boring. Jack never takes me out on dates. But *he* makes me feel exciting and desirable.

Stunned, Jack lowered the book to his lap. He stared at the rain drizzling down the windowpanes. The radio blared on, unheard. He thought about the date of the entry, a time he'd tried to forget. *Paul was four years old. That was around the time she supposedly went to visit her aunt, extended stays. Then finally, Aunt Maggie called and told me her suspicions about what Claire was doing behind my back. Aunt Maggie was right.*

He picked up the book, thumbed the back pages, and set it down again. *Claire's secret diary. She never told me the man's name. She's dead. Do I want to know?* He turned the radio off and opened the book again.

January 10—He's arranged a clever way for us to meet. He goes out of town on business trips quite frequently, so no one is suspicious. Aunt Maggie is getting old and frail, so I will visit her more often, especially since she's my only living relative. No one will think that odd. He'll get a hotel room, and I'll stay with Aunt Maggie. It'll be easy to get around her. I'm so anxious to set our plan in motion, I can hardly wait. Paul will be fine with Martha while Jack's at work. I'll only be gone a day or two at a time. I suppose I should take Paul along sometimes. He'll be okay with Aunt Maggie after I put him to bed.

January 25—Heavenly! How else can I describe it? A secret rendezvous! I feel like Ingrid Bergman.

January 26—I'm so in love with him, and I know he must love me the same way. I dream of spending the rest of my life with him. Is it possible? Is this what Fate has in mind for us?

March 13—He wants me to leave Jack. He says he can't continue these trips. He hasn't exactly said he wants to marry me, but surely he does. He said he'd get a divorce after I divorce Jack. I'm so confused. How can I love him and Jack, too? For I do; I still love Jack. And what about Paul? I can't leave my little boy. Jack would never allow me to take him. Oh, Fate, you are so cruel!

March 21—I'm so mad at Aunt Maggie! She had no right to interfere! Now Jack wants an answer. He's furious, of course. I don't know what to do. I told him I need some time to think.

My lover hasn't called. He always calls after our secret meetings. Could Jack have found out who he is? Would Jack confront him? What would my love do? Would he declare his feelings for me, tell Jack he's going to take me away?

March 23—I saw him today with another woman! I wanted to scream and scratch her face until it bled! How could I hope to compete with her? She's so glamorous! I ran away before he could see me. I'm so miserable, I want to die!

May 5—How could you do this to me, Fate? I don't deserve this! I missed my second period in a row. I have to talk to him. Surely he'll want to see me again, knowing this. It's his, of course. I'm frightened but excited, too. We'll have a whole new life. I'll have a beautiful home and a wardrobe of expensive clothes. Paul and this baby will have the best of everything.

May 20—I hate him! How could he do this to me? He was angry that I called him at work, and he was cold toward me when we met in the park. I thought he'd warm up when I told him I had a surprise. But he didn't care. He said he's finished with me! Finished! I asked him if it was that other woman, but he just gave me a disgusted look and walked away. Like I mean nothing to him! I hope Richard DeWolfe Junior drops dead!

A dagger struck Jack's chest. *Richard DeWolfe!* Bile filled his throat. He got up, threw the notebook down, and kicked a box across the floor, spilling spools of thread and bobbins. He slammed his fist into the wall, rubbed his stinging knuckles, and paced back and forth across the room before he dropped into the chair, elbows on knees, and clasped his head.

Suddenly he bolted upright.

Marah! She said DeWolfe had made a pass at her when she worked at the store. She told Claire, and he quit bothering her after that. Marah thought I took care of DeWolfe. But Claire never told me. So what happened? Claire must have confronted him herself. Did she tell him he'd made a pass at his own daughter? No, she couldn't have. Claire and I vowed we'd never tell anyone our secret.

Jack's stomach roiled.

But I never believed my wife would ever cheat on me, either. Especially not with that unscrupulous snake DeWolfe.

Driven by anger, Jack quickly finished packing up Claire's things. He carried the portable sewing machine and boxes up to the storage area under the eaves of the roof and shoved them into the farthest, darkest corner.

Only the notebook remained.

He took it to his workshop, opened the door to the woodstove, and tore out page after page of the secret diary, crumpling them so they'd burn quickly. The book slid off his lap and landed on the cement floor. When he picked it up, a folded square of paper fell out. Jack started to toss it into the firebox, but curiosity and a tiny flicker of hope forced him to unfold it. He read: "It's a girl. I'm going to name her Marah— 'bitter.' God has dealt bitterly with me, allowing this baby to be born. My life is cursed."

Jack shivered even though he sat beside a blazing stove. His fingers felt stiff and cold. "Oh, God," he moaned, "dear God ..." He closed his eyes, remembering Marah telling him that Claire had threatened to shut her in a closet and had deliberately broken Marah's favorite doll.

Jack crumpled the paper into a tight ball and pitched it into the stove. He watched it burn. Then he threw the entire notebook into the firebox, nearly smothering the flame. He jabbed at the book with the poker, opened the damper, and blew on the coals until the flames licked at the edges of the sheets, slowly scorching them from golden brown to gray ash.

As the record of Claire's sins burned, he groaned and whispered the terrible truth gripping his mind. "Claire hated Marah ... and Marah came to hate her ... and now, Marah has become a stranger. God, what's going to happen to her?"

Chapter 25

Scott slammed his locker door shut and leaned his back against it. He propped the sole of one shoe against the metal door, like he'd seen other guys do. He glanced up and down the hall, looking for Danny in the swarm of students heading home for the day. Karl and one of his sidekicks went by and made obscene gestures at Scott, being careful not to get caught by the principal. Scott pretended he didn't see them. Smells of corn chips, red licorice, and sweat mingled with the girls' perfume. He couldn't wait for summer break. Other than the jerks, he felt invisible. But he didn't mind too much. He turned and pulled his math book out of the locker and had just reached for his backpack when he heard a girl's voice.

"Hi, Scott."

A tall, slender girl with long, blond hair waved to him from the edge of the throng. It was Eileen, the girl from Nikolas's church he'd met at Easter service. He was surprised that she'd noticed him. He waved back as she swept by and disappeared.

Finally, Danny arrived and dropped his loaded backpack on the floor with a huge sigh. "Hey, Scotty. Let's go to 93 Stop-n-Go and get some lemonade, okay?"

"Yeah, but I have to get home pretty soon. Big algebra test tomorrow." He pulled his backpack out of his locker, stuffed in his algebra book along with his science and English books, and hoisted the bag over his shoulder. His friend seemed to be having trouble lifting his book bag. "Do you want me to carry that?"

Danny lifted his bag onto his shoulders with a grunt. Panting slightly, he said, "I got it. Let's go."

They reached Danny's black Mustang in the school parking lot and threw their bags onto the backseat. While Danny drove, Scott tuned in the radio and rolled down his window He looked at Danny. His friend looked pale.

"Are you okay?"

Danny turned off South Avenue onto Brooks Street. As they pulled into the drive-in, he said, "I had an AIDS test. I'm HIV-positive."

"No way!" Scott's whole body suddenly felt tingly, like he'd stuck his finger into a light socket. "AIDS?"

"No. The doctor says it could be years before I get it, and maybe never. He says they're learning more about it all the time. Developing new medicines, stuff like that. He says I need to take care of myself, eat good, exercise, stay healthy. And abstain."

"But, condoms …"

"Condoms don't guarantee anything. Think about it." Danny drove forward to place their order. "Want anything to eat?"

Scott shook his head. "I lost my appetite." He slumped against the door and stared out the window.

Danny ordered two large lemonades and eased alongside the pick-up window. After they got their order, he turned onto Brooks Street and headed for a city park in the university area. Five minutes later, he pulled into a parking space away from the playground. In the distance, they heard little kids screaming and laughing. A pleasant breeze drifted through the car.

Scott asked, "How did you know what doctor to go to?"

"I went to my grandparents' doctor. I've been to him before. He's a good old guy."

"Did you tell him you're gay?"

"I think he knew anyway. I went to him because I had a rash I couldn't get rid of. He said he wanted to test me for the AIDS virus. But it was okay, y'know? He didn't make me feel uncomfortable or anything."

Scott crimped the edge of his paper cup. "I guess this means I should get tested, too."

"Yeah."

"I don't know any doctors. I can't ask Granpop."

"You can go to the county health clinic. Not far from your place. I told my doctor about you. Not your name or anything. He said you can be tested anonymously at this clinic. It costs ten dollars, or it's free if you don't have any money. The place is called Partnership Health Care Center. You gotta do it, Scotty. Doc says the sooner, the better. They can't cure AIDS, but they can treat it, he says. If they catch it in time."

Scott heard Danny, but his words weren't sinking in. He felt like they were discussing a movie. "I just never thought it would happen to us."

"I know. I couldn't believe it either."

"Do your grandparents know?"

Danny hung his head. "Yeah. It was hard, telling them. Doc offered to do it, but I knew I had to tell them myself. My grandmother cried. My grandfather looked like he'd seen a ghost, and he didn't say anything at first. Then he stood up real straight, like he does when nobody's supposed to argue with him." Danny imitated his grandfather's austere voice and said, "'We will do whatever is necessary to take care of you. We will spare no expense.'" Danny's shoulders slumped. "In the end, it's always about money with my grandfather."

"At least they didn't throw you out, like Marco's parents."

Danny's head jerked up, and he stared at Scott. "They did? When?"

"I saw Marco in the mall one day not too long after he was at my house that night. We got to talking about what happened to him, those church guys wanting to heal him. He said after they left, his parents told him to get out and not to come back until he 'confessed his sins and repented.' They called it 'tough love.' Marco hasn't seen them since. He said he thinks about killing himself. He really misses his parents." Scott stared out the window at the laughing kids on the merry-go-round. "If Granpop knew I'm gay, he'd kick me out."

"No way. He really loves you, Scotty. Anybody can see that. But do you think Marco meant it … about killing himself?"

"I dunno. He didn't act like he was thinking about suicide now, but I think he did after his parents threw him out." He sighed. "As for Granpop, he's said enough about Marco that I know he'd hate me if he knew I'm gay. What if I get tested at this Partnership place and it turns out I'm positive, too? What if I get AIDS? Where am I gonna go?"

"What about your parents? Have you told them yet that you're gay?"

"No. Dad called again the other night. Mom keeps talking him out of telling me to come home. Now he thinks I should when school's out. But he'd change his mind fast if he knew."

"What did your grandfather say about you going back to Boise?"

"Not much he can do about it, really. Like he said, he has no legal right to say what happens to me. He doesn't want me to go, and I don't want to leave him, but he can't stop my dad from trying." Scott frowned. "Granpop can't stop him, but I can. No way am I ever going back home. I'll run away again, get a job someplace. Camp out until I can save up enough to rent an apartment."

"Promise you'll never do that without telling me first."

"Yeah, okay. I promise."

"And promise you'll get the AIDS test, Scotty."

Scott watched a robin hop across the lawn, pecking for grasshoppers in the tender young grass. Springtime. New life growing everywhere. In sharp contrast, worry of disease and death. "I don't know what good it would do," he said. "It could just make things worse if I'm positive or if I have AIDS."

"But Scotty, Doc says the earlier they catch it, the better."

"Yeah, I know. Okay, I'll get it." Scott threw his empty cup into a nearby trash can. "Let's talk about something else."

Danny started the car and pulled onto the street. After he passed through the intersection, he said, "I want to ask you a really big favor."

Scott arched an eyebrow. "What?"

"I've been thinking about what I want to do with the rest of my life. I want to help other kids. Tell them how *not* to get AIDS. Tell them it can happen to them. And I want to tell them God loves them, no matter what." He paused a beat. "It's a sin, Scotty. I really believe that now. Same-sex relations are a sin."

"Oh, come off it." Scott snorted. "You find out you're positive, and now you think it's a sin. You've got no choice about the genes you're born with."

"That's just it. I don't think it's in our genes. Well, maybe the tendency is, but we can decide not to go that way. Just like you and your dad. Remember, you told me you hoped you didn't inherit his alcoholism genes, but even if you did, you'd never let yourself become an alcoholic. I think it's the same with homosexuality. And I didn't just start believing this. I've been thinking about it for a long time. Well, for the past few months anyway."

Scott pondered. "What are you gonna tell these kids? The ones you want to help? What kids are you talking about? Kids in our school?"

"I want to start with the youth group, the one I go to at Nikolas's church. My church, too, now." Danny stopped for three elementary school kids crossing the street and glanced at his friend. "Would you help me? Talk to the kids in my group?"

Scott studied him. "You really want to tell people?"

Danny nodded. "Yeah. I want something good to come from all this."

"You talk like you're gonna get AIDS and die. You told me just because you're HIV-positive doesn't mean you're gonna get AIDS. I think you're overreacting, Danny. And besides, what about your grandparents?"

"I told them my idea. My grandmother was against it at first and worried about her friends finding out. But my grandfather approved. I was pretty surprised. He was a lot more open-minded than I expected. He said he'd made some dumb mistakes in his life, too, and he regretted he hadn't redeemed himself. That's what he said, 'redeemed.' He thinks this is, like, my chance to make up for some things I've done wrong. He got my grandmother to go along with it."

Scott mulled this over. "Sure a lot of stuff you haven't told me. What would you want me to do? I don't know about getting involved with some church … look at Marco."

Face flushed, voice urgent, Danny said, "Not all churches are like that. Not Nikolas's and my church. The preacher's a good guy. Like regular, y'know? Not the religious type, y'know? He knows about me, and he doesn't treat me any different from anybody else. In youth group, everybody just hangs out. We have a lot of fun." He glanced at Scott. "What are you laughing about? You should come and see for yourself."

Grinning, Scott said, "Do you know what you just said? You said the minister isn't the religious type."

Momentarily, Danny looked confused, then he understood. Both boys burst out laughing. As though to break the tension of their conversation, they laughed harder and longer than the joke deserved.

Finally, Scott settled down. "I guess I might come to your youth group. Just to see what it's like. But what about this idea of yours? What d'you want me to do?"

"Help me make a presentation. Write out what to say. You're on the debate team. You're good at this stuff. If you'd help me do that, I'll get up and do the talking. Once I get started, I can do it. If I have something to read from, y'know?"

Scott snorted. "That's a good way to put everyone to sleep. You can't read it, Danny. You gotta give a gut-level talk. Like it's one-on-one. If I was them, that's what I'd want."

Danny looked at him and grinned. "See? You're helping already. I never thought about it that way. You're right."

"Okay, I'll help you write up some notes. But I still think you're overreacting."

On Monday, Scott rode his bike to the county health office Danny had mentioned. The day was cool, but his palms were sweaty. He worried everyone would stare at him and somehow know he'd come for an AIDS test.

Inside the office, phones rang every few seconds, clerks hustled here and there, with papers in hand and brows wrinkled. Voices sounded dissonant and impersonal. No one gave Scott a second glance as he got in line to register. People of just about all ages filled the room but mostly young mothers with little kids. A couple of old guys. One or two guys a little older than Scott. *Are they here for AIDS testing?*

A half hour later, he was on his bike pedaling for home. The nurse who'd taken his blood was polite and businesslike. She didn't ask his name, but she'd given him a case number and told him to come back in a week for the results. The state speech meet started on Wednesday. Overnight trip. That would help burn up the time. Tough competition. He'd concentrate on his presentations for the meet.

Tuesday night, Scott tossed a duffel bag on his bed and began laying out the clothes he'd need in Helena. He heard a rustling noise. "Kitty, get out of there." Only the tip of Miss Lavender's twitching, gray and white tail poked out of the blue nylon bag.

Jack came into the room. "How's it going?"

"Great. One pair of undershorts, one pair of socks, and one pesky cat." Scott arranged his jacket, white shirt, and tie on a hanger. "I have to wear this stuff for each of my events." He gestured toward a white dress shirt still in its cellophane package. "If I make it to finals, I'll put on the new shirt you bought me."

"What do you mean, 'if'? You'll make it. Then when you go to regionals, we'll get you a new suit. And I'll tag along."

Scott screwed up his face. "Better wait 'til I get there, Granpop." He zipped up the duffel bag, leaving a small opening. The bulge inside the bag moved. A pink nose and white whiskers emerged, followed by a white paw. Then the cat's head popped through as the zipper gave way. Miss Lavender gave Scott an indignant look, leaped out, and darted from the room as Scott and Jack laughed.

At six o'clock the next morning, a car pulled up in front of the house.

"They're here, Granpop. Mr. Meyers and the other kids. Gotta go."

Jack gave him a handshake and a hug. "I'd say good luck, but you don't need luck. You have brains and skill. You'll do well."

"Yeah, I hope. Bye, Granpop."

After the speech meet, Mr. Meyers dropped Scott off at home Thursday night. Scott had no sooner walked in the door when he rushed to the phone to call Danny.

Jack objected. "Hey, hold on here. How about the speech meet? How'd you do?"

Scott paused, phone in hand. "Blew it. Placed third."

"Third place? I wouldn't call that blowing it."

"I didn't make regionals." He punched in Danny's number and pretended not to see the disappointed expression on his grandfather's face as he turned away and went outside. He knew Granpop wanted to talk about the meet, but he had to find out about Danny.

The answering machine clicked on at Danny's number. He hung up without leaving a message, went upstairs, and threw his bag on the bed, startling the cat.

"Hey, kitty, I'm sorry." He sat down on the bed and patted his lap. "C'mere." When she rubbed against his arm, he picked her up. "It's Danny, kitty. I'm scared something's happened to him. Some of the kids said his grandfather got him out of school early Wednesday. Somebody said he was taking Danny to a hospital somewhere." His arms tightened around the cat. "What if he has AIDS now? I don't want him to die."

Miss Lavender pushed herself away from Scott's grasp and sat down on the bed to smooth her fur. Scott jumped up and ran downstairs to try calling Danny again. Still no one home. He slammed down the receiver and ran out to the garage.

Jack sat at his workbench, refining the miniature horse carving. He watched Scott get his bicycle. "Where are you going?"

"Danny's house."

"It'll be dark by the time you get there. Better just call him, son."

Scott fidgeted. "All I get is their answering machine."

Jack set down his carving knife. "Now wait a minute. If they're not home, why do you want to go over there?"

"Maybe they're outside or something." Scott leaned a shoulder on the door frame. He felt his grandfather's eyes still on him, waiting. "Some kids said they heard Danny was in the hospital."

"Accident? Or is he sick?"

"No—well, I don't know. They didn't know."

"Maybe it's a false rumor."

"Yeah, maybe ... I guess."

Jack picked up his carving knife and went back to work. "You'd better wait and call him again tomorrow."

After a moment, Scott said, "Okay." *But Granpop,* he wanted to say, *Danny might have AIDS.* Would Granpop freak out? What if he told him about his own AIDS test?

CHAPTER 26

Sunday evening Jack and Kennocha locked up the Carousel and walked along the river holding hands. They found a bench flanked by willows with mahogany-colored bark, the plump buds ready to burst open any day. They sat down to watch two bright yellow kayaks zigzagging around some large rocks. The energetic young men whooped as water splashed over them. After they passed by, Jack pulled Kennocha close and stroked her cheek.

Kennocha planted a kiss at each end of his mustache. "How did Scott do at the speech meet?"

"Pretty good. He got third place. I thought he'd be disappointed he didn't qualify for regionals, but he was more worried about Danny than anything. He'd heard from some other kids that Danny was in the hospital. That turned out to be a false rumor. Scott had ants in his pants all weekend until he finally talked to Danny today. The boy's grandparents had taken him to Seattle or Salt Lake City or someplace for a few days."

"Hmm. I heard his grandparents took him out of school early Wednesday. I also heard they took him to San Francisco for a medical evaluation."

"Scott didn't say Danny was sick. I heard Scott talking on the phone, and it sounded more like a fun trip from what I overheard. But I didn't stick around. If Danny's grandparents took him for some kind of medical evaluation, I'm glad to hear it. The boy's too thin and frail looking."

Kennocha stared at the river with a faraway gaze. Then she stirred and asked, "Have you heard any more from Vic or Marah about taking Scott back home?"

"No. I'm relieved and hoping they'll let it go. But at the same time, I wish Scott had a good home and stable parents. It would be hard to give him up, but I worry about the friends he's made here."

"You mean Marco and Danny?"

Jack nodded. "Danny seems like a good kid, but sometimes I suspect he's homosexual. And I'm sure Marco is. I gave up ordering Scott to stay away from him. Marco is strange, but there's something likeable about him, too."

She had tensed under his arm. "Kids make their own choices in friends. With our knowledge or not. As for being gay, well, it turns out that maybe they don't have a choice."

"Of course they have a choice. You don't go along with that ridiculous argument they're touting nowadays, do you, that they might be born that way?"

She pulled away and faced him. "Jack, new studies have shown—"

"Nothing. They've shown nothing conclusive. I read the newspapers. Bunch of nonsense. It's a matter of right or wrong."

Her eyes flashed. "How can you say that? Why would anyone *choose* to be gay? Why risk AIDS? Why risk losing your family? Do you know how many gays and lesbians are kicked out of their homes when they tell? And then there's the harassment. It's got to be a miserable existence. Who'd ever deliberately put themselves in such a situation?"

Jack folded his arms across his chest. "There's not a person alive who doesn't have some kind of temptation to face. Okay, so maybe some are more prone than others to want to experiment. But that doesn't mean you go ahead and do it. Let it become a lifestyle. Those people *should* feel uncomfortable. They *should* worry that their families might disown them. What they do is disgusting. They're perverts."

Kennocha jumped up, stood with hands on hips, and glared at him. "I can't believe you're saying this. Even if they're not born that way, everyone has a right to make his or her own choices. Including sexual choices."

Jack was befuddled. "How can we disagree on such a basic issue? Men shouldn't have sex with men. Nor women with women. It's indecent. Morally wrong. Why would you go along with this?"

She glared at him. "You make it sound like I personally engage in same-sex encounters. Let me make this very clear. I don't. I thought you knew me better than that."

"Kennocha, please. I never thought you did anything like that." He stood and reached for her hand, but she backed away. "Please, sweetheart, let's not argue about this."

The flame in her eyes slowly faded. "Okay. We'll drop it. For now. But we clearly have some differences of opinion on basic issues. What else might there be?" She rubbed the back of her neck. "I'm tired. I'm going home."

"I'll walk with you."

"I'd rather be alone. Good-bye, Jack." She turned abruptly and began jogging away.

Jack watched her leave, despairing the possibility that she'd never want to see him again. He should've known better than to bring up that homosexual thing again. *But dammit, what's right is right and what's wrong is wrong. And homosexuality is wrong. Why can't she see that?*

CHAPTER 27

Monday, Scott couldn't get away from school until almost four thirty. He hurried to unlock his bike from the rack so he could get to the county health office before it closed.

He raced in high gear, pumping hard, dodging the mass exodus of cars and pickups leaving the high school parking lot. He zigzagged through traffic, cut across streets, and dodged pedestrians.

When he coasted up to the health office, he shoved his bike into a rack and dashed to the door. Locked. His watch showed five minutes after five. He pounded on the door.

"Hey! Anybody here?"

He peered through the glass. No lights on. No sign of life. He looked around outside. No cars in the parking lot.

His armpits felt sticky, and he stunk. His head hurt. He tried the door one more time and then gave it such a savage kick he thought he broke his toe. He limped to the rack, jerked his bike out, and pushed it along the sidewalk, eyes downcast, fighting tears of frustration.

CHAPTER 28

The same day, Jack had walked to the Carousel and spent a few hours in the workshop. When he walked home, his route took him past the county health office, on the opposite side of the street. His stride slowed at the sight of a teenager kicking the front door of the building. Jack stared. *Scott? What's he doing here?* He waited for three cars to go by. Then he dashed across the street. "Scott!"

Scott whirled, wide-eyed. "Granpop! Where did you come from?"

"The Carousel. I'm heading home now. I'll walk with you. Let's cut over a couple blocks and get off this busy street." Scott pushed his bike, lagging behind. Jack waited for him to catch up. "I saw you kick the door at the county health office," Jack said. "What's going on?"

Head down, Scott's bangs half covered his face. "I had a blood test."

All the fears Jack had kept buried, refusing them voice, rushed at him. His knees felt weak. *Blood test. AIDS. Kennocha suspected something. She was trying to tell me, but I didn't want to hear it.* "I'd have come with you, son. You don't have to do this alone." They walked a few steps in silence. "Was it for AIDS?"

The boy shot a wide-eyed look at his grandfather. "Yeah. HIV test."

Jack replayed Kennocha's words in his mind: *"Why would anyone choose to be gay?"* But this boy can't have been born homosexual. I've known him all his life. He's my grandson. Jack's temples throbbed. He saw the fear in Scott's eyes. He remembered Nikolas insisting, *"God loves everyone. None of us has the right to condemn others."* But I'm not condemning him; I just want to set him straight. For the first time, a tiny sliver of doubt entered Jack's soul. *Am I stepping out of bounds?* He recalled Nikolas's warning: *"Be careful."* He took a deep breath. "Son, I admit I'm having a tough time with this. You're young. You're—" He swallowed hard, feeling as though he suddenly had something stuck in his throat. He swallowed again and forced out the next words. "You're experimenting. You'll get over it." The words sounded phony in his ears. His knees felt weak.

Scott shook his head and wiped his cheeks and nose with the back of his hand.

Approaching a city park, Jack steered him toward a bench. "Let's sit down. My knees feel a little wobbly." He sank onto the wooden seat and closed his eyes for a few seconds in a silent prayer for help. *God, help me. I don't know what to say."*

Elbows on knees, chin in hand, Scott sat staring at the ground beneath his feet.

Finally, Jack asked, "Want to talk about it?"

Sobbing, Scott buried his face in his hands.

Jack dug in his pocket, pulled out a clean handkerchief, and handed it to him.

"I'm scared, Granpop. Scared you're gonna kick me out, and—" He sniffed and wiped his eyes with the handkerchief. "And Danny tested positive."

A chill swept through Jack's body. "He has AIDS?"

"No. But he could get it. He's HIV-positive." Scott twisted the handkerchief into a knot. "That's why it scared me when I heard he was sick." His knuckles turned white. "And besides, since he's HIV-positive ... I could be, too."

Ice coursed down Jack's spine. "You mean you and Danny have been—" The words stuck in his throat. He knew the answer. He rubbed the back of his neck. "When did you have the blood test?"

"Last week. Before I went to the speech meet. I couldn't get out of school in time today to get the results. The office was closed when I got there."

Two young boys wearing roller blades raced by on the sidewalk, yelling and laughing. Jack waited until they passed. "I want to understand this, Scott. How did you ... decide you're gay?" The words felt foreign coming out of his mouth.

"I've always been different from other guys. I never felt like I have to prove how tough I am, show off for the girls, stuff like that. I like girls, I guess, but they're just ordinary friends. But I'd play along, pretend girls turned me on, too. But they didn't, really." The handkerchief submitted to further twisting and tying. "Then I met this guy in Boise, at school, right after we moved there. Larry is like me. Different. He understands how I feel. I've never been able to talk to anyone like that before. Someone who, like, understands. We got to be good friends. Larry was with me when Mom—" Abruptly, Scott stopped.

Across the street, a man mowed a strip of lawn alongside his house. The roar of the motor faded away as he worked his way toward the back of his yard, away from the street.

"What about your mother?"

"Nothing." Scott picked at the knots he'd tied in the handkerchief. "Then after I ran away from home, I didn't care. About anything. Came here, met Danny and Marco. Danny's my best friend."

Some part of Jack's mind heard the mower's return trip, the robins chirping in the trees above him, and children squealing on the playground behind them. Ordinary sounds filtering through a very strange conversation. From the corner of his eye, he saw Scott looking at him.

"Granpop? It's not fun, being different. Sometimes I feel like a freak. And some of the guys make wisecracks. Or they act like I've got sewer breath. Or they try to pick fights. But I can't help who I am. Please don't kick me out."

Jack struggled with deep disappointment, revulsion, and anger. At the same time, seeing the misery in Scott's eyes, he wanted to protect him from pain. And from AIDS. *How soon does a person develop AIDS after they've tested positive?* He recalled things he'd read or seen on television. *Years later? Maybe never?* He fought despair. *So young. Why do they risk disease and death—for this?* "When did Danny find out he's HIV-positive?"

"Maybe a month ago."

Jack's mouth dropped open. "You waited this long to get yourself checked?"

Scott shrugged. "We never thought we'd get infected. We were careful." He groaned. "I'm sorry, Granpop. This is hard, talking to you about this stuff."

A long silence ensued. A heavy load settled on Jack's shoulders. "I'm an old man, Scott. I've seen or heard just about everything you can imagine. Homosexuality isn't new." He drew in a deep breath and continued, "You said you were careful. Condoms?"

"Yeah." Scott scowled. "But I don't know about Danny before I met him."

Jack waited, dreading worse news.

Scott continued. "I'm kinda mad at Danny. He didn't, like, level with me, y'know? I mean, Danny had told me before that this guy Stanley in California was like an uncle to him. Danny wants to go visit him this summer, but his grandfather won't let him go because he doesn't like Stanley. So I don't think he's really like an uncle. Y'know, like my uncle. Uncle Paul is great."

Jack's fists clenched. *Danny's grandfather probably has good reason to dislike the guy. He's probably the reason the boy's sick.* "How'd Danny meet this guy?"

"He was a friend of Danny's parents. Lived with them, or something like that. He took care of Danny after they were killed in a car accident, until his grandparents got custody of him. After that, Danny's grandfather told Stanley to stay away."

"How old was Danny when his parents were killed?"

"Six, I think. Or eight. Can't remember exactly."

"Did the grandparents get custody right away?"

"Guess it took a long time. I think Danny was in junior high when his grandparents brought him here to live. Y'know, Granpop, they didn't even know Danny existed until after his mother died. That's weird. But, Danny said they had disowned her—even though she was their only child—because she was doing drugs and making a mess of her life. But she wrote them a letter and left it with a girlfriend. The letter said if anything ever happened to her, she wanted her parents to know about Danny. But then this Stanley guy had some paper that he said was from Danny's parents, saying they wanted him to raise their son if anything ever happened to them. But Danny's grandfather didn't believe it and wouldn't give up. He's rich. He hired some real expensive lawyers and got custody of Danny."

"I would have done the same thing in his position. Money is only as good as the purpose it's put to. Surely they've provided a good home for Danny." *But what kind of people are they to disown their only child? Was Danny's mother that hopeless?*

Scott flicked the handkerchief at a pesky fly. "Yeah. They love him a lot. Danny says he's all they've got, and they're all he's got. Anyway, I think Danny got infected from Stanley, before his grandparents got him."

Grim-faced, Jack nodded. "Sounds possible." *But he could have been with others later on, spreading the disease, before Scott.* He put his hand on Scott's shoulder. "I like Danny, and I care about him, but I'm concerned about you, Scott. I want you to take care of yourself."

"Yeah, well, that's why I decided to get the test. It's dumb not to. Everybody can get the virus. Even if they're not gay."

"Hold on a minute. Not everybody. A lot of people are heterosexual, married—"

196

Bitterly, Scott interrupted. "Just because they're married, that doesn't mean anything."

The boy's tone of voice and words jolted Jack and brought to mind the story Kennocha had shown him and Vic's belief that Marah was having an affair. "Anything you want to tell me? About married people, someone you know?"

"No."

"Have you discussed any of this—homosexuality—with your parents?"

"No. They wouldn't care anyway."

"Now wait a minute. Your parents love you—"

Scott raised his voice. "I said they don't care!" He caught himself. "I'm sorry, Granpop, I didn't mean to yell." He rubbed the back of his neck. "You must be pretty disgusted with me. About everything."

Jack tugged at the tip of his mustache. "No, I'm glad you told me. Can't deny I have hopes for you. A career, family, kids. I want you to have a normal life and be happy. More than anything else in this world, I want all my family to be happy." Jack folded his arms across his chest. "But I want you to be realistic, son. If you were going to live this kind of lifestyle, chances are you'd always feel different, like you don't fit in. You'd have to learn to deal with people who don't approve of a homosexual lifestyle. It might affect your education, your job opportunities. And there's always the danger of AIDS. Condoms aren't foolproof."

The boy's face tensed. "There are people in the gay lifestyle who are happy. They're committed to each other and their relationship. Better than some heterosexual couples, even. And they have jobs—professional jobs. Like those guys next door. They're all going to the university. A couple of them got to talking to me over the fence one day when they were having a big barbecue. Little kids there, too. They wanted to know if you owned the Carousel. Turned out, two of those guys are a couple. One is some kind of an associate professor at the university, and they adopted two little kids who'd been in foster homes. A boy and a girl."

"Adopted? Homosexuals can't do that in this state. Where are they from?"

"I can't remember. They've only been here about a year. Those little kids were happy and playing with all the other kids. I think it's great they have a family now instead of being in foster homes."

After a moment, Jack nodded. "Guess you might be right about that. But how about you? Have you ever wanted your own family? Wouldn't you rather have your own kids?"

Scott cracked his knuckles. "I dunno. Maybe. I like little kids. Always wished I'd had a little brother or sister. Yeah, I guess I would like to have kids of my own someday. But I think it's good to adopt kids who've been dumped into society."

"But I wonder what it's like for those kids you saw at the barbecue next door, having two dads and no mom? Or the other way around? Will the kids become homosexual, too? Is that what you'd want for your kids?"

Scott shrugged. "It's their choice. I mean, their genes."

Jack planted both feet on the ground, back straight, words clipped. "Your first statement was correct. Choice. I don't think God intended men to have sex with men. Nor women with women. I don't believe people are *born* gay." He paused. "Look, I know things at home have been rough for you. You said your folks fight a lot, and I've picked up on some other things that would make it hard for a kid living in a situation like that. If your mom and dad had been getting along and your life was more normal, do you think you would have gone looking for … for a different kind of relationship?"

Shaking his head, Scott said, "You don't understand. I've always known there's something different inside me. Even when I was little and lived in Springfield. We used to go on picnics or to the ocean. We did stuff together. Mom and Dad weren't fighting in those days. But I still knew, deep inside me, that I wanted something different from what other boys wanted."

"But you could have—still can—make a decision not to give into that temptation and follow a normal course of life instead."

After a moment, Scott said, "Remember that day at the Carousel when you were helping that guy with the calliope? I was really impressed that you knew so much about calliopes, too. You could have decided to be the calliope expert instead of the wooden pony expert, right? How come you didn't?" Scott looked his grandfather square in the eyes.

Jack smiled. "I should have known better than to get into a discussion with a debate team student." He took a deep breath. "Okay, here it is. Mechanical things are pretty easy for me to figure out, but they don't speak to my soul like wood does. Wood feels alive in my hands. Screwdrivers and pliers and hinges don't."

"There, you see? You chose the thing that feels right in your soul. That's how it is with me. I don't know if it's my soul … it's more like a warm feeling in my …"

Jack kept his face straight and said, "Sex begins in your brain."

Scott blushed and didn't respond.

"C'mon, let's go home." Jack stood and feigned a stretch. "Tomorrow, I'll pick you up after school, and we'll go to the county health clinic together."

Scott stood and dug his toe into the ground, the handkerchief still wadded up in his fist. "Uh, Granpop, I just want to say … thanks for listening. And for not sending me away."

Jack wrapped an arm around his shoulders. "I'm scared of losing you. But I love you, no matter what." He gripped his grandson's shoulder. "Believe that, Scott. I love you. I care about you. I'm glad we had this talk. Now get your bike and let's go."

Scott dangled the wrinkled, soiled handkerchief at arm's length. "Do you want this back?"

Jack cuffed him playfully. "Not on your life."

Smiling, Scott picked up his backpack and pushed his bike along.

"Y'know, Granpop, a lot of guys never tell their families. They're scared of getting kicked out. That's what happened to Marco."

Something stirred in Jack's chest. *Marco. Kicked out by his family. And I treated him no better.* "I'll never reject you, Scott." *But the sooner you get over this notion that you're gay, the better.* "But I want you to think hard about what I said."

"Yeah, I will. Thanks, Granpop."

"Just one thing I'd like to know, son. Does this have anything to do with why you ran away from home?"

Instantly, Scott's mood darkened. He shook his head emphatically. "No."

Once again, Jack felt like he'd unknowingly entered a shadowy, foreboding room, one he'd been thrust into the night his grandson appeared on his doorstep, wanting to live with him. What was shrouded in that room? In his heart, Jack knew Marah was involved. Like her mother, did she harbor shameful secrets?

CHAPTER 29

The next afternoon, after biology class, Scott checked out of study hall and went to a pay phone near the gym. He dropped his backpack on the floor and called the Carousel. "Hello, is Jack Emerson there? ... No, would you just take a message, please? ... Just tell him not to pick up Scott after school ... Yeah, thanks." Scott ran a hand over his face and wiped it on his pants leg. *Granpop might get mad at me, but I have to do this alone.* He grabbed his backpack, slipped out the door, and began jogging.

An hour later, he left Partnership Health Care Center with his test results in a sealed envelope stuffed in his jeans pocket. He didn't want to go home to open the envelope. He recalled a park on the other side of the tracks, maybe a mile away, somewhere on the way up Rattlesnake Creek Canyon.

In Greenough Park, Scott crossed a bridge and then stepped away from the main path onto a narrow, meandering trail through the woods to a boulder alongside the creek. He climbed onto it, feeling safe in this hideaway under the overhanging branches.

The sound of water rushing over cobblestones soothed his pounding head. He sat still for several minutes. Then, with shaking hands, he pulled the envelope from his pocket and opened it. He stared at the words. Danny's face filled his mind. His vision blurred with tears. At last, unable to hold back any longer, he buried his face in his arms and sobbed.

CHAPTER 30

Meanwhile, in Jack's kitchen, Nikolas's voice cut into Jack's preoccupation. "Can you not sit still for even one minute? You have jumped up a hundred times to look out that window. You are expecting someone?"

Jack stood at the window, the curtain shoved to one side. "Scott should be home by now." He scowled at two vehicles speeding by. "Look at them," he muttered. "Idiots. You know what I'm going to do? Build a speed bump." He pointed toward the intersection. "Right there. That'll slow 'em down."

Jack turned to see Nikolas studying him.

"There is a problem with Scott?"

Jack sighed, dropped into a chair. "There's something I haven't told you." He picked up his coffee cup, set it down, and locked eyes with his friend. "Scott says he's homosexual."

Surprise then acceptance registered on Nikolas's face. He simply nodded.

"Danny tested positive for the HIV virus. So Scott had a blood test." Saying the words to Nikolas brought penetrating reality into his soul. "You can figure it out. He's supposed to get the results today. He didn't want me to go with him. He's late getting home. I'm worried." Ever since yesterday afternoon, he felt like someone had thrown a heavy logging chain over his shoulders. Now it felt like two.

Nikolas spoke slowly. "Jack, my friend, what can I say? What can I do?"

Jack looked up to see a tear trickle down the big man's cheek. Fighting to control his own emotions, he stood to look out the window again.

"I anticipated this about Danny," Nikolas said. "He came to me a while back, asking about my church. He wanted to know if 'different' people could go there. Does this mean Danny has that terrible disease? AIDS? Does Scott?"

"Danny doesn't have AIDS. So far." Jack told Nikolas everything about his discussion with Scott the previous day.

Nikolas wiped his eyes. "My heart breaks with yours. This disease is a fearsome thing."

"I know, I know." Jack paused. "I'll tell you something else. Kennocha thinks this homosexual business is normal for some people. Like they're born that way." Jack shook his head. "We had quite a disagreement over it." His voice dropped a pitch. "It's come between us—maybe for good."

"Because you and Kennocha do not agree, you will let that destroy something beautiful between you?" Nikolas's eyebrows met in a thick, black line above his eyes. "I do not understand. Why should this difference in your opinions end the relationship between you? Why can you not agree to disagree?"

"It's not that simple."

"Is it not?" Nikolas nailed Jack with his eyes. "I think it is a matter of pride. What if Scott were not your grandson? Would it matter then what Kennocha thinks about people in the homosexual lifestyle?"

Jack mulled over his words. "Could be you're right." He felt sheepish. "Don't get me wrong. I still can't agree that people are born this way. But I'll at least listen to her without—"

"Without being stubborn and closing your ears."

"Okay, you old Russian. I get the point. But what about you? Don't you say it's a sin?"

Nikolas laced his fingers together and leaned on the table. "I have given much thought to this recently. My youngest son tells me some of his best friends are gay couples, but my son is not gay. He has caused me to ponder. After he talked to me, I read a memoir by a famous preacher, a true biblical scholar who speaks seven languages and reads even more. This gentleman said he studied Scripture in the original languages, and he studied the historical settings. He believes Scripture is ambivalent about homosexual lifestyles. As with other things in the Holy Word, God does not tell every detail. He leaves some things for us to figure out—or to trust Him about the mysteries. I am changing my mind about this question of, 'Is it a sin?'" Nikolas paused and stroked his beard. "God sees beyond what we see. I think God places value on relationships that are born from love and integrity. Some of these other aspects are perhaps not so important."

"So what are you telling me? That homosexuals can just go ahead being homosexual? That maybe it's wrong, or maybe it's okay, or that only God knows?"

"Are we not all burdened with a tendency toward some kind of sin? Are we not all self-centered?" Nikolas folded his hands together. "Romans 3:23 says we are all sinners, every one. But Romans 5:10 says God reconciled us to Himself through His Son. The Holy Word does not have a list of exceptions following those words from God."

Jack stared at his friend. "Do you memorize everything you read in the Bible?"

Nikolas shook his head. "I do not know enough. I read my Bible every day. I study, and still I do not know enough."

Jack pulled at his mustache. "Next you're going to tell me I should, too."

"If you believe, you will want to read more, my friend."

Jack turned away, lifted the curtain, and looked down the street. Nikolas peered out, too. "We should perhaps go look for Scott?"

Jack squinted, craned his neck. "There he is!"

When Jack met Scott at the back gate, his heart fell. The boy's eyes looked red and his hair was disheveled. *Please, God, no.* He pushed the gate open.

Scott fished a crumpled wad of paper from his pocket, handed it to his grandfather, and sat down on the top step of the porch.

Jack's fingers trembled. He unfolded the paper and smoothed it. The letters and numbers on the page looked like wriggling black ants. He blinked several times until his vision cleared.

Like an earthen dam under floodwater pressure, his tension burst, and relief poured out. "Negative! Scott, you're negative!" Scott's despondent mood stopped him from throwing his arms around the boy. "What's wrong? Scott, what is it?"

Tears dampened Scott's cheeks. "At first I was relieved, you know? Then Danny's face flashed into my mind. And I wondered, why Danny and not me? Or why not me, too? Why not me instead of Danny?" He propped his elbows on his knees and buried his head in his hands. "I wish I was dead."

Jack was speechless. He felt like the father of the prodigal son, his loved one suddenly returned to him. A second chance. A new opportunity for the boy to choose life over death. But here he was, wishing he were dead and wondering why it wasn't him instead of Danny. "It's not your fault Danny's HIV-positive. He didn't get it from you."

"Yeah, but now he's all alone—"

"Alone? How so?" *Has the boy lost his mind?* "He has his grandparents. And you're still his friend, aren't you?" Scott nodded. "We don't know what's going to happen with Danny, but he's a lot better off with a healthy friend around. Think about that. And *stay healthy*."

After a moment, Scott said, "Yeah, I guess you're right."

Nikolas opened the door, coughed politely, and stepped out. "Scott, my boy. I have missed seeing you at the Carousel." He walked down the steps. "I must go. I will see you at the Carousel tomorrow, Jack. Our dapple gray is most anxious to run again."

"Hi, Nik." Scott picked up his backpack. "I've got to study for finals tomorrow." He went inside.

As soon as the door closed, Nikolas turned questioning eyes on Jack.

"He's negative. No virus."

Nikolas closed his eyes and lifted his face toward the heavens. "Thank You, Lord."

"But that paper he brought home says he should be tested every six months."

Nikolas gripped Jack's shoulder. "One day at a time, my friend. Do not waste your life away with worry. As a good man once said, 'Time will tell. It always does.'"

Jack nodded, hearing the echo of his own favorite saying.

Later that evening, Scott talked to Danny on the phone and reported to Jack.

"Danny's okay. They just got back from some private school back East. His grandfather wants him to go to school there, but Danny doesn't want to leave."

"So how is that resolved?"

"Dunno. It's like, Danny gets all the stuff he ever wants—you know, stereo, car, stuff like that—but when it comes to school and vacations, his grandfather usually wins."

"Is it a matter of win or lose? Or of what's best for Danny's future?" Jack raised an eyebrow at Scott.

"Yeah, but he should have something to say about his future, too. He's not a little kid."

Early the next evening, Marah's Cadillac pulled into the driveway. Another unannounced visit. Jack worried that she'd come to take Scott home. He hadn't even had a chance to recover his equilibrium from his grandson's revelation a few days earlier. Marah's visits always unsettled him. And Scott.

She flung open the back door, saw Scott, and opened her arms wide. "Scott, darling."

He backed away. "Did you come to take me home?"

"Dear, you know I miss you terribly. I'd love to have you home. But we don't need to talk about that tonight. I'm just here for a couple of days to visit."

Jack leaned against the kitchen counter, arms folded, watching her, wondering about her real agenda.

"That's all right, isn't it, Dad?" She smiled and kissed his cheek.

He grunted. "You might have let us know you were coming. C'mon, Scott, let's get your mother's luggage."

Outdoors, Scott said, "Granpop, you won't tell Mom, will you? About me?"

Jack deliberated his answer. "I believe your parents have a right to know you're at risk. You're underage, Scott. If you did get sick, God forbid, they would be responsible for you. Medical bills—doctors, medicine. That's part of their love and concern for you. Just because you're not getting along with them right now doesn't mean it'll always be that way."

Scott scratched his head. "Never thought about the medical stuff. But I'm not sick. I'm negative. Can't we just wait? I'll probably never get sick. If I ever do, then we can tell them."

"I'll go along with you for now. But I need to think about this some more. Let's get this stuff upstairs."

Scott set down a suitcase in Marah's room. "What did you do with the puppy? Leave it with Dad?"

Marah paled. "Oh, my puppy ..." She rubbed her forehead and murmured, "I hope Tina picked him up before Vic got home." She turned to Jack. "Dad, can I bring Tippy here next time?"

"I have a cat, remember? She doesn't like dogs."

"But Scott always wanted a dog."

Scott interrupted. "How come you asked Tina to take him? She's a druggie. She'd probably sell him if she could. Why didn't you take him to the shelter in the first place? They can find homes for puppies. Don't let Tina take him."

Marah looked confused. "What shelter? What do you know about shelters?"

Shirley A. Rorvik

"Mom, I've told you. Last summer, I helped them a couple of days every week."

"You didn't tell me you had a job." Marah rubbed her forehead, clearly not understanding the conversation.

"No, I told you I volunteer. Just because I like the animals. I've told you this before."

"Are you sure? I don't remember—"

Jack intervened. "You've had a long drive, Marah. Why don't you just rest now." As he and Scott went downstairs, he wondered about Marah's confusion. *I've never seen her like this before. Is it those diet pills?*

CHAPTER 31

Scott had a message to stop by the office after school the next day. As he read the note the secretary handed him, he tensed. *Why does she want to pick me up? I could go out the back door and pretend I never got the note.* But she'd ask the secretary. She'd find out. He crushed the note and fired it into the wastebasket. Then he shrugged into his backpack and walked out the main doors.

The note said his mother would pick him up out front. And there she was, in her white Cadillac, in the very first parking slot, where everyone would be sure to see her. She was dressed up like she was going to a party. Why couldn't she act like other mothers and wear normal clothes? Why did she always have to act so important?

CHAPTER 32

Marah tapped a nervous rhythm on the steering wheel with her polished, almond-shaped nails. Boisterous students laden with books and backpacks hurried by, some staring at the car then at her. She watched for her son.

Scott appeared at her window, his face sullen. "Why'd you want to pick me up?"

"Get in, darling. I need to talk to you."

Scowling, Scott took his time walking around the car, pulling off his pack, and climbing into the passenger seat.

"Do you like Missoula, this school?"

Staring straight ahead, he mumbled, "It's all right."

"Would you like to stay here to finish high school?"

Scott's head snapped around. "Why?"

Marah smiled. "I spoke to Mr. Owens. Do you know him, the school psychologist? Or principal, whatever he is. He agrees with me that it's best not to disrupt your education again. You're doing so well here—at least as well as in Boise."

"So what?"

She started the motor and drove away from the school. "If you want to stay, we'll talk to your grandfather."

Scott pushed the button to lower the window. He stuck his elbow out and kept his face averted. "What about Dad?"

"I can handle him. But I might need your help with your grandfather." Marah smoothed her hair. "Put the window up, dear."

He took his time finding the button to raise the window. "Granpop figures it's up to you and Dad."

"Yes, but if he knew how badly you want to stay, and how much Mr. Owens and I think it's a good idea ..."

Scott shifted slightly to stare at her. "If Dad goes for it, and Granpop too, does that mean I never have to go home?"

Marah met his gaze. "Don't you want to come home?"

Still staring at her, he said, "Why should I?"

She bit her lower lip and looked away. At the corner, she slowed to a stop as the traffic light turned red. "I know I've made mistakes, Scott, and I'm sorry. I love you, and I miss you."

"Then why are you trying to get rid of me?"

"I—I don't want to get rid of you. I want what's best for you. You're happy here. It isn't right to make you change schools again so close to the end of your high school years."

The light turned green, and Marah drove through the intersection. She hadn't been prepared for this response, and she didn't know how to counter her son's challenge. She sensed he wanted something from her, but what? An apology? But she just apologized. Did she have to spell it out to him? Bring up that ugly scene she'd just as soon forget? Couldn't he just believe her and accept that she was sorry it happened?

Scott had turned away from her again and was hunched up against the door.

When she pulled up in front of Jack's house, Scott grabbed his backpack, got out, and stood beside the car. He waited until she came around to the sidewalk.

His eyes hard, he said, "I want to stay with Granpop. I want to finish school here. I want to stay all summer. Maybe forever. But I don't believe you're doing this because it's best for me. I think you're doing it for yourself."

Marah finished a chapter in Danielle Steel's *The Perfect Stranger* and got up from the easy chair. "I'm going to make some coffee, Dad. Want some?"

Jack looked up from the newspaper's crossword puzzle. "Sounds good, with one of Nikolas's brownies. They're in the bread box."

While the coffee gurgled and dripped, Marah tiptoed upstairs, past Scott's closed door, and got a pill from her purse. Third today, or was it the fourth? But she needed them today. *Diet pills,* she told herself. She went back to the kitchen, took the pill, and waited for the coffee.

Marah returned to the living room with a brownie for her father and coffee for both of them. She settled in her chair. "I visited the school psychologist today, Mr. Owen," she said. "He's concerned about transferring Scott back to Boise."

Jack stared at her while he chewed.

She lowered her eyes, wrapped both hands around her cup, and took a long swallow. *The pill will kick in pretty quick.* "Scott's school records show that he's had a better grade point average this last quarter than he has in the last two years. I explained that I felt his poor performance in Boise might be because of tensions at home. When Vic's drunk, no one has any peace around our house. Especially Scott."

"Explain."

Hands shaking, Marah set her cup down, laced her fingers together in her lap, and looked at her father. "He goes on a rampage and starts demanding that Scott show him all his homework. Then if he doesn't like it, he makes him do it over, no matter what time of night it is. Things get very tense. I know Scott doesn't get enough sleep." She forced herself to smile. "I've never seen Scott look as good as he does now, Daddy. You've been a big help to him. And it's good to have him away from Larry."

"Scott's never said anything about Vic going on a rampage about his schoolwork."

"Oh? So what has he told you?" She held her breath.

"Very little. About anything. Seems to prefer not to talk about what goes on at home."

She exhaled and ran one hand through her hair. "So you don't really know."

"No, I don't. But I'd like to hear Vic's response to this."

Marah's eyes widened. "Surely you don't think he'd admit to such behavior?"

"I meant his reaction to Owens's recommendation that Scott stay."

"Well, of course I'll discuss it with him. I'm sure he'll agree."

Jack glanced at the gold anniversary clock on the television console. "Let's give him a call."

"Not tonight. He's at a board meeting. I'll call him tomorrow."

Jack nodded, his eyes on Marah's. "Tomorrow."

"Another thing, Daddy." Feeling she'd won, Marah began to relax. "Scott really wants to stay. He's counting on it so much, I just know how he'd be if we make him go home."

"What do you mean?"

"Oh, you know. Rebellious, moody."

"Funny, must be a different boy than the one I'm used to."

"See what I mean? He's much happier here." She smiled, got up, and went upstairs. She stopped at Scott's bedroom door and knocked softly. Without waiting for an answer, she pushed it open. Scott sat at his desk, surrounded by textbooks. She whispered, "I think Grandpa's on our side, darling."

"He said I can stay?"

"Not exactly. But close. We'll talk some more tomorrow. Good night." She eased the door shut and went across the landing to her room.

After Scott and Jack left the next morning, Marah got out of bed and went downstairs. Miss Lavender saw her and ran to the door, anxious to go out. Marah ignored her until the cat yowled. She let her out and poured herself a cup of coffee. As she swallowed two pills, she noticed a note on the kitchen table from her father, saying he'd be at the Carousel all day. Scott was in school, of course. Perfect. No interruptions.

She swallowed another morning "diet pill" and went into Jack's bedroom. At first glance, everything seemed the same as her mother had left it. Same furniture arrangement, same chenille bedspread, same floral drapes. She paused in front of her mother's dresser. Her mother's picture was gone. The glamour photo had been a favorite of Marah's.

She suddenly realized that all of her mother's things were missing from the top of her dresser. Jewelry box, perfume bottles, the porcelain rose.

Dad must've done it. Why—? Her jaw clenched. *That woman from the Carousel. She's got something to do with this.*

Anger building, she looked around. *What else has he changed?* She opened the closet. *Mother's clothes are gone! I told him I'd do that for him. Why didn't he wait? Why didn't he tell me?*

Her glance fell on a new-looking cardboard box with a Tony Lama logo. She pulled it down from the shelf and pushed the lid aside. The smell of new leather met her nostrils. *Cowboy boots?* She picked up a shiny cordovan boot with fancy stitching. The sole and heel showed some wear. *When did he buy these? And why?* She replaced the boot and shoved the box back onto the shelf. Then she saw the price tag and gasped.

214

"I don't believe this. Dad paid $140 for *cowboy boots?* And there's a cowboy hat. Dad never wears anything but that old, wool, tweed cap. What else is there?"

She reached for the shirts on hangers and slid them across the rod a few at a time. "He's gotten rid of a bunch of his clothes, too. But that's no loss, that old stuff."

She felt her pills kicking in, energizing her.

She held a blue, western shirt at arm's length and stared. Silver threads and pearl snaps. A silver bolo tie hung over the neck of the hanger. On the next hanger, she found a pair of western-cut, gray slacks, good quality.

Marah replaced the clothing, backed out of the closet, turned off the light, and shut the door. She walked to the bed and sat down. "It's got to be that woman. That red-haired woman."

With a sense of foreboding, she walked slowly toward her mother's sewing room. The room she most closely identified with her mother. *Dad interrupted me the last time I was in here. I think I found mother's diary. I have to read it.*

She shoved the door open. It banged against the wall, echoing in the barren room. Marah gasped and clutched the doorjamb to steady herself. Tears ran down her face as she stared at the empty room that once lived and breathed her mother's presence. Horrified, she whispered, "Dad, how could you?"

Twenty minutes later, fortified by another pill, Marah sat on the stool at the end of the kitchen counter, legs crossed, one foot scribing short, impatient swings while she waited for Vic's secretary to summon him to the phone. Marah willed herself to concentrate on her reason for being there—not to bring Scott home, as Vic believed, but to make sure their son stayed with his grandfather. Her personal reasons for keeping Scott in Missoula had strengthened in the past hour with her discovery of that red-headed woman's influence in her father's life. It wouldn't be easy for her father to carry on a romance with a teenager in the house, as she well knew.

At last, her husband came on the line. "Vic, darling, I went to the school yesterday. Mr. Owen, the school psychologist, strongly advised against uprooting Scott again." After ten minutes, Marah sensed she'd convinced her husband. For good measure, she added, "Oh, and darling, don't say anything to Scott—he wants to surprise you—but he might have a summer job here. He'll tell you himself as soon as he knows. Darling, I have to run. Dad invited me to meet a friend of his at the Carousel. I'll be home tomorrow or the day after ... Oh? When are you leaving? ... Well, no reason to hurry home if you won't be there ... Tina will take care of Tippy ... Yes, I'm sure Dad will let me bring the puppy over here for Scott ... Yes, of course I'll ask him ... All right, darling. Have a safe trip. Good-bye."

Marah replaced the phone and hummed as she dialed an unlisted number in Boise. Voice mail answered, but she was used to that. She left a message. "Warren, my love. Vic is leaving town this afternoon for a few days. I'll see you tomorrow night." She hung up. Time to go shopping. After just one more pill.

Feeling pleased with herself, Marah drove to the mall. Perhaps she'd buy a new nightgown. And some very expensive cologne. Scented candles. Warren liked romantic surprises.

Marah arrived at the Carousel late that afternoon. Entering the building, she looked toward the glass-windowed workroom. She saw her father with that redhead. He looked younger, vibrant. The woman tossed her head back, laughing at something he said. Marah's nostrils flared. She walked quickly past the carousel to the workroom. At the door, she took a deep breath and entered.

"Hi, Daddy," she purred. She moved to his side, slipped her arm around him, and kissed his cheek. Then she smiled at the woman on his other side, reached in front of her father, and offered her hand. "Hello, I'm Marah Giroux. Are you one of the employees?"

The woman responded with a firm handshake. "Kennocha Bryant." She smiled. "Sometimes I feel like this is my job. Actually, I work at the high school. In fact, your son is in my creative writing class for gifted students."

Marah concealed her surprise and fixed a pleasant expression on her face. "How nice."

Jack said, "And somehow she finds time to volunteer here at the Carousel. Come on, Marah, I'll show you Clarissa Mae. We're trying her out on the platform."

Marah and Kennocha followed Jack into the main room and onto the carousel platform.

"Here she is," Jack said.

He stood by the loveliest carousel pony Marah had ever seen. White with a golden mane, the animal expressed life in its eyes and action in the arch of its neck and dancing hooves. Cascades of peachy-gold roses spilled across the rear of the saddle and adorned the bridle. The pony seemed to invite its admirers to mount up and go for a ride.

"Oh, Dad, it's beautiful."

Jack grinned with pride. "Kennocha painted her."

Even with her admiration dampened by her father's comment, Marah couldn't resist stroking the horse's neck. She half expected it to whinny. "Why did you name it Clarissa Mae?"

"Don't you remember? In memory of your mother. Look, here's the plaque."

Marah leaned closer to read the small, engraved, brass plaque on the back of the saddle. "In loving memory of my wife, Claire Emerson." She straightened and looked from Kennocha to Jack. "Since it's for Mother, I'd have thought you'd paint it yourself."

Jack looked surprised. "That's not how we do things here. Besides, flowers are Kennocha's specialty."

Marah didn't hide her sarcasm. "Really."

Kennocha seemed not to notice. "Mrs. Giroux, I've really enjoyed getting to know Scott."

"Just how well have you gotten to know him?"

Kennocha smiled pleasantly. "As well as he wants me to."

Marah turned to a Fjord horse on an inside row. "This is one of those Norwegian horses, isn't it, Daddy?" She didn't hear Jack's response, nor did she care. "Will you be home soon? I'm going to make that Greek salad you like for dinner."

"No, Kennocha has invited me for supper tonight, and Scott was invited to Danny's, so you're—"

Kennocha interrupted. "Marah, please come for dinner. Your Greek salad would be good with the chicken I have planned."

"No, thank you. I'm going to look up one of my former classmates. We've been trying to get together for ages." She saw the surprised look on her father's face. "I have to run now."

Driving away, Marah clenched her jaw until her head ached. Her father acted like a teenager in love for the first time. "I despise her," Marah whispered. "And I'm going to break up this romance." Driving toward her father's house, she recalled the pony, Clarissa Mae. *In honor of Mother. The most beautiful horse on the platform. Of course. Nothing else would do for Claire Emerson. What if Daddy made a pony named for me? What would it look like? Fat. Fat, stupid, and ugly.*

Marah made her announcement the next morning, while Jack and Scott ate the pancakes, eggs, and sausage Jack had prepared. "Scott, dear, good news. Your father and I have decided to let you stay in Missoula. Subject to your grandfather's approval, of course."

Jack's eyebrows went up. "When did all this come about?"

"Vic called yesterday afternoon, while you were at the Carousel." Before her father could speak, she rushed on. "Scott can stay, can't he, Daddy?" Marah fidgeted with her rings as her father studied her. She felt like he was trying to read her mind.

Scott sat at the table, his breakfast forgotten. His eyes were fixed on Jack.

"Of course he can." He turned to Scott. "Is that what you want, son?"

Scott grinned. "For sure!"

The tension in Marah's scalp eased. "I have to go home today. Scott, dear, would you take my suitcase to the car, please?"

"Sure, Mom." He dashed upstairs.

Jack leaned against the kitchen counter, facing his daughter. "You didn't mention going home today. And it's odd you waited until this morning to tell us about Vic's phone call."

She chose to ignore his last comment. "I just decided after talking to Vic yesterday." She gestured toward the doorway, where Scott had gone. "I guess you're right, Dad. My son seems to love me more when I'm out of his life."

"I never said that, but I've been telling you, don't push him. The boy doesn't seem to trust anyone."

"Except you."

Jack nodded. "Possibly."

"He's smart. He'll never get hurt again if he's careful."

"Again? What do you know about him getting hurt?" Marah shrugged. "Everyone gets hurt, Marah. We all have to learn to deal with it. The right way."

Marah raised her chin. "I don't know what you mean."

CHAPTER 33

In Boise late that same evening, Marah and her lover, Dr. Warren Addison, lay atop rumpled sheets.

Warren mumbled drowsily, "I have to go pretty soon. Surgery tomorrow. New intern observing."

Marah ran her finger around the curve of his ear. "Is that a problem?"

He yawned, rolled over, and faced her. "Not usually. But tomorrow it is. I don't know how this guy made it through med school. He wants the title but not the work."

"What was your favorite part? In school?"

Eyes glinting, he grinned. "Female anatomy."

She kissed his chin. "And the worst?"

"Cadavers. Autopsies. All chances gone to help those people."

Marah raised up on one elbow. "Can they do autopsies on people who have been dead a long time?"

"If there's good reason and all the legal hoops have been jumped through. Such morbid thoughts. I won't let you go away anymore, coming back with such questions." He tried to kiss her, but she pulled back.

"I won't be going anyway. Dad as much as told me to stay away."

"Oh?"

"He says it's because of Scott. But I think it's because he's got a girlfriend."

"Scott?"

"No, Dad."

"Aren't you happy for him? Your mother's been dead several years."

Marah sat up. "Dad's not ready for a relationship."

"I should think your father would be the judge of that."

After Warren left, Marah swallowed two pills. Her head hurt. She wanted to escape the pain.

Marah prepared the puppy's food, but when she went to his corner where they kept his cage, he was gone. Distressed, she searched for the puppy in her sewing loft with a vague memory he'd been with her in this room sometime. But she didn't remember when. She returned to the kitchen, poured a glass of Cabernet Sauvignon, and swallowed another pill. Next she searched the cellar. The smell caused her to abandon the mission. "Forgot to clean up," she mumbled. "Have to do that tomorrow." She returned to the family room, her steps uncertain, her concentration blinking on and off like a yellow warning light.

She locked all the doors, picked up the bottle of wine and her glass, went up to her sewing loft, and curled up on the loveseat. Her mind drifted back in time. She sipped the wine and let the memories come, memories of the day when her mother had a massive stroke.

As usual when Marah and Scott visited her parents, Scott had spent happy hours with Jack doing what the eleven-year-old boy called "Granpop projects," while Marah had tried to get through each day without an argument with her mother.

On the third day of their visit, Marah and her mother had gone shopping. Marah sensed tension building when she refused to purchase a dress her mother said would make her look slimmer. Marah knew she was no longer overweight; she didn't need a dress to make her "look slimmer." Neither attempted conversation as they put away groceries, but experience told Marah trouble was coming. The attack began while Marah was peeling potatoes.

"Are you going to complete your degree," Claire asked, "or spend the rest of your life as nothing more than a housewife?"

Marah restrained herself from slamming the potato peeler onto the counter. "I'm going to wait until Scott's in high school. Then I'll see about enrolling in college."

Claire scrubbed carrots and tucked them between onions around a browned roast. She tossed in a few garlic cloves and some basil then she sprinkled on salt and pepper. "Are those potatoes ready? What are you doing with yourself these days? Any volunteer work?"

Marah handed a bowl of peeled and rinsed potatoes to her mother. "No. I don't enjoy that sort of thing."

"It wouldn't hurt you to get acquainted. It might help Vic's career."

"Vic doesn't need my help."

Claire slid the covered roasting pan into the oven, closed the door, placed her hands on her slender hips, and faced Marah. "That's the trouble with you. No vision."

"That's not fair. I—"

"That job you had in high school. You might've become a design consultant if you hadn't given Richard DeWolfe ideas. Look at the trouble you caused."

"Me?" Marah's voice went up in anger. "He created that problem, I didn't. You can't possibly think I *wanted* him to put his hands on me."

"You were so overweight, none of the boys in high school wanted you." Claire's glance swept Marah from head to foot. "When are you going to get your weight under control?"

Marah wrung out the dishcloth and slammed it on the countertop. "I've lost twenty pounds and kept it off since Scott was born. Why are you always criticizing me?" The tension she'd been holding under control all afternoon broke loose. A sob escaped. "You've never loved me, Mother. Sometimes I wish I'd never been born."

Her mother's eyes seemed to burn into Marah's soul as she said softly, "I *always* wished you'd never been born."

Marah felt a chill go through her body. She struggled to find her voice. "Then why? Why did you and Dad—?"

"He never even knew when you were conceived." Claire's mouth twisted into an ugly grimace, and her eyes turned to cold steel. "It's about time you knew. Jack Emerson is not your father. He knew that. It was *his* decision to raise you as his."

The room spun in a spiral of light and color. Marah dropped into a chair, covered her face with her hands, and waited for the dizziness to pass. When she looked up, Claire still stood, her cold eyes fixed on her. For a long moment, their eyes locked.

Marah whispered, "Who?"

Claire shook her head. "You don't need to know. He doesn't want you. He never wanted you. And after I told him I was pregnant, he never wanted *me*. If it weren't for you, I'd have had the kind of life I've dreamed of. He was—is—wealthy. We'd have been the envy of the whole town."

Trembling, Marah said, "You blame me for what *you* did. You will never love me, will you? You really do hate me, don't you, Mother?"

Claire's eyes narrowed. Without a word, she abruptly turned her back and walked away.

Marah jumped up, ran after her, grabbed her arm, and screamed, "Admit it, Mother. You hate me! But it was your fault! You *cheated* on Dad!"

Claire tried to pull away, but Marah tightened her grip.

"All the bad names you call me, Mother, you're really condemning yourself, aren't you? *You're* the 'bad, bad girl,' not me." Claire struggled, but Marah held on. She jerked her mother's arm and shrieked, "Not me!" Then, with all her strength, Marah shoved her mother.

Claire's shoulder hit the wall. Her face paled. Suddenly, she crumpled onto the floor. Her jaw fell slack, mouth open, eyes dull.

The stem of the crystal goblet broke in Marah's grip. Red wine splashed onto the loveseat. She stared at it and didn't care. The room spun as she stood and staggered to get another pill. On her way back to the loveseat, a lamp crashed to the floor. "Tippy? Did you do that?" Through the chaos in her mind, a thought came through. *Oh. I did it. Poor lamp.* She grasped the back of the loveseat to feel her way around and sit down. Then she picked up the bottle and refilled the goblet, not caring if she cut herself on the broken stem.

She remembered how she'd wanted to ask Jack about what her mother had said that day, before the stroke, but she was afraid, as though voicing the question would make it true. She wanted to know; she didn't want to know. She loved Jack, trusted him. He had never belittled her like Claire did. He always made her feel loved. No matter what her mother said, he was Dad.

But he might blame her for Claire's stroke. And her death. Then he would hate her, too.

CHAPTER 34

A month later, Jack and Nikolas worked together to repair the worn knees of the Old West Appaloosa Indian pony, complete with bow and arrows. The white and brown wooden horse bore numerous scratches and nicks from the loving attention of many children.

While Jack worked, he complained to Nikolas. "Now that the boy knows he's going to live with me the next few months, maybe longer, he's changed. Moody and messy. One day full of the dickens, fun to have around, the next day sulking and mumbling. You should see his room. Some days it looks like a tornado tore through it."

Nikolas remained bent over his work, sanding the pony's knee. "What you are saying, my friend, is that he is behaving like a normal teenager. He is comfortable with you."

Ignoring him, Jack railed on, "You know me and TV. Take it or leave it. Most of it's a bunch of foolishness anyway. Now, with Scott out of school, it'd be on day and night if I allowed it." He wiped his hands on a rag. "And those friends of his. Danny drives everywhere. Doesn't he have a bicycle? He could walk. Why should a seventeen-year-old kid have a car, anyway? I'm liking my speed bump idea better all the time." He shook sawdust out of his rag with a vengeance.

Nikolas looked up from his work. "Does Scott have a job during this season of no school?"

"That's what Vic asked me a couple of weeks ago. How is Scott's job going, he wanted to know. What job, I said. Come to find out, last time Marah was here, she told Vic the boy had a summer job lined up. But Scott says he never told his mother any such thing. 'Round and 'round. That's all these people do, go 'round and 'round. And the brass ring is in my nose. It's getting mighty sore."

A deep chuckle rumbled from Nikolas's chest. He dodged a swat from Jack's rag. "Then our boy does not have a job?"

"He's trying to find one. Got a few lawn-mowing jobs, but they don't pay much. I think he spends most of it on hamburgers, pizza, and movies. Before you know it, school will start, and he won't have saved enough to buy a pair of socks." Jack shook a can of wood putty in the air to emphasize his next complaint. "And there's another thing. No privacy. That boy wants to know every blasted thing that goes on in my life. I can't have a phone conversation or walk out the door without him wanting to know who I'm talking to and who I'm going to see."

Scratching at his beard, Nikolas gave him a knowing smile. "Yes, yes, I understand. A teenage grandson can hinder an old man's romantic endeavors." He cleared his throat. "Speaking of romance, may I assume that peace is restored between you and Kennocha?"

Putty knife in hand, Jack paused. "Yes. I took your advice for a change and apologized to her. Admitted my pride had too much influence on my comments. Have to admit, it wasn't easy at first to say anything, but Kennocha means a lot to me."

"Ah, I see now. You should listen to my advice every time you put yourself in a corner."

Jack's mood lightened. "Some help you are, you old Russian. Just you wait 'til you find some woman who'll put up with you for more than a day. You're jealous, is what you are."

"Not to worry. When I meet the right woman, I will win her heart so fast—why, you will come begging me to teach you."

"Me? Asking you? That'll never—"

Izsak called from the doorway. "Jack. Phone call for you. Sounds important."

Jack took the call in Izsak's office. It was Scott.

"Granpop, I'm at the hospital. With Danny. Can you come?"

"What happened? An accident? Are Danny's grandparents there?"

"Yeah, they're here. Not an accident. Pneumonia, they said. He can hardly breathe." Scott's voice choked up. "I'm really scared."

"Okay, son. I'll be right there."

CHAPTER 35

Jack stepped off the elevator into a bright corridor. As the smell of disinfectant penetrated his nostrils, he shuddered, remembering his vigil at Claire's bedside. He found Scott alone in a sunny parlor at the end of the corridor. He looked up with red, anxious eyes when Jack walked in.

Jack sat down beside him, tucked one arm around his back, and gave him a hug. "Have you seen him yet?"

Scott shook his head. "They just let his grandparents in a couple of minutes ago."

"I didn't know Danny had been sick."

"He wasn't, really. He's had a cold ... said his chest hurt a little, that's all. We were at his house, talking about going swimming. All of a sudden, he started coughing and couldn't stop. He passed out. His grandmother called the ambulance. Granpop, he looked awful ... like he was dead or something." Scott rubbed his face. "I never saw anybody die before."

"Son, let's just wait and see what the doctor says."

They both looked up at approaching footsteps as a slim, well-dressed man entered the room. He had prominent cheekbones and graying dark hair with a streak of white on the right side. The man appeared composed but strained.

Apparently oblivious of Jack, the man addressed Scott. "You can see him for a few minutes. He's conscious, but he might not try to speak. They have an oxygen mask over his face. He has some kind of bacterial pneumonia ... a certain kind that people with AIDS are susceptible to. Can't remember the name. Doesn't matter, I guess." He rubbed his face. "We thought ... we believed him when he'd told us he felt okay, just a cold. We should have taken him to the doctor days ago."

"Thanks. I'll go see him." Scott jumped up and hurried toward Danny's room.

Jack's eyes hadn't left the man's face since he entered the room. His heart pounded. *Richard DeWolfe. Claire's lover.* He stood, took a few steps, and faced DeWolfe. "Danny is *your* grandson?" Jack's blood boiled. Fingers curled into tight fists, elbows cocked, he advanced on DeWolfe. "You—you—worthless piece of humanity," he growled.

DeWolfe's eyes bulged. He held up his hands and stumbled backward. "What the—?" He stopped. "Jack? Jack Emerson?" He lowered his hands and gained his footing, trying to restore his dignity. "What are you doing? What is the meaning of this?"

In the man's face, fists threatening, Jack hissed, "You snake. You took my wife, used her, and dumped her like a piece of trash."

DeWolfe tried to sidestep away, but Jack's hand shot out and he grabbed his shoulder. He dug his fingers and thumb into the frightened man's flesh and slugged him in the gut with his free hand. DeWolfe let out a short cough and nearly doubled over, but Jack held tight to his shoulder, pulling him upright so he could see DeWolfe's face. "And you tried to violate my daughter."

DeWolfe gasped for air. "No! I never touched—"

Jack hung on and increased the pressure of his thumb on DeWolfe's shoulder. "Marah worked for you. She was a kid, trying to make something of herself. She wanted to be a designer. She trusted you. And you tried to molest her."

Understanding registered in DeWolfe's eyes. Jack knew he remembered.

Jack continued his pressure, pushing DeWolfe into a corner. The man's eyes flashed from Jack to the doorway.

"But Claire stopped you," Jack said, "What did she tell you?" He grabbed DeWolfe's other shoulder and slammed him against the wall.

A nurse rushed into the room. "What's going on here? Stop this immediately!"

Jack ignored her.

DeWolfe cried out, "Call the police!" The woman dashed out.

Jack backhanded him across the face. Blood trickled from DeWolfe's nose. "Answer me! What did Claire say to make you leave my daughter alone?"

DeWolfe wiped his nose with the back of his hand. "She threatened to tell my father about us ... about our ... affair." He struggled to pull a handkerchief from his pocket. "Jack, I'm sorry. It was a long time ago. I was stupid. I'm sorry." He leaned his head back against the wall, his eyes squeezed shut, mouth trembling. His voice broke as he said,

"It's haunted me for years. I wanted to apologize to Claire. But ... I waited too long." He looked at Jack, his eyes full of tears. "I'm sorry, Jack. I—"

A muscular orderly strode into the room, placed one burly hand on Jack's shoulder, the other on DeWolfe's, and pulled them apart. "Okay, fellas, that's enough. This is the hospital, not the Silver Dollar Bar."

DeWolfe looked defeated, his suit disheveled, his hair mussed as he wiped blood from his nose and tears from his face.

Jack's blood pressure lowered to simmer.

"I want you two out of here," the orderly said, "and don't come back until you can act like gentlemen." He shoved DeWolfe toward the door. He and Jack watched the man stumble into the hallway and down the corridor. As Frances DeWolfe came out of Danny's room, pulling the door closed behind her, the sad expression on her face instantly turned to alarm when she saw her husband. He barely slowed as she took his arm, and they continued toward the elevators.

Seeing Frances DeWolfe, Jack felt a fleeting sense of shame for causing her further pain. Didn't she have enough to bear with Danny's crisis? Hard on the heels of that thought, Jack knew Richard DeWolfe deserved all he gave him and more. He wanted that scoundrel to suffer.

The orderly touched Jack's arm. "Mr. Emerson."

Startled, Jack turned. "Okay, I'm going. I apologize if I disturbed any patients. It won't happen again." *Not here, anyway. If I get him in the parking lot—*

"Mr. Emerson. You probably don't remember me. I'm Ernie's little brother. I used to tag along with him to your house when I could get away with it."

Jack sucked in a deep breath and let it out. Ernie's little brother ... Realization dawned. Jack shook the orderly's hand. "I remember you now. Guess I'm lucky it was you instead of your brother who broke up this conflagration, or I'd be heading for jail right now."

"I don't think so. Just between us, Mr. DeWolfe has been a real pain around here. Whatever your reason for what you did, he must've deserved it." The orderly grinned. "But next time, please do it away from the hospital." He walked with Jack along the hall to Danny's room and then said good-bye.

Scott came out of the room, his face pale and haggard.

"He's gonna die, Granpop. I just know he is."

"Son, let's go home for a while. You can come back later."

Sniffing, Scott nodded.

As the boy moved away from Danny's room, Jack looked in. His heart wrenched at the sight of the boy's thin, frail body lying so still. *That could be Scott lying there ... cursed disease. Those fools who condone homosexuality should see Danny now, wasting away.* He fought back tears.

He turned and caught up to Scott in a few strides. Neither spoke as they stepped into the empty elevator. The doors whispered shut with a soft whoosh, like the sound of a book being closed, the story finished.

A few minutes later, Jack drove around the corner where his house came into view. Marah's white Cadillac occupied the driveway.

Scott groaned. "Oh, no, what's she doing here again?"

Silently, Jack echoed his sentiments. *What's she up to now? I won't let her change her mind about letting Scott stay.* Aloud, he said, "Maybe your dad came, too, for a visit. Long time since you've seen him."

"Dad would be driving his car. It's just Mom." Scott muttered something unintelligible under his breath. Suddenly, he sat up straight. "Granpop. Don't tell her about Danny—about—you know. Please?"

Jack pulled at his mustache. *She'll want to know why Scott's going to the hospital this evening. But she doesn't need to know the whole story. Scott has enough to handle now without his mother's dramatics.* "Okay."

They went inside and found Marah crouched on the floor with a quivering, whimpering puppy. She glared at her father.

"Your cat attacked Tippy."

"I told you Miss Lavender doesn't like dogs, and I told you I didn't want that pup. Where's my cat?"

Marah stood, the corners of her mouth turned down. "It ran into the other room. What am I going to do with Tippy? Vic doesn't think we should keep him, and Tina—she—"

Scott took the pup from his mother and cuddled it against his chest. "Granpop?" Scott gave Jack a hopeful look. "Maybe Nikolas wants a dog."

Jack sighed. *God, what kind of joke is this? With everything that's happening, Danny barely hanging on, and so many unanswered questions, and we have to deal with a dog?* "Your mother can ask him."

Scott settled onto the floor with the puppy while Jack briefly told Marah about Danny.

She said, "Pneumonia? Is that all? From the way you two looked when you came in, I thought someone died."

Jack and Scott exchanged looks.

"He's a sick boy," Jack said.

"What's euthanasia, Granpop? Isn't that when they kill people?"

Jack pulled the griddle out of the cupboard. He'd fix them grilled cheese sandwiches and soup for supper. Marah would complain, but she never ate much anyway. "Mercy killing, some call it. When all hope is gone. Some people believe in it. I don't."

"Me neither," Scott said.

"Has someone suggested it?" Marah said. "Is Danny that sick?"

"I heard Danny's grandmother tell the doctor she didn't want Danny to suffer if there was no hope," Scott said. "But she said she was against euthanasia. The doctor said it wasn't allowed in that hospital."

Suddenly intent on examining her fingernails, Marah said, "No, it's not."

Cheese and bread in hand, Jack paused to look at his daughter. *How would she know that?*

Later, shoving away her plate with its untouched sandwich, Marah jumped up from the table when Scott said he wanted to return to the hospital. "I'll go with you, Scott, and offer my support to Danny's poor grandparents. I can just imagine how they must feel."

When Jack heard this, he jerked involuntarily, spilling a spoonful of tomato soup down his shirtfront.

"We'll take Tippy over to Nikolas's on our way," Marah continued.

"Danny and his grandparents don't need strangers around at a time like this," Jack said. He went to the sink and wiped at his shirt with the dishcloth.

"Don't be silly, Daddy." Marah's chin went up. "I know how to handle these situations. I'm on the hospital auxiliary board at home. We train our volunteers for just these kinds of circumstances."

"This hospital has its own volunteers. No reason for you to go."

"And," Scott said, "Mrs. DeWolfe doesn't like strangers."

"Mrs. DeWolfe? Richard DeWolfe's wife?" Marah gave her father a puzzled look. "I know him. You know I do, Daddy." To Scott she said, "When I was in high school, I worked at DeWolfe Department Store." Her mouth curved in a tight-lipped smile. "I was one of his favorite employees. And your grandmother worked there for several years when she was young, before I was born. Didn't she, Dad?"

Jack ignored her.

"Not only that," Marah continued, "you know your grandfather worked there practically all his life. You see, darling, I'm not a stranger at all. I'll run upstairs and get ready."

After she left the room, Scott looked at his grandfather, confused. "Does she really know Danny's grandfather?"

"Not as well as she thinks." Utensils clattered as Jack dumped them in the sink. He went upstairs and rapped on Marah's bedroom door. "I want to speak to you."

"Just a minute." She flung the door open. She'd changed into a pair of ivory slacks and a green blouse. As she fastened a gold earring, she said, "I'm ready."

Sternly, Jack said, "Marah, this is not a good idea. The boy may be dying. These people need their privacy."

She tilted her head and looked at him. "You don't object to Scott going."

"The boys are friends." Marah pushed past him and dashed downstairs without even listening.

As he heard the car doors slam, he wondered, *What are Scott and Danny? More than friends, they're blood relatives.* His hatred had been burning so strong about what DeWolfe had done to Claire and tried to do to Marah, he hadn't thought about how Scott fit into this picture. Now he pieced it together.

DeWolfe is ... Scott's grandfather.

Jack struck the wall with the flat of his hand. "No!"

CHAPTER 36

Marah sat in a vinyl chair in the hospital's third-floor parlor. "Isn't it wonderful that Nikolas took Tippy? You'll be able to go over after school to play with him. It's almost like having your own dog, dear."

Scott sounded disgusted. "I'm not a little kid. Nikolas said his granddaughter wants a puppy. He's going to give the dog to her."

"Oh. I didn't hear that."

"You never hear anything except what you want to hear, Mom."

Marah stood to check her appearance in a mirror hung over a sideboard. Satisfied with her hair and makeup, she turned sideways to examine her profile. *Five more pounds and I'll be in a size 6,* she promised herself. She glanced over her shoulder to be sure Scott wasn't watching and slipped three pills from her purse. She swallowed them with a cup of lukewarm coffee. As she set the cup down, she heard low voices.

A well-dressed older couple approached the room, the woman clinging to the man's arm. The man and woman walked slowly, heads down, shoulders rounded. When the man lifted his head, straightening his shoulders, Marah suddenly wished she hadn't come. *The wolf himself. But he's as old as Dad.* Marah recalled the incident in his office so many years ago. She'd been a teenager then, inexperienced and frightened. She shuddered at the memory and pushed it from her mind.

Frances DeWolfe smiled when she saw Scott. "He asked for you, dear."

Scott's face brightened. "He's awake?"

"Just barely. Come, I'll take you to him." She glanced at her husband.

He said, "I'll wait here for the doctor."

Marah wondered if he'd recognize her after all these years.

CHAPTER 37

In the dim lights, Danny seemed to float in a white landscape, his eyes sunken and hair dark against the pillow. An eerie feeling crept over Scott.

Mrs. DeWolfe whispered to Scott, "I'm going to the chapel, dear. I'll be back in a few minutes."

Scott nodded and tiptoed to Danny's bedside. Once again, tears filled his eyes at the sight of the oxygen mask over Danny's nose and mouth, the tubes connected to his hands.

Danny's eyes opened. His voice sounded muffled beneath the oxygen mask. "Scotty." He moved his fingers.

Gently, Scott folded his hand over Danny's fingers and knelt on the floor beside him. "Hey, Danny."

Danny lifted the edge of the oxygen mask. "So tired ... I ... want it to be over."

Scott's fingers tightened. "Don't say that."

Eyes beseeching, Danny said, "Finish my project ... at church?" He held the mask over his nose and mouth and took several breaths.

Fear constricted Scott's throat. His voice cracked. "Okay. I'll try." He locked his eyes on Danny's face. *Don't die, Danny, don't die.*

"My grandparents ... Catholic funeral ... but I asked ... Fellowship Church. You ... Nikolas ... talk to pastor?" He breathed with the mask again.

"Okay, I will. We will."

"Special verse ... song ..." Danny closed his eyes then continued, " ... my journal."

Tears flowed down Scott's cheeks. "Okay, Danny, I'll talk to Nikolas, and—and we'll talk to the pastor. And I'll look in your journal for the song. And the verse. I'll do it for you, Danny. And your project, too. I'll finish it for you, the way you talked about."

Danny nodded, ever so slightly. "I'm going to heaven." His chest barely rose and fell, paused, rose and fell, and paused again.

A nurse came up behind Scott and put her hand on his shoulder. Gently, she said, "Danny needs to rest now."

Scott stood and glanced over his shoulder as he slowly walked away. The nurse caressed Danny's forehead. Would he see Danny again? *I can't go home. I'm staying here 'til ...* Scott planted himself on the floor near Danny's door.

CHAPTER 38

After Danny's grandmother and Scott left, DeWolfe seemed to notice Marah for the first time. She waited, watching him, as his eyes locked on her face. He stepped closer.

"Don't I know you? Forgive me, but I'm not recalling—"

"Marah Emerson, now Giroux."

"Marah … you're Claire Emerson's daughter." He smiled. "It's good to see you again. You've become a lovely woman." He paused. "But were you with Scott?"

"He's my son." Fighting her fear and revulsion of the man, Marah forced herself to hold her composure. "How is your grandson?" She watched him lean against the sideboard and suck in a deep breath and expel it. She noticed a bruise on his cheekbone.

"Not good. No improvement."

"Is he in a coma?"

"No, just sleeping a lot. But he seems cognizant when he's awake. One of the nurses said this sometimes happens before …"

A young nurse entered the room, her footsteps quick, energetic. "Mr. DeWolfe, the doctor will be with you shortly." She turned to Marah. "You must be Danny's mother."

Marah shook her head.

The nurse looked from Marah to DeWolfe and back. "His aunt?"

DeWolfe spoke up, his words clipped. "Danny's mother, my only child, was killed in a car accident many years ago."

"I just thought—the family resemblance—" She blushed. "Excuse me, please, I have to get back to the desk." She hurried out of the room.

The woman's words bounced through Marah's mind like a Ping-Pong ball. *Family resemblance, family resemblance …*

DeWolfe turned and poured coffee from the server on the sideboard. Marah stared at his image in the mirror. *The shape of his jaw, the nose, the eyes … that nurse is right. We do look alike. His hair—*

that white streak—like mine before I started dying it. Neither Mother nor Dad have eyes like mine and Scott's. But Richard DeWolfe does.

Hands trembling, Marah crossed her arms and tucked her fists against her sides. Her mother's unforgettable words shot through her mind. *"Jack Emerson is not your father."*

DeWolfe glanced up at Marah's reflection. She felt her face grow warm, knowing she'd been staring. Without thinking, she blurted out, "How well did you know my mother?"

DeWolfe sipped his coffee and studied the floor. "We were friends, very good friends."

Marah's heart pounded. *And lovers?*

A doctor walked into the room. "Mr. DeWolfe, let's go—"

Marah picked up her purse. "I'm leaving."

The doctor nodded. "Thank you." He looked at her. "Wait. Are you—"

"No one. I'm nobody."

Marah found Jack in his garage workshop, carving the miniature pony's tiny hooves.

She slammed her purse on the workbench. "Why didn't you tell me? You knew, and you didn't tell me!"

Jack's eyes met hers, but Marah couldn't fathom his thoughts. Did he feel guilt? Shame for his deceit? She raised her voice. "Richard DeWolfe. That's why you didn't want me to go to the hospital. You knew!"

He rubbed his thumb over the wooden pony and spoke slowly. "I wanted to protect you. You told me recently that when you were a teenager, he'd made a pass at you. I didn't want you to have to face him again."

"No, it's not that. You know what I'm talking about. You and mother never told me. I had a right to know. Why didn't you tell me?"

Without meeting her eyes, he said, "What is there to tell?"

Marah rubbed her forehead and paced. *Is it possible he doesn't know? No, he knows.* Her back turned, she said, "Mother told me. That night we argued. The night she had the stroke. She told me you're not my real father."

Marah whirled to face Jack. She caught her breath at his pale face, and her mother's sudden collapse flashed across her mind. *Not Dad, please, not Dad.* His blue eyes watered; the corners of his mouth drooped. Slowly, he set the wooden horse and his pocketknife on the workbench. For a brief instant, she regretted her words. She held her breath as Jack's shoulders heaved in a great sigh. *He's all right. He's not having a stroke. He won't die.* She let out her breath. Anger surged again.

"You know you're not my father. You must know who is. I saw the resemblance with my own eyes just minutes ago. Richard DeWolfe! *He's* my real father!" Marah struck the bench with her fist, raising a small cloud of dust. "Isn't he?"

Jack blotted his eyes and wiped his nose with a frayed handkerchief. "For years, I didn't know who your biological father is. But I'm your *real* father. I was there at your birth. I was the first to hold you. I raised you. I love you. You are my own, my very own daughter."

Marah fought against tears threatening to spill over. She loved Jack. He *was* her father. But he'd lied to her, a conspiracy with her mother. She steeled herself against her emotions.

Jack continued, "Your mother never told me who it was. I found out years later. Long after you were grown."

"Does he know? DeWolfe?"

"No. Absolutely not. We agreed to take the secret to our graves."

Marah gave a short, bitter laugh. "Not quite. She told me, remember? But not everything. Just enough to make me feel like ... like filth under her feet. She never wanted me."

Jack turned to face her. "Marah, *I* wanted you. Your mother and I decided to raise you as though you were my own. And you are."

Marah's anger wavered. "Why did you let me go to the hospital tonight?"

"I tried to stop you."

She paced from the workbench to the stove and around the rocking chair. Her head hurt. She needed some pills. She massaged her temples.

Jack said, "Did you see him?"

She gave a short, bitter laugh. "Yes. The nurse thought I was his daughter."

Jack winced. "Did he ..."

"Did he what? Act like he was glad to see me, his long-lost daughter? Oh, no. I could tell what he was thinking—about that little scene in his office when he made a pass at me."

Realization dawned. Her mouth fell open. "He *doesn't* know, does he?" She dropped into the rocking chair.

Jack slid off his stool, knelt beside her, and took her hand. "I will never understand why your mother told you. She and I had agreed to keep it a secret between us. No one else knows, Marah. As far as the rest of the world is concerned, you are my blood daughter."

Marah felt weak and shaky, like she was coming down with the flu. She clasped Jack's fingers and covered her eyes with her free hand. She couldn't stop the tears she'd been holding back since she left the hospital. She felt Jack's arms around her. He held her close, patting her back. He felt strong, secure, and safe. "Oh, Daddy, why did she hate me so? I didn't ask to be born."

"She didn't hate you, sweetheart. She loved you. But she was a troubled woman … couldn't seem to show the affection I'm sure she felt for you."

Marah pushed him away. "You always say that, but I know—"

The back door of the house slammed shut.

Jack stood and looked out the window. "Scott's home."

Together, Marah and her father returned to the house. Marah slipped into the bathroom with her purse and closed the door. She swallowed two pills, then another.

CHAPTER 39

Jack found Scott curled up on his bed, arm over his face, crying. Jack put his hand on the boy's arm.

"He's dead, Granpop. Danny died."

Jack sat down beside him and pulled his grandson into his arms. Scott sobbed against his shoulder. After a moment, the boy raised up, sniffed, and wiped his face on his arm. He swung his legs over and sat on the edge of the bed, facing the window. Jack got up, retrieved a box of Kleenex from the dresser, and sat beside him.

Scott pulled out a handful of tissues and blew his nose. "I got to talk to him for a couple of minutes then I had to leave. After a while, they let me in one more time." His voice broke. He gulped. "It was awful. One of the machines started buzzing, and nurses started running. They practically pushed me out the door and closed it." Scott took a deep, ragged breath. "I waited by his door. I was so scared. All of a sudden, it was all over. One of the nurses came out and kind of hugged me. So I knew."

Jack blew his nose. "His suffering is ended. He's with Jesus."

Scott's teary eyes searched Jack's face. "How do you know?"

"I know because—" Jack faltered. *How do I know? I believe, but I don't know how to tell my grandson why I believe.* "I believe in my heart it's true, son, but I have to admit I don't know how to explain why. I know it's in the Bible, the gospel of John. Long time ago, I could have told you the chapter and verse."

Scott picked at a hangnail on his thumb. "I just hope it's true. Danny believed it. He told me he was going to heaven. I want to believe Danny is okay now."

Never had Jack felt so inadequate to help his family. First Marah, discovering she was conceived from her mother's affair. Now Scott, looking for substance behind platitudes. And Jack didn't have good explanations for either of them.

"Before Danny got sick," Scott said, "he wanted me to help with his project. But he got sick. So we never did get it going. He wanted to tell the kids at his church youth group about AIDS, about not taking risks. 'Staying pure,' he said." Scott threw his wadded up tissues into the wastebasket. "In the hospital, Danny asked me to finish what he wanted to do. His project. I promised I would."

Hope coursed through Jack's veins, hope for Scott. Hard on its heels came doubt. Would they believe Scott if he didn't believe it himself?

"But here's what bothers me," Scott continued. "Danny said his grandfather told him that by doing good stuff to help other people, like Danny's project, he would be 'redeeming himself.' Granpop, I don't get it. In Nikolas's church one time I remember the pastor talking about redemption. He said Jesus redeems us." Scott gave Jack a searching look. "If Jesus redeems us, how can we—or why should we—try to redeem ourselves?"

"Good question. I remember pondering about that myself a long time ago. Jesus's redemption for us is his sacrificial death on the cross where he paid the penalty for our sins so we could have eternal life. We can't redeem ourselves. Only Jesus could do that because he is the only one who is perfect. And he's God's only Son. He never committed a sin, ever. Danny's grandfather could have used a different word—he could have said he was trying to correct his mistakes. That's not the same as redemption."

"Oh yeah, I get it," Scott said. "Danny's project wasn't so he could get into heaven—it's to make things fit for the way he believes— believed—before he died. He said he wanted to help other kids. He already knew he was going to heaven—because he believed in Jesus."

"Yes, you've got it," Jack said.

As though reading his mind, Scott said, "Trouble is, this isn't like debate class, where you argue something even if you don't believe it, and you convince people you do. This isn't like that. This is too—too personal. Kids won't buy it if they think I'm lying."

"Would you be lying?"

"Danny got so he was saying even if we're born gay, we can go straight. I dunno."

This wasn't the answer Jack wanted. He refused to give up hope for his grandson. "You don't have to decide about yourself right now. Give yourself a little time, son, to adjust to Danny being gone. It's okay to hurt. We're going to miss that boy."

Jack heard Marah's footsteps on the stairs.

"Granpop," Scott said, his voice gentle, "I don't think you get what I'm thinking. I believe the most important thing is that Jesus loves me. I believe that. I feel that deep in my heart. I know he died for my sins, too. But I don't believe the homosexual lifestyle is a sin."

Jack was speechless. Scott's sincerity struck his heart and mind, and he didn't know how to respond. No easy answers.

Jack knew he and Scott couldn't continue their conversation now. Truth was, he felt a little relieved. His grandson challenged his steadfast beliefs. *God, what are you doing to me?*

Marah's approach forced Jack's thoughts to her.

He worried that she would figure out that Scott and Danny were not normal friends. What would she do? Would she turn on her son when he needed comfort and love? Would she be able to cope with two shocking discoveries?

Marah came in, walked around the bed, and sat on the window seat, facing them. She had cleaned the smeared mascara off her face and seemed composed—except for one foot tapping a nervous rhythm.

"Is Danny—?"

"He's gone."

"Oh, Scott darling, I'm sorry." She leaned toward him with her arms outstretched, but he ignored her.

Watching them, Jack's heart felt like a lead bowling ball. *Will things ever be right between them?*

The simple sanctuary of Fellowship Church was filled with mourners—teenagers from the youth group, teachers from the high school, businesspeople, community leaders, and a few people from the Carousel. Several large flower arrangements flanked a large, framed portrait of Danny in front of the podium. Danny's grandparents sat in the front row. They had scheduled a Catholic service for the following day. This memorial service was in compliance with their grandson's final request.

As Jack, Kennocha, Nikolas, and Marah sat down several rows behind the DeWolfes, Scott came alongside and whispered to Jack, seated on the aisle. "Danny's grandparents asked me to sit with them. Is that okay with you, Granpop?"

Jack wanted to say no. "Go ahead, if you want to."

Scott's face looked troubled, as though he sensed Jack's reluctance.

Kennocha stood, leaned across Jack, and hugged the teenager. "You'll be a comfort to them, Scott. Do it for Danny."

He nodded and walked to the front pew.

Jack heard a hiss of breath from Marah, seated on Nikolas's far side. Did she object to her son sitting with the DeWolfes? Or to Scott asking him instead of her? Or to Kennocha's display of affection for Scott and his acceptance? Or all of the above? He hoped she wouldn't make a scene. He just wanted to get through this and get as far away as possible from Richard DeWolfe. Or strangle him.

An elderly woman sat at the piano, softly playing "Blessed Assurance" while people waited for the service to begin. Jack sensed her eyes on him and wondered if she could read his un-Christian thoughts. She smiled at him, her eyes sending a silent message of peace. Jack resolved to banish his hatred of DeWolfe. At least for the next hour.

The minister, a gray-haired man with alert, kind eyes, approached the pulpit. Jack remembered him from the Easter service. He'd also heard the man a few times previously, when Nikolas had coerced him into coming. Jack liked this preacher. Seemed genuine. Strong handshake and a manner of looking you right in the eye, almost like he could see into your soul. Unlike other preachers Jack had met, this man didn't accuse with his eyes. Instead, he gave a wide, boyish grin and said, "Hi, how are you?" like he cared. Jack hadn't admitted it to Nikolas, but if church consisted just of this man's teaching and a song or two, he'd come more often. It was the foofaraw Jack couldn't stand. Church should be church, not a platform for social announcements and endless gossip disguised as prayer requests.

After an opening prayer, the minister sat down, and a pair of teenagers came to the front as the woman at the piano played a lead-in. The boy looked like a football player. His dress shirt looked to be two sizes too small and the knotted tie too short for his long torso. The studious-looking girl beside him barely reached his shoulder. Her long, plain dress emphasized her thinness. The mismatched pair's voices blended in a beautiful melody. Jack didn't recognize the song, although he liked the words and the youngsters' clear voices as they sang.

Far beyond the understanding there's a hand that leads if you believe ... remember God loves you ...

As the young couple sat down, Scott stood, tall and handsome in a gray suit, the same one he'd taken to the speech meet. He wore his new shirt and a new tie Marah had bought for him. Jack felt Kennocha's hand slip into his. He closed his fingers around hers.

Scott peeked under his bangs at the audience, then he raised his head, swallowed, and began. "Danny is—was—my best friend." He spoke of Danny's kindness toward others, his musical talent, and his desire to help others. Then Scott glanced at his notes and cleared his throat. "Before he died, Danny asked me to read a couple of things today. The first is a Bible verse." He read the words he'd copied from Danny's journal. "For our citizenship is in heaven ... for the Savior, the Lord Jesus Christ ... will transform our lowly body into a glorious body."

Scott set aside his notes and picked up a softcover music book. "Danny played the piano and guitar. One song he really liked was written by Dennis Jernigan. He's a gay guy. *Was* gay, Danny said." Scott glanced up as several people stirred in the audience. "Danny wrote in his journal that this guy renounced his gay lifestyle and turned his life over to God. Danny said, in his journal, that he wanted to be like Dennis Jernigan." Scott opened the book. "This is the song he wanted me to read." He paused and looked up with a wry smile. "Danny knows I can't sing. This is called 'All I Used to Be.'"

I never thought that I would ever see the day that I could walk completely free. And then a cleansing rain fell over me ... the day You came raining, washing my heart clean ... pouring through my heart like a rainy day, wiping ev'ry single sin away, washing, changing me completely.

Finished, Scott hurriedly wiped tears from his cheeks and sat down beside Frances DeWolfe.

Marah fidgeted. Jack saw from the corner of his eye that she was trying to get his attention. He pretended not to notice.

The pastor stepped forward, his face calm, pleasant. "Thank you, Scott, for honoring your friend's request. I don't have much to add to what these young people have already said and sung. They spoke well. Danny's choice of verses tells me he knew his resurrection body would be whole in heaven. No disease. No suffering. That's a promise we can bank on." The pastor leaned his arms on the podium and looked into the faces of the audience. "I was just getting to know Danny when the Lord called him home. He was a fine young man." He addressed Richard and Frances DeWolfe. "I'm sorry I wasn't in town while Danny was in the hospital. I'd like to have held his hand when his soul left this earth to meet Jesus."

Throughout the minister's brief message, Jack listened intently to every word, searching for something Scott might grab onto and change his life for the better. *If Danny's early death doesn't convince my grandson about the risk in a homosexual lifestyle, I don't know what will.* From the corner of his eye, Jack saw Marah cross her legs and jiggle one foot up and down as though bored. He glanced at her. She didn't look bored; she looked nervous. *What is she thinking?* He turned his attention back to the pastor as he talked about suffering, lingering death.

"We often don't know why God allows certain things, but He is almighty God and doesn't need to explain Himself. Yet He does, to a great extent. It's all in this book." The pastor held up a Bible. "Danny trusted God to the end. Difficult as it is to see our loved ones suffer, it's not for us to say when our life or anyone else's should end. That's for God to decide."

Marah coughed as though choking on something. Abruptly, she stood, shoved her way to the aisle, and hurried to the back of the church. Moments later, Jack heard the door open and close.

Nikolas leaned forward, one eyebrow raised in a question to Jack.

Kennocha, too, gave him an inquisitive look.

Jack shrugged, as baffled as they were. And uneasy. Marah's moods were unpredictable. What was she up to now?

CHAPTER 40

One hot August day, several weeks later, in the shade of a chokecherry tree on the banks of the Clark Fork River, Jack and Nikolas lounged on a grassy slope waiting for Kennocha to return from a milkshake run to their favorite ice cream shop across the bridge. Izsak was conducting a tour in the Carousel behind them. The three had grabbed a short break until the tour was over.

Kennocha soon arrived with the treats. "They were out of licorice, Nikolas. Is the blackberry okay?" Kennocha asked as she handed it to him.

He sucked on the straw. "M-m-m, yes, indeed. This shall become my new second favorite."

Kennocha sat down and leaned back on her elbows. "Do you think we'll ever be ready for the Carousel anniversary celebration? I've barely begun painting the Indian pony."

"Nikolas and I finished the Medieval pony and moved him into the paint room today. Now we're working on the Shetland." Jack popped the lid off his cup and, using two straws, scooped out a glob of thick, butterscotch ice cream.

Nikolas said, "The Shetland is the children's favorite. It is the one their pennies bought."

Kennocha asked, "Didn't the kids design him, too?"

"Yes, they did, with Izsak's help, I am sure. But I think they chose the kind of horse and the decorations. Is that not correct, Jack?" No response. "Jack?"

Kennocha jostled him with her shoulder. "Find a bug in your ice cream?"

"What?" Jack secured the lid on his cup and poked the straws in the hole. "Sorry, I thought you were talking to Nikolas."

"You're so distracted. Is Scott all right?"

"Scott's okay." Jack scowled. "It's his mother that bothers me. She keeps making these surprise visits. Stays overnight and then she's gone again. Sometimes she doesn't even tell us she's leaving."

Nikolas stopped making slurping noises.

Jack continued, "Don't know why she doesn't stay home. Can't very well tell her that. You've seen how she hangs around down here. Feel like I can't ignore her, but it's hard to finish a job with her interruptions." Nikolas cleared his throat loud enough to get Jack's attention. His friend's eyebrows reached for his hairline.

"I may be an uneducated immigrant," he waggled his finger, "but I do know about people." He drew a deep breath. "Marah is worried about losing you, Jack."

"She can't lose me."

Kennocha held up her hand. "Wait a minute. Nikolas has a good point. Marah is possessive. And jealous." She sat up and crossed her legs yoga style. "Let's try to see this from her point of view. You said she and Vic are having problems. She may fear losing him. Her only child ran away, prefers to live with you, and is trying to distance himself from her emotionally. Her mother's dead; her brother is clear across the country with his own family. In her mind, you may be all she has left. And she sees me as a threat to your relationship."

Nikolas nodded vigorously. "Yes, that is exactly what I am saying."

Jack looked away and stared at the river, deep in thought. *They could be right. If they knew about DeWolfe and Claire, and Marah's reaction ... yes, they're probably right. Marah's so sure her mother didn't love her. Probably the only thing she's sure of right now—if she believes me—is that I love her. Although after seeing DeWolfe at the hospital that day, her anger at me, her doubt ... I don't know if she believes anyone loves her.* "I think you're right, both of you. Her attitude toward you doesn't make a lot of sense to me, Kennocha, but she's been telling me—well, her exact words were: 'While Scott's living with you, you need to concentrate on him. You can't spend time on other relationships.' She's also said it's too soon after her mother's death for me to think about another woman." He shook his head. "Guess she'd have me wait until I have one foot in the grave." He sighed. "Guess I'd better try to be more understanding with her."

Nikolas's and Kennocha's voices chorused, "No."

Jack stared at them. "What?"

Nikolas folded his hands across his stomach and nodded for Kennocha to go ahead.

"You need to establish boundaries with her. Remember the dinner party Saturday night? I went without you, because Marah suddenly got sick and asked you to take her to the emergency room. You didn't believe her, but you gave in. And the doctors found nothing wrong. They sent her home with some tranquilizers."

"You don't understand. There are things neither of you know."

Kennocha leaned forward and put her hand on his arm. "We all have problems, issues, things we must learn to cope with or resolve. No one can fix anyone else, especially someone who doesn't want to be helped."

Nikolas said, "I understand you love your daughter, my friend, but Kennocha is right. Marah comes to you when life is difficult for her. But she does not listen to your counsel." He stroked his beard. "And you know some things she has done to herself."

Jack snapped, "So what do you want me to do? Disown her?"

"Of course not," Kennocha said.

Nikolas shook his head. "No, no."

Kennocha continued, "Persuade her to get professional help." She plucked a blade of grass and ran it between her thumb and finger. "Do you think she's abusing drugs?"

"Diet pills, if that's what they really are. Maybe that's why she's so unpredictable."

"If she's abusing them—or using street drugs—that's all the more reason for her to get professional help."

Nikolas grunted. "For myself, I believe it is time for you to take a firm hand concerning your daughter."

Jack bristled. "Drag her to a treatment center?"

Nikolas cocked his head and looked Jack square in the eye. "Speak with your son-in-law. Tell him what you believe she needs. She must go home. Her husband will care for her, will he not? You told me Vic has been calling her when she's here. You said Scott is getting along better with his father and will speak with him on the phone now."

Jack stood and threw up his hands. "You two just don't understand." He started to walk away then turned abruptly. "Listen to me. I sound just like a teenager." He shoved his hands in his pockets. *Should I tell them I'm not Marah's biological father? That's why she won't leave us alone, I'm sure of it. She needs to prove to herself that I love her and won't abandon her. What am I supposed to do?*

Nikolas rolled over on the grass and got to his knees. Jack offered his hand and helped him to his feet. Nikolas wrapped a burly arm around Jack's shoulders. "My friend," Nikolas said, "you are trying too hard to make everybody happy. Some things you must trust to God."

CHAPTER 41

Late that afternoon, thunderheads formed on the horizon. The sky darkened. With the stereo in his room turned up to the maximum his grandfather would allow, Scott headed downstairs for a snack. At the sound of his mother's voice talking intently to someone on the phone, he paused on the stairs to listen.

"In my top, left-hand drawer ... no, the desk in the kitchen ... yes, that's right. It has a green leather cover." Marah laughed. "Oh, don't worry about that, Tina. He always goes to the liquor cabinet the minute he gets home from the office. He'll never notice the checkbook is gone."

Scott leaned against the wall, a sick feeling in his stomach. *Tina. That means one thing. More drugs.*

"Today. I really need the money." Irritation colored her voice. "I don't know. He said he'd see that I'm well taken care of if I'd agree to a divorce ... No, I'm not coming back yet. Dad is—well, let me just say there's a woman here who's trying to cut me out of his life. Scott's life, too. I have to deal with that situation before I come back. Now, don't forget to—"

Scott leaped down the remaining three steps and landed with an audible thud on the floor.

His mother whirled and stared at him. "Tina, I have to go now. You'll do it today, won't you? ... Okay, good-bye." She hung up and turned to face Scott again. "Hello, darling."

"Are you and Dad getting a divorce?"

"You were listening? How dare you."

"Just tell me the truth for a change."

Her eyes narrowed. "You might as well know. Your father has filed for divorce. He intends to have the papers served as soon as I get back."

"How come nobody told me? Don't I count for anything? Who's going to be in charge of me? Can Granpop?"

"That remains to be settled. You'll probably spend part of the time with me, part with your father."

"You guys are going back on your word again! I'm staying here with Granpop!" He stomped into the kitchen.

Marah followed, leaned against the counter, and folded her arms across her chest. "You might not have a choice. Do you think it would be any better living with your father? Instead of me?"

"At least he doesn't cheat on you. Is that why he's divorcing you," Scott sneered, "because of your boyfriend?"

Marah's mouth twisted into an ugly grimace. "He's been cheating on me for years. Why would he care if I do the same?"

Something snapped in Scott. His voice grew louder. "I care! Doesn't that matter? Doesn't anybody care about me? Why can't you guys just act like normal parents? I want to be proud of you—but I'm ashamed!"

He stormed into the living room, Marah on his heels.

Neither of them heard Jack come in the back door.

Scott stood in the middle of the living room and faced his mother. "Anyway, I don't believe you," he yelled. "He's not cheating on you. It's because of that guy isn't it? Dad found out, didn't he? That's why he's divorcing you!"

Shrieking foul names at her son, Marah swung her arm to backhand Scott, aiming for his face. He ducked, too late. Her ring gouged his forehead. Blood coated his fingertips when he touched it.

She raised her hand again.

"Marah! Stop!" Jack yelled. He grabbed her arm and pulled her away. She stumbled against the sofa. "What's going on here?" Jack demanded. He looked at Scott. "You're bleeding. Marah, get a bandage." He pulled a folded handkerchief from his pocket and handed it to Scott. "Hold this tight against it."

Scott complied, staring at his mother. She hadn't moved from the arm of the sofa. She seemed frozen, but her eyes were wary.

Jack said, "All right, Marah. Stay there. I want to talk to you. I'll get a bandage, Scott." He hurried toward the bathroom.

Scott glared at his mother. "I hate you!"

She stood, looked at Scott for a long moment, and her eyes filled with tears. Suddenly, she turned and ran out of the house.

Scott heard Jack call out, "Marah!" The back door slammed.

Seconds later, the Cadillac's tires squealed as she drove away.

The back door opened and closed quietly. Scott went into the kitchen to face his grandfather.

Jack said, "Let's fix that cut. What caused this?"

Scott sat at the table. "Her ring."

"I mean the argument. I heard you say something about divorce." Jack finished dressing the wound, pulled out a chair, and sat down.

"I overheard her talking to Tina. Dad is going to divorce Mom." He swallowed. "She says Dad has—has a lover. And so—" He cleared his throat. "So it's okay if she does, too. I don't believe her. About Dad. I told her I hate her."

Something changed in Jack's face, like a sudden understanding. Scott felt relief and dread. Jack looked him square in the eye, and Scott knew he had to tell.

"You knew, didn't you? About your mother? This is what you've been holding back, isn't it?"

Scott stared at the floor. "Yeah."

"Is that why you ran away? Who hit you on your back? Scott, look at me, talk to me. Now."

Scott fought to keep from crying. "What's gonna to happen to me? She says I'll have to live part of the time with her and part of the time with Dad. But I don't want to live with them. I want to stay with you."

His grandfather's eyes filled with determination. "I'll see what I can do. That's a promise. But you need to answer me."

Chapter 42

Several blocks away, Marah parked in front of a small shop and walked in. Five minutes later, she walked out with a small, brown paper bag of "diet pills." Thunderheads filled the sky as the Hellgate Canyon wind propelled them over the mountains. Wind whipping her hair, Marah dashed to her car and drove away while swallowing four pills, chased down with Diet Pepsi. Under dark skies heavy with rain, the Carousel parking lot looked deserted. But Marah saw a light in the paint room and smiled.

She found Kennocha alone, painting feathers on a bridle with a tiny brush. A denim jacket hung over the back of her stool. Kennocha looked up as Marah approached.

"Oh, hello, Marah." She stood up and rubbed her back. "I'll be glad when this one's done. Feathers are more difficult for me than flowers."

"Why do you keep at it?"

"I enjoy it." She smiled. "Despite my complaints." She bent to her work.

"I'd think you have enough to do with your job."

"Summers are pretty easy as far as my job goes. I really wanted to continue through the summer with the creative writing class, but our budget was cut."

Marah leaned against the workbench, picked up a half-pint can of green paint from the worktable, and ran her thumb over the lid. She turned the can over and over in her hands, shook it, and heard the glop of a nearly full can. "That's the class Scott's in, isn't it?"

Kennocha nodded.

"What's he write about?"

Kennocha glanced up and gave her a measured look. "Life. Problems. It could be fiction, of course." She wiped her brush on a rag and cleaned it in paint thinner.

Marah's eyes narrowed. "Could be? Exactly what does he write?" Waiting, she tossed the can from hand to hand.

Kennocha didn't answer immediately. Marah shifted her weight and stepped away from the workbench.

Kennocha straightened, pulled off her paint smock, and sat on the stool. "His best story is about a teenage boy and his parents. Specifically, his mother."

Marah's breathing quickened. "And? Go on."

Kennocha crossed her legs and clasped her knee, one heel hooked on the rung of the stool. She tipped her head back and closed her eyes as though thinking. "He describes a boy who feels betrayed by someone he loves. The boy searches for truth to overcome his pain. He finds someone he trusts and starts a new life." Kennocha lowered her head and looked directly at Marah. "What do you think of that story?"

Marah gripped the can. "How did you get him to write something like that? He wouldn't think up such a thing on his own."

"No, he wouldn't, would he?"

Marah exploded. "You witch!"

The paint can flew, striking the side of Kennocha's head. Kennocha cried out and clasped her head.

Arms outstretched, Marah rushed at her. Kennocha scrambled to get off the stool. Too late. Marah struck her with both hands and shoved her over backward.

The stool crashed to the cement floor. Kennocha's arms and legs flailed then went limp when her head struck the floor. She groaned, eyes closed.

Marah stood over her for a moment, breathing hard. "Get out of my life. Leave my son alone. And leave my father alone!" She gave a savage kick to Kennocha's side and was rewarded with another groan of pain.

Marah turned and ran out of the building. Wind and rain hit her in the face. She jumped into her car and drove as wild as the wind, cutting between vehicles, speeding. She reached the ramp to Interstate 90 and accelerated, barely staying ahead of an eighteen-wheeler barreling down the outside lane. The driver blasted his horn. She pulled ahead, weaving in and out of traffic, cutting in front of fast cars on the inside lane, and feeling the satisfying power of her car. She pressed the gas pedal and headed east, not caring where she went, just wanting the excitement of speed, the edge of control.

CHAPTER 43

Jack hoped Scott would talk to him without further prodding after he assured the boy he wouldn't let him be taken away to live with Marah when his parents divorced. *I can't tell Scott I won't let Vic take him, either. Not yet. But I will fight to keep him here.*

"I've been patient with you, son, waiting for you to choose the time to tell me why you ran away from home. Too patient, I suspect. What just happened a little while ago, your mother hitting you, worries me. I feel bad about the divorce, but my biggest concern is you. You're a minor. The courts might not be anxious to grant custody to me. I need you to tell me everything. I need all the help I can get to fight for you."

Scott stared at the salt and pepper shakers on the table. He put one on each side of the sugar bowl. Then he shoved the sugar bowl away, folded his arms on the table, and laid his head down on them.

Rain spattered the windows. Tree branches waving in the wind tapped on the house.

"I'll be right back," Jack said. He went into his bedroom and pulled a box from beneath his bed. He returned to the kitchen and pulled Scott's rolled up, bloodied shirt, out of the box—the shirt he'd found in the boy's duffel bag the night he arrived. He unrolled it, held it up, and said, "Tell me about this."

Scott raised his head. He stared, mouth open.

Jack stuffed the shirt back in the box and sat down.

Scott sat up and cleared his throat. He looked miserable. "My friend Larry, in Boise, and I stayed after school one night to help set up for a concert. We were supposed to pick up Larry's mom after work, but we were late. She works at this clinic. When we got there, it looked like everybody was gone. Larry figured she was waiting inside, so we tried to get in the front, but it was locked. We went around back. Larry went one way; I went the other. Down at my end of the building, I saw a light, so I looked in."

255

Scott's voice cracked.

"I saw her. Mom. With this guy. She was ... they were on a couch, and they were naked." His hands curled into tight fists on the table.

Jack moaned, "Oh, God, no."

"I kinda thought Dad had cheated on Mom a long time ago, before we moved to Boise. I heard them arguing. But I never thought she would cheat on him."

Jack felt like he'd swallowed a lump of clay. *Marah. Just like her mother.* "Then what did you do, son?"

Scott's expression turned from anguish to anger. "I went home and waited for her."

The phone rang. Jack ignored it.

"What if it's Mom?"

With a grunt, Jack got up. It was Nikolas.

"You have talked to Kennocha this evening, yes?" Nikolas asked.

"No, not since this afternoon when we had milkshakes together. Why?"

"I am at the Carousel. I think something might have happened. Kennocha would never leave her work area in such disarray."

An icy chill ran down Jack's spine. "I'll be right there." He hung up and quickly relayed Nikolas's message to Scott. "I have to get down there."

"I'm going with you."

Jack didn't hesitate. "Let's go."

Nikolas's Oldsmobile sat alone in the Carousel's parking lot, where the rain continued and large puddles formed on the asphalt. Overhead lights flickered on. Jack and Scott splashed across the pavement to the Carousel's back door. Nikolas was waiting for them outside the paint room.

Jack entered the room with its familiar smell of paint, linseed oil, and thinner. The Indian pony sat near Kennocha's workbench. Cans of paint and used brushes lay scattered across the surface. He moved farther inside and saw an overturned stool, with Kennocha's jacket askew over the back. Nearby, a can of green paint lay on the floor, lid intact.

"You've searched the building for her?" Jack asked Nikolas.

"Yes, and after I talked to you, I called her apartment. She did not answer."

"Would you take Scott home with you? I'm going to her apartment."

"Yes. We will tidy up here and lock up the Carousel."

"No, better leave it as it is, Nikolas. Someone might want to see it." He and Nikolas exchanged a look. Nikolas nodded.

"Granpop, I want to go with you."

"No, son. It will be better if you stay with Nikolas." *And safer for you.* "I'll call after I find Kennocha."

Jack ran from the building, splashed across the parking lot, and ran up the stairs to the bridge. He paused for a few seconds to catch his breath. Panting, he jogged to Kennocha's apartment building entrance, waved at the familiar security guard, and took the elevator up to her floor.

She didn't answer her doorbell after three frantic rings. He rapped loudly and called her name.

The deadbolt sounded a loud *click,* and the door slowly eased inward. Jack tried to glimpse Kennocha's face in the dim room as she released the safety chain and swung the door open.

"Kennocha, are you all right? Turn on the light."

She closed the door, threw the deadbolt, and flipped on the light switch.

Jack's breath caught. "Dear God, what happened?" Blood matted the hair above her ear. The old scar on her chin looked like a red brand on her white face. He reached for her, but she turned away and limped toward the sofa.

"Let me take care of you. Where are the bandages?"

She gestured beyond the kitchen. "That bathroom."

Jack hurried away and returned with a cold washcloth, a towel, and first-aid supplies. He examined her wound. "It would be better if you come closer to the sink. Your hair's full of blood."

She complied wordlessly, limping into the bathroom, sitting on the toilet lid while Jack gently washed the blood from her hair.

"You've got a cut here. I think it needs stitches."

She shook her head. "It'll be all right."

"I'll try a couple of butterfly bandages. But if that doesn't hold it ..." Carefully, he pulled her hair aside and applied the bandages.

She winced. "I hit the back of my head on the floor."

"Let me just finish this bandage." Then Jack tenderly parted her long hair and peered at the back of her head. He gave a low whistle. "This lump is big. Look at my eyes." He knelt in front of her and looked into her eyes. "They look okay, but you might have a concussion. We need to go to the emergency room."

"No, I'm all right." She took his hand and stood.

He helped her back into the living room. She sat on the sofa. "Do you want to lie down?"

"No, it hurts."

He eased down beside her and held her hand. "Please, tell me what happened."

"Marah attacked me."

Jack felt his chest tighten.

Kennocha recounted Marah's words and actions.

When she finished, Jack said, "Have you called the police?"

"No."

"She could have killed you." He got up and went to the phone. "She hit Scott this afternoon, too. Gouged his cheek with her ring. I stopped her before she could hit him again. I know a cop. I'll see if he's on duty." He dialed, and after a short conversation, he hung up. "Ernie will meet us at the hospital."

"Where's Scott? Where's Marah?"

"Nikolas took Scott home with him. I don't know where Marah is. She ran out and drove away after I caught her hitting Scott."

"That must be when she came to the Carousel. To find me."

"Come, sweetheart, let's take your car. It's closer, and you can ride the elevator down to the garage." This time Kennocha didn't protest. "I'll tell you on the way what I just learned from Scott. He didn't finish, because Nikolas called to tell us about the paint room mess. Your suspicions are right. Scott's essay is true."

The rain continued. Ernie was waiting for them at the emergency room entrance. Both he and Jack followed Kennocha and the nurse into a room. After the doctor examined Kennocha, he put two stitches in her scalp, where the paint can hit, and instructed her about possible concussion symptoms. Then he ordered her not to be alone that night or the next day.

"I'm feeling much better, Doctor," Kennocha said. "I was pretty shaken up at first, but I'm all right now."

The doctor placed his hands on his hips. "Young lady, you said you're a teacher. Do you allow your students to argue with you and disobey your instructions?"

Kennocha gave him a slight smile. "No. I'll take your instructions to heart."

After the necessary paperwork was completed at the hospital, Kennocha, Jack, and Ernie held a brief conference.

"I don't want to involve too many people in this," Kennocha said. "But I don't know what to do."

"I do," Jack said. "Nikolas already has one houseguest—Scott—and he has one more spare bedroom. Let's go to your apartment. I'll call Nikolas while you're getting your things together. He'll be very pleased to be your guardian angel tonight. And I will have peace of mind."

Ernie spoke up. "Good plan. If you're up to it, Miss Bryant, I'd like to talk with you more about what happened. And I need to see the room in the Carousel building where this happened. I'll follow you to the apartment, and after I get your statement and you're settled at Mr. Kostenka's house, Mr. Emerson can call me. We'll meet at the Carousel, and I'll take some photos." Ernie looked at his watch then at Jack. "I drove by before I came here, so I know the Carousel is closed. But any chance of someone going in there?"

Jack looked out at the pouring rain and shook his head. "Only a few of us have keys to get in the building. And I locked the paint room door when I left. I have a master key."

In Kennocha's living room, Jack sat beside her as Ernie began the interview.

When Kennocha mentioned Marah's name, Ernie's glance shot to Jack.

Jack nodded. "Yes, Marah Giroux. My daughter. She attacked Kennocha."

Ernie jotted notes while Kennocha finished her account, then he questioned Jack. "Do you know where Marah is now?"

"No. About three hours ago, she was at my house. I walked in on an argument between Marah and her son. You've met Scott." Ernie nodded. "She had hit him so hard, her ring cut his cheek. I pulled her away from him. She ran out of the house, jumped in her car, and drove off."

"Describe her vehicle, please." Jack complied.

Kennocha said, "There's something else. I think she's on drugs. I work with kids in school. I've seen how their eyes get and how they act when they're high. I'd swear Marah was using something."

Ernie's eyes questioned Jack.

Jack rubbed his forehead. "Scott says she takes diet pills. He says Marah's friend Tina in Boise is addicted. I've never seen her take pills, but I don't doubt it. She's too thin. And she's emotionally unstable."

"Could be crank," the policeman said. "Ever hear her mention that word, Jack? Maybe overhear her talking to some friends?"

Jack shook his head. "What's crank?"

"One of the street names for methamphetamine. Central nervous system stimulant. Powerful. Under the influence, a person gets paranoid, moody, nervous. Loses interest in eating. Women in Marah's age bracket get hooked by abusing diet pills first."

Jack rubbed the back of his neck, aware of Kennocha watching him closely while Ernie talked. "Six months ago, I wouldn't have believed Marah would use illegal drugs. But I never thought she'd ever make a vicious attack on anyone, either. The reactions you described fit her pretty well these past few months. She's a stranger to me." He leaned forward, clasped his hands together. *My daughter has become dangerous to others. Her son, my dear Kennocha. This can't go on.*

"It gets worse," Ernie said. "People can be extremely violent when they're high." He nodded toward Kennocha. "What she did to Miss Bryant doesn't compare with the potential for violence."

Kennocha shuddered. Jack held her hand.

Ernie said, "Look, I'm not trying to scare you. But you need to know what we might be up against." He stood. "I'll get the word out on the car. Miss Bryant, be careful. I know Nikolas Kostenka. He will guard you like a bulldog, but I expect Mrs. Giroux will return to the Carousel—or to Mr. Emerson's house."

CHAPTER 44

The porch light at Nikolas's house came on, and Jack saw his grandson come out. At the door, Nikolas stepped forward to take Kennocha's arm. "Come, let me show you to your room." They disappeared down the hallway.

As soon as Jack was satisfied that Kennocha was settled, he called Ernie and left to meet him at the Carousel, assuring Nikolas and Scott that he would be back soon to answer their questions.

Later, Jack and Scott sat at the kitchen table, while Nikolas made cocoa and filled a plate with brownies. After Jack told them what had happened, omitting some of Ernie's warnings, the three sat in silence for several long moments.

Scott asked, "Where's Mom now?"

"Don't know. Police are watching for her car."

"Will she be arrested?"

"God have mercy," Nikolas muttered.

"I don't know, son. It's up to Kennocha if she wants to press charges. She's justified to do that." He hesitated and then asked, "Do you know if she's using illegal drugs?"

"I kinda think she is. She gets those diet pills—that's what she calls them—from Tina. But I think it might be meth or cocaine. I've seen how some of the kids at school act. In Boise and here."

Nikolas refilled Scott's cocoa mug and pushed the bag of marshmallows over to him.

"Was your mother using drugs when you ran away from home? Is she the one who hit you on your back?"

Nikolas cleared his throat politely. "I will leave you two alone."

"No, it's okay, Nikolas," Scott said. He drew in a deep breath and let it out. "Like I told you, Granpop, after I saw Mom on the couch with that guy at the clinic, I went home to wait for her."

CHAPTER 45

Scott tore a marshmallow into tiny bits, dropping them one by one into the cocoa. Then he began. As he talked, about that terrible night in February, Scott felt as though he were reliving the whole thing, a festering wound breaking open, ugly pus draining out.

Hours after Scott saw his mother that day in February in the doctor's office, she arrived home. He'd been slouched on the sofa in the family room, worried and wondering what would happen when his dad found out. Hearing the garage door open, he wiped tears from face with his sleeve.

When she walked into the house and saw him, her eyebrows went up. Her eyes looked strange, like she'd been drinking. But she didn't ever get drunk like Dad. So it must be drugs.

"You're home already," she said. "Didn't you stay for the concert?"

"No."

Marah sat beside him and reached to smooth his hair, a familiar gesture.

He jerked his head away.

"Sweetie, what's wrong? Have you been crying?" She leaned forward to look at his face.

He jumped up, shoved his hands in his pockets, and shuffled into the kitchen.

"What is it, Scott? What's happened?"

Feeling his face grow hot, Scott lashed out, "I punched my best friend in the face, that's what happened."

Marah went to him, tried to put her arm around him. "Oh, Scott—"

"Leave me alone!"

"What's wrong? Tell me."

Scott yelled, "I saw you!"

"What are you talking about?"

Scott faced his mother. "I saw you at the clinic. With that guy. On the couch." He struggled for control. "Why? Why'd you do it? How could you?" His mother stood frozen, her face white. "Then Larry came around the corner. He saw you, too. He made some smart remarks. I told him to get away. But he kept looking. And smirking. And saying things about you. I slugged him."

A long moment passed. Marah drew herself up straight, lifted her chin, and said, "You are mistaken. It wasn't me."

Scott glared. "It *was* you. And your car was in the back parking lot."

She blinked and folded her arms across her chest. "Yes, I was there. At the clinic. I was late getting to my appointment, but Dr. Addison was kind enough to see me anyway." She avoided his eyes. "I found a lump. It scared me. I thought it might be cancer."

Scott snarled, "How dumb do you think I am? This isn't one of your stupid soap operas." He jabbed a trembling finger at her. "It's true, isn't it, what the guys at school say about you? They say you're a tramp and—"

Swiftly closing the gap between them, Marah swung her arm back and slapped her son across the face. "How dare you speak to me like that!"

Scott didn't flinch. "Because it's true. All those other times, in Springfield, I lied to myself, said it wasn't true. But Larry and the other guys here, they know. And now I know."

"What do you think you know? You'd believe some lying, conniving pervert instead of your own mother?"

"I saw you! And Larry's not a liar!"

"He is! They're all a bunch of lying brats!"

"You know what else they say about you? Do you, Mom?"

"That's enough! Get out of my sight! Go to your room!"

Something snapped in Scott. "I'm sick of this." He strode through the house to the foyer and reached for his jacket in the closet. It caught on his golf bag and clubs. He yanked to pull it loose and then dropped the jacket as the golf bag began to lean forward. Too late, he grabbed for the bag. It tipped onto the floor, spilling a few clubs partway out.

Marah rushed after him and forced herself between him and closet. "Where do you think you're going?"

Scott pushed her aside, still trying to retrieve his jacket from the jumble on the floor. "I'm getting out of here. I'm sick of this place. Sick of you and Dad. Sick of all the fighting and yelling and drinking and lying." He bent to pick up his jacket.

Suddenly, his mother came at him, screaming, her hands gripping a steel-headed golf club.

"You're not leaving! You hear me, Scott?" With both fists wrapped around the handle, she lifted the club above her head.

"I'm going. I don't care if I never see you again!" He turned toward the front door. A split second before the impact, he sensed a motion and saw the steel head coming at him. Instinctively, he dodged. It narrowly missed his head and struck his back with shocking force.

Scott fell to his knees. He tasted vomit coming up in his mouth and choked it down. He grasped the doorjamb and pulled himself to his feet. His mother stood close behind him, breathing hard. He looked over his shoulder. Their eyes met. He held his breath, sensed the pull of his mother's will, her power over him, almost too strong for him to resist.

An unknown strength centered in his chest, flowed up to his mind, and out to his limbs. He exhaled and took in a deep breath. Even though his mother's eyes remained fixed on his, something in his soul released him from her hold. He was free. He opened the door and walked out into the night.

Marah screamed, "No, Scott, no! I'm sorry! Don't go, don't go!"

Her voice diminished as Scott walked away, pace steady, resolve firm.

Scott looked at the mug of lukewarm cocoa. A white, lumpy mountain of melted marshmallows floated on top of the chocolate. Poking a spoon into the mound, he realized that for the first time since he'd run away, he felt a burden lift. He'd been afraid and ashamed to tell anyone, but Granpop and Nikolas listened. And believed him.

Scott straightened his shoulders. He felt like he'd reached the end of an important chapter in his life. He was ready to turn the page.

CHAPTER 46

Rain puddles glistened in the streetlights when Jack left Nikolas's house. Dark clouds hung low. Driving home, the old pickup's windshield wipers barely stayed ahead of the rain. Kennocha had awakened when he knocked lightly on the bedroom door at Nikolas's house. She told him she felt better and felt safe. Now Jack wondered where Marah was. He hoped she wasn't on the highway in this storm, but he speculated that she was en route to Boise. Ernie said the highway patrol had been alerted to watch for her car. He forced himself to quit thinking about a traffic accident that would endanger others as well as Marah; he just hoped she would arrive home safely and undetected.

He pulled up beside his house and turned off the headlights and motor. Marah's car wasn't there. He leaned his arms across the top of the steering wheel and stared into the rain-drenched night. *Marah's insane behavior. How much is from drug abuse? How much is from her dwelling on past events? Why couldn't I have seen the clues for her low self-esteem all these years? How could I have been so blind? Nikolas told me not to blame myself. Truth is, I'm at least partly to blame. Marah grew up in a conspiracy of silence.*

Jack dragged himself out of the pickup and walked to the house. A damp, indignant Miss Lavender leaped onto the porch and then dashed ahead when he opened the back door. Jack fed her, glanced at the clock, and called Vic. This bad news couldn't wait until morning.

When Vic came on the line, Jack came straight to the point and told him about Marah's attack on Kennocha.

Vic asked, "Will Kennocha be okay? Are the police involved?"

Jack filled him in on the details. "There's something else, Vic. Scott finally told me tonight why he ran away from home. And how he got the wound on his back." Jack sensed Vic's full attention. And he told him everything, including the scene between her and Scott that he broke up late that afternoon.

Vic listened without interrupting. Then he said, "I should have seen this coming. I knew Marah had mood swings, but I never once thought she would hurt Scott. Or anyone. As for the guy—there's a new development. Marah's lover dumped her. He found a new playmate according to the rumor mill. Another thing, Jack. She's done this before—disappear—usually after an argument about her extracurricular activities. She'd deny everything and then leave home for a few days. Sometimes longer."

"I didn't know. Scott never said anything about that."

"I used to cover for her. Scott knows. But he always protected her, too. One time she took off for two weeks. She finally called Scott but made him promise not to tell me where she was. This has become pretty typical of her since her mother died."

"But Vic, the stakes are higher now. The law is involved. I called the police myself."

"You've got more guts than I have."

"Marah could have killed Kennocha. I couldn't let this go on. Kennocha wanted to let the whole thing drop. I wouldn't let her. But she's still undecided about pressing charges." Jack paused. "One other thing, Vic. Is Marah using illegal drugs?"

"Yeah, she could be using again. She must be. That would explain a lot of this crap."

"Again?"

"Another one of her secrets. When we lived in Springfield, I took her in for treatment. She hated it and begged me to take her home. I let her talk me into outpatient drug counseling sessions instead. By the time we moved to Boise, I thought she was clean. But that would explain her friendship with Tina. If that woman isn't a pusher, she's got to be mighty close to someone who is. She could probably put Marah onto someone in Missoula who'd supply her, too."

"Scott said he overheard his mother talking to Tina on the phone today. He confronted her and—well, you know the rest." *Was it just this afternoon? This ordeal seems endless.*

"Well, that answers it, then. I have a little leverage against Tina through the bank. I'll put some pressure on her, see if she knows anything. And I'll see if my darling wife's made any large withdrawals from our accounts. How's Scott handling all this?"

"How do you think he's handling it? He's a kid. And he said you and Marah are going to get a divorce. True?"

"I doubt she'll file now that she's lost her boyfriend. And she needs me to get her out of this mess. I'll come over as soon as I take care of a couple of things at the office and rearrange my schedule."

"Why don't you wait a day or two, in case she's on her way home? If she is, Vic, keep her there. And get her some professional help."

As the next several days passed, Jack poured himself into preparing for the Carousel anniversary celebration in fewer than two weeks. Kennocha had recovered and decided not to press charges against Marah. She, Jack, and Nikolas spent happy hours with other volunteers at the Carousel, repairing and painting ponies, polishing brass, scrubbing the circular hardwood platform, and washing windows. Scott joined in and kept busy with the tasks at hand. Izsak supplied hamburgers or pizzas for evening work parties.

Marah had returned to Boise the night she attacked Kennocha, but Vic said she refused to see a counselor. A week later, she left home, and Vic hadn't heard from her. He believed from questioning Tina that Marah had gone to Seattle. Jack remained alert for his daughter's typical, unannounced arrival in Missoula. Several times during the past two nights, Jack received hang-up calls. His gut instinct told him it was Marah. The last time, he said, "Marah? Talk to me." A sharp *click* sounded in his ear as the connection ended.

Kennocha worked with her usual energy, but she accepted Jack's offer to walk her home at the end each day, insisting it was only because she liked having his company. Kennocha invited Scott and Nikolas, too. Then they fired up the barbecue on Kennocha's balcony or ordered in Asian food. The four bonded in an unspoken worry. Would Marah return? Or was she really in Seattle?

With the ponies completed, on the day before the anniversary celebration, many of the volunteers turned out to complete the cleaning. Kennocha and the rest of the painting crew organized cans and tubes of paint by color. Dried paint dribbles down the sides of the containers identified groups of reds, yellows, blues, and greens. They aligned cans of urethane and turpentine on a shelf, and stuck bouquets of assorted paintbrushes in tumblers. In the woodworking room, Jack, Nikolas, the other carvers, and Scott emptied the sawdust catcher, wiped off all the equipment, deposited tools into drawers or hung them on pegboards, and scrubbed the floor. Another crew washed off sticky fingerprints wherever they showed up, polished the calliope, and cleaned the floors. Then they decorated with colorful balloons and glittering streamers.

The band organ's rollicking tunes—"Seventy-Six Trombones," "The Carousel Waltz," and more—accompanied the workers' conversations and laughter. Finally, the last mop, bucket, and cleaning rags were stored away and the last piece of brass polished. Everyone wiped sweaty brows and clustered around red picnic tables in the birthday party room, pleased with their accomplishments. The carousel's hundreds of lights and brass fixtures sparkled in readiness for the grand celebration tomorrow.

Izsak had hot pizzas delivered for the group, and at the appropriate time, he brought in an insulated carrier with cartons of vanilla, chocolate, and strawberry ice cream. Someone turned off the calliope and turned on a portable radio as the group ate and talked.

Later, as darkness fell and people began drifting away, Jack, Kennocha, Nikolas, and Scott lingered to help Izsak clean up the last of the empty pizza boxes, paper cups, and plastic utensils. Afterward, they sat around a table to talk a few minutes, until Jack remembered they all wanted to return by eight o'clock the next morning. He didn't mention his interrupted sleep the past two nights and his weariness. Wary of Marah's sudden reappearance, he had insisted that Scott stay with Nikolas until Marah's whereabouts became known.

Nikolas playfully leaned on Scott's shoulder. "Drive me home, my good man. My bones are too tired to escort myself."

Scott gave him a mock salute. "Yes, sire. I shall assist you to your Rolls Royce immediately. One moment while I find your cane." He zipped out of the room and returned seconds later with a broom. Amid chuckles, the two left, Scott marching and Nikolas hobbling with the broom.

Izsak looked around, nodded in satisfaction, placed his hands on his hips, and said, "Let's lock up."

Kennocha stood and bent to reach under a table. "Oops, one more pizza box."

Izsak said, "Here, I'll take it to the Dumpster on my way out."

"I'll lock up the front," Jack said. "Leave the back door unlocked, Izsak. We'll go out that way," he called over his shoulder.

"Okay. Catch that radio, too, will you? Someone left it on over there by the gift shop. See you tomorrow." With a wave, he disappeared into the dark rear entrance hallway. In a moment, Jack heard the back door open and close, and he was alone with Kennocha.

After he locked the front door, Jack picked up the portable radio, started to turn it off, and changed his mind. *Nice music. Soft, jazzy, the kind Kennocha loves.* Radio in one hand, he flipped off the lights in the gift shop and the other rooms, one by one. Only the carousel canopy lights remained on in the main room. In the paint room, Jack saw that Kennocha had found a forgotten can of turpentine and a rag that smelled of the substance. She set them on the table when he walked in.

For a moment, they simply looked at each other. Then Kennocha said, "Let's sit beside the carousel for a minute, shall we? I love nighttime, with only the canopy lights on. The ponies look soft and dreamy."

Jack turned off the paint room light, and they walked into the main room. Jack set the radio on a bench as it began playing "Someone to Watch Over Me." He took Kennocha's hand. "May I have this dance?"

She smiled and stepped into his arms.

Jack held her close as they danced around the carousel. When the song ended, they sat on the bench, still holding hands, enjoying the ambiance of the magical carousel and mellow music.

"Before all the trouble started, I had planned to give you a dozen roses on this special night," Jack said, "because I want to ask you a question. But now, seems like things are in limbo. Because of Marah."

"I know." Kennocha squeezed his hand. "Vic hasn't heard from her?"

Jack shook his head. "She made a large draw on one of their bank accounts. She has another account in her name only. Vic found the statements in her desk. She's got money enough if she wanted to be gone for an extended time."

Kennocha's voice dropped. "You know she was trying to break us up."

"But she did not succeed. She never will." Jack slid off the bench and kneeled at Kennocha's feet. Taking both her hands in his, he said, "Kennocha, I love you. This isn't the way I planned it, I don't have the roses nor a ring, but sweetheart, will you marry me?"

A wide smile lit Kennocha's face and she squeezed his hands. "Yes!" She leaned forward and kissed him.

Jack's heart pounded in joy. He stood and pulled her into his arms. Smiling, she leaned into his chest. They embraced, their kisses long and deep while the radio played on.

Jack stroked Kennocha's face and looked into her eyes. "As soon as this Carousel party is over, let's plan a dinner date. Just the two of us. I promise you roses. But before dinner, I'd like you to go with me to choose a ring."

Kennocha grinned. "I'd love that. But I can't wait to share our news. Let's have Scott and Nikolas come to my apartment after the Carousel closes tomorrow night. We'll celebrate with sundaes."

He chuckled and hugged her. "You and your midnight sundaes. We'll do it. Do you have room in your freezer for about ten gallons of ice cream? You know how Scott and Nikolas are."

She laughed. "I'll make room. But now I really must go home. I promised to have homemade coffee cake here at eight o'clock in the morning."

Keeping an arm around her, Jack went with her to the back door. "I'll walk you home."

"I had so much stuff to bring down here today that I drove the Toyota. I'm parked just outside the door here. And you know the underground parking is secured in my building. I'll be fine." She turned. "Oh, the lights. And the radio."

"I'll take care of them and lock up." He gave her one last, long kiss. "See you tomorrow, sweetheart."

He waited in the doorway until the taillights of Kennocha's vehicle went out of view. Then he retrieved the radio. As he walked by the paint room, he thought he heard a noise. He flipped the light on and looked around. Nothing. The door to the storage room in back remained closed. He shrugged, turned off the light, and left the room. He flipped off the switch for the carousel lights, locked the door behind him, and went home.

The next morning, Jack overslept. "Eight thirty!" He flung the covers off and leaped out of bed. "Why didn't the cat wake me? Past her breakfast time," he muttered on his way to the bathroom. Then he remembered she'd stayed outside last night, prowling for mice. He showered, brushed his teeth, and threw on a shirt and twill pants. White pullover. Mustard on front. He grunted, went back into the closet. New red shirt, not ironed. "Looks pretty good." Sock drawer empty. "Yesterday's socks will have to do." He got down on his knees, groped for socks under the bed, found two, and pulled them on. He stuck his feet into loafers, grabbed his keys, and left.

Of all the days to oversleep, why today? Embarrassed that he would probably be the last of the volunteers to arrive, Jack pulled into the parking lot. A sizable crowd of visitors—mostly excited children—milled about the front door. Jack went in the back door with five minutes to spare before Izsak unlocked the front door.

Nikolas stood outside the woodworking room, watching for him. "I did not know you wanted to make a grand entrance, my friend. I would have brought my trumpet."

"You don't even own a trumpet. You probably wouldn't be here yourself if Scott hadn't gotten you out of bed." Kennocha hurried toward him, Scott on her heels.

"I was getting worried," Kennocha said. She hugged him, and he hugged her back.

Jack gave his grandson a friendly punch on the arm. "Is this old Russian keeping you awake every night snoring the roof off the house?"

Scott smiled and shook his head as he looked Jack up and down. He smirked and tried to hide a grin. Then he gave up and doubled over laughing, holding his stomach.

Jack felt his face grow warm. Instinctively, his hand went for his fly. Okay there. "What's so funny?"

"Look at your feet." Scott whooped.

"Well, I'll be darned." One black sock, one green sock, and gray plaid bedroom slippers.

They all laughed.

Playfully, Jack cuffed his grandson. "You'll never let me live this down, you rascal. Guess I'd better go home and start over," Jack said.

In mock solemnity, Nikolas shook his head. "No, my friend, you cannot leave once you are here. It is the rule for the day."

"No one will notice your feet," Kennocha said. "They're here to enjoy the carousel. Did you eat any breakfast? I'll bring you some coffee cake."

"Thanks," Jack said, "that sounds good." He sank to the bench and let his head rest against the wall.

Nikolas joined him on the bench, and Scott leaned against the wall.

Kennocha returned with coffee and a generous serving of rhubarb crisp under a pile of whipped cream. "Last piece. Just for you."

"The party's started," Scott said, looking at the front door. "I gotta help Izsak hand out party hats. See you guys later."

Rollicking calliope music greeted excited children, faces glowing in anticipation as they crowded through the doors, accompanied by parents and grandparents. The building soon reverberated with happy noise and the smell of freshly popped popcorn.

Carousel ponies pranced up and down, around and around under the canopy lights, with riders on the outside row leaning out, reaching for the brass ring while "Yankee Doodle" pealed out.

A balding, stout man and his petite, silver-haired wife approached the bench where Jack, Kennocha, and Nikolas sat watching the festivities.

"Someone told us to ask for the master woodcarver," the man said. "Would that be one of you?"

Without hesitation, Nikolas gestured toward his friend and said, "Yes, it is Jack."

"Mind if we ask you some questions?"

Jack stood. "Not at all. C'mon, let's go into the woodworking room." He tossed his paper plate and cup into the trash and led them away. Behind him, he heard Nikolas speak to Kennocha.

"This will be good for him today, to keep busy."

Jack glanced over his shoulder, taking in Kennocha's concerned look. He smiled and gave her a thumbs-up sign. She smiled back. Then he addressed the visitors. "Do you have some particular questions you wanted to ask?"

"I don't do horses, but I'm trying to learn how to carve an English setter for the wife here. We lost our Mitzi this spring, and I want to make a replica."

"We had her for sixteen years," the woman said. "We miss her so much."

"Maybe I can help," Jack said. "How much do you have carved so far?"

"I've got her all roughed out in pretty good proportions, I think. But I don't know how to get started on the hair. My practice piece looks like a bunch of crabgrass."

Chuckling, Jack led the way through a throng of people in the woodworking room. "My early pieces looked like they'd been chewed up by a lawn mower." He'd no sooner found his way to a workbench than a boy about eight years old tugged at his sleeve.

"Mister, can you show me how a pony gets started? My grandpa says they start out being a big block of wood."

"Does your grandpa come here? Maybe I know him."

"He lives in Pennsylvania."

"Aha. Your grandpa probably told you that's where some of the best carousel ponies were made many years ago. Just hang on a minute here, son, and let me help this gentleman first. Then I'll show you how ponies get started."

"No," the bald man said, "you go ahead. We're interested in that, too. We'll just follow along. Looks like you're going to be pretty busy here today. We can come back another time about the dog."

By this time several people had gathered around the workbench, all interested in the process of carving a pony. Jack noticed that Nikolas was similarly surrounded at another workbench.

Scanning the shelves, Jack said, "I don't see a body blank in here. Just a minute, folks, I'll see if I can find one in the lumber room." He figured somebody got carried away cleaning up. Body blanks shouldn't be in there, but that's probably where they put them.

In the wide corridor circling the carousel, Jack felt the breeze of the horses whirling by, heard the music and laughter, and relaxed.

His spirits lifted thinking about the end of the day, when Kennocha would invite Scott and Nikolas to her apartment for sundaes. And the announcement of their engagement. Nikolas wouldn't be surprised, he suspected, *but no one could be more surprised than I am,* Jack thought, *that Kennocha would fall in love with a plain old man like me.*

Tomorrow, he would pick up a dozen red roses, take them to her apartment, and they would go shopping for rings. And set the date. Would she be willing to elope? Probably not. He just hoped she wouldn't want him to wear a penguin suit.

The paint room was even more congested than the wood shop. Some of the painters had set up an area for kids to decorate scrap wood. A couple of the youngsters had smears of green, purple, and yellow paint on their faces. In another corner, one of the volunteers was giving a flower-painting demonstration for adults. Jack didn't see Kennocha, but in this crowd, that wasn't surprising.

He threaded his way toward the lumber room, opened the door, stepped inside, and quickly closed it again. This area was off limits to visitors. Someone had left the lights on. The small room held seven side-by-side stacks of lumber with most stacks seven feet high, separated by narrow aisles. The long sides of the stacks faced the door. He sniffed. Oddly, the air was caustic, raw, and biting. Sharper than the pitch of a freshly cut tree. *This lumber is kiln-dried. It shouldn't smell like that. What is it?*

A scuffling noise from the far corner of the room caught his attention. No one should be in there. He walked along the nearest row of stacks to the end and followed along the outside wall, looking down each aisle. A figure stepped into view at the far end, along the inside wall.

CHAPTER 47

"Marah!" His immediate reaction was relief to know her whereabouts. As he walked toward her, his breath caught and he coughed. *Turpentine!* A quick glance around his daughter showed large, wet splotches on stacks of lumber and on her slacks. Her pupils looked dilated. She held an uncapped, half-gallon-sized turpentine can in her right hand and a cigarette lighter in the left.

"Hi, Daddy." She swung the can behind her back.

Her voice sounded unnaturally high. Jack's shoulders tensed. *Drugs.* Pain shot through his gut. *Marah, my daughter.* Her hair was disheveled, and a smudge of dirt streaked across one pale, sunken cheek.

Jack grabbed her left wrist and reached for the turpentine. "Let's go home."

With surprising strength, she jerked, pulling her wrist free and splashing turpentine on herself. She backed away. "No." She clutched the can to her chest. "That redheaded woman—is she here?"

Strong fumes made Jack double over, coughing. When he stood, Marah was gone.

"Marah, where are you?" No answer. *Which way did she go?* He walked along the inside wall, past the short ends of the stacks, listening all the while and looking down each aisle. Other than muffled sounds from the paint room, he heard nothing. *Maybe she went to the corner, where I think I first heard her.* He turned around and followed along the wall to the end aisle. Just as he took a step toward the corner, he heard her again. He looked back the way he had come. Marah stood with her back to the door, staring at him as though she didn't recognize him. Jack slowly walked toward her. "Let's go home, Marah."

Suddenly, she whirled and turned off the lights. Jack stood still in the pitch-black room, listening. Nothing. He felt his way along the inside wall again, aiming for the light switch and the door. A slight noise stopped him. Another little sound. *She's hiding, hoping I'll go away. How am I going to get her out of here? Have to get out of this room, away from this smell. It's giving me a headache and making me sick.*

Jack halted at a sudden scraping sound followed by the clattering of boards. When the racket slowed, Jack shouted, "Marah! Are you all right? What happened?" He quickened his steps to reach the light switch and stumbled over loose boards. He pitched forward and landed on one knee as something moved behind him. A cascade of boards struck his head and back. He winced in pain and curled into a ball, arms over his head. When the commotion stopped, he felt around to clear away the boards so he could stand. *Thank God, this lumber is dry. Anything else might have broken my back or killed me.* An odor burned his nostrils. *Turpentine again. Is Marah dumping more of that stuff?* Jack struggled to stand, but his knee gave out and he went down again. *Did Marah start the avalanche? How would she have the strength to push over lumber stacks?* Then he remembered Ernie's words about people high on drugs: "What she did to Miss Bryant doesn't compare with the potential for violence." *Is my daughter trying to kill me?*

Jack heard her moving. Unless she turned on the lights, she couldn't know for sure where he was. He lay still, waiting.

The lights came on. Jack blinked at the brightness and tried to sit up. He elbowed several boards away until both arms were free. Then he sat up.

"Are you hurt, Daddy?"

Jack looked over his shoulder. *How could she get behind me so fast when she just turned the lights on? Did someone come in? No, I would have heard the noise from the paint room if the door opened.* Jack said, "Come help me get up."

"No. Call that redheaded woman. Tell her to come here."

She's out of her mind. I need to get hold of her and get that lighter away from her. "I can't. My knee is hurt. Come help me."

"No. You get up."

"I don't think I can stand." He kept an eye on her while he removed enough boards from his legs to attempt to stand. His knees wanted to buckle; one screamed in pain. He felt dizzy, but he forced himself to remain upright. "Let's go home."

"No. I have to tell you something."

"Okay, but let's get out of here. We can sit outside and talk."

"You don't love me anymore, do you, Daddy? Mother never loved me, ever. She loved Paul more than me. Now you love that woman more than me. And I've lost Scott to her, too."

Jack leaned against the wall, waiting for a wave of dizziness to pass. *Got to get through that pile of boards between me and the door.* He steeled himself, one hand on the wall, and staggered one step forward. His knee collapsed with the next step. He sat against the wall and looked at his daughter. She stood out of his reach. She swung the turpentine can, turned it upside down, and dumped more liquid onto the lumber, carelessly splashing it onto her feet and legs. Jack pulled a board loose and banged on the door. *Please, God, make someone hear this.*

Marah screamed at him. "What are you doing?"

Forcing calm, Jack lowered the board and said, "I'll always love you, Marah. You're my daughter, my little girl."

"Mother was the bad girl, not me." She laughed hysterically. "But I got even."

Jack's ugliest fears surged up like muddy floodwaters. The last person to see Claire alive was their daughter. "Did you hurt her, Marah?"

She stared into his eyes. Her fingers turned white clutching the lighter. "You think I tried to kill your little redhead, don't you?"

Jack's eyes burned. *Got to get the lighter away from her. Got to get out of here.* "No, I don't believe you really want to hurt anyone. You're troubled. You hurt. I can help you." He reached out his hand. "Please, give me the lighter. I'll take you home."

She tilted her head and gave him a sly look. "I could have killed her, Daddy. But not like mother."

"Let's go home. Then you can tell me about it."

Eyes wide and crazed, she continued to stare at him. But Jack had a feeling she wasn't really seeing him. The gold flecks in her brown eyes glittered. "I got even. For all the years mother was so mean to me." She fingered the lighter. "Mother opened her eyes that last day in the hospital. She looked at me. Cold, the way she always looked at me. If it had been her darling Paul, she would have smiled at him with her eyes." One eyebrow arched. "Did you know she could do that, Daddy? Look at Paul and make her eyes get all warm and then in the next second look at me and make them freeze?"

"She recognized you? She was awake?" Marah didn't seem to hear him. *Did Claire really open her eyes? I hoped, even thought she squeezed my fingers that one time. Maybe she could have recovered.* "I'm sorry your mother treated you that way. I didn't know."

Marah's voice dropped to a whisper. "That day in the hospital, I swore she would never look at me like that again. Never. What if she got well enough to come home? She'd never love me, no matter how hard I tried. Richard DeWolfe dumped her, didn't he? She said he didn't want me. But I figured it out. He didn't want *her*. So she blamed me."

Through the fog in his mind, Jack knew she was right. Claire had transferred her bitterness against DeWolfe to Marah. He knew now that Marah grew up wounded. But when his grandson arrived on his doorstep that night in February, his concern was for Scott, not Marah. The following months revealed Marah's instability. And Jack's life became a surreal carousel driven by his daughter's lies, deceit, and manipulation.

Now she stood before him, a drug-crazed woman, threatening to torch this room. He desperately wanted to repair his daughter's emotional damage. *Is it too late?*

"I love you, Marah. I want to help you."

She ignored him. A cunning look came into her eyes. "Her stroke made it easier. I poisoned her IV."

Shock hit Jack like an overwhelming wave of ice cold water. For a split second, he was stunned. Then anger surged. *She murdered her mother! And now she wants to kill me.* He gripped the board, lunged forward, and swung for her ankle.

Like a cat, she darted away. "Stop! I'll light it!"

Jack froze.

She backed out of reach. Her movements were uncanny, almost too quick to seem real.

"I killed Mother. I hated her." She moved her thumb to the lever on the lighter. "And now you hate me, too." She flicked the lighter.

"No!" Jack shouted. Too late.

Whoosh!

Flames shot up and raced along the turpentine trail toward Marah. She screamed as flames crawled up her legs. She ran toward the back of the room.

Jack threw himself away from the flames and struggled to reach the door. He coughed and choked and fought to breathe. He tried to call for help, but his voice came out in a scratchy squeak. He grabbed a board and struck it against the door again and again.

Lightbulbs exploded. Fire devoured the dry lumber. Burning stacks teetered, collapsed, and crashed to the floor. Rafters ignited and dropped, striking Jack across his shoulders and the back of his head. He fought to keep from passing out. He lost consciousness as Marah screamed in pain.

CHAPTER 48

Jack felt himself being moved, and he became aware of fresh air and someone shouting. He breathed deeply, and his mind began to clear.

Someone shouted, "Bring a stretcher! We have to get this man to a hospital!"

Jack opened his eyes. He lay on the grass, a short distance away from the smoking Carousel building. He looked around and tried to sit up, but pain and weakness forced him to lie back. So many people—sitting on the grass or standing in clusters, staring at the Carousel. Everyone looked shocked, and tears ran down some faces. The exterior walls of the building were brick, but much of the interior was wood. And, of course, the ponies were wooden. Could the fire be contained?

A man knelt beside Jack. "The ambulance is coming."

Jack tried to speak, but only a rasping sound came out. He tried to swallow and couldn't. He grasped the man's arm and pointed to the Carousel building. "My daughter," he squeaked. "There."

The man patted Jack's arm. "The fire department is here. They're inside, trying to contain it."

Jack heard Izsak's voice as he worked to control the frightened people. "Folks, everyone is out, and they're getting the fire under control. There are two main doors and two emergency exits around the building. If you haven't found your children or family yet, please stay here. My people are working around each exit to get everyone organized. We'll help you locate your—"

In the rising clamor, Izsak's voice faded away. Parents looking for children. Volunteers directing people. Children crying. Chaos. Confusion. But no sign of Marah. Suddenly, a beloved voice.

"Jack! Oh, dear God, thank you! Jack, my darling!" Kennocha raced across the lawn and fell to her knees beside Jack, crying. She stroked his face. "I thought you were—" Her words turned to sobs.

Jack reached out, touched her face, and let his own tears flow. After several moments, he looked into her eyes and willed her to understand him. He tried to force the words from his parched throat, but no sound came out. He pointed to the building. "M-m," he barely whispered. He mouthed the word, "Marah."

Suddenly, Kennocha understood. Alarmed, she said, "Marah's in there?"

He nodded.

She jumped up and ran to a fire truck.

Jack trembled. *Marah ... is she alive?*

Sirens screamed. Two ambulances arrived in the parking lot and pulled up near the building.

Kennocha returned with a cup of water for Jack. "I told them. They will tell us as soon as they know. Here, I'll help you sit up so you can drink this." She slid her arm around Jack's shoulders.

Clenching his jaw against the pain, Jack sat up. He took several deep breaths before taking a drink from the cup of water. He smiled at Kennocha. "Thank you," he whispered. He swallowed the rest of the water. "Scott? Nikolas?"

"Ah, my dear friends, I have found you." Nikolas's deep voice washed over Jack. "Scott is by the front entrance. Izsak told Scott you are safe. Then he put him to work helping with the children. He did not want him to worry about you. Scott did not know you were going to the lumber room. But I knew."

Kennocha jumped up and gave Nikolas a big hug.

Jack smiled at his friend and wiped his eyes.

Two men jogged up with a stretcher. One of them grinned at Jack. "You're a hard man to find. We've been all around looking for you."

"I don't need an ambulance. I'll be all right in a few minutes."

"Okay, but if you don't mind, I'd like to check you over." The man knelt beside Jack and began a brief examination without waiting for an answer. The other man talked to Kennocha and wrote in a notebook.

"Has anyone else been taken to the hospital?" Jack asked.

"You need to have that knee checked. It's pretty swollen. You've got some tender spots on your shoulders and the back of your head. Your eyes look good, but you should be checked for a concussion. Did you fall?"

"Pile of boards landed on me." His head throbbed, and his body felt like he'd been tumbled in a cement mixer. His throat burned, but the cool water felt good in his mouth and throat.

"Mr. Emerson, you need to see a doctor. We're here, and we'd like to take you to the hospital."

"Just help me stand up. If I can walk with this knee, I'll go see the doctor tomorrow."

"Okay, we'll give it a try." The two EMTs helped Jack to his feet.

"I'm okay, just a little wobbly. I'll be fine."

Kennocha and Nikolas exchanged looks.

"You didn't answer me. My daughter was in the same room. Her clothing caught on fire. I don't know if she got out. Did you see her?" He looked from one EMT to the other.

"No, Mr. Emerson. But we have three ambulances here. One was on the other side. Maybe that crew took care of her."

Was she taken out while I was unconscious? Jack noticed everyone's silence. "I want to see Scott. Nikolas, can I lean on you while I hold Kennocha's hand? Then I can keep an eye on you two."

Nikolas chuckled at Jack's attempted humor. "Yes, indeed. I am as solid as an ancient redwood."

"Nikolas, you are a dear," Kennocha said, "but I'll go get Scott if you'll keep an eye on Jack. He looks too wobbly to walk that far." She gave Jack a quick kiss and jogged away.

"Looks like you're in good hands, Mr. Emerson. Just get the word to us if you change your mind about a ride to the hospital." The EMTs waved and grinned as they left.

"I see some people leaving that bench." Nikolas gestured toward a bench nearby. "We will sit there."

"Yes, good place to watch the back door." Jack winced as he put weight on his injured knee, but he kept going. As Jack eased down onto the bench he said, "I don't know if I should tell Scott yet that his mother was in the lumber room. He'll have questions about the fire. Maybe I should wait until we know."

Nikolas tugged his beard, a familiar habit when he was thinking. "That is a difficult question. If I were you, I would wait and let our Lord tell you."

This time, Jack didn't pretend not to know what Nikolas meant. He knew he could have died in the fire. He didn't know yet who had pulled him out, but it had to have been someone from the paint room. Whoever it was, he or she must have heard Marah's screams. Yes, he had to tell Scott she was in there.

Jack and Nikolas watched the scene around them in silence. Apparently all the visitors, volunteers, and employees had evacuated the building. Firefighters continued to work both inside and outside.

Shirley A. Rorvik

Some parents were herding their crying children toward their cars. Many other families remained, watching with solemn faces, waiting and hoping the carousel could be saved. Newspaper and television reporters, some armed with cameras, moved about, interviewing people while scanning the crowd for other possibilities. Jack glanced at them once and then ignored them.

Soon, Jack saw Kennocha and Scott coming around the corner. When Scott saw him, he broke into a run.

"Granpop! I was so scared when I couldn't find you! Are you okay? Where were you?" He sat cross-legged on the lawn in front of Jack and studied his face.

Kennocha sat beside Jack on the bench and squeezed his hand.

With his free hand, Jack leaned over and tousled Scott's hair. "I'm fine, son. I'm very glad to see you." He let his eyes roam over Scott's face, arms, torso, and legs, making sure he was all right. *I love this boy so much ... God, help me tell him about his mother, just what he needs to know, no more. Never her terrible secret. Somehow, God, if she survived this horror, please bring healing between her and Scott.* Jack saw the worried looked in Scott's eyes and knew he was delaying too long. "Son, I need to tell you something." Jack took a deep breath. "I was in the lumber room. That's where the fire started."

284

CHAPTER 49

In the hospital the next morning, Jack sat at his daughter's bedside while Scott and Vic stood nearby. The closed curtains gave them a little privacy inside the intensive care unit. He heard quiet footsteps and low voices as the nurses monitored other patients and checked on Marah. The heart monitor at the head of her bed showed a chaotic, rapid line. Alarms sounded periodically and interrupted the wheezing ventilator as the robotic machine forced 100 percent oxygen into her damaged lungs. In, out, in, out; her chest rose and fell. She hadn't moved since firemen found her in the smoke-filled Carousel storeroom the day before. Doctors said her lung function was rapidly worsening, but the real damage was to her brain. It had swollen from anoxia, which they explained was the lack of oxygen and of carbon monoxide poisoning. Even without that, the extensive burns on her body left little hope for recovery.

She was comatose, dying. Soon, the doctor said.

When Jack told Scott yesterday that his mother was in the lumber room when the fire started, Scott's face hardened. "She did it, didn't she? Started the fire?" Jack answered yes and told him about the turpentine. Scott had it figured out before Jack told him that she appeared to be under the influence of drugs. Jack kept it brief, and Scott didn't ask any more questions.

Later, Jack told Kennocha it was as though Scott already knew the sordid story. Kennocha said, "He's probably lived through more than you and I can imagine, living with an emotionally unbalanced mother abusing drugs." With deep sadness, Jack pondered again what he could have done differently to help Marah.

The hospital room felt too familiar, reminiscent of Claire's final days. Jack forced himself to look at the IV stand, with its bag of saline. *Is that what Marah poisoned when she killed her mother?* He shuddered. He would never know.

Vic, in creased slacks and a pressed golf shirt, jingled coins in his pocket as he paced back and forth in the confined space around his wife's bed. Every few minutes he stopped at the foot of the bed, stared at her, and resumed pacing.

Leaning against the wall, Scott studied his feet, pulled up his socks, and tightened his shoelaces. He'd put on clean jeans and a Ralph Lauren shirt his mother bought for him a few weeks ago. He didn't like it when she gave it to him, and he still didn't like it, but he said he wanted to wear it today for his mother.

The teenager sniffed, wiped his eyes on the back of his hand, and went to his mother's bedside, opposite his grandfather. He spoke softly. "I don't know if you can hear me, Mom, but I have to say something to you." He touched her hand. "I forgive you for what you did to me, and to Kennocha, and to Granpop. And I love you." He leaned over and kissed her forehead. "Good-bye, Mom." A sob caught in his throat. He backed away, crying, ducked around the curtain and walked out.

Silent, Vic watched his son leave. At last, he took in a deep breath and sat down near Marah. His voice low, he said, "Is this when we say good-bye? I want to believe you can hear me. I wish we could talk one more time. What happened to us? You changed so much after your mother died. I missed the closeness we used to have. I missed coming home to—" He stopped and buried his face in his hands. After a minute, he stood, kissed Marah's forehead, and left.

Jack knew now why Vic had told him, and said again a minute ago, that Marah changed after her mother's death. Surely, Marah lived in shame and guilt after Claire died. He wanted to believe she felt remorse. He took his daughter's hand. "You have a fine son, Marah. He taught me a lesson here. I want to say something to you, too. I wish you had come to me a long time ago, when you were hurting. I'd have helped you. I've been thinking about everything, and I want you to know, I love you. You're still my girl." He stood and kissed her cheek. "May God bless your soul."

Later that evening, the phone rang in Jack's kitchen. He took a deep breath to prepare himself for the call he expected. He answered and listened. Then he looked at his son-in-law. "Vic, it's the doctor." He handed Vic the phone and walked out of the house to the workshop. The father should tell the son his mother died.

CHAPTER 50

The next morning, Vic summoned his son to Jack's kitchen table. He wanted to get Marah's remains taken care of and get back to Boise as soon as possible. Jack was in his garage, so this was a good time to talk to his son.

"Scott, we need to talk," Vic said. He pulled out a chair and sat, nodding toward the chair at the other end of the table.

Scott sat down, crossed one foot over his knee, and waited.

"Your mother didn't want any kind of funeral or memorial service. I found this note she left in her car. We'll go along with her wishes. Cremation is probably best. We can get an urn. Cemeteries have places for those." He slid the note across the table.

Scott picked it up and read his mother's scrawled handwriting.

> *I don't want a funeral, no minister, no music. God doesn't exist. I don't care what happens to my body. Burn me or bury me. But if you bury me, don't put me anywhere near my mother. She hated me, and I hate her. I didn't have a real mother, and now I've lost my father and son. And that's why I'm going to do this.*

Tears filled Scott's eyes. He looked at his father. "When did she write this?"

"I don't know exactly. Probably shortly before she went to the Carousel. I think she wanted to die in her final act of—I don't know what. Paranoia. The only thing I know for certain is that she was loaded with drugs. The ER doctor told me." He laced his fingers together on the tabletop and cleared his throat. "Scott, I failed your mother. I should have known that if she sneaked over to Tina's at least once, she'd do it again. She swore it was only one time, but in my gut, I knew better. I should have forced her into an inpatient treatment program."

"You tried that when we lived in Springfield, didn't you?" Vic nodded. "You guys didn't tell me what was going on, but I knew. I overhead you sometimes. She wouldn't stay in the program. She came back home. It didn't work."

Vic rubbed his face. "No, it didn't. She said she went to the meetings. I believed her, but if she really went, it didn't sink in. She played the game, and I think she tried for a while. But when we moved to Boise—"

"She got to be friends with Tina."

"I can't blame Tina totally. I should have seen the signs. But I was wrapped up in the new job, the added responsibility. I wanted to succeed. I admit I drank too much, worked too much. The pressure ... I didn't want to lose my chance to make it big at the bank." He looked at Scott and reached his hand across the table. "It's just you and me now, Scott. We can make it." He waited for his son's response. He expected him to comply, to be relieved, or something.

"I'm gay, Dad."

Vic jerked back, withdrawing his hand. "When did you decide *that*?"

"No decision. It's something I've always known."

Vic slammed his fist on the table and stood, muttering an expletive. He whirled around and shook his finger at Scott. "Look here, now. When we get back home, I'm sending you to a psychiatrist." He mumbled something under his breath, ran his fingers through his hair, and paced across the kitchen and back. "Crazy wife and now a fag son." He paced back and forth, hands in his pockets, jingling coins and keys. "You know if this gets out it could ruin my reputation. I've worked hard to gain my prestige. Does anyone in Boise know?"

Scott stood and faced his father. "I'm staying here."

Vic ignored him. "I'll be in Japan a couple of weeks. When I get back, you'll come home. To stay. Things will be a lot more stable now." Vic stopped pacing. He turned to speak to Scott but paused when he saw Jack coming in the back door with a thunderous look on his face and eyes like blue ice.

Scott started to speak, but Jack put a restraining hand on his shoulder.

His back straight as a steel post, Jack folded his arms and fixed his eyes on his son-in-law. "Vic, I want legal custody of Scott. The boy's staying here. This is his home." Vic started to protest, but Jack raised his voice and talked over him. "You can make it easy, or I can make it tough. I can get an attorney and prove that you're an unfit parent. Or we can do it peaceably. Which will it be?"

Stammering, Vic said, "You … you can't prove—"

"Try me," Jack said.

Suddenly, Vic felt like something collapsed inside him. He rubbed the back of his neck. "Is this really what you want, Scott?"

"Yes."

"Did you tell your grandfather what you just told me?"

"Granpop knows I'm gay."

Vic sucked in a deep breath and pulled himself together. "Okay. We'll do it your way, Jack." He brushed past Jack and walked out the door. He wished he'd gotten a motel room instead of staying at Jack's house. He needed a drink. He'd like to have a bottle and a room to himself.

CHAPTER 51

As soon as Vic's Mercedes left the yard, Scott jumped up and hugged his grandfather. Jack hugged him back.

"I'll call an attorney I know," Jack said. "We'll see what has to be done."

"Dad's going to Japan for a couple of weeks as soon as Mom is buried or ..."

"Yes, we need to talk about that. Did your dad say anything? I expect he'll want to have her service in Boise."

"Mom wrote a note. Dad found it in her car." Scott began looking around. "Dad left it here someplace." He bent to look under the table. "Here it is." He handed it to Jack.

Jack read it, sat down, and read it again. He pulled his handkerchief from his pocket, unfolded it, and wiped his eyes. "Does your Dad go along with this? No funeral? We could have a simple memorial service."

"All he said was cremation. Wants an urn to stick in a cemetery. But I don't want to do that."

"What would you like for your mother?"

"Nothing like we did for Danny. She wouldn't like that. I'm okay with cremating—but I don't want her ashes stuck in an urn someplace. She wouldn't want that. I'd like to scatter them someplace outdoors. She loves—loved—flowers and trees and ponds, like our yard, y'know? But I don't mean putting her ashes in our yard. That would be creepy." He frowned.

"How about a river?"

Scott's forehead smoothed. "Yeah. Then eventually she'd be in the ocean, and she loved the ocean."

Jack nodded, seeing his grandson come to terms with a peaceful, honorable solution in his mind. "You'll talk to your dad?"

"Yeah, if he's not too drunk when he gets back. But I know this will be okay with him. He knows Mom loved rivers and the ocean."

CHAPTER 52

A month later, Jack and Scott walked up three flights of stairs to Kennocha's apartment. Nikolas stepped off the elevator just as they reached Kennocha's door and rang the bell.

"Oh good, you're all here at once." Kennocha smiled and swung the door wide. "I'll start the pasta." They followed her into the kitchen, where spaghetti sauce bubbled on the stove, filling the apartment with the fragrance of garlic, herbs, onions, and tomatoes. The dining room table was set with ivory linen placemats and napkins and rich brown stoneware.

"I am suddenly very hungry," Nikolas said, rubbing his belly and sniffing.

"Anything I can do to help, Kennie? I mean, Miss Bryant?" Scott flushed.

Holding a loaf of French bread in one hand, she wrapped the other arm around him. "You can stop calling me 'Miss Bryant,' except in school, of course."

Scott grinned. "Okay, Grandmother."

With mock indignation, she said, "How about just Kennocha or Kennie?" She grinned and handed him the bread. "Butter and garlic are on the breakfast bar."

Hands folded in innocence, Nikolas purred, "What is it you want me to do, Miss Kennocha Bryant?"

"You, Mr. Nikolai Kostenka, can toss the salad."

"I think I'm in the wrong house," Jack said. He watched Kennocha add pasta to the kettle of boiling water. "If you call me Mr. Emerson, I'll know I am."

Kennocha gave him a long-handled fork. "Here, stir this while I think." Shoulder to shoulder, head tilted, she closed her eyes and whispered, "Mrs. Kennocha Emerson. Sounds good."

Jack sneaked a quick kiss.

Scott snickered and elbowed Nikolas as he swooned, rolling his black eyes.

The lighthearted mood continued through dinner. Nikolas, Scott, and Kennocha were well-matched in quick comebacks. Jack returned a volley now and then, but for the most part, he simply enjoyed the relief from his heavy heart. He knew these loved ones were doing this partly for him and Scott, partly for themselves. Everyone needed fun and laughter.

After dinner, they all pitched in to help Kennocha clean up the kitchen. Then they went into her living room. Jack sat in one corner of the leather sofa with his arm around Kennocha. Scott sat in the other corner, legs outstretched under the coffee table. Nikolas sank into the red suede easy chair opposite them.

Now that their appetites were satisfied and the chores done, unspoken thoughts seemed to materialize like an invisible presence in the room. Scott had said little about his mother and showed little emotion when his father said they would comply with Marah's wishes—no funeral, no service. She was cremated, her ashes placed in a simple wooden box Scott chose at the funeral home. On the second day after her death, Scott, Vic, Jack, Kennocha, and Nikolas drove up a nearby canyon, where Jack said Marah loved to go as a child on family picnics. Surrounded by the others, Scott scattered Marah's ashes in Canyon Creek. He stood for a moment, watching the current carry away the ashes. Then he tossed the box in the creek. Vic left for Boise that evening.

Jack knew that Kennocha and Nikolas wondered how Scott was feeling down deep inside. Jack figured Scott would talk when he was ready, so he hadn't tried to open the conversation with his grandson.

Nikolas opened the conversation.

"Look how tall this boy is." Nikolas eyed Scott's feet, extending to the other side of the knotty pine coffee table. "You have grown this summer, like a strong, young tree."

"Two inches since February. I'm taller than Granpop now. And way taller than Mom was." He lowered his eyes. "But I don't think she ever noticed."

Softly, Kennocha asked, "Do you want to talk about her?"

"No, I'm okay. I'm happier here with Granpop than I've ever been in my whole life. All you guys are the best family I've ever had." His chin quivered.

Kennocha slid over beside him, and giving him a hug, said, "It's okay to cry. We've all shed a lot of tears."

After a moment, Scott said, "Can I ask you something? I mean, I know it's too soon and all that, but I was just wondering—where are we gonna live after you get married? Here? Or at Granpop's?"

Startled, Jack and Kennocha looked at each other.

"We haven't talked about that," Kennocha murmured.

"We also haven't set a date," Jack said.

"My seventeenth birthday is October 1. You could do it that day. That would be a great birthday present."

"That's just weeks away! Gran would have a fit. She'll need at least six months to prepare for this event." Kennocha smiled. "She'll be tatting doilies like crazy. She'll want me to wear her lace wedding gown." She looked at Jack, eyes twinkling. "Oh, and most important, darling, she'll want you to come see her well in advance, so she can be introduced properly. And decide if you're fit husband material for me."

"Would you consider eloping?"

Nikolas boomed, "Eloping! That is not possible. This must be a *real* wedding." Nikolas stroked his beard, pleased with himself, and eyed Jack. "Scott and I will give you away, my friend."

Jack and Kennocha laughed, while Scott looked puzzled.

"What's wrong with that?" Scott said.

"No one gives away the groom. It's the bride who's given away."

"Nikolas, you dear man, I would love to have you give *me* away." Kennocha jumped up and kissed his cheek. Nikolas's black beard and mustache framed a wide grin.

"Okay, you guys, but I still don't know where we're going to live," Scott protested. "That bookcase over there would be a great place for me to set up an awesome stereo system." He grinned at Kennocha. "You like Def Leppard?"

CHAPTER 53

Late that night, Jack crawled out of bed, went into the bathroom, and swallowed two aspirin. His aching back and knee made him restless, unable to sleep. So he told himself. He splashed cold water on his face and toweled it dry.

Returning to the bedroom, he groped for his new slippers, found them, and put them on. Then he went out the back door to his workshop.

Miss Lavender, out on her nightly prowl, saw him and bounded across the yard, tail high. Jack bent to scratch a favorite spot on her back. She purred and rubbed around his legs.

"C'mon, Missy, we have a project to finish."

The cat scampered ahead to the garage and waited by the door. As soon as Jack opened it, she jumped onto the old rocking chair and began grooming her fur.

Jack sat at the workbench and picked up the miniature carousel pony and a soft cloth. With a loving touch, he wiped all traces of sawdust from the little horse and its beveled oak base. The pony's neck arched, its head turned slightly in a coquettish pose with prancing legs caught midstride. Overall, the figure stood less than six inches tall, suspended in time. Jack had carved the horse from a single block of basswood, no seams, the finest piece he'd ever done in miniature.

"What am I going to do with this now? It was for Marah." No longer able to hold back his emotions, Jack lay his head on his arms and sobbed. "My daughter, a murderer. God forgive me, but it's better that she's gone."

Suddenly, he felt a hand on his shoulder. He jerked upright, grabbed his handkerchief, wiped his eyes, and blew his nose. Then he faced his grandson. Scott was barefoot, wearing a tank top and gym shorts, his version of pajamas. "Couldn't you sleep, either? You been standing here long?"

"No, just came in. I was in the kitchen and saw your light. You okay, Granpop?"

"Yeah. Everything just caught up to me." He heaved a big sigh. Then he showed Scott the pony. "I'd been making this for your mother. A replica of Clarissa Mae, the horse I carved in honor of your grandma."

"The one with all the flowers Kennocha painted that's on the carousel now."

Jack nodded. "Now I don't know what to do with this pony."

"Can I have it? Just like it is?"

"Yes, of course. I'm glad you want it. But don't you want me to finish it? I should touch up the saddle and bridle, detail the flowers a little more. Or maybe you'd like to do that yourself?" Jack handed him the horse. Seeing the boy lovingly cup the pony in his hands, Jack knew it was meant to be.

"I want it just like it is, unfinished, like Mom." He paused. "You know that church I've been going to since Danny died? Nikolas's church? Where Danny's youth group is?"

"Yes, son, and I'm glad you're going."

"In this room where us kids meet, they have a bunch of posters on the wall. There's this one with a picture of the ocean and a little island in the middle of it. I think about it a lot. It says, 'To refuse the invitation to interpersonal encounter is to be an isolated dot in the center of a great circle—a small island in a vast ocean.' That's Mom, you know? She refused. She never let anyone get close to her. Not for real."

Jack thought about it and nodded. "Could be. I tried to get her to talk to me more, but I guess I didn't try hard enough."

"I've been reading the Bible the pastor gave me after Danny died," Scott continued. "Pastor told me to start with the gospel of John. And to pray for Mom. So I did. Every night. Even when I was mad at her, like when she hurt Kennocha. And then you. And it was right after that, I got it. I understood. Bad things are gonna happen. That's just the way life is. But God sees the big picture, and we only see our own little island. You know what I mean? All of a sudden, I just knew God loves me no matter what anybody thinks of me. I just felt like ... like Jesus wrapped His arms all around me, And I felt safe and—and loved like I never felt before." Scott sniffed and wiped the tears from his cheeks. After a moment, he continued. "And He'd have loved Mom, too, if she would've let Him. Maybe God somehow told her before she died. Do you think He could have?"

Hearing the words from the depths of Scott's heart, Jack's soul stirred, and his spirit lifted. Scott was in God's hands. As for Marah, "I certainly do think God could do that." *But would she have accepted God's love?* "As Nikolas says, 'Nothing is impossible with God.' I would like to believe her soul is at peace now. Another Nikolas-ism: 'Leave the mysteries to God, He knows everything.'" Jack drew in a deep breath and wiped tears from his eyes. "Thanks for coming out here, son. You've helped me." He wrapped his arms around his grandson in a big hug. "See, I've always said you're good for me."

Scott hugged him back for a long moment. Then he pulled away. "Let's go open that new carton of chocolate chip ice cream we got last week. Before it gets too old."

"Okay."

They walked along the cobblestone path with the scent of petunias and roses filling the clear, cool night. They stopped to find the Big Dipper. Miss Lavender purred and rubbed between their bare ankles.

"D'you 'spose Kennocha will let us have ice cream in the middle of the night after you guys get married?"

Jack chuckled. "I happen to know she loves midnight sundaes."

ABOUT THE AUTHOR

Shirley Adams Rorvik has loved carousels since she was six years old and sneaked away from home to the circus grounds to watch the elephants and their trainers set up the big tent near the railroad tracks in Helena, Montana. This book reflects her love for carousels. More importantly, the story expresses her concern for young adults in the gay lifestyle who are often rejected by the families they love, including Christian families. She gained confidence to proceed with this book after a memorable conversation with Pastor Eugene H. Peterson, translator of *The Message*. In Shirley's blended family of five adult children, two are in monogamous, long-term, same-sex relationships. When her son came out over twenty years ago, she reacted much as Jack does in this novel. By God's grace, over time, she released her son and her fears into His capable hands. Shirley and her husband, Chuck, live thirty miles from Glacier National Park, their favorite retreat for hiking and fishing. While Chuck reels in salmon, Shirley casts her fly line and watches the birds, squirrels, and clouds while pondering her current writing projects. Catching fish is optional.